KISS & TELL

Luke Murphy

KISS & TELL

www.authorlukemurphy.com

FIRST EDITION Trade Paperback

Imajin Books — www.imajinbooks.com

July 20, 2015

ISBN: 978-1-77223-089-5

Cover designed by Ryan Doan — http://www.ryandoan.com

Praise for KISS & TELL

"Luke Murphy scores big with this deep psychological thriller. Just when you think you've got things pegged, Murphy serves up another twist. Fast paced and fun, you won't want to put this book down." —Tim Green, *New York Times* bestselling author of *Unstoppable*

"An intricately detailed and clever mystery featuring a tough minded but vulnerable protagonist with more than a few demons of her own. The twists and turns kept me guessing to the very end." —Christy Reece, *New York Times* bestselling author of *Nothing To Lose*

"Luke Murphy's *Kiss & Tell* is a character driven page-turner with an interesting plot. The main character, LAPD Detective Charlene Taylor, draws the reader into her world for a ride throughout the book. This is one definitely not to miss." —Dianna T. Benson, bestselling author of *The Hidden Son*

"Luke Murphy's heroine, Charlene Taylor, is tough and tender. *Kiss & Tell* is a first-rate police procedural. Hang on. You'll have fun." —James Thayer, author of *The House of Eight Orchids*

"Luke Murphy's novel, *Kiss & Tell*, has lots of twists and turns, and police procedures where the good guy, in this case, Charlene Taylor, is not always good. The characters come to life with suspense, drama, explosive action, and an ending you never see coming." —John Foxjohn, *USA Today* bestselling author of *Killer Nurse*

For Molly—thank you for making our family complete. Welcome to the Murphy clan.

Acknowledgements

The most important people in my life: my wife Mélanie, my rock and number one supporter. My daughters, Addison, Nève and Molly, who didn't always realize that Daddy had to write, but took my mind off things with games and dancing.

I'm the first to admit that this novel was not a solo effort. I've relied on many generous and intelligent people to turn this book into a reality. I'd like to thank the following people who had a hand in making this novel what it is today. I'm indebted to you all.

(The Conception) I need to thank the creative and very brilliant Mrs. Joan Conrod, Mr. John Stevens, Ms. Nadine Doolittle, Ms. Kathy Leveille and Ms. Lisa Murphy

(The Touch-ups) A special thanks for those last minute edits and details, as well as the final nod to The Jennifer Lyons Literary Agency

(The Research) For their professional expertise, knowledge in their field and valuable information, thanks to Ms. Joanna Pozzulo (Institute of Criminology and Criminal Justice), Keith MacLellan M.D., The Los Angeles Police Department, The Los Angeles City Attorney's Office, Darron Barr (CTE Solutions), Joshua Beardsley (WEpc) and Franco Zic

(The end result) For the final look and read, a special thanks to Imajin Books

Any procedural, geographical, or other errors pertaining to this story are of no fault to the names mentioned above, but entirely my own, as at times I took many creative liberties.

And last but not least, I'd like to thank you, the reader. You make it all worthwhile.

Prologue

Dead End

He pulled the old Honda into the dark abandoned alley, killed the lights, and cut the engine. Even with the windows up, the stench of urine, vomit and waste assaulted him. The steady, dismal downpour did nothing to conceal it.

The slow, light drizzle had not diminished the latest LA heat wave, but with its subtropical-Mediterranean climate, rain was a welcomed event.

Parked next to a rusty, dented blue dumpster, Martin Taylor adjusted his Dodger hat, his alert eyes scanning the deserted area. There was nothing to see except three cinder-block, graffiti-designed walls, as the disinvested buildings had been gutted and vacated. The only sound was the relentless hum of Asian music from the back door of a Chinese takeout restaurant.

He didn't like it. He was almost trapped within the u-shaped alley, with nowhere to turn his vehicle. He'd thought about backing in because, as it was, any chance of a quick, clean getaway would be impossible. But he needed this lead. Not just for the city, but for his ego.

He checked his watch. He was ten minutes early, so Martin took the time to think about the phone call that had lured him to the area known as Skid Row, in downtown Los Angeles.

He remembered the downtown as it was in the '70s, when the sites and attractions drew both residents and tourists, but the economic downturn had changed all of that. From where he sat, he could hear the city's Metro rapid transit system running throughout the night.

Now there was a new threat in town: The Celebrity Slayer, so dubbed by the media.

The serial killer was devastating the city, taking lives and leaving angry, malicious scenes—scenes that also left behind no criminal evidence to sort.

He was killing 'B' list celebrities, but his actions, his talents, were anything but 'B' list. The LAPD's resources were running dry trying to find the guy. The media was having a field day. The paparazzi, *ETalk*, *Entertainment Tonight* and *Radar Online*, were playing to the madman's ego, feeding his narcissistic personality. He had become a celebrity overnight.

Less than an hour ago, a call had come in on Martin's cell phone, someone claiming to have pertinent information concerning the Celebrity Slayer file. He was given this address. But he still couldn't figure out how a stranger had gotten his unlisted number. That alone chilled him to the bone, but in this day and age, the internet was a highway of information and anyone could get anything. It wasn't always a positive advancement.

Movement to his left. His eyes moved quickly, darting like a cat pouncing on a mouse.

He threw on the headlights but the beams didn't cover the side wall. When he saw a form appear out of the shadows and approach the vehicle, Martin rolled down his window and touched his shoulder holster. Then the body moved into the light, and Martin released the grip on his pistol handle.

"What are you doing here?" Martin asked, a look of both concern and surprise registering on his face. He looked around the alley. "Is Charlie here? Did you follow me?"

When his questions went unanswered, Martin felt a strange sensation rise in his chest. Something was wrong, out of place.

That's when he knew. His neck tingled and the hairs sprung on his arms.

He went for his gun a second too late. The killer had a silenced weapon drawn, and had stuck it through the open window frame.

"It can't be you." Martin realized the words came out as more of a statement than a question.

"Where's the file?" the man asked in a curt voice.

"What file?" *Stall him.*

But when he looked into the eyes of the deranged killer, Martin Taylor saw that deep in the back of those eyes a hatred darker than night burned, and a homicidal maniac struggled for release.

How could I have missed it?

The last thing he thought before feeling the burning sensation of hot lead was that his daughter was in grave danger.

Book I

Double-Edge Sword

Chapter 1

Hot tears temporarily blinded her.

She stood on the soggy ground at Angelus Rosedale Cemetery roiling with emotion, looking down at the American flag-covered casket, forcing herself to face a harshest of reality checks. Denial ripped her soul.

Officer Charlene Taylor stood tall in her LAPD blues, her long, fair hair pulled back into a ponytail. Her mother and older sister stood next to her as the three women wept.

Her head throbbed, nausea overwhelmed her, and her mouth was dry.

She still couldn't believe that her father, Martin Taylor, retired Grade III Detective and Sergeant II on the LAPD, had been found dead in his car, shot point-blank. Over forty years on the force and not a scratch. He'd been retired less than five years.

Charlene never thought she'd follow in her father's footsteps, but that was all she knew—that was all he had taught her.

Her eyes wandered over the predominantly LAPD crowd. She was trying to conjure up any kind of happy childhood memory with her father when Charlene spotted Andy standing in the back of the crowd.

"What's he doing here?" Charlene whispered to herself.

"What?" her older sister asked, looking up, her eyes red-rimmed.

Charlene shook her head. She looked back at Andy, sun bleached highlights in his brown hair. He'd been a track athlete in school and had maintained his athletic physique. His charcoal eyes matched his finely tailored Gucci suit.

They'd met at NYU four years ago, in her senior year, had a fling, and Charlene was happy to leave it at that. But when she moved back to LA, Andy had followed.

They'd been on-again, off-again since that time. He treated her like a queen and the sex was great, but for some reason she just hadn't been able to make that connection she longed for. He was a good soul with a kind heart, so what was she looking for?

Her mother and Jane had fallen for Andy's charm the first time they'd met him, but Charlene's father had not taken to Andy. He had thought there was something off about him.

She wasn't sure where they stood. She hadn't heard from Andy in a week, not since he'd stormed out of her apartment, and now he showed up here. He had wanted more, but she was happy with the way they were. What was she so afraid of?

Crack!

She was startled by the loud rifle shots, a gun salute performed at every policeman's funeral, a tribute to a team member lost. Even though her father was retired, he would forever be a part of the LAPD family.

Charlene knew the drill well, knew it from attending such funerals since she'd been a child, a sad part of her third-generation cop-family routine. At every funeral in the past, she'd felt moved, part of a close-knit tribe.

But this was different.

Her blue eyes scanned the crowd. The mayor, chief of police, captains, along with many of her father's friends and former colleagues, lined up to extend condolences. Charlene shook hands and accepted hugs, appreciating the gesture, but it all felt like an empty ritual, as much for the TV cameras and police department image as anything else.

Her street partner, Officer Jason Schmidt, approached tentatively, a concerned expression on his face. Cops hated funerals. With stiff, awkward movements, Jason wrapped his arms around Charlene and she could feel her partner's warmth. He whispered in her ear. "How you holdin' up, Chip?"

She nodded imperceptibly. "Okay."

He let go the embrace and looked into her eyes, gently stroking her arms with his strong hands. "If there's anything I can do," he said, not needing to finish his sentence.

After the crowd filed out, Charlene stood with her family, but she felt alone. An awkward moment of silence passed. Jane squeezed her hand, and her mother hugged her.

"You were always his girl," her mother mouthed, barely audible, her eyes moist and sad as she attempted a valiant smile.

Charlene didn't respond. She didn't know what to say. What could she say about an absentee father? She searched for answers. There were no family vacations, no memories. Martin Taylor had been all about *the job.*

Charlene felt a deep connection with her father, but only through police work. Those were the only things she remembered—time at the station, reviewing crime scene photos, following procedures. They had nothing else. She couldn't remember a conversation they'd had that didn't involve cop talk.

He had missed her childhood. He wasn't around for the *real* times— the first boyfriend, the first date, graduation…her father had missed it all.

Tears of anger rolled down her cheeks. Rage pounded in her chest as she thought about the things she had never said to him, and now never would.

When she opened her eyes, she was alone, her mother and sister retreating to the car for warmth and dryness.

She knew it was a two-way street. She hadn't been the easiest daughter to love. Charlene was the screw-up daughter who defied her cop-dad until one day she surprised everyone by following in his footsteps.

Now, with her father gone, she'd lost any chance to make it right with him.

She tried to blink back the tears, lost the confrontation with her emotions, and struggled for self-control as she thought about the scene.

His body had been found in his car, lifeless in the driver's seat, entry wound to the chest—shot point-blank. The case was ongoing, but the leads were growing colder with each passing day. LAPD went all out for one of their own, but on day four they still had nothing.

Why would someone kill a retired cop? What had her father been doing there? No one could answer that.

She was going to get some answers…somehow.

He sat behind the steering wheel of the idling car parked in a row of vehicles, watching her through the windshield, his face hidden behind a hat and dark sunglasses.

Only moments earlier, he had been close enough to smell her perfume, to taste the salty tears that ran down her cheeks. He'd wanted to reach out and touch her. It was all he could do not to.

The crowd had departed—family and friends leaving her alone. He understood the moment was killing her. A slight smile tugged the corners of his lips. He enjoyed watching her. The way she moved, with grace and athleticism, the sadness in her eyes, the rage that was building inside her—it all brought a shiver of excitement reaching his groin.

Oh, how he wanted to be close to her, to touch her in ways she never knew.

Killing Martin Taylor hadn't been in the cards. The old man had gotten too close, had found out things he shouldn't have. He should have left well enough alone. It wasn't supposed to happen, and he didn't want to kill the old man. He actually liked Marty.

But he also liked the nickname the media have given him, even if they were a bunch of egotistical, no-nothing lackeys. He had to admit the Celebrity Slayer was kind of catchy.

The cops still couldn't connect Taylor's murder to the Celebrity Slayer, but he would get the word out. He knew just the intercessor he would use. It would be so ironic, so perfect. So…complete.

He watched Charlene Taylor's every move, studied every action, noted her every instinct. She'd been born to be a cop. It was in her blood. It was obvious, but he wanted to find out just how good she really was.

Is she as good as her father?

She hovered over the gravesite, tears slipping off her cheeks. The intensity of the moment moved him. He gripped the wheel tight, blood rushing from his hands, his knuckles whitening. He felt a stir in his pants.

She will be mine.

Chapter 2

She saw them staring at her, but she didn't care. She walked into the department and headed for the lockers. Her captain sprinted across his office, blocking her off at the end of the hallway.

"Christ, Charlene, what are you doing here?"

Charlene looked at her watch. "My shift starts in half an hour."

"Charlene, they just put your father in the ground yesterday. Take some time off."

"I don't need time off, Captain. I need my job."

She didn't want to tell him that if she wasn't here, she'd be at the bar. And that would only add to the problem.

The captain sighed. "Charlene, that wasn't an option, it was an order. Take a few days off. Spend some time with your family. All cops are provided compassionate leave for just these situations."

Charlene bit down on her lip.

The captain didn't wait for an answer. He turned and walked back into his office.

She looked around the precinct, where everyone was still looking at her.

"What are you looking at?" she asked no one in particular.

When no one answered, Charlene turned and left the department, unsure of her next move.

She knew she had to change and vowed to make an effort to be a better daughter, the kind of daughter she should have been when her father was still alive. The last few years of her life had been lonely, cut off from her family, but now, with the death of her father, Charlene realized how much her mother needed her. And Charlene did not want to let her down, again.

"I'm so happy you're here, Charlene."

Charlene stood in her father's home office, scanning the photographs on the wall as her mother sat on the couch, hovering over more than a dozen unlabeled boxes. Jane was in the kitchen, sorting through the many casserole dishes leftover from the funeral.

"There is so much stuff I don't know what to do with it all." Her mother tried to smile but it was forced.

Charlene hadn't been to the house in over a year, but her father's office hadn't changed. Awards, accommodations, and pictures with important LA officials lined the walls. There were no pictures of Charlene, her sister, or their mother. There was not one personal item anywhere in the office.

Charlene moved towards her mother and sat down beside her. She looked into her eyes, saying nothing. Then, she wrapped her arms around her and squeezed gently. She could feel her eyes moisten when she said, "I'm sorry, Mom."

Her mom squeezed back. "I know, honey. It's okay."

Charlene sniffed, the warmth of the hug surrounding her. She hadn't cried like this in so long that it felt good, as if a giant weight had been lifted from her chest. "Not just about Dad, but about me. I've been selfish and it's not fair to you. I promise to change."

Her mother wouldn't let her go. "I don't want you to change, Charlene. I want you to be you. I love you no matter what. You have to come to terms with things on your own. Don't change for me, change for you, when *you're* ready."

Charlene pulled away and wiped her nose with her sleeve. She sniffed again and then dabbed her eyes.

Her mother looked around the room and said, "It just doesn't feel right, being in your father's office without him."

"What can I do?" Charlene asked.

"You can take the desk. You would know more about that stuff anyway."

Charlene got up and walked behind the desk. There were few items on the top, no photographs, and the drawers were all locked.

Charlene shook her head. "How did you do it, Mom?"

Her mother looked up. "What's that, dear?"

"How did you live with a man that wanted nothing to do with us?"

"Charlene Marie Taylor, you watch your mouth!" Her mother looked at Charlene, sadness in her eyes. "Your dad was a wonderful husband, and a loving, devoted father."

Charlene sat down in her father's desk chair. "Why do you always defend him?"

Brenda Taylor dropped her head. "Charlene, your father tried his best. Sometimes he might have been rigid, like all police dads, but that was the only way he knew. He wasn't a young man when you were born, and he wasn't ready to be a father again."

"So I'm supposed to forgive him for that?"

"Forgive him for what? What exactly did he do?"

"Nothing! That's the point. He never did anything with us. I didn't have a normal childhood. We didn't have a family. He was so busy being the perfect cop that we had to suffer."

"Are you drinking again?" her mother asked, lines of concern drawn in her face.

Charlene let out her breath. "Don't change the subject, Mom."

"I'm not changing the subject."

"You think that's the reason I drink?"

"Isn't it? I don't know, Charlene. Tell me. Why do you act like you do?"

"I know what you're going to say, Mom. You're going to tell me that I love being a cop, but fitting in with the perfect-detective father, walking in his shadow, knowing that I'm a screw-up sends me to the bottle? Or that trying to live up to a demanding father with impossibly high expectations, to be the son he never had, was too much. Go ahead, tell me. I've heard it all before."

She could see her mother's eyes moisten.

"Do you want to know what I think? I think that father and daughter are two people more alike than they realized, and loved each other deeply, but hit a wall trying to communicate."

"I know he disapproved of my lifestyle." Charlene looked down at the freshly varnished desk.

Her mother shook her head. "Charlene, your father grew up in a different generation. Women acted differently than they do now. He just didn't understand that. It doesn't mean he loved you any less."

Brenda reached into a box and pulled out a rolled up poster. She slid off the elastic and flattened it out.

"Fernando Valenzuela," she said. "That's an old one."

Charlene looked up and hurried around the desk. She sat next to her mother and looked at the poster.

"He still has this?"

Brenda nodded, putting her arm around Charlene's shoulders.

Charlene looked at the signature on the poster. "It was the only time we had actually done a father-daughter activity. He took me to my first game. I was only six. He bought us matching Dodger hats, and I thought it was just about the coolest thing ever. That was the only time I ever felt close to him. It was Fernando Valenzuela night and we stayed after the game to get his autograph. I bet we waited for three hours."

Holding the poster, feeling the warmth from her mother's embrace, brought back memories that Charlene had missed. She picked up a scuffed baseball and felt tears threaten.

"What about the police work? He used to spend hours with you at the station. He trained you to be as good as him. Remember when he taught you to pick the bathroom lock? You were only nine years old. I was so mad. No one could get a moment's peace after that. You learned to pick every lock in the house."

Charlene tried to hide her smirk. "He only did that because Jane was in there all the time and no one else could use it. Sure, I was his little boy, the one who was supposed to be just like him. But that's it! We had nothing else."

"That's more than Jane and I got."

Charlene froze, almost tasting the bitterness from her mother. The ball fell from her hand into the box. It started to click. Maybe having a child late in life was a second opportunity for her father. He had at least tried with Charlene, but what had her sister and mother gotten? He had tried with his police work, but when it came to other parts of being a husband and father, Martin Taylor had failed miserably.

Charlene looked at her mother, who would not return her gaze. A lump of guilt caught in Charlene's throat and she swallowed it.

She placed her hands on her mother's, now trembling. "I'm sorry, Mom. I never saw it. I was always too self-absorbed, pitied my own life, that I never paid attention to who else got hurt."

"I miss him, Charlene." Her mother rested her head on Charlene's shoulder as Charlene gently stroked her hair.

"I know. Me too, Mom."

Chapter 3

She'd only been gone a few days, but when Charlene stepped back into the West LA Community Police Station on Butler Avenue, the smells of her youth assailed her. The antiseptic cleaner, covering some sort of bodily fluid discharge, and the dingy lighting hadn't changed much in twenty years. It might have turned some people off, but Charlene, as when she had first stepped into the precinct at age seven, knew what she wanted.

She changed into her uniform blues, popped a couple of Advil from the emergency stash in her locker, and met her partner at the coffee machine. Jason was polishing off his second donut, wiping off chocolate sprinkles from the side of his mouth.

Jason nodded. "You look like hell."

"Gee, thanks. It's great to be back and see you too," Charlene replied, pouring herself a cup of strong department-issue coffee.

"You forgot the Visine this morning."

"I'm all out. These lights are killing me." She squinted and blinked, her retinas assaulted. Turning, she leaned against the counter, blowing into her cup and looking out into the chaos that was the morning routine in a police station.

"I thought you were taking a few days off?" Jason asked.

"I didn't come in yesterday."

Jason chuckled. "Yeah, big break. They stuck me with Darren."

Charlene rolled her eyes. "Yikes!"

"Yikes alright, eight straight hours of talking about you. He's like a star-struck teenager. Would you throw him a bone already?"

Charlene winked. "Yeah, maybe."

Another cop entered the lunch room. "Schmidt, Taylor, are you guys on?"

Jason nodded.

"You've got a four-fifteen to follow up on."

Jason looked at his watch. "Christ. Do people not sleep-in anymore?"

They quickly signed out a car and left.

A four-fifteen was LAPD code for a domestic disturbance.

"Neighbors called it in." Jason sat in the passenger seat with a folder open on his lap.

"What do we know about the residence?"

As they wove their way to the call just outside Beverly Hills, Charlene chewed the inside of her cheek, as she always did when she was either nervous or deep in thought.

"Residents are Monica Schwartz and Charles Lefebvre. Schwartz works as a secretary at a law firm and is on her second marriage. She got the house and custody of a six-year-old girl. Father lives out of state. Schwartz married Lefebvre last year. He's a financial advisor at a bank. No priors. Probably having an argument over who gets the Audi today."

They pulled up to the curb of a well maintained, custom-built bungalow with a manicured front lawn. Parked in the driveway were a Volvo XC90 SUV Crossover and a Porsche Boxter S convertible.

"Not bad vehicles," Jason commented, stepping from the cruiser.

A woman in a house coat and hairnet stood at the edge of the grass and waved to them.

"You the neighbor?" Charlene asked.

"Adelaide Nolan." The woman extended her hand but neither officer shook it. They proceeded to the front door with Nolan following. "I heard the yelling this morning. They're normally a quiet couple, great neighbors, and they have the sweetest little girl."

When they reached the bottom step, Charlene turned. "Thank you, Ms. Nolan. You're no longer needed."

"But…"

"Ma'am." Jason gave the neighbor a nod. She took the hint and backed away.

Charlene could hear an argument inside the house. A man's openly hostile voice boomed through the thin door. She knocked firmly. The talking stopped, but no one opened the door. She knocked again, this time louder. "LAPD."

Finally the door was swung open by an attractive woman in an expensive black Prada suit, pale blue blouse, and high heels. A man stood in the background in a charcoal grey suit with a red tie.

"Is there a problem, Officers?" the woman asked.

"May we come in, Ma'am?"

The woman opened the door wider and stepped back.

"The neighbors called about a disturbance," Charlene said.

The man sighed. "Great, Monica. See what you've done?"

The woman stood tight-lipped as the man swiveled on his heels and tried to leave the room.

"Hold on, Sir. We'd like to speak with you both."

Out of the corner of her eye, Charlene saw movement past the open hallway. She turned to her partner and whispered, "I'll talk to the daughter."

Jason nodded.

Charlene found the girl in her princess-themed bedroom, sitting on the edge of the bed, staring at the floor.

Charlene knocked gently on the doorframe. "Can I come in?"

The girl didn't look up, so Charlene stepped inside. "What's your name?"

"Lauren," the girl whispered, barely audible. She still didn't look at up.

"I'm Officer Taylor." Charlene slowly approached the bed. "Can I sit down with you, Lauren?"

Lauren, without looking up, slid over to make room.

Charlene sat down gingerly. "This is a pretty room. Do you like princesses?"

The girl finally looked at Charlene, a slight smile tugging at the corners of her lips. "Cinderella is my favorite."

Charlene looked at the little girl. The neighbor was right, she was a doll. But there was sadness in her eyes that Charlene didn't recognize.

"Why is Cinderella your favorite?"

"Because she's beautiful, and she was better than her evil stepmother."

"Well, I like Cinderella too. But my favorite is Belle, from Beauty and the Beast."

"Why do you like her?" Lauren asked, now completely interested in Charlene.

"Because she's also beautiful, but because she's compassionate and helps those in need. That's what police officers like to do."

The girl finally smiled, revealing a cute set of teeth with the two front ones missing. "Yeah, she's pretty cool too, I guess."

Charlene nodded. "What grade are you in, Lauren?"

"I'm in grade one. Mrs. Hopkins is my teacher."

Charlene pointed to a colored drawing taped to the mirror. "Looks like you're pretty talented."

Again Lauren smiled, revealing those missing teeth, and Charlene felt it in the pit of her stomach.

"What were your parents arguing about, Lauren?"

Lauren shrugged. "I don't know. They yell at each other a lot."

"What do you do when they argue?"

"I come in here and look at my books."

Charlene turned to find a row of fairy tale books neatly placed on a short white bookshelf.

"Okay, Lauren. Maybe when I come back I can bring you a new book for your collection. Would you like that?"

The girl nodded shyly and smiled.

"Great," Charlene said, getting up from the bed. "Give me a high five." Charlene held up her hand, palm out.

When Lauren raised her hand high in the air to give the high five, and her shirt lifted from her waist, Charlene saw shades of bruising on the girl's abdomen.

Charlene dropped her hand. "Lauren, how did you get that bruise?"

Lauren jumped to her feet, pulled the shirt down past her waist, and walked to the corner of the room, standing with her back to Charlene.

Charlene walked quietly to her. "Lauren, I need you to lift your shirt."

Lauren shook her head, but didn't speak.

"Please, Lauren. I can help you."

There was a long, intense moment of silence. Charlene could hear Jason talking in the other room with the parents. She turned to head that way when Lauren spoke.

"You mean help me like Belle does?"

Charlene turned back and approached Lauren. She placed her hands gently on the girl's slender shoulders and slowly turned her around. She could still see the sadness in Lauren's eyes, but this time it was mixed with fear.

"Yes, Lauren. I'll help you like Belle."

When Lauren lifted her shirt, Charlene gasped. Tiny bruises and welts were scattered over the child's abdomen.

All of the marks were in well-concealed areas, hidden to the public eye. Whoever had done this had been cautious, with the ability to cover the evidence.

"How did you get these, Lauren?"

The little girl stayed quiet.

Nausea burned Charlene's throat. She made a fist as she felt her blood rise.

"Jason," Charlene called out. "I need you in here."

Charlene kept Lauren's shirt raised, and when Jason rounded the corner, he stopped abruptly, closing his eyes and turning his head.

"Oh, Jesus."

"What's the problem, Offi—" When Lauren's mother entered the room, she covered her mouth with her hand. "Lauren," she said, quickly closing her eyes and turning away. "I can explain this." She was about to go on when Lefebvre stepped into the room.

He didn't hesitate. "Lauren is a very clumsy girl, Officer."

Charlene looked back down at Lauren, whose head was now lowered. Charlene saw a large teardrop hit the floor at Lauren's feet.

Charlene looked at Jason, who shook his head, but the anger had already pushed its way back into her throat.

The stepfather continued, "We try to tell her to be more careful but…"

Charlene exploded off her feet. She rammed the stepfather against the wall, pinning him hard, her forearm jammed forcefully against his throat. She could see his face turning blue as he struggled for air.

"No, please," the mother wailed.

Jason was quick to react. "Charlene," he screamed.

He pried Charlene from the man and separated them.

"I'm fine," Charlene said, smoothing out her wrinkled uniform with her hand.

"Are you fucking crazy?" the man screamed, holding his throat as color returned to his face. "That's harassment. I'll have your goddamn badge."

Jason whirled quickly and stuck a finger in the man's face. "Not another word or you'll find yourself in handcuffs in the back of our car."

The man must have seen something in Jason's eyes because he closed his mouth and left the room. The woman scampered after him.

Charlene returned to Lauren, who was now shaking. Tears streaked down her face. Charlene wrapped her arms around the six-year-old, who was shivering.

"It's going to be okay, Lauren. I will help you."

"Charlene…"

When Charlene looked at her partner, he stopped mid-sentence. She ducked her head to her collar and used her radio to call it in, looking for backup. Then Charlene wrapped Lauren in a blanket and carried her outside. She placed the child on the passenger seat of the cruiser.

Charlene and her partner stood outside the car. "We need to call child welfare."

Jason nodded, sweat beads peppering his forehead.

"I can't wait to lock up this scumbag."

Jason nodded again. "We can't avoid what happened in there. What if he files charges?"

"Do you think I care about what happens to me?" Charlene said. "All I care about is this little girl."

Jason nodded, put his hand on Charlene's shoulder, and said, "I've got your back."

"I can't believe there's nothing we can do," Charlene said as she and Jason headed back to the precinct.

"That's our US legal system. We let the state handle it. There has to be an investigation before charges can be laid."

"What about Lauren?"

Jason didn't have a response.

Charlene didn't say another word until Jason parked the cruiser outside the precinct.

"You mind taking this one?" she asked.

Jason nodded. "I'll go file the incident report. You hang here."

When Jason disappeared inside, Charlene opened the door to let in some air and turned on the radio. She put her head back on the headrest and closed her eyes. Her head was still aching, she was dehydrated, and the sun was stinging her eyes.

Jason returned and hopped in the driver's seat.

"What a morning. How about lunch?"

Without opening her eyes she said, "Absolutely."

They stopped at Murphy's Law Irish Pub for lunch and enjoyed the sunny California weather on the terrace of the downtown eatery. The restaurant was a regular hangout for cops, but on that day, Jason and Charlene were the only officers there.

The silence was heavy at the table, and Charlene wanted nothing more than to order a stiff drink and forget about the last two hours. But she had never crossed the line of drinking on the job. She had kept a promise to herself that no matter how bad things got, she never would.

"Did the captain say anything?"

"You mean did the guy call?" Jason smiled.

"Yeah, something like that."

"Nope, nothing. I don't think we'll hear from him."

"I'm already fighting for a position in a man's world. I can't afford to mess up on the job."

The waitress arrived to take their order. When she had left, Charlene said, "I can't stop thinking about Lauren."

Jason asked, "The Dodgers win last night?"

"Five-four in eleven." Charlene was grateful for the change of subject. She could talk baseball all day.

When their shift ended that evening, Charlene expected the office to be empty. She just had to grab some things from her locker before heading home.

But when she walked in, Charlene saw her captain still in his office, surrounded by a billowing cloud of smoke, looking annoyed. Smoking in public buildings appeared to be illegal everywhere except the captain's office.

During her four years as an officer, all under supervision by Captain Edgar North, Charlene had come to respect and admire the man. Captain North was a forgiving, mild mannered man who would back his officers no matter what. At sixty-two, North still had a full head of black hair with glints of silver. He was Charlene's height and kept himself in shape with weekly trips to the local gym. Charlene had never seen the captain in anything other than his police uniform, always neatly pressed and clean.

The captain got up from his desk and stood in his doorway. "Charlene, a word?"

Charlene and Jason exchanged looks. Jason shrugged.

"See you tomorrow, Chip."

She took a deep breath and entered the captain's office.

"Shut the door." His restless blue eyes remained on her.

The captain's expression was inscrutable. She quietly sat down and looked at the captain, who was perched on the front of his desk. She waited, chewing the inside of her cheek anxiously.

"How is everything?"

She shrugged "Fine, Sir."

"Sorry I wasn't in this morning for your first day back. How was your time off?"

"Fine."

"How are your mother and sister?"

"They're getting by, Sir."

The captain seemed to drift off. Charlene followed his gaze to a scene in the lobby. Two uniformed officers booking a large biker were having trouble controlling him.

The only sound in the captain's office was from the steady, low hum of the air-filtering system.

"Look, Charlene, I've got a problem." He returned his attention to Charlene, who shifted uncomfortably in her chair. "Since your father's death, I've held daily conferences with LAPD across the city. Not only did we lose your father, but Donnie Bradley was badly injured in the line of duty and forced to retire. Anyway, during our talks, your name came up for possible promotion."

Charlene was sure her expression registered one of surprise, but didn't say anything.

"You've been a great cop since joining the squad. You could say you have a perfect record." He still didn't smile.

"Thank you, Sir. I hoped—"

"Please, let me finish. The guys, the ones who aren't threatened by a woman on the force—don't worry, I can tell them apart—appreciate your work, and frankly, I agree." He went on. "Last night I had a three-hour conference call with the Board of Police Commissioners, the chief of police and Captain Dunbar from RHD. That's right, all the big dogs. I told them my feelings about you as a police officer and as a person."

Charlene was stunned, her expression blank. "Sir, I don't know what to say."

That Captain North would overlook her flaws, and the corporate board of police officers and the chief of police were all behind her, made Charlene swell with pride.

He put up his hand in a halting motion. "Don't get too excited just yet. I thought I was making the right move, but after today, I'm not so sure."

Charlene's heart dropped in her chest. Her mouth went dry and she couldn't swallow.

"What *did* happen today, Officer?" He spoke in a pacifying tone.

She didn't respond.

"We got a call from some guy screaming police brutality, claiming that you tried to choke him."

Charlene sat up at the edge of her seat. She didn't deny anything. "The son-of-a-bitch is physically abusing his stepdaughter."

"You have proof of that?"

"I saw the goddamn bruises."

"And she said he did it?"

"Not in so many words"

"Just how many words did she use then?" He didn't wait for her to answer. "The State is looking into it. I read Schmidt's report, and he claims everything was on the up and up, and I have to take his word for it. The last thing this precinct can afford right now is a lawsuit and public humiliation."

Charlene sat back and closed her eyes. "The bastard deserves more than he got."

The captain shook his head. "That's the problem, Charlene. You wear your heart on your sleeve, and you let your emotions control your actions. I think you'll make a great detective someday. Maybe even better than your father. But I don't know if you're ready."

She opened her eyes. "I am, Captain."

He pursed his lips and shook his head. "I can't have a powder keg protecting my streets. You're a tripwire, one step away from detonation."

"I admit, I got a little carried away this morning. It has never happened before and it won't happen again."

"Damn right it won't." The captain never swore and the word coming out of his mouth sounded out of place. "I should write you up on a CUBO—conduct unbecoming an officer."

Charlene waited.

"This guy said his wife saw the whole thing. But it's their word against ours. I think we can lean on him. But if word got out about what happened, do you know how it would make me look, after recommending you for a promotion?"

Charlene dropped her head. "I'm sorry, Sir."

The captain took a deep breath and relaxed his shoulders. "Did I ever tell you about the first time I met you?"

Charlene looked up, trying to recall. "I don't think so."

He crossed his arms. "Christ, it must be twenty years now. You were probably only seven or eight at the time. Even at that age, we could see your athleticism and toughness. Because of that, and your haircut, most of us at the department mistook you for a boy. Plus your father called you Charlie."

"Yeah, that's me, his little tomboy."

"I remember the first day you came to work with your father. He was so proud. When you first walked in, you were clung to his leg, and I thought you'd never last the day. Most kids that age would have been terrified, but you seemed to be drawn to it."

He stopped and waited for a reaction, but Charlene wanted to hear the rest of the story. Although she remembered the moment, she wanted to hear it in North's words.

"As your father read his files, you studied the room. You already had a keen sense for detail. We had a good laugh because you kept trying to grab your father's gun from his holster. I remember thinking to myself that this kid will be a hell of a cop someday. Nothing scared you, only interested you. You belonged right from the start. You have a gift,

Charlene. You are like him in every way, a chip off the old block. That's why we started calling you Chip."

Charlene knew that was one reason, but many called her that because they thought she had a chip on her shoulder.

"So what happens now?" Charlene asked.

He stood up and paced the office. "Just think of what a promotion could do. You'll be using a weapon under a caseload with high violence, not to mention the stress of taking on a new role, added to the death of your father. You'll be working with a team that depends on your clear-headedness, who will be putting their lives on the line for you."

"What are you saying, Captain?"

"Your promotion is contingent on psychological counseling and a report from the LAPD psychologist. Because RHD is so short on manpower right now, you will be eased into a minor role, interviews and paperwork only, to ease the caseload and free up some things. We'll see what happens when we get the psychologist's report."

Charlene raised her arms in exasperation. "Come on, Cap, a psychiatrist-seeing detective? I'll be the laughing stock of the department."

"This is the only deal, Charlene. Consider the alternatives." He gave some time for Charlene to answer. When she didn't, he went on. "If anyone asks, this is standard police procedure for someone who has lost an immediate family member. We'll say it's an extension of your return from compassionate leave."

She knew the captain had put it all on the line recommending her for the position. But this wasn't the way she wanted it. She was grateful, but now Captain North had this on her, so the carpet could be pulled out from under her at any time. She would always have to be cautious. Charlene also realized that she was being given this leeway because of her father.

"I won't let you down, Sir."

"I know you won't. Don't forget to call Dr. Gardner and schedule a session."

"Yes, Sir," she said, faking enthusiasm.

Chapter 4

She cleaned out her locker quickly and hustled from the building, avoiding conversation with the few evening-shifters who were loitering. Once word got out of her promotion, the retrograde male egos she worked with would do anything to bring her down.

They would think this had come too soon, too easily to the young officer, even with the stipulations and circumstances that surrounded it. But Charlene had been overlooked for a promotion a year ago. She thought it was because of her gender, or maybe her carefree lifestyle, but either way, she had deserved that job.

Her father had tried to settle her down. He told her to bide her time, work harder than the rest, and it would happen.

She didn't care what anyone else thought now.

Since Parker Center was no longer their headquarters, Charlene headed to her new home in the new LAPD Administrative Building, the Detective Bureau on 100 West First Street. During the drive, Charlene thought about the statistics. Out of the seventy-six sworn detectives and five civilian personnel in RHD, only six were women. Charlene was the only detective under thirty.

Ronald Dunbar, Captain III and Commanding Officer of the Robbery-Homicide Division of the Detective Bureau, was in his office, seated behind his desk sipping coffee, the *LA Daily News* spread out in front of him. A fat cigar hung from the side of his mouth and noticeable sweat stains were present on his shirt. A pair of rimless reading glasses perched the end of his nose.

He looked up from his reading and waved her in. She peered around the cloud of smoke that formed over the captain's desk and bit her lip nervously.

"Sit down, Taylor." The captain was a husky, burly guy. He spoke like a kid from Brooklyn.

Dunbar's dark, greasy hair was matted and combed over a bald spot. He had a sharp chin, his nose was crooked and his face deeply pitted from teenage acne. The reading glasses barely covered his black eyes. Because of the captain's badly deviated septum, Charlene could hear him breathing from across the room.

He closed the paper, threw it on his desk, and mopped the gritty sweat from his forehead. He slid his glasses into his breast pocket. He sat back in his chair, inhaled deeply from what smelled like a knockoff Cuban, and blew smoke rings in the air. He looked like he was having trouble focusing, his forehead creased with concern wrinkles.

"I'm not sure I've done the right thing," he finally said. "Captain North has put his professional reputation on the line for you. Can you handle that?" He looked at Charlene.

She swallowed and nodded. "Yes, Sir."

"I was your father's boss for a long time. I've seen him work, and North seems to think you possess those same traits that made your father a successful detective. You have your father's instincts. You have an eye and nose for the work. And I couldn't care less about what other people think. I decide who is on my team. All I care about are results." He let out his breath. "Goddamn air conditioner is broke again," he snarled, pulling his clingy shirt from his body. "No bullshit, Taylor. Are you ready for this?" He looked at her with raised eyebrows.

She answered without hesitation, "Yes, Sir."

"Did Captain North lay out the conditions of your promotion?"

"Yes, Sir."

"I'm up to my eyeballs in shit here. Our caseload is exploding and manpower is down, so I need to know the truth. R&H has the highest level of stress in the department. It's just going to get worse. Can I count on you or will the bottle win?"

Charlene shouldn't have been surprised by the captain's candor, but was stunned that he knew so much. Had her dad mentioned something to him when they had worked together?

"You can count on me, Sir."

He studied her for a long moment. Charlene fidgeted in her chair, waiting for a response.

"The only reason you're here is because, with this current heat wave, crime is rising. I'm sure you know that the Celebrity Slayer case is front and center. Even though everyone thinks this guy is a "B" list killer and will eventually slip up, I think this is only the beginning. I'm already short two detectives and I need to fill those positions. I attended a morning meeting with the mayor, who has declared a city-wide alert. Every LAPD department will now work together, share information and manpower on the Celebrity Slayer case. My department workload has just tripled. Don't make a fool of me, Taylor."

"No, Sir."

"With your promotion will also come some blowback from the men in this department. I can handle those assholes, but can you?"

"I've been doing it my whole life, Sir."

Dunbar nodded. "Good." Without taking his eyes off her, he reached into his desk and threw a badge and set of keys onto the top. "Take your father's desk. I'm assigning you to Homicide Special Section with Senior Detective Lawrence Baker. Light duty, Taylor. You'll observe only. Do you understand that?"

Charlene nodded. "Yes, Sir."

"Welcome to the team." He extended his hand and her new captain's crippling handshake almost brought Charlene to her knees. "I already set up an appointment for you with Gardner. Tomorrow morning, eight sharp."

"Thank you, Sir."

She made her way to her new desk, where she would take on some of the bloodiest and nastiest crimes in the city.

She was both glad and sorry to have her father's desk. Did the captain want to test whether she was sentimental or did he assume he did her a kindness? The desks in the RHD were pushed together to form pairs, so she was right next to her partner.

Teaming with Larry Baker was a compliment, since he was the most senior detective on the force. Or did it mean she needed a babysitter?

When she sat in her father's chair, the irony of only having a chance at his job because of his death washed over her. There was guilt from accepting the promotion, but she deserved it. Sitting there now, she missed her dad and knew that he was looking down on her, watching over her.

She had to get her energy up no matter what. The average rate of murder in Los Angeles was almost double the national average. And Charlene was finally getting her chance.

"Oh!" One last orgasmic scream to the ceiling and full-body shiver.

Charlene let out her breath, dismounted, and rolled over onto her back. She was lathered with sweat, and the booze buzz in her brain sent the room spinning.

She turned to Andy lying beside her, the mounds of hair on his chest rising and lowering as he caught his breath. She got up and pulled a robe over her naked body, her nostrils flaring at the cologne saturated air. She turned on the floor fan.

"I have an early appointment, Andy. I need to get some sleep."

He lunged across the futon and snagged her hand as she was walking by. "Move in with me, Charlene," he said.

"Are you crazy, Andy?"

"Why not?" He looked hurt.

She sat down beside him. "Look, Andy, I like the way things are. Why ruin what we have?"

"Because I love you," he said.

Charlene got up and walked into the kitchen. Behind her, she could hear Andy turn on the bedside lamp, rise from the bed, and pull a pair of torn jeans over a taut body.

"Did you hear what I said?" Andy moved towards her.

She stood at the sink but didn't turn around. She looked out the window and recognized a man sitting on a motorcycle outside her building. He was holding a helmet in his lap and staring up at her apartment window.

Andy grasped her shoulder and turned her around.

"I heard you, Andy." She couldn't look him in the eye.

"What are you so afraid of, Charlene? Why do you keep pushing me away?"

"I'm just not ready. It's not a good time. I just made detective and I'll be over my head with a new workload."

"Not ready? What's it going to take, Charlene? When we finished school, you weren't ready because we didn't yet have jobs. When you were sworn in with the LAPD, it was a bad time because you were starting a new job and trying to get your feet under you. And now this. Well, Charlene, it will never be the perfect time. You'll always have some excuse. Sometimes you just have to take a chance and trust somebody." Andy's face was red and he was gritting his teeth.

"I think you should go, Andy."

He tried to put his arms around her but she moved away.

Andy finished putting on his clothes and said, "Wow, your dad has really messed you up."

He slammed the door on the way out. She went to the window and watched him leave, driving away with a squeal of the tires.

That's when she noticed the man still on his motor bike, staring directly at her. She left the apartment and headed down to the front of the building.

She went through the front door and crossed the street. The man never took his eyes off her, and he grinned from ear to ear. He was cute, lithe, but Charlene could not recall his name.

"Can I help you?" she asked.

"Who was that? Your boyfriend?" he said sarcastically, motioning towards Andy's late model BMW sedan that had disappeared.

"None of your business. What do you want?"

The man shrugged his shoulders and said, "You." He still hadn't gotten off the motorcycle.

Charlene snickered. "Me?"

"I miss you, Charlene. I thought we had something."

"Miss me? We were together one night, a long time ago. We were both drunk and needed a release."

"It meant something to me."

"Look, we both got something out of the deal. We both needed someone, and we were there to comfort each other."

"I can't forget that night," he insisted, his voice rising. "But I guess it meant nothing to you. You just fuck every guy you meet at a bar?" he sneered.

"Look, what we had was special, but it was one night. I thought we both knew that there were no strings."

Then she had an image in her mind and remembered seeing his bike somewhere before, but never registering its importance. "Have you been following me?" she asked. Her breath quickened at the thought.

"You're playing a dangerous game, Charlene." Now his tone had turned callous. The vein in his neck pulsated. He started the engine, slid on his helmet, and closed the eye shield.

Charlene took a step towards him but he opened the bike up, pulled out into the street without signaling, and zipped away.

She turned and watched the chopper vanish, realizing that her hands were curled into tight balls. She wiped the spit from her mouth and noticed that she was shaking. Was it from anger towards her confrontation with two separate men, or fear that what one, or both, had said was closer to the truth than Charlene wanted to believe?

Charlene was jolted awake, blinking several times. Her head throbbed, and it took her a minute to gather her bearings. She rubbed her eyes, noticing that she had fallen asleep in her bathrobe.

All of the lights and the TV were on. *Last Call with Carson Daly* told Charlene that it was very early morning and still pitch black outside.

What had wakened her? She thought of her confrontation earlier in the evening and made a fist.

She rolled off the futon and moved to the kitchen where she popped a couple of Advil and chased them with a cold glass of water. She was stumbling towards the bathroom when the phone rang.

That's what had awakened her.

She moved back to the living room, which doubled as a bedroom, pushed aside the empty beer cans from the coffee table, and grabbed the portable phone, checking the caller ID. It indicated *private caller*.

"Hello," Charlene answered after three rings.

"Hello, Charlie!" an eerie, scratchy voice said.

Charlene hesitated. Only one person called her Charlie and he was six feet in the ground. Was this someone's idea of a sick joke? The silence was broken before she could speak.

"Do you know who this is, Charlie?"

"If I had to guess, I'd say some loser who had nothing better to do at two in the morning than jerk off in his parents' basement."

"Oh, you're a feisty one. I like that."

"Alright, perv, thanks for the call."

She was about to hang up when the voice said, "I saw you at the funeral."

That gave her pause, and a slight shiver.

He continued. "You looked so sad. I wish I could have consoled you."

"Who is this?" Charlene demanded.

An evil laugh echoed in the phone. "I'm an admirer."

"Great. Just what I need." She laid the sarcasm on thick.

"You're a lot like your father," he said in an imperious tone. "The old man should have stayed retired and minded his own business. I really had no choice."

"What are you talking about? Who is this?"

Charlene's mind was in overdrive as she quickly brought up a mental image, sorting through the faces at her father's funeral. The only people she knew to be there were family, friends, cops, and politicians. Had he really been there or just read about it in the papers?

He went on. "I do hope you'll be more of a challenge. Martin got old and slow." He spoke softly, not a hint of rage in a voice lacking human emotion.

"You killed my father?"

He laughed again. "Oh, this is fun. Are you having fun yet?"

"Fuck you."

"That might be fun too. But for now, let's just be friends. I'm not who they think I am, Charlie."

"What are you talking about?" Charlene was lost. The room spun, she felt dizzy and out of sorts.

"I'm going to show them I'm for real. Not just some B-level butcher."

"The Celebrity Slayer?" She wasn't sure if she said it aloud or to herself. The phone almost fell to the floor.

He let out a cackle before ending the call.

She sat there for minutes, the phone pressed against the side of her head, a loud dial tone ringing in her ear.

When she finally hung up and set the phone on the table, she moved, in a trance, to the bathroom.

Had that really been the Celebrity Slayer? Had the Celebrity Slayer killed her father? But why? Her dad wasn't a celebrity. What did he mean her father should have stayed retired?

All of these questions were racing through Charlene's mind when there was a discreet rap on her apartment door.

A knock on the door at this time of night was a worry on its own, but after receiving that call, she wasn't taking any chances.

She finished emptying her bladder and grabbed her gun from the closet. She slowly crept towards the door and put her eye to the peephole. After seeing nothing, she pushed the door open a fraction, keeping the chain lock in place. She could see nothing through the narrow slit, so she unchained and opened the door wider, always keeping her gun in the ready position.

She scanned the hallway, checking behind the staircase exit at each end. When she returned to her apartment, she noticed a tiny, gift-wrapped box had been left outside her door. She looked around again.

There was no inscription on the box. Had Andy left this, as a way of apologizing for their earlier dispute?

She picked up the package and entered the apartment. She gently lifted the box to her ear and shook it. It was extremely light and nothing moved when she jiggled it. She removed the bow string, unwrapped the ribbon, and removed the lid.

The box contained only a single sliver of paper with an address written on it. Charlene didn't recognize the location or its significance.

She was searching her memory, when the faint buzzing of her pager went off. Charlene picked up the phone and dialed the unfamiliar number.

"Detective Baker," a voice answered.

"It's Charlene Taylor."

"We've got a homicide at 1100 Lindblade Street."

As Charlene looked down at the paper in her trembling hands, her heart dropped in her chest.

Chapter 5

Culver City comprises approximately five square miles in western Los Angeles County. It has been a significant center for motion pictures, including Columbia Pictures, situated in the former MGM studio on Washington Boulevard, so it was no surprise to Charlene that the Celebrity Slayer would strike there. If this was, in fact, one of his.

Charlene hadn't been back to Culver City since her father's burial, and when she passed the Angelus-Rosedale Cemetery where her father lay, she felt a twinge of guilt.

A patrol officer with the tedious task of brushing back onlookers waved her through at the scene. She watched her colleagues in uniform completing the usual assignments—interviewing neighbors, going through garbage, and taking down plates. Those monotonous jobs weren't hers anymore.

The trash media were already circling the area like vultures. She saw news vans for *ETalk*, *National Enquirer*, and *ET*, as well as local news stations.

Exiting the car, she popped a breath mint and ran the gauntlet of cameras and hysteria, the flashes stinging her retinas.

A throng had formed behind the crowd-control barriers, some whispering while others snapped pictures from their iPhones. Teenagers took selfies with the crime scene pasted behind them.

She watched the crowd, checking to see if anyone was paying too much attention to her. Was he here? Did he want to see her in action?

She immediately spotted an LA County Sheriff's vehicle parked in the driveway and wondered if there was any jurisdictional conflict.

As she moved towards the house, Charlene saw her partner make a beeline in her direction. He was shaking his head and mumbling under his breath.

"Not ours, Kid," he said as he brushed past her.

She stopped and turned. "What do you mean?"

"The captain gave it to another team."

"That's bullshit," Charlene said, and continued for the entrance.

She could hear Larry panting as he tried to catch up. "Where are you going?"

"To buy our tickets inside."

Even with their backs turned, Charlene recognized the captain and two homicide investigators standing at the doorway sipping Starbucks coffee and talking. They were smoking energetically and laughing, and she could smell the stench of testosterone waft in the air.

She could overhear the conversation. The taller of the two investigators was reading from a notepad.

"Looks like one of his. The victim is Vanessa Jackson. Female, Caucasian, twenty-three years old, single and living alone. Same MO— butchered in the bedroom, major facial disfigurement. We're not yet sure just how many stab wounds and cuts, and we don't even know which ones were made post-mortem. We'll have to wait until we get her cleaned up."

"Post-mortem? What are you, a fuckin' medical examiner, Harris? Talk like a cop for Christ's sake."

Detective Harris's face reddened slightly, but he continued. "At first glance, the ME says it looks like the same routine, low pressure bleed out, lots of pain. He wanted it to last long so she'd suffer. A mirror was set up so the victim could see what he was doing to her. Sick bastard! It's like he just kept going. She's another former child star with blonde hair, blue eyes, and fake breasts. She was the lead in an eighties sitcom, but hasn't done anything meaningful since, basically bit-acting in B movies. She was..." The detective noticed Charlene standing behind the captain and stopped.

The captain turned around.

"Captain," Charlene said and nodded.

"Taylor. I've decided to put Berkley and Harris on this one."

Charlene looked at her captain, then at her two colleagues who refused to make eye contact. She turned to Larry who shrugged his shoulders, a disgusted sneer on his lips.

Charlene found it odd that the captain would put two detectives, relatively new to the department with minimal experience, on the case when her partner, with thirty years of experience, was already working the Slayer case. The Captain must have seen the questioning look in her eyes.

"You haven't been cleared for duty yet."

"I'm already involved, Sir."

Charlene removed a Ziploc baggy from her pocket and handed it to the captain.

"Where'd you get this?" he asked, reading the contents.

The other detectives strained their necks to see.

"It was left in my apartment this evening."

"By who?"

"I'm not sure. It could be the Celebrity Slayer."

"Oh, you know him personally, do you?" The captain handed the bag to one of the detectives. "Get this to Forensics."

Charlene shook her head. "I think he called me tonight. Someone who claims to be him, anyway. Then this was left at my door. He invited me over."

"Oh really." Her captain didn't look impressed. "Why would he target you?"

"I don't know. He also told me that he killed my father."

The captain looked confused. "Your father? Your father was shot and killed in his car."

"I'm aware of that, Sir."

"The MO isn't even remotely the same. Your father was a cop, not an actor. He was shot. The Slayer uses knives, aggressively, on all of his victims. Someone's yanking your chain, Taylor."

Charlene nodded. "Then why the phone call, Sir?"

"That could have been anyone. Maybe some punk trying to get his jollies by teasing a cop. Who knows?"

Charlene decided it was time to shut her mouth.

"You're dismissed, Taylor," her captain said, turning back to his detectives.

But Charlene still didn't move.

Detective Harris spoke. "But the question is, why here in West LA? All the previous murders were in Hollywood, now he all of a sudden changes venues. Geographically, it's a throw-off."

Berkley chimed in. "I agree that it's not Hollywood, but it is a center for movies. Normally I'd say he is trying to throw us off geographically, but he didn't change his MO. It's now officially a serial case."

Charlene was aware that with correct protocol, cases weren't deemed serial until four bodies were discovered and connected. California had the highest number of serial homicide cases in America.

"He's taunting us," Charlene said. "He killed my father and now he wants our department to start investigating the murders. He wants me to be a part of this."

The captain turned back around. "Taylor, are you still here? I thought I told you to—"

"Captain!" A uniformed cop came running up to the group at the house. "We've got a problem."

The group turned and saw that two cameramen had broken the barricade and were sprinting towards the house.

The captain blew air through his closed lips. "Jesus Christ. Goddamn paparazzi. Taylor, go home." Then the captain quickly moved towards where the commotion had broken loose.

The LAPD SID team was busy hustling around.

With the captain gone and the detectives inside processing the scene, Charlene faced the first decisive moment of her career. She grabbed Larry by the wrist. "Let's go."

"What?"

"I want to get a look inside."

Larry reluctantly followed, ducking under the yellow crime scene tape and into the house.

Chewing on her lip, Charlene moved straight to the bedroom, which was packed tight with techs and SIDs. A team member was working the adhesive specimen mount to lift powders from surfaces for spectroscopy analysis back at the lab. Another was working the Luma-Lite, checking for bodily fluids such as blood and semen that would become luminescent upon detection. A videographer was taping the scene.

She could smell the blood before reaching the top of the stairs. When she entered the room, Charlene's stomach lurched.

"You okay, Kid?" Larry asked, grabbing her shoulder to hold her up.

"Fine," she replied, shaking away his hand.

She looked again at the massive blood shed quickly studying the scene, cataloguing the images, understanding the kind of psychopathic rage it took to commit such evil—blood spatter on the walls and ceiling, bed sheets soaked in red, and the body chopped to pieces.

If the body had been found in the woods, it would have taken dental records to identify it. But since it was in this house, enough information was found to identify the victim. The walls, floor, and bed sheets were smeared with blood. It was all very messy, the Celebrity Slayer's style. It usually took DNA analysis to generate an identity.

Charlene needed fresh air.

As she left the house, she thought about the phone call she'd received. Now that she thought about it, it was very hard to believe that the person who had committed this crime had also killed her father. Maybe the captain was right, that it had been some kid playing a prank.

But what about the note?

She could have tried to grab a couple of hours of sleep when she got home, but what was the point? Her meeting with the LAPD shrink was in a few hours.

She was exhausted, but more frustrated with her captain. She'd driven to the scene excited, in anticipation of working her first case. And with the note, she was directly related to the killing. How could he ignore that?

And why would he assign two new detectives, still wet behind the ears, when she and Larry were more than capable? Why was that? What was the captain hiding, or trying to protect her from?

She trudged up the stairs and when she turned the corner, noticed that the lock on her door had been tampered with.

Dread flooded her as panic slithered up her spine. She pulled out her sidearm.

The neighbor's door opened and a man stepped out, adjusting a burgundy tie. When he saw Charlene, his eyes bulged, and he quickly stepped back inside. Charlene had lived in the apartment for three years, but didn't know any of the neighbors.

She slowly stepped inside her apartment and stood still, her ears on alert. She didn't hear anything. Charlene searched each room methodically. The small bachelor pad was quick to search.

Confident that she was alone, Charlene began to look if anything was missing, when a ripple of fear swept over her skin.

She'd always had the ability to keep panic at bay, but Charlene's heart almost stopped beating, her breath caught in the middle of her chest. Her futon had been made and an LA Dodgers ball cap had been placed neatly over the bedspread.

The hairs rose on her neck as she secured the apartment one more time, returning cautiously to the bed.

Even with the sudden urge to act, adrenaline squeezing her stomach into knots, Charlene followed police procedure. Using a dry cloth, she carefully lifted the hat and examined it.

She kept her own Dodgers hat at the station, and this one was set at a bigger fit.

She noticed a couple of hairs tucked inside, so she placed the hat into a plastic Ziploc bag. Later, she would take the hat to the lab to test for hair fibers, comparing them with her father's. She would also test the hat for fingerprints.

This was a message.

She was now definitely too wired to sleep. She picked through the dirty clothes hamper, still replaying the last couple of hours in her mind. She checked the clock—two hours before her appointment.

Charlene found her black bicycle shorts and sports training bra and pulled them on, throwing a track suit on over top. Grabbing her iPod on the way out, she left the apartment, making sure to lock the door, and took the flight of stairs down to the parking lot.

She took ten minutes to stretch, making sure her quads, hamstrings, and calves were loose. She didn't see any suspicious vehicles in the area, so she placed the headphones over her ears and started out at a leisurely pace on her regular route.

She'd always been boyishly nimble, which had impressed her father, and running every morning made sure she remained that way.

Once she turned off Maryland Street onto South Lucas Avenue, she picked up the pace, pushing herself. She passed the Good Samaritan Hospital where every morning the crowd outside would wave to her.

Charlene used these morning runs to sweat out the hangover, forget her problems and just run. This was her time to hate herself, to make herself stronger, better.

The sun was starting to peek over the horizon when she arrived back at her apartment forty-five minutes later, feeling half human again. She was impressed that her breathing was only slightly labored.

She let herself in and shed the sweaty garments on her way to the bathroom. She entered now fully awake, the booze sweated out of her. Starting the shower, she leaned her head over the sink, splashed cold water over her face, and used a hand towel to wipe away the combination of water and perspiration.

Catching herself in the mirror, she admired her new haircut. Her father would have hated it. He didn't believe women should have short hair, but she needed a change. Her dirty blonde locks now hung only inches below her ears.

She turned around and inspected the large tattoo on the middle of her lower back, remnants of a night of binge drinking and regretful decisions. The butterfly was wrapped in a broken-linked chain.

She turned back towards the mirror. The heavy drinking, sleepless nights, and her careless lifestyle were beginning to wear her down. She needed to turn her life around.

Her deep blue eyes were now bloodshot from last night's binge. Bags were beginning to form below them. She'd been a police officer for only five years and she'd been working herself to the bone. The life of a detective wasn't going to get any easier.

After a quick shower, Charlene dressed and grabbed her belt and holster that hung from the treadmill. She could grab a coffee and bagel on the way.

Chapter 6

On her way to work, Charlene called her mother to check in, something she had never done before. Step two to making things right. They had a nice talk and exchanged pleasantries. It felt good to be a daughter again.

She arrived at the Detective Bureau before seven, squeezed some Visine in each eye, and entered the building. She was surprised that the doctor had agreed to meet so early. With them it was usually, "I have a slot available, take it or leave it."

But Dr. Edward Gardner had spent thirteen years tending to cops, knew their reservations, their quirks, and he accepted the responsibility of complying with his patients' peculiar wishes. He was the lone member of the LAPD Detective Bureau Psyche staff and had made some enemies on the force due to his intellectual arrogance.

He had seen cops come and go, counseling emotional employees who put their life on the line every day. Police work had the highest rate of suicide of any occupation.

The forty-two-year-old psychiatrist was also the LAPD psychological consultant for many of their serial cases. He was currently assisting the Hollywood Division in the Celebrity Slayer case, and Charlene was hoping to find out what he knew about the psychological balance of the killer.

While many LAPD members were cynical about assurances of confidentiality from law enforcement psychiatrists, Gardner had a solid reputation for professionalism and discretion.

Charlene waited in the corridor, looking at pictures of former cops—those who played major roles in the LAPD's past. One photo in particular caught her interest.

In 1910, the LAPD appointed the nation's first female policewoman with arrest powers. Alice Stebbins Wells was a policewoman for thirty years and became a Sergeant in 1934 before retiring in 1940.

Charlene heard footsteps on the stairs and saw the doctor appear. He looked more like a hippie from the seventies, with a long gray pony tail and beard. He wore a dress jacket and scarf and had a novel tucked under his arm.

"Sorry I'm late, Detective," he apologized, taking a second glance into her eyes.

He unlocked the door and let Charlene in. She followed him, passing his desk, across the room, but didn't sit down. Gardner removed his jacket and hung it on a coat rack in the corner. Underneath his jacket the psychiatrist wore a short-sleeved buttoned shirt exposing a bulging vein running down his left arm. The doctor's body was wiry, well sculpted from his LAPD weight room membership.

He grabbed a pen and pad off the top of his desk and sat in a high-back chair facing Charlene. He chewed on the end of his pen and surveyed her with gray eyes, giving Charlene a shiver.

Neither said a word. It was a staring contest. Charlene picked at some dead skin on her fingers.

Finally he said, "Please sit down, Detective."

Before sitting, she said, "Look, Doc, I have no interest in being here. The captain says it's mandatory, so be it. But it doesn't mean I have to like it." She noticed the edge in her voice, well practiced from years of developing defense mechanisms with her father.

The doctor smiled. He had a prominent Adam's apple and Charlene watched it move when he spoke. "I understand, Detective. How do you feel about the stipulations of your promotion?"

"Great," she said sarcastically. "A detective delegated to menial work and seeing a shrink. I'm a department joke."

"So you don't feel all of this is necessary?"

Charlene shook her head. "Doc, I don't have a drinking problem."

"Opinions vary."

"Yeah, my colleagues. They think it's weird that I came back to work so early after my father's death."

"Work can be therapeutic."

"That's what I said." At least someone was on her side.

"Did you have a drink last night?"

Charlene diverted her eyes, looking around the spacious office, decorated with frigid elegance. The walls were covered with the doctor's awards and accolades, a diploma from Columbia University and pictures of the doctor shaking hands and mingling at various functions with LA celebrities. A long, oak-stained bookshelf covered an entire wall and was lined with books on police conduct, police procedures, crime scene processes, and psychological reference textbooks. The padded leather sofa was positioned with mathematical accuracy, but she had chosen a straight-back chair, sitting tensely.

She turned back to the doctor, the inside of her cheek tightly clasped between her teeth.

"I had a couple to blow off some steam. There's nothing wrong with that."

"You're right," he agreed. "There is nothing wrong with blowing off a little steam from time to time. But we need to talk about frequency and quantity."

Charlene silently nodded.

He went on. "Do you miss your father?"

"What kind of question is that? Of course I do."

Don't be so defensive.

"Let's talk about your relationship with Martin."

She shrugged. "It was normal."

He leaned back in his chair, looking to relax a little more. He steepled his fingers. "So you never felt the pressure of living up to his example?"

"Maybe a bit. But pressure can be a positive thing."

"If handled correctly. What about your home life?"

"Look, Doc, I get the feeling that you already know that my father wasn't much of a dad and we didn't bond. He was rarely home, and he was married to his work more than his family. Let's not waste each other's time."

"How did it make you feel growing up without a male role model?"

"I was fine with it."

"What about your mother and sister?"

"You'd have to ask them. They might have had a problem with it."

He smiled again. "No, I mean, how was your relationship with them?"

"I never understood my mom, how she could put up with my dad. My sister and I never had much in common. She is the Barbie doll, drama queen, make up and boyfriends type. But I'm working on rebuilding that."

He nodded. "Boyfriend?"

"I'm seeing someone."

"Is it serious?"

Charlene shrugged her shoulder. "Not as serious as he would like, but I'm satisfied with the arrangement."

"What about your friends?"

"My best friend lives in New York, and with my life, I don't exactly have the opportunity to make new friends."

Neither said a word for almost five minutes. Charlene began to fidget and moved to the edge of her seat.

"So what do you think, Doc?"

After a pregnant pause, he answered. "I think you're drinking heavily, you're emotionally shut down in your personal life, and almost too emotional in your professional life. You're isolated from family and possibly friends as well. You have trust and commitment issues. You have a personal demon—your father's death means you can never repair that relationship. You can never make it right with him."

She let out her breath. "Wow! That was quick."

"There are five stages of grief, Detective. Denial, anger, bargaining, depression, and acceptance—and there is no timeline. It's my job to help you get through them and then we'll go from there."

"What about my job?"

"I'll talk to the captain. I think we can work something out."

Her partner was at his desk when she got upstairs. His computer was off and the *LA Times* was open. There was a pile of LAPD Detective manuals on Charlene's desk, and a thin folder with a post-it note resting on top.

"Get any sleep?" Larry asked.

She sat down and removed her jacket and holster. "Some," she lied. "So what should I do?"

"Go through those manuals," he nodded at the pile, "and get caught up with our policies and procedures. Then go through that folder."

"What is it?" Charlene asked, lifting it off the pile and opening it.

"It's a copy of transcripts taken from neighbors of one of the cases I'm currently working. I've been pulled off the Celebrity Slayer case to babysit," he grunted. "We have a shitload of older cases to go through."

Charlene could clearly see the look of disgust on her partner's face. She didn't reply. What could she say?

"You smoke, Taylor?"

She shook her head.

"Wonderful, another non-smoker. What is it with this generation? You think you'll live any longer than the rest of us? I'm going out for one. When I come back, we'll get at it."

He heaved his large bulk out of his seat and waddled across the room, finding a fellow smoker and ushering him outside.

When Charlene grabbed a pen from Larry's desk, she accidentally bumped the sliding keyboard drawer, moving the mouse, and the computer came to life. An ongoing game of solitaire appeared on the screen, and no other links were open. The solitaire was on hour thirty-eight.

She opened the first manual and had just started reading when Larry returned.

"I'm going to pound the pavement, Taylor."

She looked up from her reading, closed the book, and jumped to her feet.

"Where are you going?" Larry asked.

"With you."

"I don't think so. You need to go through that stuff. You haven't been cleared yet."

"Come on, Larry. We both know this is a waste of time."

"That's true." He smiled. "Sorry, Kid, captain's rules. Here's my cell number, use it if you need anything. Plug it into your phone."

She blew out her breath and sat back down, saving Larry's number in her phone. She watched her partner leave, and when Charlene was certain he wasn't returning, she closed the book and got up.

It was only a ten minute drive to the Hertzberg-Davis Forensic Science Center at California State University, but Charlene didn't want to be seen leaving the building when she'd been given strict orders to stay.

The Hertzberg-Davis Forensic Science Center is home to the LAPD's Scientific Investigation Division, the LA County Sheriff's Department Scientific Services Bureau and the University's Criminal Justice program.

She opened her cell and placed a called.

"And to what do I owe this honor?" the responder said.

Charlene smiled. "Hello, Dana."

"It's about time you called. I thought now that you were a hot shot detective you were too good for us lab rats."

Dana Davis and Charlene had joined the force at the same time and went through training together. Dana had spent her first two LAPD years as a patrol officer, and she and Charlene had immediately hit it off. But when Dana landed on the CSI team three years ago, Charlene saw less of her. Dana worked for a special task unit in the Trace Evidence Lab, handling and testing important evidence for most big cases.

"Sorry, been kind of busy," Charlene said.

"I didn't get to talk at the funeral. I'm so sorry, Char."

"Thanks."

"But we need to celebrate this promotion, girly."

"I know, I know."

"So, what's up?"

"Are you working today?"

"Charlene, I'm always working."

"Any chance you could go for a drive?"

"I'll be there in ten."

Charlene hung up and went downstairs, retrieving her evidence bag from the car. Seven minutes later, Dana's Red Prelude screeched around the corner and braked sharply in front of the building.

Charlene handed the bag through the open window.

"High priority," Charlene said.

"Huh, who do you think you are, Detective?" the CSI tech said and then smiled.

"Someone with a best friend in high places," Charlene responded. "I also have a hair sample from my father's brush." She handed it over.

"Seems like you have all the bases covered. Shouldn't take long."

"Call me with the results."

Dana squealed out of the parking lot and merged into traffic without signaling or checking her mirrors.

Back in room 637, Charlene found Detectives Berkley and Harris huddled around the coffee machine.

"You guys still working the Slayer case?"

Berkley looked at Harris, and then nodded.

"Any details connected to my dad's case?"

"Are you still on that theory?" Harris asked. "There isn't one shred of evidence that links your father's murder to the Celebrity Slayer."

She didn't intend to get into a pissing match with the detectives, so she returned to her desk. She knew they were still eyeing her, so she sat down and opened up a manual.

But she couldn't concentrate, flipping the pages unconsciously. She kept the detectives in her line of sight, and when they had left the building, she got back up.

She glided across the room and walked down the back hall. She walked into the twenty-by-twenty filing room and closed the door. Every case file was recorded both electronically and in hard copy.

She knew what she was looking for, but was unsure where to find it. The old filing cabinets were unmarked, and she didn't want to risk using a computer to retrieve the information, since her account would be detected.

She rifled the first cabinet case files, always cautious of any approaching sounds. Fifteen minutes and two cabinets later, Charlene found it.

She shut the drawer quietly and placed the folder on top of the cabinet. Charlene heard a noise and froze, her nerves cracking with every sound. When no one entered the room, she opened the file and quickly examined the black and white photographs of her father's crime scene and the scene inventory and notes.

The detectives hadn't lied. There was nothing in her father's case file directly related to the Slayer.

She heard footsteps outside the door and quickly shut the file. She had to move.

Charlene shoved the folder inside her shirt, tucking it inside her waistline. She buttoned her shirt and exited the room, making sure to lock the door on the way out.

Charlene walked past the receptionist and approached the photocopy machine in the empty copy office. She quickly removed the contents of the folder and slid them in the machine, making sure to replace her father's original file, and took all of her papers to her desk.

She had just opened the report when her name was called. She looked up to find her captain standing outside his office, waving her inside.

Had he seen her? Impossible.

She shoved the file inside her desk and quickly walked across the room, biting her lip in anticipation.

He didn't tell her to sit down. "I just got Gardner's report from your first meeting."

She gulped, held the back of the chair for support, and waited.

"He cleared you for full duty." He waited for her reaction. When there was none, he went on. "A lot of psychiatric mumbo-jumbo bullshit. His report concluded that in his opinion, you're not an alcoholic, but did overindulge and you have a sincere desire backed by commitment to get it under control. As long as you continue with weekly visits, you're eligible for full duty. Does that sound about right?"

"Yes, Sir."

"You know what I think?" He didn't wait for her to answer. "I think you caught a break, Kid. Don't fuck it up."

"Yes, Sir." She didn't wait to be dismissed. She left, hiding a hint of a smile.

Her phone was ringing when she got back to her desk. Her heart was still pounding and sweat pelted her upper lip.

She recognized Dana's cell phone number.

"What did you find?"

"These hair samples are an exact match to your father, Detective."

Charlene sat back in her chair. Now she was sure of it…the Celebrity Slayer had killed her father. But why? Wrong place, wrong time? But that wasn't how the Slayer operated. From what she'd heard, the killer was careful, methodical, everything planned out in advance. He must have known what killing a cop would do.

She listened as Dana continued. "There were two sets of fingerprints found on the hat. I ran them through AFIS. One belonged to your father, but the database didn't find a match to the other."

If the print wasn't in the Automated Fingerprint Identification System that meant it belonged to someone who had never been charged with a crime.

"Thanks, Dana."

"What should I do with this?"

"I'll pick it up later."

Charlene had just hung up the desk phone when her iPhone chirped. She unclipped it and answered. "Detective Taylor, Robbery-Homicide."

"Meet me at the Mojo for lunch. You know the way?"

"Yep."

Chapter 7

Mel's Mojo was the smallest pub in LA and a second home for LAPD. After stopping at the Forensics Center, Charlene arrived at the downtown pub before Larry, selected a corner booth, and sat facing the door, a paranoid habit she'd caught from her father.

He was easy to spot coming through the door, his large, bulky frame squeezing through the afternoon crowd.

At six foot even and two hundred twenty pounds, the detective was a little thicker around the middle than he used to be but his police instincts had not waned—his sharp brown eyes never missed a clue. He had wide, thick black eyebrows, matching bushy sideburns to the earlobe, a nose a little out of proportion, and gray hair never combed. He was overweight, but it had never hindered his reputation as having one of the highest solving rates in the state.

The fifty-eight-year-old detective was gasping for air when he finally reached the booth, grabbing the table with one arm to steady himself. After catching his breath, he squeezed into the booth across from Charlene.

"The captain called, said you're good to go."

Charlene nodded.

"Did you order?" he asked, looking at the glass of water in front of her.

Charlene shook her head. "No, not yet."

They gave their order to the waitress, and when she had left, Charlene asked, "When do you think we'll get on the Slayer case?"

Larry smirked. "You're kidding, right? You won't be allowed within a hundred feet of that file."

Charlene leaned back in her seat and pouted.

"I know you think this guy killed your old man, but all you have to go on is what some crank caller told you."

Charlene unzipped the black LAPD satchel she had with her and removed the plastic bag containing her father's Dodgers hat.

She threw it on the table. "He left that in my apartment."

Larry lifted the hat and examined it as Charlene continued. "My dad was wearing that hat the night he was killed, I'm sure of it. He rarely went anywhere without it since he'd retired. The person who killed him, who claims to be the Celebrity Slayer, left that in my apartment for me to find."

Larry studied the bag. "Fingerprints?"

"My father's prints and an unknown."

"Interesting. Anything else from it?"

"The hairs match my father's. SID couldn't find anything else from it."

Larry smiled. "You move fast, Kid. I'm impressed. Guess you weren't reading those manuals this morning." He handed it back to Charlene.

She could feel her face burn. They sat in silence for a few minutes, and she was about to say more when their food was served—a Cobb salad for Charlene and a cheeseburger with fries for Larry.

Larry flipped his tie over his shoulder and took two healthy bites.

"With all of your work with SID, did you get to the transcripts?" he asked with his mouth full of greasy burger.

"I didn't get around to it."

He put his cheeseburger down. "What have you been doing all morning?"

She pointed to the Dodgers hat.

He took a large drink from his Dr. Pepper and smiled.

"What?" Charlene asked.

"You're just like your dad. He hated the paperwork too. He would rather be on the street."

This was the first time he had mentioned her father. Not only had they been best friends, but Larry had been a pallbearer at Martin Taylor's funeral.

"You ever been partnered with a woman before, Larry?"

"No, Ma'am. This is a first for me."

She could sense Larry squirm, uncomfortable with where the conversation was heading. Charlene changed it.

"Tell me about the Slayer case?"

"This guy is sick. I'm from Brooklyn, grew up in the Bronx, and I've seen some whack-jobs in my life as a detective, but this sicko has them all beat."

She watched Larry eat and listened to his stories. His face and voice showed the strain of over thirty years on the job. Baker was a hard-nosed, old school detective who didn't like the bureaucracy of the department.

"Do you believe he killed my father?" Charlene asked.

"I believe what I can prove. And right now, we ain't got jack."

"What *do* we have? What are they saying at the monthly LAPD detective meetings?"

"Kid, you ain't got the years for that information. Besides, because of you, I'm off the Slayer case." He ate the rest of his fries. "You done yet?"

She looked down at her salad, and she had yet to take a bite.

"We're going over those transcripts this afternoon, maybe even visit the crime scene." He sucked in his gut to escape the booth. "I hope you brought money, because I forgot my wallet. I'll get the next one. I'll meet you back at the office. We'll grab the transcripts and head out."

He left before she could answer.

She stopped at her parents' house after work. Although she did want to check on her mother, something else was niggling at the back of Charlene's mind, and it led her home. It had been something the Celebrity Slayer had said during their phone conversation.

Her mother must have heard the car pull up because she opened the door and stepped outside, greeting Charlene as she walked up the walkway.

"Charlene, what's wrong?"

"Nothing, Mom." Charlene wasn't exactly the pop-in kind of daughter, so any unexpected visit had to be a surprise.

"It's so good to see you," her mom said. "Come in."

Her mother put her arm around Charlene and pulled her inside. The house still smelled like home, the scent of her mother's pot roast wafted through the air, as if it was permanently installed.

"I'm so happy you stopped by."

"Did Jane go back yet?"

Her mother shook her head. "No, she's sticking around for a while to help out. She went to the store to pick up a few items. It's so good to have both my girls close by."

Charlene smiled and handed her mother a Styrofoam cup. "I stopped and got you one of those lattes you like so much from the café down the street.

"Thank you, Charlene. You didn't have to do that." She accepted the cup and sipped gratefully.

"I was wondering if I could look for something in Dad's office?"

"Well, of course, honey. What are you looking for?"

"I'm not sure yet." She stepped past her mother, heading towards her father's office. "Are all of dad's things still here?"

"Yes." Her mother followed. "I haven't yet decided what to do with it all."

Charlene found much of his work had already been boxed, but not sealed. She opened each one, carefully sorting through all of her father's papers. She looked for any key words or any clues that any of the files had to do with the Celebrity Slayer. Had her father really been working on the case as the Slayer had alleged?

She didn't see any papers in the eight boxes that could be associated with that case. She walked to her father's desk and jiggled the locked drawers.

"Do you have a key, Mom?"

Brenda shook her head. "Your father was always so private with his police affairs. He never wanted me—or you girls—to be privy to such information. He always tried to protect us."

Charlene grimaced. "Do you have a screwdriver?"

"Your father has a tool box in the basement."

Charlene took the steps to the cellar, an unfinished basement that consisted of her father's work bench and storage space. Power tools hung on the wall, and the tool box sat on her father's work table. A large oil-burning furnace in the corner kicked on.

Her father hadn't exactly been a handyman, but he had all of the necessary tools to be considered a man's man.

She opened the box and rummaged through, finding a small-slotted screwdriver. She returned to her father's office and jiggled the screwdriver in the drawer slot, snapping the inner-lock and pulling open the drawer.

"There's that lock-picking skill. What are you looking for?" her mother asked.

"A certain file."

Nothing in the top drawer. After quickly snapping the bottom drawer lock, she opened it to find a row of manila folders lined up. They were labeled and named, with dates and case numbers. All old cases. Still, nothing on the Celebrity Slayer.

She rifled through the folders, knowing that every detective had certain cases that dogged them, and her father was no different. Most of these cases were still ongoing. They had a case number, but no one was actually investigating.

She threw the folders back into the drawer and let out her breath. Was she chasing a lie?

"Did you find what you were looking for?"

Charlene shook her head in response to her mother's question. She was trying to think like her father. Where would that file be?

"I heard about your promotion."

Charlene looked at her mother, saw the sadness in her eyes, and immediately felt guilty. "I was going to call. I…"

Her mother raised her hand. "It's okay, Charlene. I'm happy for you."

Her mother said it, but Charlene could hear the anxiety in her voice, and knew what she really had wanted to say.

"Mom, this has always been my goal."

"I know, honey. But ever since your father…" She didn't finish the sentence, and Charlene could sense her mother had drifted. But before Charlene could speak, her mother continued. "I've just been so worried about you. I don't want to lose another member of my family to that police department."

"I know, Mom. I promise to be careful."

"Remember the time I caught you playing with your father's gun?"

Charlene smiled to herself. She had only been a toddler. "I remember."

"I was so angry with him, and he just laughed, picking you up and placing you on his lap. Somehow, no matter how much I tried to ignore it, I knew you would follow him. I never denied that, or fought it. I'm not going to try to talk you out of this; it's your decision and you're a grown woman. So congratulations, honey, but don't expect me to share your enthusiasm. But I'm happy you got what you wanted."

Charlene didn't know what to say. She knew her mother was just acting like any loving, protective parent would. Even after everything they had been through, as cruel and hateful as Charlene had been, a mother's love was enduring.

A long, uncomfortable silence fell.

"Mom, is there anywhere else where dad might have stored his police stuff?"

"The last few weeks, before his death, he spent a lot of time in the basement. I never knew what he was doing down there."

Charlene returned to the basement. Searching the dark, spider-web infested corners, she came across a door she had never noticed before. Not that she had spent a lot of time in the unfinished basement.

She could hear her mother's footsteps overhead.

There was a padlock on the door so Charlene grabbed a claw hammer from her father's tool box. After three swings, the lock blew apart. She pushed open the door.

The room was pitch black. She swiped the wall for the light switch, but couldn't find it. She opened the door wider, to allow the minimal light inside, and stepped in, only to be greeted with a mouthful of dusty, stale, mildewed air. She coughed it out, moving further inside, walking directly into a cobweb. As she swatted it away, her hand brushed against a string dangling from the ceiling. She tugged on it and the room lit up.

The sudden light from the hundred-watt bulb temporarily blinded her. Once her eyes had adjusted, Charlene stood still, a lump gathering in her throat.

The converted cellar was now a shrine. The walls were lined with newspaper clippings, pictures, and maps. A desk was littered with papers, folders, and notes. A collage of items was tacked to a cork board. Charlene recognized her father's scribbled writing on a chalk board that had been screw-nailed to the wall. Newspaper articles, with dates, had been cut out and taped up.

For every detective, there was always that one case that stuck out, the one that *got away*. This must have been her father's.

His homicide investigator's textbook was on the counter and she started reading his notes when her mother appeared at the door. "Oh, my God! What is this?"

"A case that dad was working on."

"But your father was retired."

"Cops never really retire, Mom. I'm taking it all with me, the computer too."

Charlene went to step past her mother when she felt a firm grip on her forearm. She had never felt her mother's physical strength like that before.

"Charlene, please don't."

"I have to, Mom."

"No, you don't. Don't you see? This is what killed your father?"

"Mom, I don't think…"

"Don't lie to me. You know as well as I do that he was killed because of this case. I may only be a lonely, stay-at-home housewife to you, but I was married to a cop for forty years. Don't you see how dangerous this is?"

"I have to do this, Mom."

"Why? Do you really believe that if you catch this guy you will make everything right with your father? I know you, Charlene. I know that you're the type of person who will take all that pent-up emotional energy and become obsessed with finding his killer, seeking redemption for yourself."

"What are you so scared of, Mom?"

"That you'll stop at nothing to get what you want. That's what scares me. But I don't know that what you'll find will heal your wounds. It will never end."

"I don't have a choice, Mom. I promise to be careful."

Charlene turned and headed upstairs. She went into her father's office and flipped through the wooden rolodex on his desk. She found the number and dialed.

"Jim Duggan."

Charlene only knew the man through her father. Duggan was a veteran homicide detective with the LAPD Hollywood Division, and he was also the man heading-up the Celebrity Slayer Task Force.

"Mr. Duggan, this is Charlene Taylor."

"Charlene." She could hear the surprise in his voice. "I'm sorry I never had a chance to talk to you after the funeral. Your father was a good cop, and an even better friend."

"Cut the shit, Jim. I just found your file."

Duggan was silent.

"What did you get my father involved in?"

"Charlene, I don't know what…"

"Enough lies!" Charlene screamed into the phone. "Or the next call I make will be to my captain."

"Okay, hold on." There was silence on the line and she could tell Duggan was stalling. "This goes no further."

"Agreed."

Duggan let out his breath. "I approached your father about a month ago. We had just finished our monthly LAPD detective meeting, and we all agreed we were nowhere on the Slayer case. After the meeting, I called your dad and asked him to meet me at the City Hall Park. That's when I asked him to assist on the Slayer case."

"You bastard! You got him killed!"

"Look, Charlene, he didn't have to accept the task."

"Bullshit! You and I both know he would never turn down a job. He was a cop for life. It's what he loved."

Again, silence invaded the phone call.

"When did you talk to him again?"

"After the next detective meeting. We met again at the park, and he said he had some irons in the fire. He had some real leads but he wasn't sure they would pan out. That's the last I heard from him."

"He didn't give any more details?"

"No. Sorry, Charlene."

"Who else knew he was working the case?"

"As far as I know…nobody."

She didn't have anything else. "Thanks for getting my father killed, Jim."

Charlene hung up. Bile caked the corners of her mouth. She wanted to throw the phone but resisted. She heard the front door slam shut, and through the window, saw her mother beginning her evening walk. Had she overheard the conversation?

She returned to the basement, wanting to load all of her father's things in her car before her mother and sister returned.

Before she left the house, she had one more thought. Since her mother hadn't moved a thing from Charlene's room since childhood, she ran up the stairs to her old bedroom and grabbed something she knew would be there.

It was after eight when she finally got to the apartment. She hadn't eaten supper and was famished, but instead she unloaded the car. Once everything was inside, she pulled a beer from the case and tucked the rest in the back of the fridge.

Entering the large six-by-six walk-in closet, she unhooked all of the hanging clothes, bundled them up, and threw the pile onto her futon. Then she removed everything from the floor of the closet—bags, shoes, sports equipment, and anything else that had been thrown there. The last item to be moved was the chest of drawers containing her undergarments and the rest of her clothing. She slid that out and pushed it against the wall in the living room.

Once the closet was empty, she began to arrange her father's files. She started by tacking the city maps to the wall. Then she pulled her father's old filing cabinet in, along with a desk and folding chair. She rested her laptop on the desk, and then ran an internet line and power bar. She filed away her father's notes and tacked the crime scene photos and case files to the board.

Then she added everything she had photocopied from RHD on her father's murder—reports, pictures, and notes.

She grabbed a second can of beer and sat down at the desk. She needed to cross-reference her father's murder case to those of the Celebrity Slayer. She had to find a connection.

She thought about her father's murder and a rush of emotion hit her. Why had he been there that night? It had to be about the Slayer case. He'd been killed because he'd been following a lead.

Who else knew her father was working the case? Larry had shown no clue. But the LAPD was a tight-knit community, and word usually spread quickly.

His papers were in perfect order and Charlene easily found his note on the meeting. There was no name mentioned, just the fact that he had an 8 PM meeting scheduled in the back alley behind Imperial Palace Chinese Buffet with someone who possibly had some information. Rather vague. Had it been an anonymous?

She looked at the case file.

The next morning his car was found parked in a hidden alley near Sunset Boulevard in Hollywood. The car was in *park*, the ignition on and the window down. Post-mortem lividity suggested that his body hadn't been moved.

Her father had been extremely intelligent, diligent, and a first class detective. There was no way he could be lured into danger by a stranger and tricked by a complete fool.

Charlene had the details of the report memorized, and had spent hours at the scene after everything had been cleared, so with a clear head and all of her information, she closed her eyes and pictured what she thought the scene looked like, as if she'd been there.

Her dad sat in the idling car in the alley, waiting for his informant. He was there to gather information. Out of the shadows, someone approached the car. Martin Taylor either rolled down his window or it had already been down. He trusted the person, maybe even knew him or her. The killer stood outside the vehicle, never getting in or touching the door handle. Words were exchanged, and then the individual drew a gun. Before her father could raise his hands in defense, the killer stuck the weapon inside the car and pulled the trigger. The bullet hit him in the chest, killing him instantly.

Of course, it was all speculative. But that's how the detective saw it happening, in her own mind.

Cartridge casings found at the scene, as well as the bullet pulled from her father, were from a .45. Interviews showed that no one had seen or heard anything from the alley. That meant the killer had to have used a silencer. Not many people owned silenced pistols. Ballistics was run through IBIS, the Integrated Ballistics Identification Systems managed by the Bureau of Alcohol, Tobacco, and Firearms, but no hits were matched.

Martin Taylor's body was found by a restaurant employee who'd gone to the back to use the dumpster. Charlene wanted to interview that man, because to Charlene, the first witness at a scene was automatically considered a suspect. There were no other witnesses in the report.

Since his body was found on Sunset, the Hollywood division was handling the case, but Charlene's precinct was assisting.

Because Martin Taylor was a cop, the case was a high priority. Her father's body was immediately autopsied and the car explored for evidence, but nothing was found, so they released the body to give him a proper burial.

She took a swig of beer, and removing a magnifying glass, studied her father's crime scene photos in precise detail. Then she cross referenced those pictures with ones taken from the Celebrity Slayer scenes. Nothing jumped out as connecting, but she didn't expect it to. She had to dig deeper.

She stared at the photos until her vision blurred.

After two more beers and an hour of meticulous studying, she flung the magnifying glass on the desk.

Fuck!

The murders were premeditated. The killer's method had been planned with meticulous detail. She still had two more of her father's folders to go through, but tonight would be pointless. She had nothing left.

She took the time to file all the information away neatly, storing it in the filing cabinet in an order that she could find quickly, then she shut off the light.

Book II

Case #1

Chapter 8

She'd just fallen asleep when the ringing of her cell phone woke her. Charlene rolled over and grabbed her iPhone off the floor, reading the time. Her eyes were glazed and the room was spinning, but she managed to clear her head. *10:15 PM.*

She answered. "Hello?" Her voice was hoarse.

"We caught our first case, Kid."

"What's up, Larry?" she asked, getting out of bed and rummaging through the bundles of clothes on the floor, bed and chairs. A drum beat a steady rhythm in her head.

"We have a four-nineteen on Westwood Boulevard."

"Is it a celebrity?"

"Kind of."

"What do you mean, kind of?"

"I'll tell you when you get here. We have our work cut out for us."

"I'll be there in ten."

As she scribbled the address down, she recognized the area, a peaceful upper class suburb, not exactly the kind of location where the Celebrity Slayer victims had been discovered. But she wasn't ruling anything out.

She flicked on the lamp and found the least wrinkled pair of khakis and a button down shirt from the bundle of crumpled clothes on the floor. She strapped on her shoulder holster, put a Colt .38 in an ankle holster, grabbed the keys, and left.

She opened the door and ran into the hallway where Andy was standing with his arms extended. He was holding a take-out bag from their favorite post-sex Sushi place.

"Peace offering," he said.

"Not tonight, Andy," Charlene replied, and sprinted past him. "Sorry," she called back. Charlene stopped at the closest twenty-four-hour coffee shop and grabbed two coffees, and used hers to wash down two Tylenol. Then she opened the glove compartment and popped two Antipoleez breath mints into her mouth. She'd discovered the breath mints in college, the only thing that concealed the odor of alcohol.

She tuned the radio to KFWB 980 LA News and checked for updates on ongoing cases, including what she could expect at the crime scene. Placing the cherry on the Volvo roof, she sped away. She needed to get to the scene before a mob contaminated it.

It took eight minutes. The "traffic" on site was dense. She recognized some faces, and was waved through to the doorway.

Before getting out of the car, she used the rearview mirror to apply lip gloss and a touch of blush.

She clipped on her ID and directed McHale, a burly cop she hadn't worked with before, to start the canvas and look out for someone standing around and watching too intently. Killers did sometimes hang around the scene.

She quickly inspected the crowd. The cars parked in the driveway were a silver Jaguar and a baby blue Ford Fiesta.

There was a box of latex gloves resting on a stool inside the door of the house, and Charlene slipped on a pair. She pushed her way through and looked for her partner.

The first detail she noticed was the strong scent of vanilla that hung in the air. She inventoried the room as she moved towards the body.

Over the victim's body, the ME was hovering a UV light which was intended to visually enhance evidence, including sub-dermal bruising, and a photographer was removing video equipment from a bag. Charlene looked over the coroner's shoulder at two perfectly placed bullet holes in the victim's chest.

Charlene detailed the vic's stats—white, male, over six feet, about one hundred eighty pounds, well dressed, handsome with no distinguishing marks—layers of bruising on face and hands. Reasonably fit, with black golf slacks, no tie, and tufts of dark hair at his unbuttoned collar. His pockets were pulled out.

The coroner looked up at Charlene. "You lead?"

She nodded, in order to make that true and to get to work immediately. Then Larry came out of a back room with the captain. *Great!* What had she missed? She focused back on the coroner.

"Whoever shot this man was either very lucky or a top notch marksman. See here," he said, using a thermometer as a pointer. "Two bullets in the chest, side by side, while the victim was moving towards the shooter."

"Time of death?"

With his rubber gloved hand, the coroner pulled the victim's eyelids all the way open. "The corneas haven't blurred over yet and the blood's still warm. I'd say he's been dead less than two hours."

She checked her watch, *10:36 PM.* Less than two hours. That was good. The killer was just recently here, maybe leaving evidence and clues that could still be detected. Most of the neighbors would have been home from work and not yet gone to bed.

Charlene had to move quickly. She noticed minor bruising on the victim's face, possible signs of a struggle. She found the same on his knuckles.

"How recent are those marks?" Charlene asked.

"Some of these are older than others. Some bruises take days to appear, but these look newer than those. Plus, the perp had a gun, unless it had been dislodged and there was a struggle. The cuts on his fingers are pre-mortem, I'd say about four to five hours old."

Charlene digested the coroner's information. A possible fight prior to the murder.

Charlene needed to ID the victim ASAP and establish a timeline. When the Medical Examiner began dusting the body, Charlene asked, "What are you doing?"

"The best way to contain the prints is before moving the body."

Larry left the captain and approached her. She handed him one of the covered coffee cups. "Wasn't sure how you took it. Sugar and cream are in the bag."

"Black, thanks," he grunted. "The Dodgers win tonight?"

She shook her head. "Lost bad." She nodded at the body. "This ours?"

Larry nodded.

Charlene smiled, her lip lodged between her teeth.

"Found these on the deceased." He held up a plastic, see-through LAPD evidence bag as he sipped the coffee. The bag was labeled with the case number, date, and time. Charlene quickly scanned the items that came from the victim's pockets. Black leather wallet, car keys, pack of juicy fruit gum, and some loose change.

"What do you know so far?" she asked.

"Not much," he answered, flipping through his notepad. "Two shots to the chest, close range. We didn't find any cartridge casings, so unless the killer picked them up, we're guessing a revolver, not a semi-auto. By the size of the holes in the victim's chest, I'm guessing nine millimeter. We won't know for sure until Ballistics check the bullets. But why pick up the casing if you're going to leave the bullets?"

Charlene realized that Larry was speaking from over thirty years of experience.

"What's with the vanilla?"

"You smell that too, huh? Scented candles in the bathroom, about a dozen of them lit. The bathtub was overflowing when the first cop on the scene arrived," Larry said as he took a large gulp of coffee.

"What's that about?"

Larry shrugged. "Recognize the vic?" he asked.

She moved closer, peeking over the coroner's shoulder. She'd seen the face before but couldn't place him. She shook her head.

"The deceased has been identified as Dr. Ken Anderson, Professor at UCLA." He stopped and looked at Charlene. The name still didn't register with her. Then he continued. "Married to Beverly Minor, no children. They live at 414 Melrose Avenue, West Hollywood."

"What's he doing here?" Charlene asked.

"Not sure. But did you hear what I said? The name?"

Charlene shrugged.

"Beverly Minor. Carl Minor's daughter."

"The billionaire?"

"The same."

That name alone justified the captain's presence at the scene. Now Charlene understood why Dunbar was well dressed and ready to make a statement to the press. And that was why the victim looked so familiar. This case would be high alert.

"Okay, so why is Beverly Minor's husband here?"

"The house belongs to Lloyd Gladstone."

"What's his connection to Anderson? The name doesn't ring a bell."

"It shouldn't. He's nobody. We already contacted Gladstone who lives in Glendale. He said he's been renting out the house since he acquired it in '98. New tenants this year."

"What about the vehicles?" Charlene asked.

"The Jag belongs to Anderson, and the Fiesta is registered to one of the renters." He looked at his notepad. "According to Gladstone, the renters are UCLA students, Jessica Philips and Ashley Stanley. No sign of either of them yet, but we're already running a check and have put out an APB."

"Next of kin been notified?" Charlene asked

Charlene knew that ninety percent of murders were spousal related and usually had something to do with love or money. Of these murders, fifty-five percent were committed by the wife. But the victim's wife, Beverly Minor, was already a wealthy woman. Did she have another reason?

"Not yet," Larry said.

"The ME said that some of those bruises could be a few hours old. Let's use the GPS on Anderson's phone to see where he's been."

"Good thinking," said Larry. "He didn't have a phone on him, so it could be in his car. I'll send someone to look now."

While Larry was attracting the attention of one of the on-site officers, Charlene looked around the living room. The house looked to be furnished in elegant, high-end furniture. If it wasn't for the empty pizza boxes and school text books scattered about, there would be no reason to believe that college students lived there.

"Pretty nice for college students," Charlene remarked when Larry got back.

"I agree. My first college apartment consisted of duct-tape patched beanbag chairs and dirty mattresses."

Larry pulled the wallet from the evidence bag and handed it to Charlene. She studied Anderson's California State driver's license and made a mental note of the address.

Larry continued. "Eighty-three dollars found inside, meaning this wasn't a robbery gone bad, it was a planned execution."

"So who found the body?" Charlene asked.

"Phone-in." Again Larry studied his notes. "Anonymous nine-one-one. No words spoken, phone left off the hook. We made the trace and the first officer on the scene found the door open and called it in."

"You think the killer called the cops?"

"Why would he?"

"Or she," Charlene corrected her partner. "Who was the first on scene?"

"Davidson." Larry fingered a young officer standing by the staircase and signaled him over.

"You found the body?" Charlene asked the cop who couldn't have been more than twenty.

"Yes, Ma'am."

"This the way you found it?"

"Yes, Ma'am." The kid shifted his weight from left foot to right. "I followed procedure. Make sure the vic is dead. Seal off the scene. Check for witnesses. And call it in."

"You alone?"

"No, Ma'am, my partner was outside for backup."

"Anything touched?"

"No, Ma'am."

"Okay."

Charlene glanced over the room quickly. She wouldn't get anything done with the mess of people. She had to get them out of the house so she could start her inspection.

Her partner acted as if the same was on his mind. "We need to find these girls, and Anderson's connection to them." Larry turned to the ME. "Hey, Don, you got a smoke?" The ME handed Larry his pack of cigarettes, and the detective promptly lit one and waved out his match.

Carl Minor's involvement would ensure a high-priority autopsy.

"SID has started collecting evidence," Larry stated between puffs.

"Okay." She caught the attention of a tech from the Scientific Investigation Division and summoned him over. "Where's Dana?"

The tech looked annoyed. "She didn't get this one. The boss sent me."

She acknowledged the newbie. "Let's get everyone out of here and get the crime scene unit in. Detective Baker and I will take this room. Send your team over the rest of the house. We also need a unit outside to scour the yard." She was getting into it when a young officer approached them from behind.

"Detective Baker?" They turned and saw a young, white cop jogging through the doorway. He looked at Charlene. "Hey, Chip."

Charlene grimaced and nodded. "Darren."

Then he turned back to Larry. "Jessica Philips is here."

Charlene looked over Darren's shoulder and found a young white woman with a look of concern and confusion on her face. The girl appeared to be in her early twenties, thin, well dressed and well groomed.

When the cop noticed Philips in the house, he sprinted towards her, grabbing her tightly by the arm. "I told you to wait outside."

"I'm sorry, I…"

"Darren," Charlene stepped in. "Let her go. It's fine. Have the cars impounded and towed back to the precinct to have the team go through them."

Larry and Charlene approached the woman. Charlene examined the suspect. Moderately attractive, black hair, blue eyes—about five seven, one hundred ten pounds. She didn't move with the grace of an athlete, but, from the empty pizza box, Charlene guessed Jessica Philips didn't worry about her weight. She wore blue jeans, a white T-shirt and white sneakers. Her eyes were red and swollen.

"Jessica Philips?" Larry asked.

"Yes," the woman replied, clearly shaken.

"I'm Detective Baker and this is my partner, Detective Taylor. We're with the West LA Robbery-Homicide Division of the LAPD."

No response. Philips looked entranced by the scene, engulfed by LAPD officers inspecting her house.

"Ms. Philips."

"Oh, sorry." Jessica looked at Charlene. "What did you say?"

"Detective Baker was wondering if you'd mind answering a few questions."

"Okay," she agreed tentatively, her eyes still showing signs of uncertainty. "But what is this all about? What's going on? Why is Professor Anderson's car in my driveway?"

Charlene looked around the room. Everyone was still watching them. Even the Captain had stopped what he was doing and had edged closer. They were all watching Charlene, on her first case, as much as they watched Jessica Philips. Charlene could feel the intensity of the stares.

"Let's take her to another room," Larry suggested.

Chapter 9

They led Philips upstairs and into one of the bedrooms, closing the door, eliminating the noise.

"Would you like something to drink, Ms. Philips?" Charlene asked.

"No, thank you. Where are Sandra and Ashley?"

Charlene looked at Larry, who asked, "Who is Sandra?"

"My sister," Philips answered.

"Is your sister staying with you?" Larry asked.

"She moved here two weeks ago."

Larry referred to his notes. "Your landlord, Lloyd Gladstone, said that only two of you live here."

Philips looked a little weary. "I hadn't told him yet that my sister had moved in."

Larry wrote something in his notes.

"Ms. Philips," Charlene started. "As far as we know, nothing has happened to your roommates. We're looking for Ms. Stanley now."

"Then who is out there?"

Charlene looked at Larry, who shook his head imperceptibly.

"Have I been robbed?"

As a cop, Charlene understood how most people came to this inaccurate conclusion. Being robbed meant someone using violence to steal something from another person. In this case, it would have been a B&E.

"Why don't you take a look around to see if anything's missing? Go with her," he said to Charlene.

Charlene followed Philips as they went room to room. On their way back to the bedroom, Philips shrugged and said, "I don't notice anything missing. But it's hard to tell."

When they entered the bedroom, Larry asked, "Where were you tonight, Ms. Philips?"

"I went for a walk to clear my head."

"Were you with anyone?"

"No."

"Did anyone see you?"

She shook her head. "I don't think so? The streets were bare."

"Where did you go?"

"I went to the park around the corner and sat on the bench. I like to go there to relax. Then I came home."

"How long were you gone?"

"A couple of hours."

"That's a long walk," Larry looked at Charlene.

Charlene had been sitting back quietly, observing Philips and letting Larry run the interrogation. Now she asked, "What was bothering you?"

"Just personal stuff."

"Where are your roommates?"

"Ashley has a softball game, and Sandra is at a meeting."

Charlene checked her watch. "Do they always stay out this late?"

Philips nodded.

"Excuse us, Ms. Philips," Larry said, summoning Charlene to the hallway and closing the door.

When they got out, Larry asked, "What do you think?"

"Pretty vague."

"I agree."

"I know I'm new to this, and you're the lead, but let's remember this is just preliminary questioning. We don't want to lose her trust. She's not a suspect, yet."

"Yeah, good. We need to make sure she feels at ease with us. We need her to relax, so we can trap her in any inconsistencies. That's why I think you should do the talking."

"Why me?"

"You're a woman, and young. You can relate to each other. She might open up to you."

"Okay." Charlene took a deep breath and blew it out.

"Don't worry, I'll be there to guide you. You'll do just fine." Larry smiled. "You ready?"

Charlene nodded and they went back into the room. Philips stood up from the bed.

"Do I need a lawyer?"

"If you want one, but I assure you, Ms. Philips, this is just routine. We really appreciate your cooperation and any information you give us that will help find out what happened here tonight would be very helpful," Larry said.

"I don't even know what happened here," she replied.

But Larry's words of encouragement seemed to work because Philips sat back down. Charlene could see her shiver and offered a blanket to wrap around her. They had to keep the conversation casual.

"I really want to know who is out there!" She started to rise from the bed.

"We need to be certain first, Ms. Philips." Charlene replied evasively. "Why don't you walk us through your day?"

"Nothing unusual happened. I went to school this morning. At lunch, I went to the bank. I had to get money out for our cleaning lady. She comes every Friday. Went to my usual classes, came home, inspected the work the cleaning lady had done and paid her. That's about it."

They could confirm the time with the housekeeper.

"So your roommates haven't been home since you got back from school?"

Jessica shook her head. "I wasn't expecting them. They get home late on Friday nights."

"How did you know that the car in the driveway belonged to Ken Anderson?"

Jessica looked at Charlene, and the detective thought she had struck a nerve.

"Professor Anderson is my teacher at UCLA, and I also work as his assistant so I recognized it."

"Did you see Professor Anderson tonight?"

"No."

Quick response, Charlene thought.

"When was the last time you saw him?"

"He hasn't been at school the last few days. Maybe Monday or Tuesday."

"Would he have any reason to come to your house?"

Jessica hesitated, and then said. "Maybe to drop off papers to mark. That's part of my required duties as his Teaching Assistant."

Charlene looked at Larry, who just shrugged and urged her to continue.

"Has Professor Anderson ever come by your house before?"

Philips shifted uncomfortably on the bed before answering, "No."

Charlene was thinking of her next question when Philips stood back up. "Detectives, what is going on? Why are you asking about Ken?"

Ken? Charlene looked at Philips. Not many students are on a first name basis with their professors.

"Ms. Philips, Ken Anderson was shot and killed in your house tonight," Larry said.

Philips put her hand to her mouth, and tears erupted from her eyes. If this was an act, to Charlene, it was a hell of a performance. It looked genuine enough.

Charlene found a Kleenex box on the computer desk and handed it to Philips.

"Thank you."

Charlene again looked at Larry, who mouthed, "Keep going."

Charlene sat down next to Jessica. "If you weren't home, if no one was home, then how did Ken Anderson get into your house?"

"Maybe the door was unlocked."

"Do you often keep it unlocked when no one is here?"

Jessica shook her head.

"Did you lock it tonight when you left?"

"I can't remember."

Charlene saw Larry roll his eyes.

Larry grabbed Charlene by the arm and pulled her to the corner of the room. He whispered, "Let's test for GSR right away, while you have her cooperating."

"Can we do that without the presence of a lawyer?" Charlene asked.

Larry grunted. "Yes, we can test for it without probable cause, and it will stand up in court. It's a good idea to do it now. Ninety percent of gun powder residue is gone after the first hour. We'll never get this chance again."

"Ms. Philips, we'd like to run a test to remove you as a suspect to Ken Anderson's murder," Larry said.

"What kind of test?"

"Well, we know that the person who killed Ken Anderson fired a gun and sometimes trace evidence can be left on that individual. It's just a test on you and your clothes that will tell us if you've recently fired a gun."

Philips nodded.

Larry left the room and returned a minute later with a gloved lab tech holding a small kit. He nodded towards Philips and the tech used an adhesive lifter to swab her shirt and hands.

"What's he doing?"

"He's just testing for gunshot residue."

The man concluded his work and looked at Larry. "I'll fill out the information sheet and get this to the lab for testing. Time frame of results will range anywhere from two to six hours." Then he left.

"Any idea when your roommates will be home?" Larry asked.

Philips shook her head. "I can try to call them."

"That would be helpful."

Philips pulled out her iPhone and punched numbers. When she looked up she said, "Both calls went straight to voice mail."

"Thank you for your time, Ms. Philips. We appreciate your cooperation. Do you have somewhere to stay for a few days? Your house will be off limits," Larry said.

"Yes, we can stay at a friend's house."

They left the room and headed for the front door.

"You want to wait for the roommates?" Charlene asked.

Larry shook his head. "Who knows when they'll be back? I'd rather do some background checking and be more prepared for our next visit."

"We better notify next of kin."

The driveway lights were on when the detectives wheeled to a stop in front of the Anderson home. A long, black limousine was parked outside, and the chauffer was leaning against the door, smoking a cigarette and refusing to look in their direction.

Every light in the house was on.

"Looks like they're all up. I guess we got here late," Larry said.

Charlene checked her watch. "It's 2 AM. That's weird."

They got out of the car and walked up to the door.

Fulfilling this moral obligation as a cop sent chills through Charlene. She rang the bell, and the door was opened by Beverly Minor, wearing a baggy blue bathrobe. Charlene barely recognized the woman. Behind the makeup and fancy clothes, Minor looked like a normal person with dark bags under her feline green eyes, looking like someone who had come to terms with aging. Her brown hair was pulled back too tightly and white roots were beginning to show. The lines of worry at the corners of her eyes were prominent. This was not the woman Charlene had seen only months ago, looking picturesque in the newspaper in her expensive, over-done wedding dress. Today, the widow looked every day of her forty years. She also looked slightly medicated.

Charlene could hear Larry approaching from behind, his heavy wheezing blowing hot air on her neck.

"Mrs. Anderson?" Charlene flashed her badge. "I'm Detective Taylor and this is Detective Baker, with the LAPD. May we come in?"

If she was surprised to find LAPD detectives at her door in the middle of the night, Minor didn't show it. She didn't exactly beckon them in, but turned and headed inside herself.

"What did my husband do this time?" she asked, as she turned her back and showed the detectives to the living room.

They followed her.

"Let me do the talking," Larry muttered.

They entered a family room furnished with high-end furniture, Persian carpets and expensive paintings. The room was lit by an enormous antique glass chandelier.

A balding man with a thin straight nose and an expensive suit sat on the sofa, and another stood at the window looking outside. When the man at the window turned, Charlene saw that it was Beverly Minor's father, sixty-seven-year-old real estate tycoon Carl Minor, the self-made billionaire.

"Detectives," Carl Minor said and nodded. He lit a cigar and sat across from the detectives. The smell of expensive Cuban smoke filled the air as he blew out rings.

Charlene studied the billionaire, dressed in a sharp, cashmere, double breasted navy blue blazer and gray flannel slacks. His self-assured presence lingered like perfume. She wondered about his presence at two in the morning.

Charlene waited, wondering if Larry was going to speak. She looked at him and shrugged, but Larry was staring at Minor. Finally, Charlene elbow-jabbed her partner.

Larry looked at Charlene then at the widow.

"Mrs. Anderson, we have some news about your husband."

Beverly's face tightened, quickly turning her head, looking at her father who sat motionless on the chair. Charlene studied both their reactions, the billionaire suddenly interested in the conversation.

"What is it?" Beverly asked.

"Mrs. Anderson, a few hours ago your husband was shot and killed. We found his body in a house on Westwood Boulevard. His identity has been confirmed."

The room grew still. Beverly Anderson did not cry. Her eyes never fluttered. Again she looked at her father, as if requesting permission to react.

Carl Minor broke the silence. "Do you have any leads?"

The two detectives exchanged glances. Nobody in the room seemed to feel any remorse for Anderson's death. So far, the mysterious man on the seat had said nothing. No one had even introduced him.

"Mrs. Anderson, where were you last night?" Charlene asked.

Beverly glanced at the man on the couch and inhaled sharply.

Larry grabbed Charlene's jacket sleeve and pulled himself into an upright seated position. "This is just a routine question we have to ask, Mrs. Anderson."

Charlene looked at Larry, but he didn't look back.

The man on the couch nodded to Beverly.

"I was driving around. I do that sometimes. It relaxes me."

"Was anyone with you?"

Beverly shook her head.

Again, Larry was silent, so Charlene pressed the issue. "When did you last see your husband?"

Beverly shrugged. "This afternoon."

"Mrs. Anderson, how would you describe your relationship with your husband?"

"Well, Detective, I'd say that Ken and I had the same relationship that all newlyweds have. We were in love and crazy about each other."

"Any arguments, disagreements, or fights recently?"

Larry tried to stand but Charlene imperceptibly pulled him back.

Beverly smiled. "Detective, you mustn't be married." She looked condescendingly upon Charlene. "Of course we had disagreements. Show me a couple that doesn't and I'll show you a couple that's lying."

Larry finally spoke up. "Your husband's body was found in a house rented by a Ms. Jessica Philips. Do you know Ms. Philips?" He handed her a picture.

The widow accepted the photograph and studied the image, shaking her head and handing it to her father. "Not that I'm aware of."

"She is your husband's teaching assistant at UCLA," Larry said.

Beverly pursed her lips. "If you say so. My husband and I rarely talk about his work here at home."

"Is this woman a suspect?" Carl Minor asked.

"Not at the moment," Larry answered.

"Do you know of any reason why your husband would be at Ms. Philips' house?" Charlene asked.

Beverly shrugged her shoulders. "Like I said, Detective, I don't know the girl and as for my husband, who knows what he does when he's not here? He's a grown man."

Larry spoke next. "Mrs. Anderson, do you know of anyone who would want to hurt your husband? Does he have any enemies who you are aware of?"

Beverly looked uncomfortably at her guests then turned to face her father. As she opened her mouth to speak, Carl Minor gave a facial sign and the man on the sofa stood up. "Okay, I believe I've heard enough."

"Detectives, this is my attorney, Ian Johnson," Carl Minor announced.

The attorney continued. "What are you trying to do to my client?"

"We just want to make sure we know everything. And let her know that her husband was shot and killed at Jessica Philips' house last night. We'd also like to establish a timeline starting from when he left this house," Charlene said.

"Detectives," Beverly looked disgusted, "are you implying that I killed my husband?"

"Easy, Beverly, let me handle this," her lawyer chimed in. "Is this really the time? Mrs. Anderson has just found out that her husband was killed."

Charlene mumbled, "I think she knew before that. She…"

"Okay, we're done here. Thank you for your time." Larry stood up. "I trust that we can come back if we need to?"

"Anything else you need from my client can go through me, and we can make it official downtown. Thank you for coming."

"Detective Baker, could I see you alone for a minute?" Carl Minor beckoned towards the back room.

Charlene looked at her partner who just shrugged. Larry and Minor disappeared from the room. The attorney guided Charlene to the door.

"You can tell your client that we'll be in touch," Charlene said.

The attorney was about to answer when the men returned.

Larry shared their condolences and promised to keep them up to date on the investigation, but Charlene suspected Carl Minor would keep himself well informed. They left the house and headed for the car.

As soon as they were outside, Charlene asked, "What was that all about?"

Larry shrugged. "Nothin' much. He just wants to make sure we do everything we can."

They got in the car and shut the doors. Larry started the car and smiled towards the doorway, where Minor and his attorney were still standing. Under his breath he said, "Don't ever do that again. I told you to let me do the talking. You almost blew everything up."

"I was letting you talk, but I think your lips were too swollen from kissing Minor's ass," Charlene replied.

He backed out of the driveway.

"Listen, Kid, I loved your father like a brother. He was a great cop, but sometimes he tried to push too hard. I see a lot of him in you. You can't just go at everything head-on, sometimes it takes a little finesse. I've been doing this for thirty years and you'll get there. Not every case will be solved in a day."

Charlene nodded. "Sorry."

Larry chuckled. "I don't think Carl Minor likes you very much. What do you think of the widow?"

"I don't know if she killed her husband, but she's definitely hiding something."

Larry nodded.

"And not only that," Charlene continued. "Minor is hiding something, and it's apparent he didn't like his son-in-law one bit."

Chapter 10

"Yes, Sir." Captain Ronald Dunbar sat back in his chair, the phone call set on speaker, his face reddening with each insult thrown his way.

"Listen, Captain. I don't want this Charlene Taylor, this snot-nosed rookie, running this investigation!"

"But, Sir…"

"Don't 'but sir' me. I'm Carl Minor and I won't tolerate a rookie handling my son-in-law's case."

"But, Sir, Detective Taylor is not lead. She's working alongside one of our most experienced and most successful detectives." He looked at Charlene's partner, Larry Baker, who sat in the seat in front of Dunbar's desk. "Detective Baker's record speaks for itself, and I'm confident that he and detective Taylor, working together, will be successful. Or I would have never put them on this case."

"Well, she sure seemed like the lead this morning. Threatening my daughter with wild accusations."

"Mr. Minor, once Detective Baker and Detective Taylor get in this morning I'll have a talk with them and find out what happened. If something inappropriate was said or done, I'll get to the bottom of it and handle it internally."

"I don't like having a rookie involved. She seems like a loose cannon who can't follow procedures. Her father was just killed a few months ago. I'm worried about her emotional state. I also heard she likes the sauce."

Dunbar grimaced and shook his head. "I assure you, Charlene Taylor is in fact a rookie, but she's a more than capable detective and she has this precinct's full support and cooperation. Don't worry, Sir, this case is in good hands."

"What about the FBI?"

"Mr. Minor, murder is not a federal crime. We have jurisdiction. Trust me. We're doing everything possible to find your son-in-law's killer."

"I hear you have a suspect. I want this Philips girl arrested immediately."

"Sir, Philips is not a suspect. She's a 'person of interest' but that's all."

"I don't care, Captain. Bring her in. This case should be top priority and I want it closed and put to rest. Lord knows my daughter has been through enough. I don't want her to have to endure anymore. You got that?"

"I understand completely, Sir. But..." Before the captain could say more, Minor had hung up.

Dunbar hung up the phone and stared at it for a long, silent minute.

"Well, that was a pleasant call. You have something brown on your nose," Detective Baker said.

"Fuck you, Larry. I don't like taking orders," Dunbar replied. "How did Taylor do this morning?"

"It was beautiful. She ruffled some feathers," Baker answered. He and Dunbar smiled. "But Minor lawyered up. We won't be able to touch him or his daughter with a ten-foot pole. We'll need some heavy artillery to line her up again."

"I like the thought of that tight-ass Carl Minor, with his money and power, getting worked up by a rookie, female detective. Taylor might just have that young, cocky attitude we need on this case. What do you think of her?"

Baker shrugged so Dunbar continued. "Charlene is the son her father never had, athletic and tough. When it comes to police work, she acts on hunches and instincts, like her father. But I truly believe she might be better. Her record speaks for itself."

Dunbar swiveled in his chair and ripped off a precinct manpower list that hung on the wall. He scrolled down the chart, mumbling to himself as he crossed off names.

"Christ! Who'll work with her, Larry? I've got a fuckin' serial killer on the loose, and I'm being ordered to assign as many as I can to some rich kid's murder. Not only that, but I have a department full of egotistical, testosterone-pumping jackasses who won't take orders from a woman. My ulcer is on fire."

"She doesn't make friends easy," Baker said. "She carries that chip on her shoulder. Man, it's hot in here." He pulled at the collar of his shirt.

Even with the steady hum of the high-powered office air conditioner, beads of sweat streaked down the back of both overweight men, and their shirts clung uncomfortably.

"Berry and Clayton won't have a problem with it." Dunbar highlighted the two names and continued to scroll down when there was a knock on the door. Dunbar and Baker looked up to find Officer Darren Brady standing outside, his dark brown eyes half covered by curly brown bangs.

Dunbar waved him in. "What do you want, Brady?"

"Sir, if you need extra hands with the Anderson case, I'd like to volunteer."

"Oh great," Baker said, heavy sarcasm in his voice.

"Let me handle this, Larry." Dunbar looked at Officer Brady. "This isn't to get into Taylor's pants, is it?"

The officer's face reddened. "No, Sir."

"Well then, I'll let you know."

The young officer, new to the force, nodded and left the office, shutting the door behind him.

"What do you know about Brady?" Dunbar asked Baker.

"Very little. A transfer from Hollywood. Seems to have a perpetual hard-on for my partner. But..."

"Captain Klaver in the Hollywood division has nothing but praise for Brady. He's a good cop, organized, methodical and even obsessively clean from what I've heard. And he is willing to work with you guys. What do you think?"

Baker sighed audibly. "Why not? What a dream team."

She was thankful that she'd ignored the fresh case in the fridge when she'd gotten home this morning from the Anderson notification. The demons had been reaching out for her, and it took all she had not to get pulled in.

Charlene showed up for work early Saturday morning, anxious to get started on her first case. She'd only had a couple of hours of sleep, but she didn't care. She knew she was constantly being watched, given an extremely short leash that could be pulled in at any time.

The news on the car radio hadn't been encouraging. The press had been briefed and were swarming, already taking the case over, smelling the scent of blood. The names hadn't been released because, at that time, next of kin had yet to be notified. Once the mention of Anderson's name hit the streets, all hell would break loose.

The precinct was buzzing, already in full swing. She entered the department and found Larry in the captain's office, sharing a cigarette. She rushed in before going to her desk.

"Anything new?" she asked.

"Taylor, come in," the captain ordered. "How'd it go at the Anderson home?"

Charlene shrugged. "Fine."

The captain looked at Larry then back at Charlene. "Baker said you did a good job."

She looked at Larry. "Thank you, Sir."

"Baker says that all of the reports are done and on his desk. That would be a good place to start."

"Yes, Sir."

Larry and Charlene left the office.

"Did you tell the captain that Minor is hiding something?" Charlene asked Larry.

"Oh, yeah, that's the first thing I said when I got here. We should pull Carl Minor in for questioning in his son-in-law's murder. Gee, Kid, I know I look like Brad Pitt, but this isn't a Hollywood movie script. You can't go after big sharks like Minor on suspicion."

"But you agree, right?"

Larry didn't respond.

Charlene immediately booted up her computer and entered her password, but Larry grabbed his stained mug and headed for the coffee room.

Seeing the three reports completed and on Larry's desk made Charlene realize how high profile this case was. Everyone, including the Medical Examiner, Ballistics Team, and Crime Scene Unit, would be reporting to her and Larry, and they had all worked through the night.

When the screen booted up, Charlene noticed that the date and time of her last entry indicated last night. But she hadn't been in the department. Who had been inside her account? How had they gotten in and why?

This was the first time she'd been in the account so she had no files or anything to hide, but the fact that her privacy had been breached gave her worry.

Maybe it was the tech that had set up the account.

Charlene picked up her phone and dialed the captain.

"What?"

"Captain, when was my computer account set up?"

"What do I look like to you, Taylor, a computer geek? How should I know? Call the tech center."

She hung up and called downstairs. She was informed that her account was set up yesterday morning, that her last log in was in fact last night and there was no error. Charlene hung up.

She looked around the room but no one was paying attention to her. Were they keeping tabs on her?

She plugged the case information into the computer, looking for a match to the Anderson murder. The FBI VICAP System—the Violent Criminal Apprehension Program—was a computer database of every homicide that had occurred within the city of Los Angeles—and throughout the rest of the country—since 1985.

First, she scanned the database of the LA County Homicide Cold Case Department for a link. Then she checked the CAS VICAP for California State matches and then switched to the federal level. While the computer searched, she picked up the case book and sorted through the papers. Each case book included a page on the victim.

She read.

Victim—Kenneth Vincent Anderson—was killed between the approximate hours of 8 PM and 10 PM, Friday, May 26, from multiple— two—gunshot wounds to the chest. The bullets pierced vital organs and victim died almost instantly. Evidence found on person—body—legally withdrawn and placed in concealed plastic envelope, stapled to document.

Charlene checked the file but found no such evidence. Then she saw the staple holes at the top of the folder. Someone had removed the evidence. She looked around the room quickly but no one gave her a second look. Who had tampered with her crime scene and investigation?

She read on and noted that Anderson's preliminary toxicology report showed that his blood-alcohol level to be at zero point one eight, well above the legal limit in Los Angeles of zero point zero eight percent. At that level, Anderson would have undergone severe emotional swings, and a major loss in reflexes, reaction time, and gross motor control. He would not have been able to defend himself.

The victim's Jaguar as well as Philips' car had been vacuumed and combed through, but nothing in the way of evidence for the case was recovered. His phone was recovered in the car and was currently being scanned.

Charlene opened the ballistics report. The bullets pulled from Anderson's body were from a nine-millimeter, just as Larry had guessed. No other bullets, holes, or casings were found at the scene, meaning the killer had only fired the gun twice—perfect shooting.

Forensics found no fingerprints on or around the body. Only four sets of prints were found in the house. One belonged to Anderson and the other three were unknown. Charlene assumed the three leftover belonged to the girls living there, but because they had never been arrested, their prints weren't on file.

There were several hair fibers found on Anderson clothes, belonging to a female. Those hairs could have been left on Anderson anywhere, at anytime. But Charlene would still have to test them against the female suspects in the case.

She quickly scribbled on a sticky pad to have Larry send someone to fingerprint the girls to compare the prints they'd pulled from the scene. Then she stuck it on his computer screen.

Turning back to her desk, she found the folder stuffed with transcribed interviews of neighbors. Most people had been home, but no one saw or heard anything that night, not even gun shots. Silencer? But how many people owned a silencer? As easy as it was to obtain a firearm in LA, it wasn't the same for a silencer.

The GSR Test on Philips' hands and clothing came back negative, eliminating her as having fired a gun that night, unless she changed clothes and washed thoroughly before getting back home. It was a possibility. She could have discarded the garments during the time she'd left the house.

The computer chimed, completing its search. Two hundred eighty-six matches were found in the state of California dating back one year, but that was understandable. A gun was a common weapon, easily accessible. Charlene then focused her search on LA murders only. The computer found forty-eight. Then to narrow it further, she typed in 'two bullets in chest.' The computer came back with eight matches.

"Find anything?" Larry asked, handing her a warm mug.

"Eight matches in LA."

"What do ya got?" Larry slipped on a pair of reading glasses and looked over her shoulder, as Charlene read off the list.

"Looks like…" Charlene scrolled down the screen. "Four are gang/mob related, two robberies, and two are closed, both shooters in prison for life without parole."

She looked at Larry who was rummaging in his pocket.

"ME found this in Anderson's breast pocket after we left." He set a zip lock bag on top of Charlene's keyboard.

She picked up the bag, which was labeled with the case number, date, time, and details of where it was found. Examining the contents, she noticed the staple holes at the top.

She heard Larry grunt and rip the sticky note off his screen, but pick up the phone and call forensics. Charlene smiled to herself.

Inside the bag were multiple black-painted rose petals, although they were now wilted and a bit mushy from the moisture. The color of the rose was significant, because a black rose meant *death* or *farewell*.

When he'd hung up the phone, Charlene asked, "How many petals?"

"Thirteen," Larry said, giving her a look.

Thirteen roses meant *secret admirer*.

She looked at her partner. "Thirteen black rose petals? Mob hit?"

"Could be. They've already been dusted but there are no prints. They pried the bullets from Anderson and are running them through the system, hoping for a cold hit."

"I know that black rose petals placed in the victim's pocket is a calling card for LA's version of the mafia. But it just doesn't feel like a mob hit."

Larry grunted and nodded. "I hear ya. Let's go talk with the roommates. They've checked into the Hilton on South Grand Avenue."

"The Hilton?" Charlene gave her partner a blank stare. "How the hell can college kids afford the Hilton?"

"Good question. Maybe we should ask them."

Charlene was putting on her jacket when the captain called for them. "Baker, Taylor, come in here."

The captain was pacing the floor, as if something major had broken. Charlene saw Jim Flanders, the department PR guy, sitting quietly on the couch.

"Sit down," the Captain scowled.

Charlene could see the captain's TV turned to a news report. A handsome female Asian reporter was positioned for dramatic effect outside Philips' house, but the volume was down and Charlene couldn't read the caption.

"I don't have to tell you the impact this case will have on the city. You know Carl Minor. The media will have a field day with this. So far, word hasn't gotten out on who the victim is, buying us some time. But it will. So we need to get ahead of it." He sighed. "Because of the Celebrity Slayer case eating up time and manpower, I can only assign those three officers to your unit. They already know and are awaiting instructions."

"What three officers?" Charlene asked.

Larry smiled. "You're going to love this, Kid."

"Berry, Clayton, and Brady," the captain responded.

Charlene didn't reply, instead she looked at Flanders. "How are we handling the press on this one?"

It was the captain who answered. "Don't worry about the media. I'll take care of them." He gave the PR guy a look and received a silent nod.

"I'll drive," Larry said, leaving the office and heading to the reception desk to check out a unit vehicle.

"What about Berry and Clayton?"

"Have them look into Anderson and the toxicology report."

Charlene nodded and jogged across the room. She spoke faster than she should have. "Clayton, you and Berry find out everything you can on Ken Anderson. Talk to his attorney and find out about his will. Then head over to UCLA and speak with some of his colleagues. Find out where he was drinking last night and who he was with."

She slipped past Darren's desk without being seen.

Before reaching Larry, she swung by her desk and grabbed the preliminary background report.

As they reached the door, they could hear Darren calling them. Charlene stopped to turn, but Larry pulled her sleeve.

"Pretend you didn't hear him."

Chapter 11

They checked out a car and, as they pulled out of the underground parking lot, Larry merged onto 100 West First Street before taking a left onto South Grand Avenue.

"Looks like they're doing some renovations on the Museum of Contemporary Art," Charlene noted as they passed the historic MOCA building.

"They can do all the renovating they want, but they'll never get me inside," Larry said. "Tell me a little about Sandra Philips and Ashley Stanley so I know what I'm going into."

Charlene opened the file.

"Not much on either of them. We ran their social security numbers. Stanley's from San Diego. She's a twenty-one-year-old freshman at UCLA. It says here that she's an only child and her parents are both doctors who graduated from UCLA."

"That's it?"

"That's all that's in the system."

Larry didn't take his eyes off the road, but Charlene could see the confusion on his face. "Not much there to go on."

"Guess she hasn't done anything to report about."

"Guess we know how they're stayin' at the Hilton—mommy and daddy. What about the Philips' sister, other than the fact she's from Chicago?"

Charlene turned the page. "Oh boy!"

"What?"

"Sandra's a rape victim."

"How recent?"

"Very. And guess who she accused?"

"Anderson?"

"Bingo. According to this, on May twenty-fifth, two nights ago and one night before his murder, Sandra Philips filed sexual assault charges against Anderson. A unit was sent to Anderson's home but they couldn't find him. He wasn't seen again until we found him…dead with two bullets buried in his chest."

"Interesting. What else?"

Charlene flipped back from the rape report. "From Chicago, eighteen years old, currently employed at the Beechwood Country Club. Look here, it says that Sandra was a member of the Chicago Gun Club. Joined a few months before moving to LA."

"I'd say that's interesting too."

"And pertinent. This report gives Sandra Philips means, the ability to handle a gun, and motive, the rape."

"I'm glad we have that information. Every gun club in America has to register their members in our database. Makes it accessible."

"I think I have a job for Darren."

"Do it," Larry said.

Charlene scanned the signed name at the bottom of the page and opened her iPhone. "Darren, it's Charlene. I need you to contact Detective Adrienne Jackson with the Rape Special Section Unit. Ask her about the Sandra Philips' case, get as much information as you can, and leave a full written report on my desk."

"Funny you should mention her," Darren said. "I think Jackson was just up here looking for you. I saw her at your desk and writing something down, probably leaving you a note. Do you want me to check?"

"No, she probably knows we're working the Anderson case and we would want to know about the Philips' incident. Give her a call and get the details."

Darren was saying something when Charlene hung up.

"Ah, hell," Larry said

"What is it?"

"I don't want to have to talk about this. Maybe you should take Philips, and I'll take Stanley. Then we can reconvene in the car and go over our notes."

"That's probably a good idea, Larry."

He finally took his eyes off the road and looked at her. "What's that supposed to mean?"

"Nothing."

"Hey, I can be just as sympathetic as the next guy. It just makes me uncomfortable."

"It's okay, I got it, Larry." Then she thought of something else. "Didn't Beverly Anderson tell us that her husband was at home yesterday afternoon?"

"Yes, she did." Larry rubbed his eyes. "I need a smoke."

They pulled up to the downtown hotel located in the heart of the business and financial district. The historical downtown building from the 1920s was the area's only European-style Boutique hotel.

A mob of media, as well as the rubber-necked public, gathered outside the hotel. Larry didn't bother swerving to avoid anyone. They squeezed through the cameras and questions, flashed their badges, and were led inside by a doorman in a green suit and hat.

"It's been like this for the last couple of hours," the doorman said.

"Goddamn vultures!" Larry spat the words from his mouth like a bad taste.

"What happened?" Charlene asked Larry.

"Has to be Minor," he said. "This is about to get big, Kid."

"Like OJ in '94?"

"Maybe bigger."

The detectives crossed the gleaming marble lobby and approached the welcome desk hidden by an assortment of scented floral displays. They flashed their badges again.

"We're looking for Jessica Philips' room," Larry said.

A pretty, dark blonde woman in a green blazer typed at a keyboard. "I'm sorry, we don't have anyone by that name."

"How about Sandra Philips or Ashley Stanley?" Charlene said.

Again the woman typed rapidly. "Nope."

"Jesus Christ," Larry groaned.

Charlene turned around and watched a young bellboy sorting luggage on a cart.

"You," she said. She showed her badge. "We're looking for three young college girls who checked in this morning."

The boy looked at the woman behind the counter, and then said, "Room 324."

Larry turned back to the woman behind the counter. "We're gonna need an empty room."

"Let me get the manager."

She slipped into a back room and returned within minutes.

"Detectives," said a short man with slick hair and a waxed mustache. "What is the problem?"

Larry nodded towards outside. "What do you think, genius? We need to use a room to question a witness," Larry lied.

"Oh, then in that case, you may use our meeting rooms. Each room is set up with a…"

"Great," Larry interrupted and grabbed Charlene.

They were directed to the elevators.

"Nice one," Larry said when they were inside.

"Never underestimate a boy and his penis," Charlene replied.

As they rode the elevator, Charlene said, "I saw Carter out there."

"Prick."

Paul Carter was the new *LA Times* cop-beat reporter. His hennaed, slightly disheveled hair and matching goatee stood out amongst the crowd. His pear-shaped build showed the diet of an on-the-call reporter, and his beady eyes were constantly on the lookout for the next big story.

Since joining the *Times*, the thirty-eight year old man had quickly made a name for himself as an aggressive, tell-it-like-it-is reporter who had already made a few enemies on the police force because of his low-ball tactics. Carter was only motivated by fame and fortune, not the real story. He was looking for the "big story," then the book and movie deals that might follow.

"Third floor, this is us," Charlene announced.

They stepped off the elevator and approached the door.

"Should we have called ahead first?" Charlene asked.

Larry smiled. "You're cute, Kid."

He banged on the door with his fist.

The door was opened by a younger version of Jessica Philips, petite and striking. The family resemblance was evident, although this woman was more attractive, even with the noticeable shades of bruising on her face and a bloodshot eye. She had a 'spider bite' labret piercing the left side of her bottom lip.

"Detective Baker, Detective Taylor," Jessica Philips' voice came from the back of the room.

Philips, and the woman Charlene presumed to be Ashley Stanley, were standing behind Sandra Philips. The TV was on and showed the Channel 4 news team helicopter hovering over the crowd gathered outside the hotel, their eye-in-the-sky focused on the Hilton.

The woman at the door stood aside and the detectives moved in. The room was a double, with matching queen-sized beds.

Jessica made the introductions. "This is my sister, Sandra, and our roommate, Ashley. Have you found something new on the case?"

"Afraid not. But we'd like to ask Sandra and Ashley some questions."

Sandra was quiet, but Ashley spoke up. "Of course, Detectives, whatever we can do to help."

Charlene stayed in room 324, while Larry and Ashley Stanley headed to the conference room on the first floor.

Jessica changed into workout clothes and headed for the fitness room downstairs, to give Charlene and Sandra some privacy.

Before starting the interrogation, Charlene sat back and studied her interviewee—nervous, apprehensive, and almost scared to a point of avoiding eye contact. Charlene could see the similarities with Jessica, but also the differences.

Sandra had been blessed with elegant beauty—well-proportioned features, long flowing auburn hair, blue eyes, a petite frame and flawless skin.

They were seated at a round wooden table at a custom-designed work area in the corner of the room.

"I can't believe this is happening!" Sandra shivered, looking as if she was about to break down, but composed herself. "I should never have come to LA."

"When did you move?" Charlene asked.

"A few weeks ago. Mom and Dad are both gone, and Sandra is all I have left. Things were going so well. I was with Sandra again, I had a job, and was making friends, and then…"

Sandra nodded, sniffed, and dabbed her eyes and nose.

"Are you okay?" Charlene asked.

Sandra nodded. "Ask me."

"Where were you last night?"

Sandra looked away from Charlene. "I was at class."

Nothing in Sandra Philips' bio indicated she was in school or taking classes.

"Where?"

"It's a night class at West Los Angeles College."

"What are you taking?"

Sandra stood up and walked over to a table with a mirror. There was a jug of ice water and a coffee machine on top. She grabbed a clean glass and poured some water.

Before drinking she said, "It's a class for rape victims. It started at nine and ended at eleven."

Charlene's mouth went dry. West LA College was located in Culver City, so Charlene knew that if Sandra had been at that meeting, which could be easily verified, then there was no way she had time to commit the crime at her house.

Charlene could have found out the details of the rape from the lead investigator, and she would, but she also wanted the direct story from the victim so she could examine Sandra's body language.

"Sandra, I know this is difficult. But I need to hear what happened on May twenty-fifth."

Sandra returned to her chair, curled up, and hugged her knees to her chest. Charlene could see the fear in her eyes.

"It's okay, Sandra. Take your time."

"But I already told Detective Jackson everything, twice."

"I know, Sandra. But I need to hear it myself. Sometimes people forget things immediately after a traumatic event and then, as time goes by, little details come back."

"Okay." She hesitated.

"Just start from the beginning."

"I was watching TV when I heard a knock on the door."

"What time was this?"

"It was late. Probably close to midnight. Jessica and Ashley were at the library. I opened the door and Professor Anderson was there." Sandra spoke as if she'd memorized the story and had told it a thousand times before.

"Did you know him?"

"Well, of course."

Charlene didn't say anything, and Sandra must have seen something register in the detective's eyes, because she recoiled, closing her mouth. "I thought you knew."

"Knew what?"

"About Jessica and Professor Anderson."

Charlene had suspected. "Please go on, Sandra."

"Is this going to get Jessica in trouble?"

"Not if you tell the truth, Sandra."

She took a deep breath and continued. "Jessica had never brought him around, and I knew their affair was supposed to be a secret. But I recognized him from the Country Club where I work so I didn't think much about it. When I opened the door I could smell alcohol and cigarette smoke."

"What did he say?"

"He asked if Jessica was there, but his speech was slurred. When I said no, he smiled and pushed his way inside. The way he looked at me gave me chills."

"Other times you associated with Ken Anderson, how did he seem? How did he act?"

Sandra shrugged her slender shoulders. "The only other times I saw him were at the Country Club. I never led him on, if that's what you mean, Detective."

She was getting defensive and angry.

"Not at all, Sandra. I just want to get a feel for your relationship."

"I never saw him outside of the Club. There was no *relationship*."

Charlene nodded.

"I was dressed for bed, in a striped pajama bottom and a mini half-shirt, and I could tell he was looking at my pierced naval. I didn't like it, and I tried to cover myself, but he pinned me against the desk. I started to freak out. I told him I didn't know when Jessica would be home and he should leave. But he just stood there."

"I tried to slip by him, but he lunged at me. I tried dodging him, pushing him away, but he was strong. I begged him to stop. I pulled his hair and scratched his face. And then he called me a tease, and said that nobody turned *him* down."

"Then he hit me. I fell to the floor and before I could get up, he was on me. He tore off my clothes…" She started to shake.

Sandra was sweating now, her face paling. She was gulping in chunks of breath, and tiny sobs slipped through her closed lips.

"That's okay, Sandra. You don't have to say any more."

"But I want to." She looked at Charlene. "When he was done, he pulled up his pants and stared down at me. I couldn't look at him. I closed my eyes, but I could feel him kneeling next to me. I wish I had been unconscious, because I wouldn't have heard him."

"It's okay, Sandra. Don't."

She shook her head emphatically. "I want you to hear. I want you to know. He whispered into my ear, I could smell the alcohol on his breath. He said, 'Keep your mouth shut'."

Sandra full-body shivered. "I still hear those words in my head."

Charlene's heart was pounding. She couldn't imagine a woman, a child like Sandra, let alone anyone, having to go through that. Bile rose in her throat.

Sandra continued.

"Telling Jessica was the hardest part. I hated keeping it from her. I wanted her to know. She had a right to know."

As Charlene stood, Sandra said, "I don't know if I could have done it without Detective Jackson. She was so sympathetic, so comforting. I could tell she really wanted to help. She told me I was brave. And I liked that. No one had ever called me brave before. She promised me Ken would never hurt me again, hurt anyone again…and I believed her."

"Thank you, Sandra."

Charlene was starting to write something down when Sandra's words brought her head up from her notepad. They met eyes.

"Detective Taylor, do you really believe that time heals all wounds?"

"Yes I do, Sandra," Charlene answered, thinking it ironic that she could tell another woman that but not herself.

"No matter how hard I try, I can't get rid of the memories, the nightmares. When I close my eyes, all I see is Ken. The fear is constant."

"You'll get through this, Sandra. I promise." But Charlene couldn't believe her own words.

"Do you own a gun, Sandra?"

Sandra hesitated slightly before answering, "No."

Charlene put her hand on Sandra's knee. "Thank you for your time, Sandra, and your honesty."

Larry was already in the car when Charlene left the hotel. He had his notepad out and was flipping through it.

"What did you get?" Charlene asked.

"A whole lotta nothin'. A lot of nervous fidgetin', anxious and apprehensive looks, easy to see the impact this situation has on Stanley. She's taking it hard."

"I got the same thing from Sandra."

"Stanley said she was playin' in her competitive women's softball league last night. The game started at eight and lasted a couple of hours. I'll follow up on that. She admitted knowin' Anderson professionally, as her professor, but outside of that she didn't have any contact with him." He hesitated. "Jessica Philips was boppin' the Professor." Larry smiled at his discovery, as if it was a mind blowing proclamation.

"Sandra told me the same thing. The affair was supposed to be a secret, but I wonder who else knew about it?"

"That's what I was thinking. It would explain Anderson's presence in the house. Could have been a lovers' tiff?"

"It wouldn't be the first time, but I'm not feeling it."

"Yeah, I agree. I don't see Jessica Philips as a possible suspect. Not yet, anyway."

"I always suspected more than a teacher-student relationship," Charlene admitted. "We have to find out what else Jessica Philips is hiding."

Charlene opened her phone and called Officer Berry.

"Are you guys still at UCLA?"

"Just leaving."

"Try to retrieve Ken Anderson and Jessica Philips' class lists, and interview some of the other students. See if anyone knew if Jessica was dating anyone. We're heading there now, so we might run into you."

Charlene hung up and looked at Larry. "You know, this doesn't just give Sandra motive."

"I know, I know." Larry looked disturbed. "If Beverly Anderson knew about her husband's affair, then she too had motive."

"And what about Carl Minor? Would he tolerate a cheating son-in-law?"

The UCLA Department of Psychology was housed in Franz Hall, a three building facility located on the east side of campus. The detectives entered by Westholme Avenue, badged their way past the campus security guards and parked in the designated visitors' parking lot number two, close enough to cross campus on foot.

They stopped by the dean's office to show the search warrants and receive the key to Anderson's office. After showing their badges, the receptionist, a cheerfully overweight woman with a trained smile, indicated that the dean was away on holidays and wouldn't be returning until Monday. When asked about his home number, the detectives were politely told that the dean was in Bermuda. The secretary called campus safety to escort them to Anderson's office.

As they walked to the professor's office, located on the third floor of the old building, the campus security guard went on about always dreaming of being a cop, but a hearing impairment disqualified him from applying.

They followed the guard up three flights of stairs to the office. They had brought along their investigative kits, and campus security left the detectives, ensuring they would lock up when they left.

Charlene and Larry slid on protective gloves and tossed the room. There was no safe, so all of Anderson's papers were scattered chaotically.

Even though it wasn't the crime scene, vital details could be in the office to lead the investigation. Who had visited Anderson? What was he into?

They dusted the entire room, starting with the doorknobs and moving to the desk drawer handles. They collected all the papers and threw them in a bag. It would be easier to investigate everything with a few more sets of eyes at the office.

"Look at this, Taylor." Larry held up a pocket-sized black book.

She approached him curiously. "What is it?"

"Looks like the professor's little black book. The pages are filled with women's names. Jessica and Sandra Philips are both here under 'P'."

"So he considered Sandra's rape as a notch on his bed post?" Charlene was disgusted, but she wondered how many of those names were added after his marriage. Then she had a thought. "Is Ashley Stanley in there?"

"Stanley, S… Let's see." Larry flipped through the pages. "Stanley, Stanley, Stanley… Nope, not here."

They retrieved the rest of the material in the office, locked up, and headed for the precinct.

Chapter 12

After visiting Anderson's office, they spent the next three hours going through the stuff they'd confiscated and writing out their daily reports.

After work, Charlene took a detour on her way home. She circled Lauren's neighborhood several times, looking for any indication of a disturbance. She prayed for a sign that would give her probable cause to barge into the house.

She parked on the side of the road, staring at the house, picturing little Lauren inside the dragon's layer. How was she coping? What could Charlene do to help?

The images of Lauren's bruised body consumed Charlene.

Ever since that morning, Charlene had been keeping tabs on Lauren and her family and the ongoing social case. Charlene doubted that anything would be done and didn't see Lauren being removed from the family.

Charlene would have to think of a way to get her out.

She got out of the car, walked to the door, and knocked.

It was opened by Charles Lefebvre, the man who had almost caused her to lose her job. Lefebvre stood at the door with a smug look on his face, showing no ill effects of their run in. Charlene would have liked to wipe it clean.

"What do you want?" he said. Charlene could tell that he recognized her even out of uniform.

Just seeing his face stirred something deep within Charlene. "I'd like to see Lauren."

"What about?"

"That's between us."

Lefebvre hesitated, obviously trying to goad Charlene into doing something stupid, but she wasn't taking the bait.

"Who is it, honey?" Monica Schwartz's voice came from behind and then her head appeared over Lefebvre's shoulder. When she saw Charlene, she didn't say a word.

"Officer Taylor!" Lauren's voice boomed from behind her mother and then the little girl squeezed through two sets of legs to meet Charlene. The six-year-old wrapped her arms around Charlene's legs and squeezed tightly. "You came back." Lauren smiled and Charlene could see that her two front adult teeth were starting to come in.

"I told you I would," Charlene said. She looked at Schwartz and Lefebvre who were still standing at the door watching.

"Let's go, honey." Schwartz pulled Lefebvre by the shoulder but he didn't leave immediately, staring at Charlene one last time before shutting the door.

Charlene bent down and hugged Lauren. "How have you been?"

"Great," Lauren squealed. "Mommy bought me a new bike and I can ride it all by myself...no training wheels." The girl's contagious smile was ear-to-ear.

"That's so great, Lauren. You're a real star." Charlene showed Lauren a book she'd brought along. "My mother gave me this book when I was about your age."

Lauren took the book and read the cover, her eyes growing wide with excitement. "*Beauty and the Beast*. Wow!"

"It's all yours."

Lauren looked at Charlene. "Really?"

"Yep. You can read about Belle every night before you go to sleep."

"Cool, thanks, Officer Taylor."

Just as Lauren was giving Charlene another hug, the front door opened and Lefebvre said, "Lauren, it's time for your bath. Your mother has the tub ready."

"Okay." The girl smiled, waved playfully at Charlene, and skipped into the house.

Lefebvre stepped outside and shut the door. "I don't ever want to see you back here again. You've already done enough to this family."

Charlene stepped closer to Lefebvre, right in his face almost nose to nose. She could see sweat seeping out of his pores. Lefebvre squirmed, taking an involuntary step back.

"Actually, it's Detective Taylor now." Charlene smiled. "I'll be driving by this house every night until you're either behind bars or dead.

If I see one reason to stop, I won't even hesitate. And this time, I won't have a partner to stop me."

Charlene turned around and headed back to her car. Lefebvre was still on the doorstep when she drove away.

After being caught in evening rush hour, she traipsed through the door at almost eight. The fridge had been freshly stocked, so Charlene grabbed a Bud and flipped on the TV. She cleaned out her jacket pockets and noticed she hadn't put Anderson's car keys back in the evidence bag. She threw the keys on the kitchen counter and used the remote to turn on the TV.

Listening to the nightly news report, she got undressed. As a cop, she was always interested in the kind of attention a case garnered. As expected, the Anderson murder was the lead story. America loved drama, and to Charlene, this case reeked of it.

The media had already ranked the case with some of the more famous ones LAPD had investigated—Manson, Kennedy, and OJ.

Ken Anderson's personal life, his in-laws, led the story, and Jessica Philips' name was mentioned as a highly involved suspect. They were making Ken Anderson out to have been a saint, and Jessica a killer. But to Larry and Charlene, she wasn't even a possible suspect.

Captain Dunbar appeared and gave a brief, candid speech, spouting the regular mumbo-jumbo, "The police are doing all they can to get to the truth." Then Carl Minor was interviewed to say that he would do all he could to help. Charlene assumed he would also throw some money and clout around.

She shook her head and flicked off the set. The politics of the case would become a burden and a hurdle.

She was getting undressed when the phone rang. Charlene contemplated answering. She looked at the sweating bottle in her hand and took another swig. She sat on the futon and clicked on the phone.

"Hi, Charlie."

"You again."

"You didn't think I was going away, did you?" He spoke with a voice devoid of emotion.

"Hoping, more like it." She took a drink. "Why don't we meet?"

"Are you interested, Charlie?"

"Sorry, I don't go for little dicks. And don't call me that." She could feel her temperature rise.

"Temper, temper, your doctor wouldn't want to hear about your short fuse going off again. I saw the guy you attacked. What a shame." He let out a wicked laugh.

Charlene felt beads of sweat pierce her upper lip. She bit her bottom lip. How does he know so much?

"What do you want from me?" Charlene snapped back.

"You're going to help me get my message out."

"What message?"

"Now that you're officially a detective, I think it's time to play a game. Are you in the mood for a game, Charlie?"

She composed herself. "So you've been watching me."

"I've been waiting for this day."

"You have?" Charlene sounded surprised. She wasn't sure why she wasn't. "Why's that?"

"Now we're working on even ground. It's a fair fight. Now, I can compare the two Taylor detectives." He let out a low laugh.

Anger surged up from within her. She'd been unconsciously holding her breath and let it out. She went to a machine she had attached to the phone and turned it on.

"Are you going to give me a hint?"

He ignored the question. "You better put on a shirt, Charlie. You look cold."

Charlene froze, her heart dropping in her chest. She got up and slowly moved towards the window. She peeked out to the darkened side street, but with no streetlights, her vision was limited. She thought she saw a gaunt figure in the shadows inside a sidewalk phone booth, but couldn't be certain. There were so few phone booths still remaining that she was always surprised when she passed this one.

"Do you like what you see?" she asked.

Charlene furtively removed her gun from the holster. Holding the portable phone to her ear, she tiptoed to the door and into the hall of her apartment building.

She heard him squeeze out a low laugh, but she could tell that she had triggered something.

"Oh, Charlie, I really can't wait until we get closer. I know everything about you. But my favorite part is your tattoo."

Her breath caught in her throat. He knew everything, even her most secret, intimate details.

"Tell me, Detective. Is that a sign of freedom—breaking from the chains of your father?"

She had to keep him on the line. "You seem to know a lot about me. I don't know a thing about you. For all I know, you're just some pervert who peeps in women's windows."

She was only two flights of stairs and the corner of the building away from the booth. But she was moving slowly, cautious not to frighten him or give away her position. Charlene was scared herself, but her police mentality, her instincts, kicked in. Her heart pumped.

"I don't think so, Detective!" Charlene could hear the anger growing in his tone. She had touched a nerve. This guy was an attention seeker, loved the spotlight. He wanted her to know who he really was. But as quickly as he angered, he just as quickly caught himself and regained his frighteningly calm, reasonable voice. "You'll soon realize that I'm the man I say I am." Then the connection was broken.

She dropped the phone and sprinted down the remaining flight of stairs. She rounded the corner with her pistol drawn and grasped tightly. She sidestepped towards the phone booth hunched in a marksman's crouch. Fear urged her on, her nerves tingling. Charlene quickly shifted her body and swung out, blocking the front of the opened booth door.

Empty.

If someone *had* been in there, he or she was now gone. The telephone receiver dangled in mid-air, and the remnants of a shattered light bulb lay scattered on the floor. She scanned the area and listened, seeing and hearing nothing.

How did he know so much? Did she know this guy?

A car honked, and she raised her gun in time to see a car full of young men, their heads out the window, screaming and cheering at her. Then she realized she was still in only a bra.

She examined the scene a little longer, taking ten minutes to make sure it was clear, and then holstered her weapon.

"I need a drink."

Charlene rolled off him and grabbed the Budweiser from her night table. She took a sip—too warm—and bounced off the bed. Ignoring her underwear, she pulled on one of Andy's old NYU T-shirts that was way too big for her and headed for the kitchen.

"Wow, that was amazing," Andy said. "And I thought I was just coming over for sushi." He smiled.

She came back holding a Styrofoam container and sat cross-legged on the bed beside him.

"I owed you for the other night," she answered, popping a piece into her mouth.

"Move in with me," he said.

"Not this again." Charlene scooped a piece of sushi out of the container and slid it into Andy's open mouth.

He chewed, swallowed, and then said, "Why not?"

"Andy, I'm not having this discussion again. I'm not ready, and that's it." She got up and headed back to the kitchen.

"I'm not giving up on us, Charlene. This is going to happen. I want us to have a life together."

"Do as you please, Andy, but I don't have time for a life. You have to go now. I have work to do."

"What kind of work do you do at one in the morning?"

"Real work." She opened the fridge and removed a cold bottle.

"You have real issues, Charlene." She heard his feet hit the floor. "Every time I bring up our future, you push me away."

"So I've been told, repeatedly."

Andy got dressed and let himself out without saying goodbye. He slammed the door hard.

Once he was gone, she opened the beer and entered her new, homemade office.

Her father's file had been awaiting her. She set the beer on her desk and sat down, opening the three-inch folder. She read over her father's case—police files, crime scene photos, ballistics reports, and autopsy protocols.

She checked the witness list. Only one. Ren Cheung was working the late shift at the Imperial Palace Chinese Buffet that night. He'd called it in. Charlene knew that sometimes killers would come forward as witnesses. It gave them a sense of power, and helped them find out how much the police knew. The first witness should be the first suspect.

She threw the papers back on the desk and took a drink. "This means nothing unless I'm at the scene," she said to herself.

She checked her watch, threw on an old pair of faded jeans, grabbed a red sweater off the floor, and headed for the door.

She passed through "Guitar Row," aptly nicknamed because of the number of guitar stores and music industry-related businesses, before parking in front of the Imperial Palace building, just a few blocks down from the Viper Room, a nightclub once owned by actor Johnny Depp. Imperial Palace was closed, so Charlene pulled a flashlight out of her glove box and walked around to the back alley, which was black and pungent. The stench assaulted her nostrils.

Without the aid of her iPhone flashlight, Charlene would never have found her way around. Either the killer had a light, or was so familiar with the area that he could maneuver in the dark.

She scanned the corners of the alley with her light then changed her mind. She returned to her vehicle and brought it around, entering the alley from the east wing, as her father had done. She parked in the exact location where her father's car had been found.

She turned off the engine, rolled down the window, and sat staring through the windshield. Except for the light exiting the back of the

Chinese restaurant, the lot was quiet and empty. Charlene knew the restaurant had closed at midnight, and the night-timers—dishwashers, bus boys, and cleaners—were busy preparing the inside for another day of business.

She stared around the alley and noticed that the darkest, most hidden part of the alleyway was to her left, in an unlit corner. That would have been the best place for a stalker to watch his unsuspecting target and be able to move in undetected.

She looked at the passenger seat where two things rested—the case file and a new six-pack of Old Milwaukee. She grabbed the folder and had just opened it when a door slammed to her left. Charlene was so startled that she almost reached for her weapon, when she saw a short, older Asian man, with two black garbage bags slung over his shoulders, heave the sacks into the adjacent bins.

"Hey, you!" Charlene called, opening the car door and stepping out.

The man turned, so Charlene removed her badge and approached him.

"I'm looking for Ren Cheung."

The man snickered, obviously at her pronunciation of the name.

"Ren is in restaurant."

"Can you get him for me?"

The man nodded and bowed slightly. He had small eyes and saggy jowls, and what little hair remained was parted to the side. He turned towards the opening and yelled something in Chinese. Words were exchanged before an extremely tall, thin Asian man, ducking through the doorway, exited the kitchen and joined Charlene.

Since Asian men were known for their small stature, Charlene had to do a double take.

Cheung had a face deeply pitted from acne, a silver stud in his chin, and thick lips. He was stoop-shouldered, maybe from the fact that he was a foot taller than his colleagues. Again, the man said something in Chinese to Cheung, before leaving them and rejoining the kitchen staff.

"What did he say?" Charlene asked.

"He say, 'Don't get pregnant. Have short kids'." Ren smiled.

"Funny. You're the one who found the police officer?"

He nodded. "Yes, Ma'am. I tell cops everyting I know."

Charlene nodded. "Yes, I read the report. Can you tell me again?"

"I come out with garbage, see car. I go see, find dead guy. Call cops."

"You didn't see anyone else?"

"No, Ma'am."

"You didn't hear any noise, like gunshots?"

"No, Ma'am."

"Silencer," Charlene whispered.

"Pardon?"

"Nothing. You didn't see any other vehicle around?"

"No, Ma'am."

"How often do you come out here?"

"On busy night, maybe every two hour with garbage."

"Any smokers?"

"Oh yes, many."

"Do they smoke out here?"

"Yes. They start at nine, and rotate every thirty minutes."

"So the killer must have known the schedule."

Cheung started to shift back and forth on his feet, with continuing glances towards the door. Charlene saw the older gentleman staring out at them, wondered if he was Cheung's boss, and didn't want to get the young man into trouble.

"Was there anything different that night that sticks out in your mind?"

"You mean other than dead guy?"

She nodded. "Thank you, Ren." She stuck out her hand but the man ignored it, instead bowing.

As he turned to leave, Charlene said, "Can you do me one favor before heading back to the kitchen?"

Cheung turned back around. "What's that?"

"Go sit in my car?"

"Huh?"

"Behind the wheel."

Cheung shrugged his slender shoulders and headed towards the parked Volvo. As he was moving back the seat, his back turned, Charlene slipped into the darkened, black-shadowed corner and watched him.

Cheung sat down and shut the door. When he looked out, he panicked. He quickly twisted and turned his neck, intensely searching the alley for Charlene.

"Detective?" he asked.

Charlene stepped out of the shadow, and Cheung looked at her.

"You couldn't see me, could you?"

"No, Ma'am."

"That's all. Thanks."

Cheung didn't question, he just nodded and headed back to the kitchen.

When Cheung had disappeared, Charlene walked to the unlit corner, from where she suspected her father had been observed. Using her flashlight, she searched for any signs that someone had been there—cigarette butts, chewing gum, tread mark from a shoe, a piece of fingernail, piece of thread, used coffee cup or broken glass—but there was nothing.

That would have been too easy.

Trash littered the edge of the walls and around the dumpster. Charlene wondered how long it had been there.

She walked over to the dumpster and lifted the lid. The odor stabbed her like a punch to the trachea. The dumpster was filled with bags that had been gutted—either animals or LA's version of the homeless.

There was no warrant needed for garbage-abandoned property, and she wondered if it had been checked. There was no point now, since it would have been emptied several times over since her father's murder. She closed the lid and returned to her car.

Chapter 13

On Sunday morning, Charlene stood on the concrete steps of the Our Lady of Fatima Catholic Church on South Barrington Avenue. She had attended the morning service with her mother and sister, the first time she had been to church since she was old enough to make her own decisions.

"I'm glad you came, Charlene. It means a lot to Mom," Jane said, standing beside Charlene as they watched their mother outside the church, making the rounds to fellow worshippers and saying hello.

"It feels weird being here. It's been so long." Charlene tugged at her clothes.

"You need to come more often."

Charlene nodded. "Sometimes, with the things I see on the job, it makes it hard to believe there's a God."

"I guess so. You look great." Jane smiled.

"Thanks. Of course, you look stunning as usual."

Jane had always been a looker, and she had grown more beautiful with age. Her long brown hair was tied back and her perfect complexion lightly colored from blush. Four months pregnant with her first child and starting to show—the glow of pregnancy on her cheeks. She had on a new Bloomingdale's pant suit, all black.

"Thanks, but I feel fat." She patted her tiny round lump of a belly. "Did the Dodgers win last night?"

It was a failed but valiant attempt. Jane wasn't the athletic type and had never liked sports. She was the older, critical sister. They were as different as night and day. Jane was the beautiful one, the responsible one, born to be a wife and mother.

"They didn't play." Charlene smiled.

"Oops." Jane laughed. "How are things with you and Andy? Mom and I think he's perfect for you."

Charlene bit her lip. "I'm not sure. I just don't feel that spark with Andy. I can't put my finger on it. Dad hated him."

Jane giggled. "But Dad hated everyone we dated."

"Not Richard," Charlene reminded Jane.

Richard was Jane's husband. They had been married for four years and Richard was an architect in Colorado, where he was now awaiting Jane's arrival.

"That's true."

"So when do you go back?" Charlene asked.

"I fly out tonight."

"Look, Jane. There is something I've been meaning to tell you."

"What is it, Charlene?" Jane looked worried.

"I'm sorry"

"For what?" Jane now looked confused.

"Everything." Charlene hesitated and then continued. "I haven't been a good sister. I haven't been there for you when you needed me the most. We missed out on a lot of 'sister' experiences, things that we could have gone through together. I've been selfish and I'm trying my best to change. I want to be a better person for you and mom, make it as right as I possibly can."

Jane took Charlene by the hand. "None of us is perfect, Charlene. We can only do the best we can with the cards we're dealt. I love you no matter what. You're my sister, blood, and that's more important than anything."

They stood and hugged, holding the embrace until Jane quickly pulled away.

"Ooh," she said, touching her belly. "I think we have a future soccer player on our hands."

Charlene placed her hand on Jane's stomach and felt it too.

Jane looked into Charlene's eyes. "You have to promise to come to Colorado when the baby is born."

"I promise," Charlene said. "Nothing would make me happier."

She called Larry from her car and told him she was going directly to the crime scene, and he said that he would try to meet her but was following up on some things they'd found in Anderson's office.

Charlene already had the SID reports from the scene, but she wanted to take everything in with her own eyes, get inside the mind of the killer. She still didn't think that Jessica Philips was guilty of anything, other than falling for the wrong guy.

After parking the Volvo, she removed her investigation kit from the trunk and followed the walk-way to the front door. Yellow plastic tape stretched across the doorframe still warned the area was a crime scene. Charlene blew into a latex glove and slipped it on, opened the door and stepped underneath the tape, checking the door handle and frame. No scratches, scuff marks, or damage—no signs of forced entry. The locks were fastened and secured.

Charlene reached into her pocket and pulled out Anderson's car keys. She'd brought them on a hunch. Trying several, one slipped into place and turned, springing the lock.

"I knew it," Charlene whispered.

Anderson had a key. Of course he had. He'd been committing adultery with Jessica Philips. But just how many people knew about the affair?

Since the LAPD Crime Scene Unit had already searched, swept, vacuumed, cast, excavated, and printed the entire house, Charlene focused her attention on the exact point where Anderson had been shot. She circled the large puddle of dried blood, which had darkened to almost black from the heat. Charlene stood three feet from the stain, facing the wall. With no sign of a blood trail and directed by the blood spatter, SID had determined the exact position where Anderson had been standing when he was shot.

She heard a car door slam, and considered waiting for Larry to get inside. But when she went to the window, she didn't see any vehicle other than her own.

Charlene returned to her spot and closed her eyes to run through possible scenarios in her head, her lip lodged tightly between her teeth.

"From where the body was discovered, and knowing the impact that a round from a nine-millimeter has, that would mean the killer was standing right about here," she said aloud to herself.

With her eyes still closed, Charlene took six steps forward and opened her eyes. She turned and stuck out her hand, as if holding an imaginary gun. She closed her eyes again, picturing the killer, faceless, standing with the gun drawn.

Anderson was in good shape. He looked quick and agile. How could someone with a gun sneak up on him? He was highly intoxicated, and that would have slowed down his reaction time.

Charlene looked around the room quickly, nothing looked out of place. She stood on the bloodstain and then worked in a spiral out from the body.

Although everything had been done, and she was confident of the LAPD SID Team's capabilities, Charlene reexamined the bookshelves and the front hallway. No signs of a struggle. She looked through day planners and phone messages, nothing from Anderson.

She relaxed her eyes, unfocused, and let her head wander. It took her a couple of minutes to realize that her drifting eyes had picked up on something. She pulled out a tiny flashlight and got down on her knees.

With all of the commotion in the house during the initial crime scene examination, with so many bodies milling about, details sometimes got overlooked.

Tiny scratches on the hardwood floor led from the doorway to the living room. Scuff marks that could have been made from anything or anytime, but looked fresh. The marks were surrounded by what looked to be chalk dust. There was no mention of it in the reports.

Charlene stood and looked at a wooden-framed chalkboard attached to the wall. It was meant to be a decoration, but there were phone messages written on the board, none of any significance. The chalk and brush had been neatly placed on the ledge.

A struggle could have caused the chalk and brush to fall to the floor. If there had been a struggle that meant the killer could have been male because not many females, from the look of Anderson and the fact that he was a gym member, could have out-muscled Anderson, no matter how intoxicated he was. Also, the wounds on Anderson indicated he had been recently attacked.

The bullet pattern in Anderson told her that the gun hadn't accidentally gone off during a struggle. It was shot with precision.

Charlene noted everything in her report. She knew she was reaching, but at this point, she was desperate.

After another hour of exhaustive investigative research, with nothing added to her hard evidence but thoughts and theories, Charlene replaced the crime scene tape and locked the door.

The sun made her eyes water as she scoped the neighborhood, following the cracked concrete path.

As she reached the car, Charlene noticed a Caucasian man across the street walking a dog. There was no reason for Charlene's internal alarm to sound, but for some reason the man gave her pause. She hesitated with her hand on the door handle.

Was he staring at me? Had he been there when I got here?

She couldn't remember seeing him when she had first arrived, and waved it off as her paranoia since the Celebrity Slayer calls had started.

She got in the car and was inserting the key when she spotted an unlabeled beige ten-by-thirteen manila envelope on the passenger seat. The hairs on the back of her neck sprang to attention and dread exploded up her spine.

From the driver's seat, she turned in all four directions and noticed the dog walker still in view, looking back in her direction. She looked around but saw no one else. Charlene caught her own reflection in the rear-view mirror and noticed she had paled.

She knew protocol and knew what she was expected to do. There could be anything inside the envelope. A bomb. A note. A warning. Evidence.

She withdrew the latex glove box from the slot on her door. She slid into a pair again and lifted the envelope from the seat. One word was written on the outside in neat handwriting, "Charlie".

Her skin prickled. Charlene noticed the envelope wasn't sealed, which meant whoever had put it there hadn't licked the edge—no DNA.

She removed the contents, about a dozen black and white, eight-by-ten photographs, and a sheet of white printer paper. She pulled them out and sorted through. As she scanned the pictures, Charlene's chest tightened.

The first four were close-ups of the four Celebrity Slayer victims, their headshots. Then there were also pictures of the murder scenes, before the cops had shown up when the victims were still alive, and could have only been taken by one person...the killer. She mentally scanned the scenes from her own pictures, trying to make comparisons, but she couldn't. She would have to take them home to be sure.

The next set of pictures was of the same four women and looked like surveillance footage, as the predator stalked his prey. The women were stunning—beautiful actresses who had come to LA looking for a shot. Charlene knew that serial killers were always fantasy-motivated, and wondered if that was the reason the killer had chosen his victims.

Did he fantasize about making love to these women?

But there was no evidence of penetration or sexual degradation of any of the women. Was the killer impotent?

She looked at the computer print out. The words were written in the middle, in black, bold-face lettering. "**I need you Charlie.**"

Charlene stared at the words, reading them over.

She stuffed the menacing photos back into the envelope and scanned the neighborhood again, seeing the dog walker's back as he made his way down the sidewalk. When she went to grab the door handle, she noticed that her fists were curled tight. She jumped from the car and took off in a sprint.

"Excuse me, Sir?" Charlene called, but the man didn't turn around.

Is he speeding up?

Charlene quickened her pace and called again, "Excuse me, Sir? LAPD." She tucked her jacket inside her holster flap, giving her easy access to her gun.

This time the man stopped, but didn't turn around. Charlene had her badge out as she approached him. When he finally turned, Charlene came face to face with a middle-aged man about a foot taller than her. He had black arched eyebrows, pitted cheeks, and a heavy overbite. He was walking an overweight, brown and black pug that sniffed at Charlene's feet and wagged its curly tail with enthusiasm. Charlene immediately thought this guy had the kind of looks that would make him uncomfortable and withdrawn around women.

The man wore an all-weather jacket and Italian loafers. His tense, nervous expression could have been from anything, especially the sight of an LAPD detective's badge.

"LAPD." Charlene flashed her badge. "I'd like to ask you a couple of questions."

"About what?"

"Do you live around here?"

He pointed with his index finger. "Three houses down. Number six-eleven."

"What's your name?"

"Ted."

"Do you have a last name?"

The man pursed his lips. "Elliot."

"Can I see some ID, Ted Elliot?"

"I don't have my wallet. I only brought Myles out for a walk."

At the sound of his name, the puppy started to whimper.

"Did you happen to see anyone inside my car while I was in the house?" Charlene asked.

The man shook his head.

"Are you sure?"

"Yes, Officer." He looked at the dog. "Can I go? Myles is getting impatient."

Charlene looked down and saw the dog sitting at attention.

"Did the police question you about the incident that happened here a couple of nights ago?"

"Yes. I gave them my report. I wasn't home so I didn't see or hear anything."

She knew she could easily verify this from the crime report.

"Why don't we go get that wallet, Ted?"

After verifying the man was who he said he was, Charlene headed to the department.

Chapter 14

"Well, that was a waste of time." Officer Nick Berry put the car into drive.

"You didn't really think Anderson's lawyer would give us anything did you?" Berry's partner, officer Brad Clayton, responded.

"Then why did Baker send us there?"

"Dotting the I's and crossing the T's. It's called going through the motions of a homicide investigation. At least we got something from Anderson's colleagues."

"Yeah, but confirmation won't be easy."

The officers had discovered that Anderson's favorite hang-out was O'Brien's on Wilshire, a small, low key pub that would conceal Anderson's identity.

As they neared the bar, Berry cracked the window and lit a cigarette, keeping one hand on the steering wheel and blowing smoke outside.

"So, are you going to be okay with this?"

"Okay with what?" Berry asked, already knowing.

"Don't give me that, Nick. Are you going to be okay working for Taylor?"

"Actually, *we're* working for Baker. But to answer your question, am I pissed off I didn't get the promotion? Hell, yes. Do I have more mouths to feed at home? Hell, yes. But this is my job."

Clayton nodded. "You know that smoke really annoys me," he added, after swallowing a mouthful of Greek salad.

"I know, but it helps me calm down. I got no sleep last night. Are you almost done with that? We're here."

"Almost."

"Why can't you just have McDonalds like the rest of us? You think you'll live longer?"

"I'll take my chances."

Berry pulled the car into the vacant parking lot and shut down the engine. He looked at his partner. "So, what about you?"

"What about me?"

"Do you think you got overlooked again for a reason?"

"Why, because I'm gay? Let's not get into this. Let's go."

By mid-morning, the bar parking lot was sparsely occupied. They were met by the soft sounds of Irish jukebox music and an older gentleman standing behind the counter with a bar towel slung over his shoulder. He stood only about a foot above the bar and wore a green and white striped, button down shirt.

"Good morning, Officers."

The men approached the bar. As the senior, Berry took the lead.

"We're looking for the manager."

"You're looking at him. Sam O'Brien." The man stretched out his hand and the officers shook it. "What can I do for you?"

If the man was uneasy at the sight of cops in his bar, he didn't show it.

"Ken Anderson."

The man nodded, his lips puckered in a remorseful grimace. "We knew him as Rick. He was a good customer." Then he turned to a young woman, who wore the same striped shirt, mopping the floor around the pool table. "Kathleen, can you take over?"

He turned back to the officers. "We can talk in my office."

The manager led them past the pool table, down a long, narrow hallway into a comfortable looking office with glimmering hardwood flooring and leather furniture.

"Come on in."

The cops sat down while the bar owner sat behind a mahogany desk.

"I've been wondering when you'd get around to stopping in."

Berry spoke while Clayton took notes. "When was the last time you saw Anderson?"

"Ken was in here Friday night. I had no idea who he was, but when I saw his picture on the TV the next morning, I knew it was him."

The officers looked at each other. "You didn't think you should notify the police?"

The bar owner shrugged. "Figured you'd get around to seeing me. I can't believe he'd been coming in here for so long and I didn't even know who he was. He told me his name was Rick, but I guess that's why he came here."

"Why's that?"

"I didn't recognize him, and I doubt any of my clientele would either. He's married into one of the richest families in America and came in here with a new women each time. If he wanted to remain anonymous, this was the place to do it."

"Who was he with on Friday?"

The owner shook his head and smiled. "That's the strange part. That's the first time he's ever been here alone."

"You recognize any of these girls?" Clayton handed the manager pictures of Jessica Philips, Sandra Philips, and Ashley Stanley.

The bartender examined them closely and shook his head. "Nah. Doesn't really seem like Ken's type." He handed the picture back. "Did one of them kill him?"

Berry ignored the question. "On this particular night, how did he act?"

"Same as always, quiet. The only change was that he didn't have a woman with him."

"Can you tell us anything about him?"

"Sure, I'm a bartender." The man smiled. "That's what we do." He leaned back in his chair. "Ken liked his liquor, always the good stuff from the top shelf. He didn't talk much, especially when there were sports on the TV. I think he gambled a lot. He'd hide himself in the corner, drink and watch sports until closing time, and then stumble out with his arm around a different babe."

"Did you notice any marks on his face Friday, like maybe he'd been in a fight?"

"Didn't really notice, but then again the lighting isn't so good in that section so his face was hidden."

"Did anyone talk to him?"

The man shook his head. "I tried to approach him but he waved me off. So I knew he was having a bad night."

"Who served him?"

The owner swiveled in his chair and checked the employee schedule. "That'd be Kathleen."

Berry nodded to Clayton, who quickly left the room. He turned back to the man behind the desk. "Did you see him leave?"

"I watched him most of the night, thought he was acting peculiar. So I guess I saw him leave."

"Did he leave with anyone? Did anyone follow him out?"

"No, he left alone."

Clayton returned. "Waitress said she remembers serving him, but he never looked up from the table when he ordered."

"So that's all you have for us?" Berry turned back to the manager.

The expression on the man's face tensed, tightening. "I don't really want to get involved."

"If you know something, Mr. O'Brien, then withholding information is an obstruction of justice. Punishable by law" Berry said.

"I know the law, Officer."

The bar owner opened his desk drawer and withdrew a bottle of Crown Royal. He poured himself a shot and drank it. Then he removed a package of cigarettes.

"You mind?" he asked, holding up a cigarette.

Both cops shook their head, so he lit up and inhaled.

The cops were getting annoyed. "So are you going to tell us, or are we going downtown?"

"Alright, alright." He crushed out the cigarette and leaned back in his chair. "I guess I should have reported it when it happened."

"What was it?" Berry moved to the edge of his seat.

The bar owner looked at a calendar pinned to the wall behind his chair. "I can't remember the exact date, but it was the night the Heat came to town and blew out the Lakers." The man looked at the cops, as if relaying a silent message from one LA sports fan to another. But neither Berry nor Clayton followed basketball.

"Go on."

"Ken was here with one of his blondes."

"Did you recognize her?"

"Nah, they all look the same. She was new, but fit Ken's tastes— blonde, fake breasts, lots of makeup—looked out of it, maybe even a little stoned. I call them the 'flavor of the month club'." He smiled, then quickly remembered the relevance of the story and discarded the grin.

He continued. "Anyway, they sat at the bar, and Ken asked me to turn on the Lakers game. Guess he had some money on it."

"How did he do?"

"The more the Heat increased their lead, the more he drank. The Lakers didn't even come close to covering the spread."

"How much did he lose?"

The owner shrugged. "He didn't say. But he buried his head like someone had shot his dog. I told him that he should probably go and I offered to call him a cab."

"Did he leave?"

"Not right away. But he should have." The owners eyes grew large, a look of terror slashed across his face. "Two guys came in."

"Can you remember what they looked like?"

"Couldn't forget if I tried."

"Describe them."

"They were huge and dressed in full black—leather jackets and jeans, dark hair pulled into ponytails, goatees, dark sunglasses, and black shirts unbuttoned to expose hairy chests. They were at least six three, the black cowboy boots making them six five easy. They looked serious."

"Did they say anything?"

"I asked them what they wanted and they simply looked at Ken. I didn't ask questions."

"How did Ken react?"

"Almost as if he'd been expecting them. He got up and walked outside. Just left the girl on the stool. I watched them leave then ran to the window to look out."

"Where did they take him?"

"The alley out back. There's a window that gives a clear view of it."

"Take us out there."

"You sure?"

"Yeah. Let's go."

The owner led the cops to the back of the bar, exiting through a push-barred back door marked *Emergency Exit Only*.

The scent of garbage, vomit, urine, and stale beer permeated the quiet twenty-foot-wide alleyway. A blue dumpster, overloaded with garbage, was pushed up against a spray-paint graffiti brick wall. Garbage and broken liquor bottles lay strewn throughout the alley.

Berry turned to Clayton. "No witnesses, the perfect location for a beating."

"I watched the whole thing from that window." The owner pointed to a small barred window at the back of the building.

"What happened?"

"Let's just say they laid a beatin' on him."

The cops noticed dried blood stains on the dirty pavement.

"Have you ever seen these men again?"

"No, Sir, and thank God."

"Would you be willing to come down to the station and work with a sketch artist to recreate a likeness?"

"Nick," Clayton said. "I have a feeling these guys are already in the system."

"Maybe come down and view some mug shots then, Mr. O'Brien?"

"Like I said, Officers, I don't want to get involved."

They should probably have told O'Brien that he was under an obligation to do so, but the officers were so excited to have their first real lead that they just thanked him and left.

Chapter 15

Charlene grabbed a late lunch at a Greek deli. Before heading to her desk at Robbery-Homicide in the new Police Administration Building on West First Street, she stopped by the Hertzberg-Davis Forensic Science Center where Dana was working in the lab.

She gave Dana the envelope and pictures, and told her that nobody saw the results but her.

She arrived back at her desk to find a copy of the *LA Times* spread across it, the front page covered with the Anderson murder investigation. She quickly skimmed the contents and then folded it up and threw it on the desk.

The reporter, Paul Carter, had about as much information on the murder as the cops had. In fact, he had too much. Carter had a rundown on Jessica Philips' life, as well as Ken Anderson's relationship with Carl Minor. Charlene was fuming.

Goddamn leaks!

She picked up the newspaper and marched into the captain's office without knocking.

The captain was also reading the front page article.

"Captain, I want to put a gag order on everyone connected to this case."

He looked up. "I'm sorry, who's running point on this one? Where's Baker?"

"I just got here and haven't seen him yet."

"Well maybe you should discuss these things with your partner before yelling out stupidity. You're a rookie, Taylor, don't forget that."

She stormed out of the office and took a deep breath, allowing her rage to pass. She opened the paper back up and read the article in its entirety, finding nothing she didn't already know, which sometimes happened in this city, and then quickly flipped to the sports section to see how the other teams in the Dodgers' division had fared in last night's games.

She found Larry at his desk, where Darren was leaning over the computer.

Larry was sitting back with his legs up, holding a paper cup of coffee.

"What's up?" Charlene asked.

"My computer was acting up, so I asked officer computer geek to help me out. He had it fixed within minutes. Thanks, Brady."

Darren looked at Charlene. "It was nothing really. All I had to do was..."

"Thanks, Brady," Larry said again.

Darren took the hint and returned to his desk.

When he was gone Larry said, "Those hair fibers found on Anderson didn't match the samples we pulled from Stanley and the two Philips girls."

"Do you think we can get a sample from Beverly Minor?"

Larry smirked. "Doubtful. Her lawyer won't allow it and I don't know if it would have any bearing. She's his wife, so of course he'd have her hair on him." He threw a folder on her desk. "Clayton and Berry dropped this off."

Charlene opened the folder. It was the complete file on Anderson.

"Did they find anything?"

"I just looked through it quickly. They went for coffee."

Charlene started to read through it when the officers got back and told her what they found.

"We've established a timeline. After our initial interviews and using LUDs, we're pretty sure Anderson went to Jessica Philips' house directly from the bar. We doubt he had any contact with anyone in between. It's all in the report. "

LUDs were the local usage details from Anderson's iPhone records.

"We also talked to his lawyer, whom he doesn't share with his wife. Not much there. Anderson didn't have a will."

"Really?" Charlene said.

Barry shrugged. "He was one of those guys who thought he'd live forever."

"I saw something in here about an incident at the bar," she said.

The officers told them about Anderson's run in with two unknown acquaintances. They detailed the physical description.

Charlene jumped to her feet. "I'll find out who works that beat to see if these characters are anyone they're familiar with."

"Sit down, Taylor," Larry said. He turned towards the officers. "Thanks, guys. Take the rest of the night off and meet us back here first thing in the morning."

The men left.

When they were gone, Charlene said, "Larry, let's go. We need to find out who these guys are."

"I already know who they are." Larry swiveled in his chair and using his computer mouse, dragged an ace of spades across the screen.

"Then who are they?" Charlene asked.

Larry closed the game. "They work for Alberto Bianchi."

Charlene sat back in her seat. "Oh boy!"

"Let's sit on it for the night, so we can figure out how to approach it," Larry said, getting out of his seat and throwing his empty cup in the garbage.

Charlene didn't move. A ripple of fear coursed through her veins.

They walked out together. Charlene watched Larry squeeze into a white Honda Civic and pull away. But she had no intention of going home.

She called ahead to make sure Dana was still there, and then pulled onto South Main Street. It took only minutes to turn off the San Bernardino Freeway and into the designated parking area on the CSULA campus.

She met Dana inside and followed her into the glassed-in lab.

"I don't have much for you, Char."

"What do you mean?"

"The guy used a standard, traditional fifteen by twelve beige manila folder. No chance of a tracing record. It has never been used before, because the two prong metal clasp and eyelet in the flap have not been damaged. No DNA, because it hadn't been licked."

"What about the paper?"

"Not much better. No fingerprints, standard twenty pound copier paper, no watermark, printed on a traditional laser copier. No luck."

Dana handed the material back to Charlene.

"Thanks, Dana."

"How about that drink?"

"Rain check? I'm not quite done yet for the night."

"Do detectives ever have a five o'clock punch-out?" Dana smiled.

"I wish," Charlene said.

There was a brochure on Charlene's windshield when she got back to her car. The Sigma Nu Fraternity was having a keg party on Friday, five dollar entry, and it promised to be "a night to remember." She smiled, reminiscing, then crumpled the pamphlet, got in the car, and started it up.

She exited the campus parking lot and headed for the San Bernardino Freeway. She had fifteen minutes, maybe twenty-five with traffic, to decide how she would approach her next move.

Charlene was sure that Carl Minor was hiding something, and his bloated ego wouldn't turn her away.

As she picked up speed on the Hollywood Freeway, Charlene passed the Hollywood Bowl, the famous amphitheater that showcased so many memorable live musical performances, before she turned off and entered the Hills.

Traffic was light but steady as she took her time making the drive up through the Hollywood Hills into a gated community. She listened to a message on her iPhone from her mother checking up on her, but decided not to call back.

She hung up and steered the long 1999 Crown Vic through the windy Hollywood Hills. She didn't like the Crown Vic, and cursed that the department still hadn't made the transfer to the new SUVs, like many of the other LAPD departments.

The sun was weak as dusk was descending when she reached the peak of the hill. Carl Minor's house came into view, the last one on the dead-end street. The detective had never actually been inside, but she'd seen photos in magazines and knew that the home had recently made the cover of *Architectural Digest*. She slowed at the iron-gate where visitors were instructed to buzz for admittance. She found a group of tourists standing outside, snapping photos of the elegant landscaping.

She identified herself and showed her badge to the camera. The gate gently opened and Charlene entered, followed the long, paved driveway that encircled a lawn of groomed Bermuda grass, and parked in front of the house.

The chauffer, who'd been at Beverly Anderson's home the morning Charlene and Larry had made the next of kin notification, was standing outside with a smoke in his mouth and a water hose in his hand, washing down the already shiny limousine. Another of Minor's hired hands was working in a flower garden the size of half a football field.

Minor himself was standing outside on the front step. The billionaire was dressed more casually than at their last encounter, his beige shorts and white golf shirt almost making the man look normal. The sixty-seven-year-old's body showed the results of years of manicures, pedicures, and pampering. He was thick around the waist, but his thin, pale legs showed he was not overweight.

Charlene smiled, strode confidently up the walkway, and shook Minor's hand.

"What can I do for you, Detective?" He looked annoyed.

"I'd like to discuss your son-in-law's murder."

"Where's your partner?"

"He couldn't make it."

Minor checked his watch, looked around his twenty-three-acre property, and nodded with a grunt. They stepped inside.

"Honey, we'll be in the study," he called out, his voice echoing, but Charlene didn't see Mrs. Minor.

They crossed the hardwood floor, passing a curved staircase made of varnished oak, into a large, arch-ceilinged room with a grand piano and wall-sized open-shelved bookcases. Although it was not cold, the marble fireplace burned intently.

Minor closed the double-French doors and offered Charlene a seat. She looked around the large library, filled with old money furnishings, before choosing a Molina brown leather chair. Minor sat across from Charlene, in a tall-back leather armchair.

A butler appeared from a side door. "Can I get you something, Mr. Minor?"

"Bourbon, Edgar. Detective?"

She was off the clock. "Gin and tonic."

Minor seemed to nod at Charlene's request, giving a short sneer.

The butler nodded and disappeared through a side door as Charlene continued to appreciate the fine architecture of the room. The shelves were stacked with hardback books. A large, burgundy oak desk sat in the middle of the room with a computer resting on the corner. The furniture was all leather, and the floor was stained hardwood.

The butler returned quickly, holding a silver tray with the drinks. He handed Charlene a tall, thin glass with ice-cubes and a wedge of lime floating on top. Minor grabbed his snifter as the butler opened a wooden box, revealing a row of Cuban cigars. Minor chose one, as the butler clipped the end and lit the tobacco.

When the butler vanished again, Charlene watched the billionaire's demeanor, trying to read his body language. He dipped the cigar into his bourbon and took a long, satisfying puff. He clinked the ice cubes in the glass, holding the detective's stare for a long, tense moment, his small, suspicious gray eyes bearing down on her. With her eyes, Charlene followed the trail made by the ice cubes, as they danced in what looked to be, and what Charlene expected to be, very expensive liquor.

Charlene sipped with restraint.

Minor sighed. "What do you want, Detective?"

"I want to talk about your son-in-law."

"What would you like to know?"

"Are you sorry he's dead?"

Minor stared at Charlene for what felt like minutes. He didn't speak, and Charlene met the billionaire's stare. Finally he relented.

"In the past, Detective, I had a habit of getting to know my daughter's acquaintances."

"What do you mean, 'getting to know'?"

"I had them checked out. You probably think that sounds overprotective, but I have my reasons. I didn't do that with Ken."

"Why not?"

"I didn't have time. Christ, they were barely dating when he proposed. But I knew enough not to trust him."

"Why's that?"

"Come on, Detective. I'm Carl Minor. I've worked damn hard to get to where I am and I won't let some punk take it away. Maybe it was a gut instinct or a father's perception, but I never trusted Ken."

"Did you tell your daughter this?"

"Of course I did. But Beverly was in love and having a family was the most important thing to her. I suggested a prenuptial agreement, but it never happened."

He set the drink down on an antique end table and turned on the brass lamp.

"Did your opinion change after the wedding?" Charlene asked.

"He was my son-in-law and potentially the father of my grandchildren. I left it at that." He shrugged his shoulders noncommittally.

Charlene didn't say anything, but she didn't believe him. She took a drink. She waited. She pretended to write some notes down, stalling. She knew Minor wanted to talk.

"Look, Detective, it's no secret how I felt about Ken," he said, an iciness in his voice.

Charlene looked up as he continued.

"He was an arrogant, self-absorbed, son-of-a-bitch who cared for no one but himself. The man abused money, alcohol, and women. I tried to talk Beverly out of marrying him. But she was in love, and, as a father, I supported her decision. Even though I knew it was wrong."

"What do you mean 'abused'?"

"I often saw marks on her. He had a sort of hypnotic control over her that I could never figure out. The man had an addiction to gambling, and it was usually his drinking that augmented the problem."

"When was the last time you saw Ken?"

"I guess it was a week ago." He leaned back in his seat, in concentration, trying to recreate the event. "He came to me looking for money, again. A sure thing, he'd called it."

"How much?" Charlene was scribbling notes, trying to keep up.

"Fifteen thousand. But I didn't give it to him," he said, with no remorse in his voice. "I bailed him out enough times."

"Where were you the night Ken was killed?"

Minor smiled. "I was here, Detective, all night, hosting a get-together with friends."

She wrote it down. It would be easy to authenticate his alibi.

"Who was your son-in-law in debt to?"

He was about to answer when the door swung open and Minor's lawyer, Ian Johnson, strode in, sporting a black-tie tuxedo. "Okay, Detective, this interview is over." He looked at Minor. "Your wife called, and it's a good thing she did. What are you thinking, Carl?"

The billionaire said nothing.

As they were escorting Charlene out of the library, she thought of something.

"Mr. Minor, how is your daughter holding up?"

The old man looked at her. "She's coping. She's tough, she's a Minor. This is the best thing that could have happened."

"Carl, enough!" the attorney interrupted.

They opened the door and Charlene stepped out onto the front step, followed by Minor's attorney. "If you need to talk with my client again, I suggest you contact me first, or there will be repercussions." He handed Charlene a business card and shut the door.

Chapter 16

Her better judgment told her not to go alone. She called Larry, who was pissed, and he insisted on joining her. She didn't argue.

Alberto Bianchi was the closest thing LA had to the mafia. No one knew his real name, or his real bio, because no one was still around to confirm it.

Rumor had it that Bianchi was born in Brooklyn, and when his mother disappeared after his birth, he was adopted by a top man in the NY Mafia. Growing up under the wing and watchful eye of his adopted father, Bartolomeo Bianchi, Alberto quickly inherited the man's name and was shown the tricks of the trade. With one of the most influential and powerful men in the underworld as an adopted father, Alberto graduated quickly through the tiers of the mob, becoming a top gun. When he became a legal adult, he was shipped to LA to run the Bianchi crime-family's West Coast business.

He was a mob son, second generation crook, which meant Alberto Bianchi was established and connected.

At forty-four, Bianchi was simply known as *the man*. He had a long rap sheet, but no convictions. He was high on the LAPD priority status, but so far they had come up with zilch.

Everyone in LA, including the cops, knew that Bianchi ran an underground gambling ring out of his pizzeria in Lincoln Heights, but couldn't prove it. The pizza place was a legitimate business on paper and perfect cover. He was one of the largest bookies in the city, with a bad reputation. Murder was not his forte, but Charlene realized that he was not above it to get what he wanted. When opportunities arose for the LAPD, witnesses either disappeared or refused to come forward.

There were a number of reasons for Charlene to suspect Bianchi—Minor's confession that Anderson owed money, the bar owner's testimony of Bianchi's men attacking Anderson, and the black rose petals found in Anderson's pocket.

As she crawled through Lincoln Heights, she got caught in a short delay as the young, handsome, strong men on the LAFD performed a practice run outside of the Fire Station on Pasadena Avenue. She didn't mind the scenery at all.

Darkness was falling when Charlene turned onto North Broadway. Larry was waiting on the curb, and he opened Charlene's door when she pulled up in the LAPD-issued vehicle.

"What are you doing? I told you I would handle this."

"Carl Minor just told me that Anderson owed a gambling debt. Add that to the description of Bianchi's men roughing Anderson up, equals an automatic meeting with Bianchi."

Larry was pulling at his hair. "Carl Minor! What were you doing talking to Carl Minor?" His face looked like it would explode. "Are you out of your mind?"

Charlene ignored Larry, brushed past him, and headed for the pizzeria. She could hear Larry's heavy footsteps running to catch her, and Charlene was afraid he might keel over from a heart attack.

"Okay, wait." Larry grabbed her by the coat sleeve. "If we're actually goin' through with this, then we have to do it right. We're walkin' on thin ice here. Let me do the talkin'."

Charlene rolled her eyes, but let Larry pass, following him, hoping the bulge from her Glock wasn't noticeable.

When she walked in, Charlene recognized the owner immediately, and anticipation buzzed through her blood.

Bianchi stood behind the counter, with a hairnet pulled over his greased-back hair, and beads of sweat pelting his forehead. The man was well tanned, stood at least six five and easily tipped the scales at two fifty, with little of that being body fat.

He was kneading a roll of dough when the detectives walked in, and Bianchi met their eyes. He smiled. His affable demeanor did not fool Charlene. This man was one of the cruelest, most feared individuals in the city.

"Detective Baker, *Benvenuti*, it's been a while. Are you here for a slice of LA's finest?" Because Charlene knew Bianchi was born in Brooklyn, she was aware that his thick Italian accent was faked.

Charlene looked at Larry who refused to make eye contact. *How does Bianchi know Larry?*

"I see you have a new partner. *Che bella.*" Bianchi kissed the tips of his fingers and blew it into the air.

They approached the counter.

Larry dropped his voice to a whisper. "Alberto, we need to talk."

"What's this Alberto thing? What, we strangers now? Call me Al."

"We need to talk," Larry echoed.

"So talk." Bianchi now had the dough in the air, impressively spinning the uncooked crust.

Charlene was waiting to be introduced, but when Larry didn't move, Charlene said, "Detective Taylor."

The mobster stopped playing with the dough, set it on the counter, and walked around the front, cleaning his hands on his grease-stained apron. He checked Charlene up and down. He looked into her eyes, and if it hadn't been for the gin and tonic in her bloodstream, she might have been edgy.

"Taylor? You mean Marty's kid? Well, I'll be." He let out a quiet snort and turned to the customers in the room. "Hey guys, this here's Marty Taylor's little girl. *Sembra come lui.*"

The men nodded. He turned back to Charlene. "Kid, me and your *padre* go way back. He was a good cop, a good man."

Charlene had no idea under what circumstances Bianchi would be acquaintances with her father. It made her stomach sick to think that Martin Taylor had conducted affairs with the mobster. But then again, she hadn't known her father that well.

Bianchi turned back to another man who stood behind the counter. "Anthony, take over. Me and the detectives gotta talk."

Bianchi escorted them to a quiet corner booth in the back of the shop, away from the endless chatter of Italian men conversing loudly, using their hands as props. He removed the hairnet and Charlene noticed that not one strand of hair from his black, gel-stiffened head moved.

"Would you like a slice of pie, Detective? It's the best in town," Bianchi asked, focusing on Charlene.

She shook her head.

They sat down at the booth, Larry and Charlene on one side, Bianchi across from them. Bianchi moved first, choosing the side facing the front door. His large bulk took up most of the seat and was squeezed in, looking completely uncomfortable.

"Al, we need to talk about Ken Anderson."

As Larry spoke, Bianchi stared at Charlene. She could feel his black, beady eyes dissecting her, and her nerves tingled.

"Would you like a drink, Detective?"

Charlene shook her head.

"Man," Bianchi said. "Look at you. The eyes, the nose, even the jaw. Kid, you're the spittin' image of your father."

"Al, please," Larry raised his voice and caught a quick stare from Bianchi, cutting him short. The men at the front table stopped talking, staring at the corner booth.

Charlene froze, wondering if she would need to draw her gun. How fast could she get to it squeezed into the booth?

Bianchi looked at his customers, raised his hand and nodded imperceptibly as the men went back to their conversation. Larry was sweating immensely.

"Yes, Detective, let's talk." Bianchi finally looked away from Charlene and sat back in the booth, looking fully relaxed. He pulled a pack of cigarettes from his apron and offered one to the detectives. Charlene shook her head but Larry popped one into his mouth. Charlene wasn't sure, under United States regulation, if smoking was permitted inside the restaurant, but Larry lit the cigarette as Bianchi continued.

"Should I know this Ken Anderson?"

Charlene produced a photo.

"Ah, yes. Ken Anderson. The man loved pizza. I believe he always ordered the meat-lovers. He's a good customer." He looked at Charlene. "Do you talk? I see you over there biting your lip, as if you wanna say somethin'." He lit a cigarette and blew smoke from the corner of his mouth.

Charlene would have liked nothing better than to reach over the table and grab the over-sized gangster, and probably would have if Larry wasn't with her.

"Al, we need information on this Anderson character," Larry said.

Bianchi looked at Larry but didn't respond. Then he looked at Charlene and said, "I want her to ask the questions."

She could tell Larry was about to protest so Charlene said, "Look, Mr. Bianchi…"

"Please, call me Al. All my friends do," he suggested with a toothy grin.

Charlene refused. "Mr. Bianchi, we know Ken Anderson was a gambler who owed a lot of money. We also know that a couple of days before his murder, Anderson was seen outside O'Brien's on Wilshire getting the shit beat out of him by two of your thugs. We suspect that you were looking for a payment." She almost rose from her seat but felt Larry's hand on her forearm.

Bianchi smiled. "Now there's the Taylor fire. Larry, put that dog on a leash. *Lei è pazza!*"

"We also found this in Anderson's shirt pocket." Charlene set a picture of the rose petals on the table.

Bianchi looked at the picture, but didn't pick it up. He chuckled. "Nice flowers." He sighed, as if bored. Then he leaned over, face to the table, as if talking to it. "I don't know anything about being a bookie. I run a respectable, legitimate pizza franchise here, that's it."

Charlene sat back, without realizing she'd been sitting forward. "Look, Alberto, I don't care about a gambling ring. I'm a homicide detective, in charge of a murder investigation. That's all I care about."

"I like you, Detective, so for your sake, just to help you out, let's say I did some gambling in my spare time, which I don't. If this Anderson guy owed me money, which he didn't because I'm not a bookie, but if he did, I wouldn't kill the man. Maybe rough him up a little, but you can't squeeze money out of a dead man."

Charlene didn't believe him, but he had a point. Anderson couldn't pay a debt if he was dead. Torture, but not death. Anderson's murder didn't benefit Bianchi.

"Where were you two nights ago?"

"Why don't you ask your friends?"

"Uh?" Charlene was confused.

Bianchi went on, with a wave of the hand. "Never mind. I was here, working most of the night. Went out for a sandwich and came back. That's what happens when you own your own business. Twenty-four seven."

"Was anyone with you?"

Bianchi smiled, waving his hands around the room. "Take a look around, Detective, these guys are always here. *Io sono sempre al lavoro.* Ask any of them."

Bianchi, as usual, had an alibi. He gave them a complimentary pizza to take with them. But Charlene wasn't hungry.

How did Bianchi know her father so well? Was the man that much of a stranger to her?

As they were leaving, Bianchi called out, "And, Detective, say hi to your friends outside for me. *STRONZOS!*" He flicked his chin in disgust.

This was the second reference to Charlene's 'friends'. What did he mean? Was he talking about the other cops on the force?

After seeing Larry to his car and watching him drive away, Charlene crossed the street to where she had parked.

She opened her door and was stepping in when she felt a firm tug on her arm. She turned but was too slow as two men in black suits grabbed her by the shoulders and aggressively pulled her around the corner of the building. Charlene tried to pull away and reach for her gun, but the men overpowered her.

She was physically moved to the alley and shoved into a white, government-issued van, the door sliding closed behind her.

She sat in a seat facing the back of the van, across from an older gentleman in a freshly pressed suit with glasses perched on the end of his nose and a receding hairline. The van was idling and a man with short black hair and dark glasses sat behind the wheel. He did not turn around or look in the rearview mirror.

Charlene turned back to the man across from her. He was reading a black notebook and then looked up at Charlene, his small, alert eyes studying her, his thin lips unsmiling.

"Relax, Detective Taylor, this will only take a minute."

As he reached into his jacket pocket, Charlene flinched. He pulled out his wallet, opened it, and set it on Charlene's lap. She took the wallet and read the credentials.

"FBI?"

"That's right," he replied, taking his wallet back. "We've been investigating Bianchi for six months, and you're about to blow our whole operation. We have that whole place wired and a twenty-four hour detail on Bianchi." He pointed to the pizza shop. "And we're close, just waiting for a mistake."

Charlene looked out the tinted windows. Two agents stood at the door. She looked towards the building facing the pizzeria, envisioning a surveillance team, cameras hidden behind the closed blinds and a room full of sweaty, coffee-breath agents who'd been cooped up in a tiny room for months.

"Do you have anything on him?"

He shook his head. "Bianchi's smart. He likes meeting in open spaces, realizing too much could be captured within walls. Now, Detective, you know I can't go into detail about this sting, but I'll answer a few questions just to keep you away from Bianchi." He picked up a file and read from some papers. "The day before Ken Anderson's murder, he paid his debt. We watched, listened, and recorded the whole conversation. Of course, he said he was paying off a pizza tab and no amount of money was mentioned. Bianchi didn't kill him. In fact, he was nowhere near Anderson on the night of the murder, and none of his colleagues were either. I can't tell you where they were as that's confidential. Stay away from Bianchi. This is our case."

"Can I have the tape?"

He shook his head. "I don't think so."

She was about to protest when he knocked on the window, and the door slid open. The two agents grabbed Charlene, pulled the detective out, and jumped inside. The van quickly sped away.

Charlene snarled as the vehicle disappeared. She dropped her shoulders in exhaustion, a perfect ending to a perfect day. Maybe she could catch the end of the Dodgers game at the bar.

So those were the 'friends' Bianchi had been referring to. The mobster knew he was being wire tapped.

As she was getting into her car, a text message appeared on her iPhone. "See JC ASAP!"

So much for a cold beer.

Because she already had all of the necessary paper work in her car, Charlene sat in the parking lot at 210 West Temple Street and wrote out her daily reports, noting everything they had on the investigation. Her iPhone buzzed, telling her once again to "See JC ASAP."

She looked around the area and smiled, amazed at how quickly the civic roadway could become abandoned. During regular business hours, the county and federal courts, hall of records, city hall and other civic structures built along Temple Street were alive with bustling civilians. Now all was calm.

Once the forms were completed, she slid the papers into a colored file folder and sealed it. She entered the building and took the elevator to suite 18000. The secretary was gone and the suite was empty, but Charlene could see the light in Jeffrey Clark's office. She lightly rapped on the outside of the door and let herself in.

The district attorney was seated at his desk, typing on a computer. When Charlene stepped in, the DA poked his head over the open laptop. "Have a seat, Detective."

"Where's Detective Baker?" Charlene asked.

Without looking up from his typing, the DA answered, "He called and said he couldn't make it. He said you could fill me in."

Bastard!

She sat down close enough to smell his aftershave and watched Clark type.

The man projected confidence. There was no denying that District Attorney Jeffrey Clark was extremely handsome, even in a city full of gorgeous celebrities. At forty-three, he looked to be in his late twenties. Jet black hair, clean shaven stubble, sizzling hazel eyes, and a strong jaw made up facial features that could melt a woman. He was exceedingly cultured and could work a room like a trendy host—intelligent, funny, with a salesman's smile. He was tall and lithe, worked out in a gym five days a week, and was a former track star at Harvard. He was always impeccably dressed, and tonight was no different—a charcoal striped suit with a quiet tie. He had been named most eligible bachelor in the state of California for 2010.

Many cops didn't like Clark because he was self-absorbed, pushy, with a no-bullshit way of handling cases, and he expected perfection. Because of his initials, JC, most of the force referred to him as Jesus Christ because of his larger than life image.

Before she had a chance to study Clark's office, he shut the laptop and sat back in his black, leather, high-back seat. He interlocked his fingers and stared at the detective.

"What do we have on the Anderson murder?"

She rose from her seat, handed the closed file to the DA, and sat back down. She watched him open the case and slide the documents out. As he was looking through the papers, Charlene relayed everything they knew so far—the interviews, evidence, suspicions.

He read the documents while listening to Charlene's spiel. When she had finished, with Clark still looking over the file, he asked, "Do we have enough on Jessica Philips?"

Charlene tried not to look shocked. "Jessica Philips?"

"Yeah, I hear she was having an affair with Anderson, and he had raped her sister, a lot of motive there." He still hadn't looked up from the papers.

"Sir, with all due respect, we have nothing on Philips. Actually, we have nothing on anyone at this point."

He laid the papers down on the desk and looked at the detective, his penetrating, dark green eyes smiling at her—casually flirtatious.

"I want this manner handled quickly, Detective, and I told Detective Baker the same thing."

"Well, Mr. Clark, I don't see how that is possible. We don't have a murder weapon, a witness, or forensic evidence. We both know that motive isn't enough to convict a killer."

Charlene finally understood. Minor had gotten to Clark. Jeffrey Clark was just the kind of ass-kisser to agree to anything Carl Minor suggested.

"We will," he said confidently, holding the folder in the air. "I'll have my secretary make copies of everything and have it back on your desk by morning. You're dismissed, Detective," he said politely, but with authority.

Chapter 17

She woke up Monday morning, at six fifteen, feeling drowsy and a little perplexed. Yesterday had been an excruciatingly long day, and the up-and-down emotional rollercoaster of her first case had taken its toll. She'd limited herself to only four drinks last night.

When she opened her eyes, she was stung by the first light of dawn filtering through the blinds.

She was slipping into her running clothes when Charlene noticed a white envelope on the floor in front of the front door. The envelope hadn't been there last night when she'd returned. It wasn't labeled, and this one was sealed.

She opened the door and looked out into the hallway. Someone must have slipped the mail under her door either late last night or early this morning.

Another Celebrity Slayer message?

She went back inside and shut the door. Because she didn't have any thin gloves in the apartment, Charlene used hands-free utensils to transport the envelope from the floor to the kitchen counter. Using a steak knife, she slit the envelope open, and with a pair of tweezers, removed the tiny paper. She laid it on the countertop.

The paper contained an out-of-state phone number and the words 'Re: Alberto Bianchi'.

She hesitated for only seconds before picking up the phone and dialing the number.

The man who answered must have been waiting for her call. "Charlene Taylor?" The voice sounded wide awake for six in the morning.

"Yes," Charlene said hesitantly. She didn't recognize the voice. It wasn't the Celebrity Slayer. "Who is this?"

"Who I am doesn't matter. What I know does."

"Oh, how cliché." Charlene rolled her eyes. "What do you know?"

"I've been on the Bianchi task force for the last four years."

A Fed. Charlene tried to bring back the images of her encounter last night. The two guards outside the van and the driver, but when she closed her eyes, she couldn't form faces. "What about it?"

"I have to tell you this because I don't think you should remove Bianchi as a suspect on the Anderson murder."

"Why not?" Charlene cradled the phone between her shoulder and ear, searching hastily for paper and a pen.

"The night Anderson was killed, Bianchi gave us the slip. We picked him up about an hour later. He was on the other side of the city, so the timing is pressed, but possible."

"I thought your boss said Anderson paid his debt?"

"That's what he would have you believe."

"How did a guy like Bianchi manage to give the FBI the slip?"

"He's smart and he has connections. That night we tailed him to a sandwich shop in Century City."

"What time was this?" She scribbled notes.

"It was 9:36 PM." Charlene was impressed with the agent's accuracy. "We could tell he was on to us because he continually shifted lanes, and we knew, from our research teams, that his father had trained him to spot a tail. We followed protocol—stayed four cars back, even made vehicle switches every two miles. We have his phone bugged so we heard the call he made to the sandwich shop. We're good at our jobs, Detective, but that night Bianchi was better." Charlene could detect the disgust in the man's voice. "When he went inside the sandwich shop, he must have switched clothes and slipped out the back because ten minutes later a man matching Bianchi's physical description, wearing Bianchi's clothes, came out the front."

"Did you not see his face?" Charlene couldn't believe this story.

"He had his hat pulled down and used the large, take-out paper restaurant bag to shield his face. He got into Bianchi's car and drove off. About an hour later, we got a look at the driver's face and pulled him over. About twenty minutes after that, we located Bianchi driving an '82 silver Dodge truck."

"So he had over an hour without a tail?"

"That's right. I don't think that would have given Bianchi enough time to cross the city, kill Anderson, and cross back. We found him in Rancho Park. That's a pretty good commute in that time span, especially in an old truck."

This story just put Bianchi back on the suspect list. "Tell me about the task force."

"The inner-agency task force was set up fifteen years ago, when Bianchi first arrived in LA. We knew his father had sent him here for a reason, we just didn't know what. We put heavy surveillance on his home, work, and three vehicles. But he knows how to conduct his business around the taps. The devices are state of the art, but from our intel we also know he has a man on his payroll who is quite handy at deciphering our work, and we've been keeping an eye out for him."

"What do you have on Bianchi?"

The man snorted. "Not much. And trust me it's not from a lack of trying."

"What do you mean?"

"The list of Bianchi followers includes the FBI, CIA, and IRS. And now, since the Anderson murder, you can add the LAPD."

"Why are you telling me all of this?"

"Because I know you met my boss last night. This whole slip-up has been an embarrassment for the Bureau. They're trying to cover it up and keep your department away from Bianchi."

"Can I call you from time to time to check in?"

"No. When I hang up, this number will be disconnected." With that, the man was gone.

Charlene laid down the phone. This case was moving quickly, with information popping up all over the city.

She went for a run to clear her head.

Charlene sat at her desk, sucking on a breath mint while reviewing crime scene pictures and the Anderson report.

"The signed search warrants for Anderson's house finally came in," Larry said, dropping a stack of papers on the two desks.

"Huh," Charlene said, looking at the papers. "Only took two days."

Larry didn't respond and Charlene wondered if Larry felt as she did—that someone or something was inhibiting the progress of the investigation.

"Give 'em to Berry and Clayton," Larry said.

She found them huddled around the coffee machine and waved them over.

"Here are the search warrants for Anderson's home. Carl Minor's lawyer will probably be there so show him the paper work. Search the entire house and subpoena anything that may be evidence. Get his PC too. You guys know what to look for."

They nodded and left. If they were put out by taking orders from a woman, they didn't show it. Charlene wondered why Larry was giving her so much responsibility.

Charlene was about to say something when three well-dressed men walked by, followed by the captain.

"Who are they?" Charlene asked.

Larry shrugged, lifting his suit jacket from the back of his chair and throwing it on.

Charlene caught Detective Berkley scampering by and pulled him over.

"Who are the suits?"

"The Feds have just joined the Slayer case."

Charlene pictured the 'perfect storm' brewing from a clash of egos, but remained quiet.

"Taylor!"

Charlene was swung around in her chair by the captain. One of the FBI agents was standing behind him.

"This is Agent Higgins."

He swapped the briefcase from his right to left hand and shook Charlene's.

The captain continued. "They'd like you to join the multiple homicide briefing."

"Why me?" Charlene asked.

The agent answered. "We've been told that the killer has been in contact with you."

"That's right."

"Then we'd like you to join us and share your insight."

"I'll wait outside," Larry said, trudging away.

Charlene followed the men into the conference room, which had now been assigned to the Celebrity Slayer Task Force. About a dozen men and one woman sat around a large cherry-wood conference table. A large screen had been set up in the corner and a laptop hooked up to a projector was on the table.

The introductions were quickly made, Charlene took a seat, and the light was turned off.

Special Agent in Charge Myles Cunningham, from the FBI Behavioral Science Regional Unit in Los Angeles, stood, and with the aid of a PowerPoint presentation, began the meeting. When the first victim's photo came on the screen, it felt like all the air was sucked out of the room.

"We're just joining the investigation this morning but we started a profile from what we have so far. There are four kinds of killers and from what we've seen so far, and this is only preliminary, he's a 'thrill' killer. We've looked quickly at the files and this is what we see.

"If we look at the evolution of the kills, we see that this UNSUB is gaining confidence. We know that serial killers in general grow, learn from their mistakes and increase their risk-taking. This guy has a narcissistic personality, preoccupied with issues of personal inadequacy, power, prestige and vanity. Most killers don't stop until they're caught."

"But we'll need to review the crime scenes, reports, interviews and analysis. Let's make this clear. It is *not* our intention to catch this guy. That's your job. We will simply assist you where to focus your investigation, and then suggest proactive techniques to draw out the killer."

He went on to discuss the procedure by which they worked—about stepping into the mind of the killer and putting themselves in the place of the victim. When he had completed his slide show, he looked at Charlene.

"Detective Taylor, it is my understanding that you have had contact with this guy."

"That's right," Charlene said and nodded.

She went on to tell them about the frequent phone calls, as well as the items he had left—the address of a victim, her father's baseball hat and the pictures in her car. She knew this was the first her captain had heard of it and could feel his eyes trained on her. Charlene did not mention her father's involvement in the case, or that she had all of his notes in her apartment.

"We'll need all of that stuff to have it analyzed," the agent said.

"Already done," Charlene answered.

The agent smiled. "You've been busy, Detective." He turned back to the rest of the group. "Okay, sounds like this guy might have killed Martin Taylor too. If that's the case, it will change the profile."

Charlene smiled and looked at her captain, but he refused to make eye contact with her.

The lights were turned back on.

"We should have a profile by the end of the day. In the meantime, let's send some people to the funeral to videotape. I want faces and license plates. Who knows, maybe the killer will want to watch."

The meeting was adjourned and everyone dismissed. Charlene retrieved the evidence from her locker and handed it over to the Feds.

Darren was having a conversation with Larry when she got back to her desk.

"How was that?" Larry asked, with Darren looking very eager and curious.

"About what you would expect."

"Do they know who it is yet?" Larry asked sarcastically, obviously not a fan of the FBI.

"Anything new?" Darren asked earnestly.

"Darren, don't you have something for us?"

When he left, she caught Larry grinning ear-to-ear. "What?" she asked.

"I think Brady is in love. He came over here to see what you were up to. Watch yourself, Taylor."

Charlene rolled her eyes and changed the subject. "So what about Bianchi?"

"What about him?"

"Larry, I don't know what kind of relationship you have with him, but we need to take a closer look."

Before he could answer, Charlene picked up her phone and called Dennis Watson who worked Vice Division and specifically organized crime. Watson was a former veteran undercover cop before being promoted to an office job.

"Dennis, it's Charlene Taylor in Homicide. I need everything you have on Alberto Bianchi and I need it ASAP."

"He has a list of KAs. You want those too?"

"Send everything on his known associates. Thanks."

"So, even after our visit to Bianchi last night, you still think he's guilty?" Larry asked after she had hung up.

She didn't tell him about her encounter with the FBI, or the phone call this morning.

"I wouldn't call him a rock solid lead but I think he's worth looking at. I have my doubts. I think the rose petals in Anderson's shirt were staged."

"How's that?"

"I believe they were put there with the intent of deflecting our investigation away from any logical suspect. They want us to look at Bianchi. But that's just my hunch."

"What else can I do?" Darren had returned and dropped a thick sheaf of papers on Larry's desk.

"What's that?" Charlene asked, looking at the stack of papers.

"Everything I could get on the Philips' rape. Twelve pages."

"Twelve pages! Jesus, Darren, all I wanted was a brief description from the lead investigator."

"But…"

"Never mind."

"Brady, call the Chicago Gun Club and ask for Instructor Fred Spooner. Find out what you can on one of his former students, Sandra Philips," Larry said.

"Yes, Sir." Darren saluted sarcastically and turned.

"And here, Brady," Larry said, flinging a book in the air. The officer caught it skillfully.

"Find out what you can about Anderson's women. Who they are and where they were on the night of his murder. Check alibis, bios, and their present relationships."

Darren opened it, skimming from front to back. "But there's gotta be over a hundred names in here!"

"Is that a problem?" Larry asked, raising his voice.

"No, Sir." Darren turned and headed to the table that had been set up for their team.

Larry looked at Charlene and smiled. "That should keep him busy for a while."

Charlene returned the smile. "The Dean at UCLA is supposed to be back today."

"I was thinking the same thing." Larry stood up.

"I just want to review the file Berry and Clayton put together first."

Larry nodded. "Okay, I gotta take a leak anyway."

When he left, Charlene plugged some information into the computer and then searched everything from the file, made by her officers, to the material found in Anderson's office.

She didn't want to make eye contact, but Charlene could feel Darren staring at her from across the room. Was he still pissed about his assignment?

Berry and Clayton had conducted an extensive, thorough search and had compiled facts on everything, from phone records and bank statements to a personal profile of the victim.

These were the facts.

Anderson was born in San Francisco in nineteen seventy-six. He was thirty-six years old, six two, two hundred five pounds, and a graduate of Princeton University in the top fifth percentile of his class. He dropped out of med school after two years and had been a College Psychology Professor for the last eight. He was once married to a woman who lived in San Francisco whom he no longer saw, no children. He owned a nineteen ninety-eight Jaguar. He remarried last year. He was a member of Gold's Gym and the Beachwood Country Club.

This is what wasn't in the bio.

Anderson was a drunk who loved women and gambling. He was in an unstable marriage, hated by his father-in-law, and in debt to a demanding bookie. He had an affair with his TA, raped her sister, and had a book full of women he either dated or slept with. Charlene could think of a number of reasons and a number of people who would be better off with Anderson dead.

He was at O'Brien's on Wilshire on the night of the murder, left the bar alone, and apparently saw no one on the way to the house. He made a call from his cell phone to Jessica Philips and it was connected at 8:57 PM. The call only lasted a few seconds. Less than an hour later, Anderson was shot twice in the chest at Philips' house and the killer called nine-one-one. Then there were the rose petals, but with the news from the FBI, Charlene didn't think Bianchi had had the time to commit the murder, although one of his men could have. To Charlene, the petals were a maneuver to throw the cops off. Bianchi was low on the suspect list.

Jessica and Sandra Philips, Carl Minor, Beverly Anderson, and Alberto Bianchi all had motive and opportunity.

As she reviewed her notes, Charlene noticed something interesting.

Why had Anderson, a top professor in the Department of Psychiatry at USC, transferred to UCLA? It meant less pay, a drop in seniority, and half the benefits package.

Larry returned, drying his hands on his pant legs. Charlene mentioned her suspicions.

"Apples and oranges, Taylor," Larry answered. "One school's private, the other public. USC is located in the slums—the Southern fringe of downtown LA by Exposition Park. UCLA is on the West Side, near Beverly Hills. UCLA is deemed the 'cooler' school—more famous and prestigious."

"That's your opinion, Larry."

"That's a good point and one we can bring up with the dean."

Charlene still thought there was another reason behind it.

"Call the Dean at UCLA and tell him we're on our way."

Before they left the precinct, Charlene dropped a couple of bucks in the department coffee-fund jar, confident Larry hadn't done it.

Chapter 18

By midmorning they were in the fast lane, of the Santa Monica, heading towards UCLA.

"So what do you think of Darren?" Charlene asked.

"Oh no, Taylor, don't tell me Brady is getting to you?" Larry had a sneer on his face.

"He's kind of cute, you know, in a boyish way."

"Brady's a punk. He's been in the department for what, a year? He hasn't made any friends."

"He's the shy, quiet type," Charlene said.

"And who transfers from a plush job in Hollywood to this shithole?"

"Larry, he loves being a cop and wants to be a part of something. What's his story?" Charlene was aware that cops, even the male ones, loved to gossip.

Larry shrugged, while keeping both hands on the wheel. "He's twenty-three, two years in Hollywood, one here. Hollywood dicks never retire. Why would they with a cushy job like that? I think he transferred here for a speedier promotion. I always catch him reading police procedural books, and he's always signing up for extra courses. Still lives with his parents. Oh yeah, and he has a twenty-four/seven hard-on for you."

"Interesting," Charlene said.

"Oh no, he's gotten to you."

"I'm just saying."

After checking through campus safety, they parked in the Administrative Building parking lot and locked the doors.

The receptionist wasn't at her desk so Charlene and Larry showed themselves down the hallway to the dean's office. Charlene followed Larry, passing the framed pictures, on the hallway walls, of UCLA celebrity Alumni, from James Dean to Rob Reiner to Kareem Abdul-Jabbar.

Dean Lawrence Murray was both a dean and a professor in the UCLA Department of Psychology. The fifty-five-year-old was massaging his temples when the detectives rapped on the door. He lifted his head from a stack of paperwork and summoned the detectives inside. His thinning gray hair was combed over a bald spot and he had a knobby nose with tired and worn brown eyes. On his anorexic frame, his brown suit hung limply. His tie was pulled tight.

"Sorry for the mess, Detectives. I get back from my holiday only to find my best professor is dead. His poor wife and family. Reporters have been calling every twenty minutes, and trying to replace a highly qualified, experienced professor like Ken isn't an easy task. I've had to cancel his classes this week."

Charlene couldn't help notice the dean's perfect diction.

"That's why we're here, Dean Murray," Larry said. "I'm Detective Baker, and this is my partner, Detective Taylor."

"Please, sit down." He ushered them to a couple of comfortable, leather chairs in front of his desk. He returned to his seat.

Larry got right to it. "My partner and I were wondering about Ken Anderson's transfer from USC. It seemed short notice, almost unexpected."

The dean hesitated, looking out the window to where two students were skateboarding across the parking lot. Then he spoke. "Ken's transfer was a surprise to everyone, including me. Of course, I was delighted to have a professor of Ken's status here at the school. He's one of the youngest professors to ever grace our school, and one of the best. I never thought we could afford him, but when he agreed to our terms, we were quite pleased."

"What were his reasons for wanting to leave USC?"

"I never asked, and he never said. It was actually Dean Brown who approached me. Hubert and I are good friends, golf together twice a month. When he came to me with the proposal, I thought it was a dream come true. I assumed it was to be closer to his family."

Charlene still didn't believe this. From what she knew, Anderson wasn't exactly a family-man and didn't seem like the kind of person to make a decision for someone else's benefit. Most things he did had an ulterior motive. And he definitely wouldn't have done it to be closer to Carl Minor. Plus, why would a degenerate gambler take a pay cut?

"Dean Murray, did you know Professor Anderson was having an affair with his TA?" Charlene asked.

The dean pushed back in his seat, his eyes bulging. "I had no idea, Detectives, honest. Trust me, if I had known, there would've been severe repercussions. We don't tolerate that kind of behavior at UCLA." He was quick to protect the integrity of the school, a defensive note in his voice.

"Did it not strike you as odd that Anderson would take such a significant pay cut?" Larry asked.

The dean sighed, starting to look annoyed. "Of course it did, Detective, but as I said, I never questioned it. I was happy to have him. We had a position to fill and he filled it. Quite capably, I might add. I couldn't have hand-picked a more qualified candidate. Let's not forget something, Detectives. The Department of Psychology at UCLA is one of the largest in the country. We receive millions of dollars in funding annually, and it's a world class research institution."

"So you didn't know about his personal problems—a bad marriage, not to mention his abuse of gambling, booze, and women." Now it was Charlene's turn to press the matter.

"Look, Detective Taylor," the dean said as he rose from his seat. "I try to make it a point of knowing what my professors do with their personal lives, but Ken was different. He was a great professor, and of course you know who his father-in-law is."

"Ignorance is bliss," Charlene interrupted.

The dean went on. "I don't hide the fact that I thought the school could benefit from a Carl Minor donation. I kept my nose out of his business, as long as his private life didn't interfere with his professional career. And it never did...until now." He seemed to lose his train of thought but caught it quickly. "If you want to know more about Professor Anderson, perhaps you should talk to Dean Brown over at USC. He and Ken were quite close."

"Our list is growing," Larry was saying when they jumped into the car. "We're spending a lot of time in the car when there's a lot to do. I suggest we split up."

Charlene didn't argue.

"Drop me off at the department. While you're at USC, I'll chase down our backgrounds and alibis. Cut our time in half. Are you okay with handling the interview on your own?" Larry looked genuinely concerned.

"I think it's a good idea." Charlene always liked being on her own.

She dropped Larry off and then, knowing she wouldn't be returning to the precinct, traded in the Crown Vic for her Volvo.

She followed the directions she'd received, turning onto the campus at entrance six and following Vermont Avenue at 36th Place.

Charlene had confirmed the meeting by phone, and Dean Brown, an older, distinguished looking gentleman with thick, chalk-white hair, closely spaced blue eyes, and a permanent tan, was waiting at the front of Parking Structure "A". The sixty-five-year-old kept in good shape and was dressed in a USC Cardinal and Gold V-neck sweater pulled over a white dress shirt, with beige slacks. His smile was genuine, and he wasted little time leading Charlene into the building.

"When I heard about Ken, I couldn't believe it," the dean said as they made the short walk to the Psychology Department, located in the USC College of Letters, Arts & Sciences. Dean Brown moved in a quick, fluid motion, his pace never slowing.

They entered a building adjoining the Dornsife Cognitive Neuroscience Imaging Center and entered the dean's office.

"Please have a seat, Detective," he gestured. "I just have a call to make."

Charlene sat and studied the office. The walls were littered with plaques and pictures from past USC achievements and former student-athletes. Charlene recognized some of the players who were now highly acclaimed professionals. She saw a picture of two African-American men in Trojan jerseys, Marcus Allen and Calvin Watters. Allen was older than Watters and went on to claim success in the NFL, but Watters, who'd been expected to be an NFL stand-out, had disappeared after college. Charlene wondered what ever happened to Watters after his career-ending injury. She knew his older brother was an LAPD detective with a different branch.

Like UCLA, the USC walls were plastered with famous people— John Wayne, Tom Selleck, John Ritter, Neil Armstrong, and Will Ferrell. A set of new Calloway golf clubs sat in the corner of the office beside an artificial practice putting green. The dean's desk looked freshly varnished, and a computer and phone were the lone articles resting on top.

"Now, Detective," the dean said as he hung up and snapped Charlene back to attention. "What can I do for you?"

"Do you have the stuff I requested?"

The dean handed her a folder. "These are all the files we have on Ken when he worked at the school."

Charlene quickly opened them and flipped through. The file contained personal information—address, identification, and signed contracts with USC. It also had Anderson's class schedule, awards and achievements he earned during his tenure, as well as pictures of him with various students from school events. Charlene noted that most were women.

"As you can see, Detective, Ken was a well-respected, top-notch professor."

Something didn't sit right. She shut the folder and looked at the dean, her lips pursed. "Let's talk about what's not in the file."

The dean cocked his head and squinted. "What do you mean?"

"What am I missing? Ken Anderson left a job and took a transfer to another school for less money, fewer benefits, and a drop in seniority. With his lifestyle, Anderson needed money."

The dean said nothing, shifted uncomfortably in his seat and looked away, gripping the arms of his chair. "Ken did marry Carl Minor's daughter. There should have been more than enough branches on that money tree."

"Come on, Dean Brown, work with me."

Again, the dean looked away. The silence lingered, and Charlene decided to let the moment run its course.

Then the dean rose from his chair. "I guess it doesn't matter now."

He moved to a corner of the room and took down a framed painting, revealing a hidden safe. He quickly turned the knob, entered the code, and opened the safe door. He removed a file and returned to his desk.

"I was supposed to dispose of this. I knew it would come back someday," he said, handing the folder across his desk. "I'm now glad I didn't destroy it. The story needs to be told."

Charlene quickly read over the top document. When she finished, she looked back at the dean, a glint in her eyes. "Tell me about it."

The dean leaned back in his chair, letting out a deep breath. Then he started. "My job here is to oversee the undergraduate educational mission of the college. When something happens in the Psych Department, to an undergrad, I'm in charge of handling the problem, not the President. That document came across my desk two years ago. The student's name was Margaret Conners. She was a freshman." He hesitated, setting the mood, and then added, "She claimed Ken raped her."

"What did you do?"

"I held a private meeting with Ken. He denied it. We had a school doctor examine the victim and evidence was found that she *had* indeed been raped." He closed his eyes. "I wanted to believe my professor, but we had an eye-witness seeing Ken enter the dorm earlier that night. Margaret Connors was a first year student, straight 'As' with no reason to lie. We threatened to put Ken on administrative leave, which meant his professional conduct would be looked at."

"Who was the eye witness?"

"Anonymous tip and we never followed up."

"Why not?" She looked through the rest of the file. There was no police report, only a signed agreement. Without reading the form, she looked back at the dean. "There were no charges filed?"

The dean sighed again, closed his eyes for a couple of seconds, and looked at Charlene. His sharp blue eyes had saddened. "No. That's why we never followed up on the phone tip. The cops were called. By whom, I never found out. But they were sent away without a report. The student's parents are members of the school alumni. They took it exceptionally hard. We talked them out of following through with a grievance. I had them agree, if Ken was removed, that no mention of the event would be brought up. We suggested Ken take a sabbatical, but he immediately transferred to UCLA and the situation was dead and buried."

Now it was Charlene's turn to sit back in her seat. She was disgusted. She could see why the dean had done what he had, to avoid a lawsuit and public scandal. That press would have killed the school. The case sounded a lot like the Sandra Philips' rape, bringing new suspects with motive. "Do you remember the officers' names?"

The dean shook his head. "I can't remember. I've tried to put the incident behind me and move on. Now you come around, stirring up muddy water. But I do remember one cop continued to come around after, for a follow up. She was quite adamant but nothing transpired."

"I need to talk to Margaret Connors."

"Look, Detective, we've all worked hard to put it behind us and this will only bring up old wounds, scars that have taken a long time to heal—if they have at all. Don't wake up sleeping ghosts."

Charlene stood up, placing her hands on the desk and leaning forward, almost nose to nose with the dean. "Where's Margaret Connors?"

Chapter 19

It was only a fifteen minute drive from USC to Boyle Heights, where Margaret Connors lived with her parents in a suburban community. Charlene called Larry from the car to fill him in on the interview with Dean Brown.

"Sounds like a solid lead, Kid. Good work," Larry approved. "I'll add it to the Investigating Officer's Chronological Report which I'm filling out now. I'll leave it on my desk if you want to take a look to make sure I haven't forgotten anything. I think I might have something on Beverly Minor's alibi too. I'm just waiting on a phone call. You okay in Boyle Heights alone?"

"Sure," Charlene answered.

"Good. We'll meet here tomorrow morning and review everything new."

Charlene hung up, her body vibrating with anticipation. Things were finally starting to happen.

She was surprised to hear that Connors lived in Boyle Heights, since ninety-five percent of the community was Hispanic and Latino, and it had also been the home to former gangster, Mickey Cohen.

She followed the dean's directions through a working-class neighborhood before pulling up to an older bungalow with an attached garage, a white-stuccoed house starting to show signs of its age.

Charlene parked in the driveway behind a navy blue Nissan Pathfinder, got out of the vehicle and approached the front door, ringing the bell twice and waiting.

The door was opened by a smiling man who looked to be in his late forties. His sandy brown hair had traces of white and there were stress lines around his blue eyes. His body looked naturally muscular and lithe, and was hidden underneath a white golf shirt and khaki shorts.

"Can I help you?" he asked.

"Detective Taylor, LAPD." Charlene showed her badge.

"What's the problem, Detective?"

"I would like to speak to you about an incident at USC a couple of years ago."

The man didn't flinch. "Come in. I'm Margaret's father, Eric. "

Eric Connors turned, and Charlene followed him inside. She removed her shoes and was shown into a comfortably furnished living room. The inside of the house looked dated, unchanged in years.

"Margaret's in her bedroom, I'll get her. Please, make yourself comfortable."

He left the room, and Charlene studied the surroundings. There was a small fire burning in a fireplace with a dark red mahogany mantle, displaying framed photographs, ribbons and trophies won by a younger Margaret Connors. A thirty-two-inch TV was tuned to the local news, volume muted, and a John Grisham novel was on the coffee table, open and resting face up beside a half cup of coffee. A pair of slippers sat in front of the couch. There was a Bible and rosary on a night stand, along with a ceramic statue of Jesus Christ.

The man returned with a petite girl, who didn't look to have hit her twenties, clinging tightly to her father's side. She looked like someone whose faith in humanity had waned. Her brown hair was swept back in a French knot, and a large purple and gold sweatshirt, almost to her knees, hung off her body. In large bold writing the words '82nd Annual Pig Game Champs' were displayed across the chest, and underneath those, in smaller letters, were the words 'The oldest high school rivalry west of the Mississippi'. Margaret Connors had inherited her father's blue eyes.

"Detective Taylor, this is my daughter, Margaret."

"Nice to meet you, Margaret," Charlene smiled, extending her hand slowly. The girl gave Charlene a doleful smile, but didn't shake her hand, instead slinking away. Charlene remembered seeing that same fear behind Sandra Philips' eyes.

"Is this your wife, Mr. Connors?" Charlene pointed to a pretty woman in a picture.

"Yes," he said, his eyes dropping to the floor. "Beth passed away last winter from cancer."

"I'm so sorry."

"Thank you. Please, sit down." He went on. "Doctors said the cancer had been there for years, dormant, but really spread quickly. The stress didn't help. We had a tough year," he said, looking at his daughter and stroking her hair. He turned back to Charlene. "What would you like to know, Detective?"

"Ken Anderson was murdered two nights ago."

"Yes, we heard," Connors replied. Charlene saw no signs of remorse in his face.

"Dean Brown told me what happened to Margaret. I'd like to hear your version." She directed her question at Margaret, but expected her father to respond.

Margaret Connors sat so close to her father it reminded Charlene of a six-year-old who still wasn't comfortable around strangers.

Eric Connors sandwiched his daughter's hands in his own, and looked her in the eyes. "Are you up for this, MagPie?"

The girl looked at Charlene, then back at her father. She nodded slightly.

"Okay," he whispered.

Charlene listened to Margaret's story, identical to Sandra Philips'.

A drunk Anderson had pushed his way inside the dorm room, thinking because of who he was he would get away with it. And he had.

Margaret insisted that she hadn't led him on and had firmly said no, but Anderson was like a man possessed.

Charlene asked, "Why didn't you press charges?"

Eric Connors held Charlene's stare. She could tell he was torturing himself. He seemed to hesitate. "If I could go back, I'd do it differently. Beth and I are, were, USC graduates, alumni, and we didn't want to drag the school's name through the mud. It was Anderson who needed to be punished, not the school. I believed in Karma and felt that God would take vengeance. I've known Dean Brown for a long time and I respect his opinion. Looking back now, I should have gone to the police."

Charlene put herself in his shoes, thought about how he must feel knowing his daughter had never recovered, and that just maybe, if he'd pressed charges, sent Anderson away, his daughter might have been able to turn a corner. And that might have relieved some stress from his wife, who was unknowingly dying of cancer. The man carried the weight of the world on his shoulders.

"I'm sorry, Mr. Connors," Charlene said. "I just don't buy the fact that you didn't press charges because you and your wife were such devoted alumni."

Connors' jaw tightened. He closed his eyes and let out his breath. When he opened them, he said, "We signed a non-disclosure agreement with Carl Minor." He got up off the couch, a look of disgust on his face.

He turned his back and walked towards the window to look at the street outside.

"Hush money," Charlene mumbled to herself. Now it was starting to make sense. "But your bank accounts and financial records would have raised red flags."

Eric Connors turned back towards them, his eyes now wet. He shook his head. "He didn't pay us directly."

"What do you mean," Charlene asked.

"Carl Minor covered Beth's medical expenses. He paid each installment in full."

Charlene was silent.

Margaret interrupted Charlene's thoughts with a quiet voice. "I agreed."

Charlene turned and looked at Margaret, who seemed so small to Charlene.

She continued. "We were in a bind, I knew that. We didn't have any medical insurance and Mom was getting worse each day. Dad had to stay home to take care of her, and no work meant no money. So I pleaded with my dad to take the deal. It was best for the family."

Charlene digested the information. "I understand the cops were called anyway?"

Again, the answers came from Eric Connors. He nodded dejectedly. "Yes, Margaret's roommate called the police. But we sent them away. They didn't take it well."

Charlene got up and approached them. She placed her hand on Margaret's. "I'm so sorry for what you've been through, both of you. But I do have one more question that I have to ask." She looked Eric in the eye. "Where were you on the night Ken Anderson was murdered?"

Eric Connors stood up, swiping Charlene's hand away. "We were here."

"Is this true, Margaret?"

The girl nodded.

"Was there anyone else with you?"

"No one," he answered. "Just the two of us, like it always is."

Charlene nodded. "Thank you for your time. It was nice of you to let me in and it took a lot of courage to tell your story, Margaret."

Connors walked her to the door. As Charlene was slipping into her shoes, a framed photograph on a hallway table quickened something in her memory. Goose bumps sprouted on her arms. She picked up the frame—two girls at a Halloween party. One girl was clearly Margaret Connors dressed in a Ketchup costume, and the other girl, although hidden in a Mustard bottle outfit, looked vaguely familiar.

"Margaret, who is this in the picture with you?"

"Who?" the girl asked, moving closer to Charlene and looking at the picture. "Oh, that's Sarah, my roommate from school."

"Sarah who?"

"Sarah Crawford."

Charlene could have sworn the girl in the picture was someone else. The hair was a different color and shorter, but the facial features were similar.

"She's the one who called the cops," Eric Connors said.

"Do you mind if I borrow this for a couple of days? I promise to give it back," Charlene asked.

"Sure," Margaret replied, shrugging her shoulders.

Charlene removed the picture from the frame, thanked them again, and left. There was something oddly familiar about the woman in the picture.

She hung her coat in the front closet, and choosing beer over Jack Daniels, checked her messages. Three missed calls—her mother, sister, and a private caller.

There was only one message. Jane had arrived safely in Denver and she was just checking in.

Charlene hung up and checked the clock. She dialed her mother's number, but was greeted by voicemail. She left a quick message to tell her mother she was in for the night if she wanted to call back.

She twisted off the beer cap and took a drink. The Dodgers game was over—another loss. They were on a lengthy losing streak so Charlene wasn't sorry she was missing the games. She quickly finished the beer and tossed the empty into the recycling bin and grabbed another.

Drained, Charlene lay on top of the futon, fluffed up her pillows, and channel surfed before settling on a rerun of *Gunsmoke*. The TV played, but she couldn't concentrate.

The case consumed her. She removed the picture from her pocket and looked at it again.

Who was the girl with Margaret Connors?

Charlene rose from the bed. She poured a shot of Jack Daniels and chased it with the cold beer. She returned to the hall and opened the walk-in closet, flicking on the light.

She booted up the computer and stared at her father's files in the cabinet. She still had two folders to get through that she hadn't yet had a chance to look at.

Charlene logged onto the internet and googled 'Ashley Stanley'. Over twenty million hits came up—Facebook pages, LinkedIn profiles, Twitter accounts and Myspace sites. Charlene skimmed the first fifty hits, but none were for the Ashley Stanley she was interested in. She clicked on 'google images' but couldn't find any pictures matching her suspect.

Then Charlene googled 'Sarah Crawford'. This time over forty-five million hits, an even more common name. Charlene went through the same routine, and still couldn't find the woman she was looking for.

She blew air out of her cheeks in frustration.

With this case, Charlene hadn't the time or energy to focus on her father. She knew she should be sleeping, resting up for what would be a long day tomorrow on the Anderson case.

She took another slug of beer and plugged wires into her father's laptop, which was so old it didn't have wireless. Once it was running, Charlene opened the internet and went to her father's 'favorites'. She spent the next hour following her father's internet trail, to see if she could retrace his steps. But none of the websites he had visited seemed to be connected with the Slayer case, or at least she couldn't make the connections yet.

Charlene shook her head. She changed direction.

Instead of focusing on her father's murder, and trying to match it to the Slayer murders, she searched the known Slayer victims, and tried to tie those to her father's investigation.

She opened the filing cabinet, removed her father's notes and scanned the personal crime lab she'd established for her father's case. The walls were jumbled with reports, photocopied documents, newspaper clippings, and crime scene pictures from not only her father's notes, but also everything the LAPD had on the Celebrity Slayer. Scrawled notes rested on the desk beside her laptop, and folders were filed neatly on the closet shelf, everything labeled and columned.

The pictures from the five murder scenes had been formed into a collage for Charlene to contrast and compare.

Look at it like you're looking at it for the first time. What's missing?

Nothing stood out.

She stood in front of an enlarged map of LA tacked to the wall. Colored pins displayed the location where each victim had been found. She chewed the inside of her mouth. Choosing a crime site had geographical logic, but through the geographical profile there was no sign of an area pattern. The body dumpsites were splattered in random locations. Now the killer had moved from Hollywood to West LA. *Why?*

Location and timing were important in all serial cases, but Charlene couldn't find the significance here.

She sat down at the desk and opened the file, reviewing the autopsy protocols and post-mortem reports. The common thread for all of the victims was the brutality of the way they were killed. Multiple knife wounds applied over the entire body and face. No sexual assault.

Okay, Charlene. Don't look at what he's doing. Look at why *he's doing it.*

Every murder should make sense, even if the killer was a psychopath. She removed the copies of the photos from the package that had been left in her car and spread them out across the desk, matching them with the photos taken by the police.

Is he trying to tell me something?

Using a magnify glass, Charlene compared the photos taken from the Slayer, to those taken by the LAPD, looking for a common denominator, anything that separated the photos.

There were no physical traits that connected the victims. Both men and women were killed—different hair color, eye color, height, weight, length of hair, skin color.

Charlene knew that serial killers rarely crossed racial lines, but this guy had no prejudices. Serial killers dehumanize their victims. These were all beautiful people, and the heavy knife slashes to their face told Charlene that their looks were definitely a trigger. The only thing that connected the victims before death was their line of work.

Each victim had almost identical wounds, in identical areas. Defensive wounds and the MEs said that death was prolonged, almost wanting the pain to last. Definite overkill.

She turned to the back of each case file and found the investigative chronology, following the steps each detective took in investigating the murder. They had been thorough.

She threw her head back in frustration. All she could do at this point was look for patterns and eliminate theories.

She pounded her fist on the desk, and papers from the final folder she hadn't yet gotten to scattered to the ground. When she bent to pick them up, Charlene noticed that her father's notepad was open to the middle. One word her father had scribbled was underlined and gave Charlene pause. She shivered, picking up the notepad.

COP?

Did her father think the Celebrity Slayer was a cop? Did he know who it was?

Underneath that single word was a short list of names. Was her father making assumptions? Did he have proof?

Charlene recognized some of the names and shivered at the thought. Most were retired, but some still going strong.

Charlene turned to the first page of her father's notes and flipped through.

He had cut out newspaper articles in which the police were quoted as saying, "at this time, no information can be reported in order to successfully continue the investigation," which basically meant the police had nothing.

On the third page, Charlene found something interesting that her father had noted from a shoeprint found outside the house of one of the victims. It was either a man's size eight or a woman's size ten. A small man's foot or a large woman's foot. He also suggested that the killer had a forefoot strike gait—toe to heel, ball of foot lands first—with no limp, which can be read from the depth and location of the footprints.

Charlene leaned back in her chair and stretched. There was one burning question.

Why celebrities?

Serial killers don't normally choose high-profile victims. But from what Charlene had seen, the Celebrity Slayer was anything but normal. Even though these victims were B level stars, they would have better security and more people watching them than the average man.

Did the hunt matter?

Book III

Motive

Chapter 20

Berry and Clayton had confiscated boxes of material from Anderson's home and were sifting through the documents in the back room when Charlene arrived at the office Tuesday morning. They were also going through the contents taken from Anderson's office, but so far nothing of significance had been found.

Alberto Bianchi's file sat on Charlene's desk. The folder was thick with hunches and possibilities. Bianchi was involved, allegedly, in a lot of schemes, including the gambling ring, but not murder. This didn't feel like a mob hit to Charlene, but she wasn't about to eliminate anyone at this point.

Larry still wasn't in, so Charlene looked through the Bianchi file herself and found something interesting. She buzzed Dennis Watson in Vice.

"Dennis, it's Charlene."

"Did you get the file, Detective?"

"Yeah, thanks. It says here that Bianchi has a daughter."

"That's right, allegedly."

"What does that mean?" Charlene sat back in her chair.

"Well, rumor has it that Bianchi knocked up some New Yorker when he was seventeen. His old man, embarrassed and outraged by the whole thing, paid the woman to disappear and shipped her to the West coast. When Bianchi was old enough, his pop sent him out here to be closer to his daughter. But since Bianchi arrived, over fifteen years ago, no one has seen proof of a daughter or a woman that age hanging around. We don't even have a picture. She could be any twenty-seven-year-old walking the street."

"Who's the mother?"

"Don't know that either. Bianchi's father went to great lengths to keep it a secret."

"So you have no idea who our missing women are, mother or daughter?"

"Like I said, Detective, we don't even know the mother's name or if a daughter even exists. It's all speculation and hearsay. The mother could have remarried. The daughter might be using her step-father's name or her mother's maiden name. In all honesty, we don't even know if Bianchi's daughter knows who her real father is."

"What about the FBI? Do you think they have any idea?"

He chuckled aloud. "Even if they did have that information, they certainly wouldn't share it with us."

"Thanks, Dennis."

Charlene hung up, wondering if Bianchi's daughter was in Anderson's black book. There would be no way to know, without DNA samples, and the department didn't have the funds, or the time, to test every woman in the book.

She quickly picked the phone back up and tried the phone number left in her apartment by the anonymous Fed.

No dice, number disconnected. Charlene slammed the phone down.

It had been four days since Anderson's murder. Charlene found the Investigating Officer's Chronological Report on Larry's desk and looked through it. Larry had all the bases covered.

She went over again what they had on the Anderson murder, the facts looping around in her head relentlessly. Who benefited the most from the professor's death?

Jessica Philips was having an affair with the victim. Anderson refused to leave his wife, knowing that his marriage into one of the richest families in America had its advantages, but not enough to keep him from cheating. Then he raped Jessica's sister, Sandra.

Sandra Philips, one of the rape victims. Not just the physical damage, but the emotional hurt and humiliation alone was enough to send any woman over the edge, wanting to exact some sort of revenge. From Darren's call to the Chicago Gun Club, Charlene knew that Sandra was an expert shot. The bullets found in Anderson's chest were perfectly placed, while he was in motion. But Charlene also understood that shooting at targets in a gallery was significantly different than aiming at a human. The gun got a little heavier, the trigger a little tighter, and the instinctive shaking made the firearm difficult to aim.

Of all the suspects associated with the case, Ashley Stanley bothered Charlene the most because there was absolutely nothing on her. Stanley was a roommate and close friend. If the woman in the photograph taken from Margaret Connors' home was indeed Ashley Stanley, as Charlene suspected, that meant Stanley was directly linked to Anderson at the time of both rapes. That gave Stanley double motive.

Charlene knew that rape is a crime of violence, not sex. How far had Anderson pushed and had he pushed the wrong person?

All three women in the house had both opportunity and motive.

According to her father, Beverly Anderson had been beaten and abused both mentally and physically. With a cheating husband and no prenuptial agreement, Anderson's death was the only way out of the loveless marriage without a major financial impact.

Carl Minor hated his son-in-law more than his fiercest competitor and would do anything to protect his daughter. He also had the money to hire a top hitman to eliminate Anderson, although, with the phone call to nine-one-one, Charlene doubted a hired assassin committed the murder.

Bianchi was also a suspect, albeit a weak one, because of the flower petals found in Anderson's shirt and Anderson's gambling debt. The phone call yesterday from the unknown agent was also confirmation that Bianchi wasn't solidly alibied.

Charlene shook her head and grimaced. She just didn't buy it. The flower petals looked more like a decoy, but she couldn't eliminate Bianchi because of what he was capable of. She thought about his carefully scripted exhibition at the pizza shop, as if everything he'd said had been rehearsed.

Now add two more suspects to her list.

Margaret Connors was also an Anderson rape victim, and there's no telling how many more there could be. Most women never come forward.

Margaret's life had been shattered. She'd quit school, moved home and lived a tortured life, with the everyday torment of her past. She would never be the same again.

Her father, Eric Connors, also suffered the consequences of the rape. He lost two women, his daughter mentally and his wife physically. He probably blamed both on Anderson's vicious act, if not directly, then at least indirectly. How far would a loving father and grieving husband go?

Eight suspects with motive. This case was moving at dizzying speed, with no sign of slowing down.

Charlene's opinion was that no MO match existed in the state files or the FBI's VICAP database. Jessica's admission that nothing had been taken told Charlene this was not a robbery gone astray, but a planned, premeditated kill by someone close to the victim. Someone who could fire a gin with expert precision. Charlene was sure that Anderson had known or had preliminary contact with the murderer prior to that night.

Taking the time to put the flower petals, already dyed in black ink, in the victim's pocket in an attempt to frame the mob also suggested the killer was organized and prepared. Maybe a seasoned professional or at least someone accustomed to death.

This was not random. It was personal. That thought kept circling in her mind.

She got up to stretch her legs and saw Darren returning to the case desk. It looked as if he had just come back from fixing himself up in the bathroom. He had a file tucked under his armpit.

"Darren, how's it coming with the black book?"

"I'm sorry, Chip. I need a little more time." The officer slumped in his chair. "There are a lot of names."

"While you're checking the names, try to track down any more rape victims connected to Anderson. We know about two for sure, but I bet there are a few more that haven't come forward. You might even check rape records with unidentified suspects. You never know, we might get lucky."

Charlene returned to her desk and tried the Sarah Crawford angle again, punching the name into the computer. She checked the NCIC Database, DMV, INS, IRS, and SS files with no luck. It made no sense.

Charlene saw Larry lumbering across the lobby floor, holding back an obvious smirk.

"Nice of you to join us," Charlene said sarcastically.

"Reviewing background material and alibi checks is the real police work. The past is a guide, Taylor. Don't forget that." His smile was more obvious. He read from his notes. "Sandra Philips was, in fact, at her rape seminar, and it did end when she said it did. Ashley Stanley was at softball. Her coach and captain verified the team checklist."

So far, Charlene hadn't heard anything promising.

Larry went on. "Beverly Anderson did go to her yoga workout that night."

Charlene slumped her shoulders. "I thought you said…"

"But," Larry interrupted, "the teacher or sensei or whatever the hell he's called said she left class early."

Charlene jumped out of her seat and held herself back from giving her partner a hug.

Larry held up a set of keys. "I'll drive."

During the ride, Charlene read from a file she'd pulled on the Andersons.

"I wish we'd had this on our first visit," she said.

"What is it?"

"A police report. Beverly called nine-one-one a couple of weeks ago to report her husband on a drunken rampage."

"What happened?"

"What seems to happen with Anderson. When the cops showed up, Beverly said it was all just a misunderstanding."

"Man, this guy was playing with fire. Rape, spousal abuse, adultery."

"Yeah and it looks like he finally got burned."

"I'm going to hit up a few neighbors to see if they have any information. You start with Beverly Minor and then I'll come in," Larry said.

"Gladly." Charlene bit the inside of her lip in anticipation.

Beverly opened the door before Charlene had a chance to knock. The widow was dressed in spandex. Her hair was tied up and she was carrying a blue, rubber Yoga mat. "Oh, you startled me, Detective Taylor!"

"Sorry, Mrs. Anderson, but you never gave me a chance to knock."

"I was just on my way out. I'm already late." Beverly impatiently checked her watch.

"Please, Mrs. Anderson, this'll only take a minute and it's very important."

They went inside and sat on the couch. Charlene was amazed at the almost overnight transformation. Beverly no longer looked like a woman fighting her age. Her skin had been tightened by Botox treatments and the bags around her eyes were gone. No makeup emphasized the widow's impossibly high cheekbones and elegant bone structure. Her brown hair had been freshly colored and small gold spheres dangled from her lobes.

"Mrs. Anderson," Charlene began, "I was filing through old reports and came across a nine-one-one call you placed a couple of weeks ago."

Beverly hesitated, as if thinking. "That was all a misunderstanding."

"So I've read. I'd like to hear about it."

Beverly crossed her legs, looking uncomfortably tense. Her eyes wandered around the well-furnished living room.

"Fine, Detective, I have nothing to hide." She looked at Charlene, as if waiting for a response. When Charlene didn't give in, she continued. "As soon as he walked in the door that night, I could smell the perfume. I knew he'd been with a woman."

"Did you confront him?"

She looked at Charlene and the detective could see desperation in the woman's eyes. "I never had before. I didn't want to face the reality, to be another statistic. Plus, I didn't want to admit my father was right. But…I'd had enough."

She stopped talking, trying to catch her breath.

Charlene waited.

"He didn't deny it. He didn't say anything. I got in his face, issuing dire threats of divorce, told him I would go straight to my father. That seemed to get his attention."

She went silent. Charlene urged her on. "Let's go back to the night you called the police."

"There was something in his eyes." Beverly looked off, fear on her face, as if seeing her husband again.

"Did he hit you?"

Charlene's words broke Beverly's trance. She looked at Charlene, a small smile spread on her face. "Not at first. He tried to calm me, but I was on a roll. I wasn't thinking—I was just reacting. I had so much frustration, held my tongue for so long, that it was all just coming out. When I charged at him, that's when he lost it."

Charlene let her go.

"He hit me." A single tear rolled down Beverly's cheek. "He'd never done that before."

Charlene got up from her seat and sat beside Beverly. The detective took her by the hand.

"He wasn't like that when we first met." She smiled, her eyes reliving better times. "We were madly in love and had so many plans—marriage, kids, grow old together. Once we got married, the honeymoon ended. It all fell apart. I tried to hold it together, and maybe I fooled myself for a while. Deep down, I knew I couldn't change him. He crossed the line that night."

"Tell me, Beverly," Charlene urged.

She brought her hand to the left side of her face, as if feeling the blow. "I was stunned, more humiliated than hurt. He grabbed me by the arm and squeezed. He said, 'You bitch! You mean nothing to me. I never loved you.' He said it with such casualness that I knew he wasn't lying. That it had all been an act. After he was done humiliating me, he threw me to the ground."

She lifted her shirt to reveal a large bruise that was just starting to yellow.

Charlene looked at her files. "I don't see anything in your report about a hospital visitation."

"I didn't go to the hospital. I was too humiliated."

"It's not your fault, Beverly." Charlene shifted closer. "So *you* called the cops?"

She nodded. "Then I called my father, told him what happened. I didn't want to involve him, but that night my husband scared me."

"What did your father say?"

"He told me to send the cops away and he would take care of everything. But we never had to file the divorce papers because Ken was killed."

This just upped Carl Minor's motive. A divorce would have cost millions.

"Why didn't you tell us you left yoga class early on the night of your husband's murder?" Charlene watched for a reaction.

Beverly looked to be deep in thought. "I forgot about that. I had a hair appointment."

"So if I call your stylist she'll confirm your appointment? Where do you go?" Charlene removed her notepad and pen.

Beverly crossed her arms and pursed her lips. "Fine, I didn't have a hair appointment." Her skin paled noticeably. She looked like she might be sick.

Charlene didn't act surprised because she wasn't.

"I lied to protect a friend."

"What friend?"

She hesitated slightly. "I had an affair," she said with real regret. "He's married and I didn't want to drag his family into this. They don't deserve that."

Now everything was beginning to fall into place. "Did your husband know this?"

She hesitated, shaking her head. "Not at first. He…"

There was a knock on the door.

"That's probably my partner." Charlene left Beverly and rushed to the front door, seeing Larry on the other side.

"We've got a live one," she said as she hurried back to Beverly.

Larry chose the love seat, his bulk sinking in with a soft moan from the leather. He squirmed and opened his pad.

He didn't wait for pleasantries. "Mrs. Anderson, your neighbors claim they heard shouting and loud noises comin' from your house the night before your husband's murder."

Charlene interrupted. "Last time we spoke, you told us that you and Ken were in love. Why did you lie to us?"

Beverly blew air from her cheeks. "Come on, Detective, I'm not an idiot. I know how that would've looked."

"What about your lover?" Charlene asked.

Larry said, "Lover? What did I miss?"

Charlene said nothing and neither did Beverly.

She looked beaten. Beverly closed her eyes and sighed. "Ken caught us in the bedroom. I guess in reality I wanted him to. I wanted him to feel what it was like. They started yelling, sizing each other up."

"What happened?"

Ten minutes later, as they were walking to the car, Larry said, "I guess we know where Anderson got the bruises. Do you think Beverly offed her husband? Or had this Marcus do it?"

"I don't know," Charlene answered, "but I wouldn't blame her if she did."

Chapter 21

When they got back to the department, Charlene quickly glanced at her watch—11 AM. She pulled the car to the curb and kept it idling. Larry stepped out and looked back. "You comin'?"

"Give me an hour, Larry."

Through light, late-morning traffic Charlene made it to 1831 West Washington Boulevard by eleven forty. She'd been avoiding the place, but not for the same reasons most cops avoided cemeteries. Charlene hadn't been back since the day they'd put her father in the ground.

She parked outside the gates behind the familiar black Focus. She followed the brick pathway, through the cast iron gate opening and past the sign welcoming people to the Angelus-Rosedale Cemetery.

The sign in front informed Charlene that the cemetery was founded in 1884, was the first cemetery opened to all races and creeds, and there was a list of notables who were buried on the site, including those in politics, the military and entertainment.

She followed the paved walkway towards her father's plot near the back of the sixty-five acre expanse, passing half a dozen pyramid crypts. Her mother was already there, kneeling in front of the monument, pulling weeds and tending to the flowers. Charlene stopped and watched her. She could hear her mother's quiet sniffles.

"Hi, Mom," Charlene whispered, not wanting to startle her.

Her mother turned and smiled. "Hi, honey."

The smile looked tired and forced. Charlene noted how she'd aged in the last month. Her hair showed signs of gray, the crow's feet around her eyes were prominent, and her heavily lined forehead showed wrinkles of worry and distress.

Did I cause this?

Charlene approached the tombstone. She stood beside her mother, both women admiring the monument.

"He really did love you, Charlene. He was so proud the day you were sworn in as an officer. I'd never seen him happier."

Charlene's eyes moistened, and she blinked hard. She felt her mother's arm wrap around her, and it didn't feel awkward.

"He had a funny way of showing it," Charlene said.

Her mother threw her other arm around Charlene, pulling her tight. Charlene could feel her mother's heartbeat against her own.

"That was your father. He had trouble showing his affection. But you were his girl." She hesitated, waiting for Charlene, and then continued. "Remember when he was studying for lieutenant and you spilled coffee all over the manuals?" Brenda smiled with both her mouth and her eyes. "Anyone else and he would have lost it. But not with his little Charlie."

Charlene pulled away, wiping her eyes with the sleeve of her shirt. She remembered.

"I stopped off and got this," Charlene said, handing her mother a potted plant she knew nothing about. "The florist said they're called Fairy Roses, and the sun will actually fade the flowers to bluish white."

"They're beautiful, Charlene." Her mother accepted the flowers and immediately made a place for them at the head of the monument.

Charlene watched her mother work—determined, unfazed, with only love. She wished again she could make up the years she'd missed, but knew that she could only start over.

Still on her knees, her mother turned and looked at Charlene. Charlene could see a smudge of dirt on her mother's forehead from where she'd rubbed her sweaty brow with a gloved hand.

"How have you been, Charlene? Really."

"I've been good."

Charlene wasn't sure if her mother believed her, but she didn't respond. Her eyes wandered to the holstered Glock on Charlene's hip and she shook her head.

"I could never get used to those things," she mumbled, going back to the gardening.

Charlene could hear the anxiety in her mother's voice.

Charlene knew that her job was slowly killing the woman who'd already lost a husband to police work.

She could lie. Tell her mother she didn't like it, was thinking of giving up being a cop and switching careers. But her mother would never believe her. She had always known Charlene was too much like her father. Stubborn to the core and born to be a cop.

Charlene didn't say any of those things. She just stood there, speechless.

Her mother got up and inspected her handy work. Then she looked at Charlene and smiled with damp eyes. She put her hand on Charlene's cheek then gently squeezed her chin, tracing the deep scar-line. "That scar makes me think of your father. I'm glad you came, Charlene."

"Me too, Mom," Charlene replied.

"Why don't we have dinner soon," her mother suggested.

"I'd like that, Mom."

She kissed her cheek, and Charlene watched her mother walk away. Her pace had slowed, her movements heavy.

Charlene placed a finger on her chin, rubbing the tiny 'V' shaped scar, a memory of her childhood.

Six years old. A game of cops and robbers. She'd been so excited to find her father hiding under the back porch that she'd tumbled down the wooden staircase and split her chin open. Although there was plenty of blood, Charlene hadn't cried. Instead, she'd slapped the handcuffs on her dad's wrists. The memory seemed like yesterday. Her mother, hysterical, had condemned the game.

Charlene smiled to herself.

Her father's sunset black granite stone showed a cross and two roses engraved on the left side, and the black and white etching took up the rest.

Martin Scott Taylor
1941-2012
Husband, Father, Cop

Charlene stood alone staring at her father's engraved stone. She'd seen people in movies talking to headstones, as if the deceased could hear their words. But Charlene never believed that. Besides, what would she say? She knew that nothing she *could* say now would ever make things right. She was too late for reconciliation. She would never have that chance now.

Without a word, Charlene turned and walked away.

She'd passed Larry on the way in. He was having a smoke outside with half a dozen other cops huddled around a sand jar.

At her desk, Charlene punched Marcus Lopez's name into the NCIC database, and did a full background sweep, including arrest and conviction records.

While she waited, Officers Brady, Berry and Clayton had written statements in hand and were ready to give their oral accounts.

They started when Larry got in.

Darren went first. "So far I've found nothing from the black book. All the women are accounted for, but nobody admitted to being raped."

"Most women won't come forward," said Charlene.

"I also followed that lead you gave me and spoke with Sandra Philips' shooting instructor. He said that Philips was at the top of her class after only three months of instruction. She was better than men who'd spent a lifetime at lessons. He confirmed that she owns a gun."

Larry sat up and turned to Officer Berry. "Find that gun and check with Ballistics. You might need to…"

"Already been done," Darren cut him off. He smiled at Charlene. "It's a .32, perfect weapon for a woman—small enough to fit in a purse, but with enough pop. We took it to the shooting gallery where it was fired and tested the bullets to the ones pulled from Anderson. No match. We also entered the gun and bullets into the database but found no match to any previous crimes. We gave Philips a small fine, registered it, and gave it back."

Charlene was impressed at how thorough and disciplined Darren's procedure had been. She thought about Sandra, the gun, and the perfectly placed bullet holes in Anderson's chest. She could tell that Larry was thinking the same thing. Knowing that Sandra could shoot with such pinpoint accuracy made her worth looking into further. Anyone could acquire a gun on the streets.

"Good work, Darren. Stay on the names in the book and let me know if anything else comes up."

Larry nodded to Berry and Clayton, who just shook their heads.

"Nothing in Anderson's home. No pertinent papers, and the neighbors said they rarely had visitors, no one suspicious. We went through phone records but nothing jumped out."

Larry looked at Charlene. "You have anything for them?"

Charlene shook her head. "Let me make a phone call first."

"Go back to your desks and we'll get back to you," Larry said.

As she was dialing the number, Clayton lingered around the desk. She hung up the phone.

"What is it, Officer?" Larry asked.

"Detective, I hate to bring this up, but this is our fourth day. We've been treading water for three days now. We don't seem to have any more leads."

Charlene knew where he was going. They'd spent more time and resources on this murder than most. Were they starting to feel resentment for being given so much time for this one case because some rich kid had gotten popped, when they have dozens of other cases that deserved time and attention?

Larry grimaced. "We stay on it as long as the captain says. Something will come up."

Clayton nodded and retreated to his desk.

Charlene opened Sandra's rape file and saw Detective Adrienne Jackson's signature at the bottom.

Charlene knew very little about Jackson, only that she was relatively new to the Rape Special Sections Unit. She'd seen her around the department and could picture her—stocky, about five three, one hundred thirty-five pounds, never wore makeup, revealing scarred cheeks from adolescent acne. Her fiery red hair was always tied back and her probing green eyes were constantly on edge.

She'd heard rumors that Jackson was a genuine patrol officer, sometimes too intense for the line of work.

Charlene picked up her desk phone and was transferred to the RSS Department but a man answered Detective Jackson's phone.

"Rape Special Section Unit," he said.

Charlene was caught off guard. "Oh, sorry, I was looking for Detective Jackson."

"Well, this is her desk phone, but Detective Jackson is off today. Can I take a message?"

"Sure. This is Detective Taylor in Robbery-Homicide. I was just looking for information on one of her cases. I would like her to contact me ASAP."

"Well," the man stuttered. "Since it's important, I actually saw Adrienne in the department weight room finishing up a workout. I know for a fact that after each workout she hits the shooting gallery downstairs to fire off a few rounds. You can probably find her there."

"Thanks," Charlene said. "That's what I'll do."

She hung up and got out of her chair. "I'm going to talk with Jackson about the Sandra Philips rape, see if anything stands out."

"Good thinking," Larry replied. "I'm going to look up Marcus Lopez."

She crossed the lobby and banged open the steel door, heading down the stairs to the basement.

Charlene signed in, passed on the gun challenge and grabbed a set of ear protectors. She entered the sound proof galley and stood behind the bulletproof pane glass watching Adrienne Jackson firing off rounds.

It was a small gallery, only three lanes, and Jackson was the only shooter today.

Jackson started with fixed targets, and after dropping a clip on those, set her sights on moving boards. After she had finished off another clip, she turned in time for Charlene to flag her down before starting another round. Jackson motioned for Charlene to come around and join her.

Charlene left the lobby and headed out into the gallery. She removed the head set.

"Detective Jackson?" Charlene asked.

"That's me," Jackson said.

"Detective Taylor, Robbery-Homicide."

Jackson had yet to look at Charlene. She was busy reeling in her used targets.

Charlene couldn't help but notice the impeccable accuracy displayed by Jackson on both idle and moving targets—perfect chest shots in a circular pattern.

Charlene whistled. "Nice shooting."

Jackson smiled. "Lots of practice." She ripped the targets off the wire and finally turned to face Charlene. "What can I do for you, Detective?" Jackson's voice was deep and husky.

"It's about one of your cases, the Sandra Philips' rape. I know you have a lot of cases to deal with, so if you want to go back to your office to get that file, that works for me."

"No need. I was wondering when you'd get around to seeing me. I know you're working the Anderson murder, and Officer Brady had called about Sandra Philips."

"What can you tell me about it?"

The LAPD sex crimes expert didn't hesitate. "Dr. Landry at the Good Samaritan called it in. He told us he had just admitted a rape victim to the ER. Since Philips was spending the night, we showed up first thing in the morning. This usually gives the victim time to remember the events clearly."

Jackson paused, but when Charlene didn't say anything, she continued.

"Nothing we haven't seen before. But we see some ugly shit around here. Much of Sandra's bruised face was covered with gauze and bandages. Her upper body was badly damaged—dressed ribs and deep shoulder cuts."

She seemed to stop to let what she'd said sink in.

Charlene was amazed at Jackson's recollection of the case, since RSSU had so many cases on the go at one time. Charlene thought Jackson was on too much of a roll to say anything to slow her down.

"At first she wouldn't talk to us. They rarely do. Like most victims, Philips was showing a clear sign of what we call disassociation. That's psychological refuge from the memory of a traumatic event. Most victims are too afraid to come forward. But she came around."

"So what was your next move after leaving the hospital?" Charlene asked.

"I looked up Anderson. Handsome, white collar, married, good job at a distinguished school, no prior record. There's no typical profile on a rapist, that's what makes this job so challenging. Rapists are not physically identifiable. They may appear friendly, normal, and non-threatening. Many are young, married, and have children. Rapist types and traits however can be categorized. Over seventy percent of rape victims know their attackers, and over seventy-five percent of the rapes reported involve persons of the same race."

Charlene quickly cut Jackson off before the detective recited every national rape statistic.

"What about Anderson?"

"We called UCLA, but Anderson had called in sick. So Johnson and I drove directly to his house. Anderson's wife didn't know where he was. We never found him until his body was discovered. That's where you come in. Any breaks in the case?"

"Nothing yet," Charlene answered.

"Of course, we continue to follow up with Sandra, as we do all of our victims. Rape has a devastating effect on the mental health of victims. Over thirty-one percent of all rape victims develop rape-related post-traumatic Stress Disorder. More than one in ten…"

"Thank you for your time, Detective Jackson." Charlene turned to walk away but Jackson kept talking.

"You know what surprised me the most, though?"

Charlene stopped and turned back around. "What's that?"

"The person who seemed to be affected the most by the rape, even more than Sandra and her sister, was Philips' roommate, Ashley Stanley. She was irate over the whole situation. We had to calm her down a couple of times."

Charlene processed this news. "Thank you, Detective."

"I mean, I thought we were going to have to put her in restraints. She wanted blood."

Charlene opened the door but stopped to look back at Jackson. "Very interesting. Thanks for your time, Detective. Even on your day off."

Jackson shrugged. "No problem. If there's anything else I can do, let me know."

Charlene got back up to her desk where the CPIC computer had finished printing out Lopez's lengthy sheet. Larry was reading it out.

Lopez was born an American citizen to Latino parents, a street punk with a rap sheet a mile long. Raised by his unmarried mother, spent time in juvenile detention centers, dabbled in shoplifting, loitering, vandalism, assault, and drug trafficking. Like the majority of ill-fated immigrants pouring in from Latin America, he dropped out of school and joined a gang.

Charlene would have liked this guy for Anderson's murder, but Lopez had been clean for twelve years, on paper. It looked like he'd put his adolescent years behind him. He had a steady job and was married with twin girls. Why risk that?

Lopez was twenty-six-years-old and listed at six three, two hundred pounds. His photo showed rugged good looks, dark skinned complexion, long, untamed black hair, a strong, defined jaw, and dark piercing eyes. His white teeth dazzled against his dark complexion.

Larry jotted down a contact address and waved over Berry and Clayton. "Check this guy out. He had an altercation with Anderson the night before the murder. If your cop alarms go off and you think we need to investigate this guy further, I'll work on the warrant."

Charlene scribbled an address of her own from the Lopez file and grabbed her jacket.

"Let's go, Larry?"

They found themselves in the part of the city where East LA rookie cops walk the beat. It was a cruel initiation.

Charlene checked the address and pulled the cruiser to the curb, parking in front of an old, sign-less white-brick building. Weeds sprang from the cracked pavement and broken liquor bottles littered the sidewalk.

"What is this place, Taylor?" Larry grunted as he got out of the car.

"This is where Lopez hung out as a kid."

"Looks like a dump."

The Lincoln Boys Youth Center was located in Lincoln Heights, east of downtown Los Angeles, situated between a vacated drug store and closed flower shop. Adjacent to the building, two African-American boys, in baggy jeans and tank tops, played basketball on a court built of cracked pavement and chain-hooped nets.

The detectives let themselves into the quiet, one room office. Phones rang, papers were scattered about, and the office looked like controlled chaos as three employees, one male and two female, ran the operation. A lone chair next to the door was taken by a teenage Hispanic girl with too much makeup, smoking a cigarette.

Charlene saw the lone male employee seated at his desk reading the *LA Times*, and thought it must be her man. He had narrow, hunched shoulders, a trimmed beard, and his black hair showed comb marks. His hazel eyes were hidden behind a pair of reading glasses. He wore a white ACDC T-shirt and jeans. She approached and said, "Russell Evans?"

"Yes?" the man replied, eyeing the detectives.

Charlene took out her badge. "LAPD, I'm Detective Taylor, this is my partner, Detective Baker."

The man didn't flinch, accustomed to frequent police visits. "Please, come to my office, Detectives." The man guided Larry and Charlene to a partitioned-off desk in the corner of the room.

"So this is what they mean by open-concept," Larry mumbled.

Evans ignored him. "What can I do for you today?"

Charlene asked. "You were Marcus Lopez's counselor?"

The man's facial expression registered surprise. "Wow, that's a very long time ago."

"So you were?"

A window air conditioner hummed behind him. "Yes," he nodded. "I was his street counselor for three years."

"Can you tell us a bit about him?"

He didn't need to check any files. "Like most Latino kids, Marcus was a good seed but got in with the wrong crowd. Dropped out of school and joined a gang at the age of ten, committed his first crime at eleven, smoked, did drugs, and drank heavily as an adolescent. I did my best to turn him around."

The counselor spoke with a sense of pride. Charlene noticed a colored picture tacked to the partition, Evans with a group of Latino kids.

"Did it work?"

"Marcus was one of our success stories. Once my kids leave me, I keep track with the police. What's this about, Detective? Has Marcus done something?"

"We're investigating an altercation Marcus had with a guy who's now dead," Larry said.

"Can I show you something, Detectives?" Evans asked.

When they both nodded, Evans grabbed a set of keys from his desk and led them out of the office.

"I'll drive," he said.

Larry looked at the Crown Vic parked against the curb, then at the Pinto parked in front of it. He gave Charlene an 'are-you-out-of-your-fucking-mind' look. Charlene couldn't hide her smile as Larry slid his bulk into the backseat of the compact, two-door Ford Pinto.

They drove three blocks, passing Lincoln Park before turning down a menacing, slummy, one-way street. Trash cans were toppled over, small houses, meters apart, were in ruins and buildings had been vacated. Gangs of kids, bandanas on their heads, stood on the corner sidewalk, smoking cigarettes and sipping from bagged bottles. There was a homemade street sign made from a cardboard box that read 'No Cops.'

Evans stopped at a stop sign. Charlene was grateful that they hadn't brought the cruiser.

"This is where Marcus was born and raised. As you can see, there wasn't much chance for a young boy. He turned to the gang for protection. Most of these kids will never make it past fifteen. It's my job to make sure they have an opportunity. But there's only so much three people can do."

Evans waved at the gang of kids, and a few waved back.

When he took off he said, "These are the odds Marcus beat. He wasn't a good kid, he got into a lot of trouble, but he has conquered his past. He has a good job, a loving wife, and two beautiful daughters. Why would he risk that?"

"People do stupid things all the time," Larry said. "Or I wouldn't have a job."

Evans didn't reply. They circled the block, back to the Youth Center.

"Is there anything more I can do for you, Detectives?"

Chapter 22

On their way back to the detective bureau, Larry said, "What about Jessica Philips? Have we found anything on her?"

Charlene shook her head. "Still nothing. But Minor is putting pressure on us to."

"Okay, we have a dead body in her apartment, no weapon and no fingerprints except for hers and her roommates."

"Larry, you can't timeframe a fingerprint. The girls live there."

He continued by ignoring Charlene's remark. "No witnesses saw her leave the house and she has no alibi. Nobody saw anyone else enter or leave the house. As for motive, she was Anderson's lover...the man who raped her sister. Phone records indicate that Anderson had called the house only minutes before his murder. Philips knew he was coming."

"I asked her about that. Anderson was on his cell phone, and Jessica said that all she could hear was loud music, static and slurring. We know that Anderson was at the bar and was heavily intoxicated. Philips said she left right after the call. We know the call only lasted seconds. If you want to talk motive, what about Beverly Minor, who was facing a lengthy and expensive divorce. Or Sandra Philips, the rape victim. Carl Minor, Marcus Lopez, Alberto Bianchi, Eric and Margaret Connors...we can make a goddamn motive case for them all! Just as concrete as Jessica Philips'."

"How did that interview go?" Larry asked.

Charlene filled him in about Eric and Margaret Connors.

Larry unbuckled his seatbelt and let out his breath. "Jesus. There's no end in sight."

Berry and Clayton were sitting on the edge of Larry's desk when they got back.

"We found Lopez down on Fifth, where he's working construction. His boss was pissed when we pulled him, but Lopez didn't seem surprised. He has a nasty shiner and his knuckles are bruised and scratched. He tried to come up with some bogus story about how he got them, but when we told him we knew about Anderson, he confessed."

Charlene's eyes grew large as she bit her lip and held her breath.

Berry cut in. "To the fight and the affair."

Charlene exhaled.

"Lopez claims he was with Beverly Anderson the night of the murder. No witnesses. I got the opinion his story had been rehearsed. Cop alarm."

Larry looked at Charlene. "Beverly might have tipped him off that we were looking for him."

Charlene nodded.

Berry continued. "I also sensed tension in his voice. Of course, this is all just speculation. But as a long time cop, I like to think my instincts are pretty accurate."

"What about a murder weapon?"

"He said he doesn't own a gun. Here's the report. If you get a warrant, we can search his house and car."

Berry handed the report to Larry, who gave it to Charlene.

"What should we do?" Clayton asked.

Charlene looked at Larry, who checked his watch. He said, "Berry, go home and spend some time with your wife and daughter. Clayton, go home and do…whatever it is you do."

The officers nodded and left.

"Here are the search warrant applications. Do you know how to fill them out?" Larry asked Charlene as he slid the papers onto her desk.

With the fight and admitted affair, they had enough on Lopez to garner a warrant, but Charlene knew the process could take days.

"I think so," she replied, but knew that her voice lacked confidence.

Larry slid on a pair of bifocals and wheeled his chair next to Charlene's. He went over the application with her, showing her where and what to insert and initial.

When the forms were completed, she left them on Captain Dunbar's desk.

"I'm going to call it a night, Kid. Meet you back here in the morning? Don't be gallivanting tonight." He smiled.

"Goodnight, Larry." Charlene smiled back.

She returned to her desk and called Darren, surprised he was still at the bureau after hours, and told him that, when Dunbar was finished signing off on the documents, to find a judge. He complained about finding a judge this late in the evening, but she hung up.

Charlene checked the database for the Margaret Connors rape file, but no charges were laid so a file wasn't opened. There was no proof of the incident.

"Dead and buried." Just as the dean had admitted.

The only people who truly knew what happened were Margaret Connors and Ken Anderson. With no file, there was no way for Charlene to know which officers had even been assigned to the case.

Another dead end.

When she stepped inside her apartment, something didn't feel right. Her Taylor-Cop alarm was ringing.

Charlene checked the security alarm, but it was still active. She disarmed it, slipped out her weapon and checked each room carefully. Nothing. She examined the windows and locks for any sign of forced entry. Nothing.

She picked up the phone—no messages—and hit number one on her speed-dial. She ordered a dinner-for-one, gave her name, phone number and address, and hung up.

She hadn't heard from Andy since he'd stormed out, which seemed to be a common thread in their relationship. It wasn't healthy and Charlene wasn't sure why he kept coming back. What was she so afraid of? Andy was a good guy and loved her. What more did she want or need?

It was a travel day for the Dodgers, so Charlene, knowing she had time before her food arrived, changed into her favorite sweats, attached her IPod to her waistband, pulled the headphones over her ears and took to the streets.

Since starting the Professor Case, as it was being called around the office, Charlene had been ignoring her runs. It felt good as she increased her pace.

As she ran, she still had that inkling that someone was watching her. She continued to glance around, sometimes perceptibly, but sometimes not. That sense of being followed dogged her right back to the apartment.

She stretched in the parking lot to cool down, continuously scanning the surroundings. She didn't notice any suspicious vehicles.

When she rounded the corner to head upstairs, Charlene saw what looked like the same biker from the other night. He was parked in the same spot, only this time his helmet was still on and his visor flipped down. His head was turned towards her and his stare gave her a shiver. He sat there staring at her and when she made a move towards him, he gave a quick salute and pulled away from the curb. If that guy was stalking her, he didn't conceal it very well.

An Asian boy in his teens was standing outside her door when she reached the top of the stairs. She grabbed the bag from his hand, tipped him generously and then let herself in.

She stripped, hopped in the shower, and slipped into a pair of pajama shorts and Andy's extra-large NYU T-shirt.

Charlene grabbed a beer from the fridge and spread out the Anderson case file. She studied everything again, wanting to get a clear picture in her mind before turning in for the night.

Eight suspects with eight motives. Except for Jessica Philips, they all had alibis, albeit loose ones, but Charlene knew that sometimes only the guilty could produce the perfect alibi.

"Okay, follow evidence and eliminate suspects," she told herself.

For the next forty minutes, Charlene twirled noodles with chopsticks and information with her brain.

Ashley Stanley and Sarah Crawford were the missing links. The cops knew everything on everyone else, but these women were ghosts.

The google searches were useless. It was just too broad a database and the names too common. But someone, somewhere, knew.

First, she placed a call to the dean at UCLA to request all of the information on Ashley Stanley be sent to the precinct. Next, she called the dean at USC and requested that everything they had on Sarah Crawford also be sent to the precinct.

Charlene's last thread of hope lay in something in the two records overlapping.

Before falling asleep, the detective programmed herself to dream about the case.

Chapter 23

Early Wednesday morning, Charlene grabbed the case files, locked up and took the building elevator to the basement parking lot.

As she unlocked the car door and got in, Charlene immediately spotted it. Her guts tightened.

A gold chain hung from the rearview mirror, spinning in midair.

She looked around the dark vacant subbasement.

She eyed the chain. She knew that she shouldn't touch it, that it was probably some sort of evidence that needed to be examined proficiently. But what if they didn't have time?

She grabbed a Kleenex from the console, reopened the door, allowing the interior light to come on, and gently removed the chain with the Kleenex. Holding it close to the light, Charlene noticed a small locket at the end of the chain. The initials engraved on the back were T.L.S.

She pried the locket open and was met by a brown-haired woman with a dimply-faced smile. Although the picture was miniscule, Charlene didn't think she recognized the woman.

It had to be another message from the Celebrity Slayer. But how had he gotten into the secured underground parking?

After further inspection, Charlene closed the locket and slipped it into her jacket. She needed to get to the station, have the photograph blown up and try to positively ID the woman.

The Slayer wanted to be in the spotlight, needed to be heard. And he was using her to achieve his goals. Charlene was starting to feel like a pawn in the Celebrity Slayer's chess game.

When Charlene stormed into the precinct, she saw the Anderson task force unenthusiastically assembled at her desk. She brushed past them, making her way towards the captain's office.

"What's up," Larry asked.

"Walk with me." She entered without knocking and threw the locket on the desk.

The captain dropped the morning newspaper and looked down at the locket. "What's this?" he said, picking it up and examining it.

"I found that in my car this morning."

Charlene told her captain what she thought.

He seemed to take her more seriously now. "So you think this is another vic.?" He was already getting out of his seat.

"Probably."

"Then why hasn't it been bagged and tagged?"

"Come on, Cap." Charlene was growing exasperated with the lack of cooperation she was receiving. "We both know the killer isn't stupid enough to leave any trace evidence."

Charlene could tell the captain was respectfully taking in what she said, which made her feel a little better.

"Give it to tech. Have them blow it up and send out a bulletin to the local news stations. Have them run the picture and tell them anyone with information on this woman is to contact the police immediately. I think that's the fastest way to find out who T.L.S. is."

"You think this T.L.S. is still alive?"

"Doubtful."

"I'll get on it ASAP. How's the Anderson case?"

"We're working on it."

"Well let's work a little faster and get this thing nailed shut."

"Yes, Sir."

"Captain," Larry said. "This is starting to get serious. I think we should tighten security at her place."

Charlene first thought he was joking until the captain said, "I think you're right. Let me make a couple of calls."

They left the office. Charlene still hadn't had her morning coffee and was feeling worn-out, but she wasn't sure whether it was from the Celebrity Slayer or the Anderson case.

She studied her team.

Darren was the only one who looked upbeat. The young officer was always chipper, on alert and ready for action, no matter the circumstances or time of day.

Clayton, as usual, looked more like a stockbroker than a policeman. Neat, thin, always well maintained, his uniform freshly pressed, without a brown gelled hair out of place.

Berry looked the worst. With a two-day beard and bloodshot eyes, Charlene realized this time-consuming case was keeping him away from his family, and with a newborn at home, his nights were probably sleepless. He never complained. Charlene was sure she spotted baby drool on the shoulder of his uniform.

"Here, guys." Larry handed the papers he was holding to Officer Clayton. "This warrant was signed last night." He turned to Darren. "Thanks, Brady."

Darren smiled, looked at Charlene and blushed.

Larry turned back to the senior officers. "Since it's only good for twenty-four hours, you better hit Lopez immediately. Brady, go back to your desk and I'll let you know when I have something for you."

Charlene collapsed in her chair, at a stalemate—five days on the case with nothing to show except suspects with motive and lack of evidence to support theories.

"I got an interesting phone call last night," Larry said. "Ashley Stanley's alibi doesn't hold up."

"Go on." He now had her full attention.

"Her softball game had ended early because the pitcher twisted an ankle. Since there was no backup, they called the game. The coach remembered that last night and called me, thought it might help. According to the time line, that'd give her opportunity."

Another piece of circumstantial evidence. They still couldn't place Stanley at the scene at the time of the murder. In fact, there was still no concrete evidence placing any of the suspects at the scene of the crime during the time of the murder.

"Have you ever heard of a woman named Sarah Crawford?"

Larry shook his head.

"That reminds me. Did you check messages this morning?"

"Didn't get a chance yet," Larry said.

She got up and went to the front desk. The clerk came out of the back room. "Mornin', Detectives."

"Good morning, Henry," Charlene said. "Anything for me?"

The man turned and checked her in-box and pulled out a sheaf of papers. "Fax from UCLA." He handed the papers to her. "I also transferred a call from USC to your desk this morning. You going back to school, Detective?"

Charlene smiled. "Hardly."

She read the papers as she walked back to her desk, where Larry was still waiting.

"What is it?" Larry asked.

"I called the schools last night to fax everything they had on Ashley Stanley and Sarah Crawford."

Larry shifted his eyes, as if in thought. "I know that one of those girls is the roommate. Who's the other?"

"Not sure yet."

"What's there about Stanley?"

"Nothing we don't already know. Let me check my voice mail."

She sat at her desk and picked up the phone. She went through the process of retrieving her messages and listened as a woman's business-like voice cleared her throat and said, "Good morning, Detective Taylor. This is Danielle Patterson from Human Resources at USC. Dean Brown forwarded your message to me and I've looked up your request. There is no student in our records by the name of Sarah Crawford. I've gone back as far as five years and there is no indication that a student by that name has ever been a student at USC. If you have any further requests, please don't hesitate to call."

Charlene wrote down the contact number left by the HR representative and deleted the message. This case—and this woman— was getting stranger by the minute.

"What did the message say?" Larry asked.

Charlene shook her head, as if to shush him. She logged onto the internet and went to the USC website to check some stats.

She looked at Larry. "What are the odds that professors at USC would remember one young woman out of forty thousand students?"

Larry laughed out loud. "Depends on the girl."

"That's what I thought," Charlene said. "And I doubt Sarah Crawford wanted to be noticed." She slumped in her seat.

"Are you going to tell me who Sarah Crawford is?" Larry asked again.

Charlene forgot she'd never mentioned that aspect of her interview at the Connors' house. She removed the picture from her desk and handed it to him. "I saw this picture at Margaret Connors' place. The woman's name is Sarah Crawford."

Charlene told Larry about the rape connection with Anderson. Once he processed this new information, he checked the picture.

"Is that Stanley?"

Charlene smiled. "That's what I think. But I can't seem to verify it."

She picked up the phone and dialed Eric Connors' phone number. It was answered after six rings.

Charlene first identified herself. "Is this a bad time?"

"Not at all, Detective."

"Is there any chance I could speak with Margaret? It's about her former roommate."

Charlene could hear Eric Connors voice talking to Margaret in the background, and there was a thump as he set down the phone. She closed her eyes and said a silent prayer that Margaret might have some tiny piece of information that would help them track down Sarah Crawford.

Margaret came on the line. "Hello."

"Hello, Margaret. How are you?"

"Fine." The voice hadn't changed. Margaret Connors was still unsure of herself.

"Margaret, I was wondering if you would know where I could find Sarah Crawford."

Margaret hesitated. "Is Sarah in trouble?"

"Not at all. We would just like to speak with her."

"I don't really know, Detective. Sarah never talked about herself or her family. We were only roommates for a few months."

Charlene gritted her teeth. "Do you remember anything about her? Anything she said or owned that might tell us something?"

"Actually, she did give me a sweatshirt. Well, I don't know if she gave it to me, but she disappeared so quickly I didn't have time to give it back."

Charlene rolled her eyes and blew air from her cheeks. *Great, a sweatshirt.*

"It was the one I had on the day you visited."

Charlene closed her eyes and pictured the interview. Seeing Margaret on the couch huddled closely to her father, the gold and purple sweatshirt dangling down to her knees. There was something written on the front. What was it?

Charlene's head snapped up in recognition.

She sat up. "The Pig Game?" Charlene asked.

"Yes, that's right, but…"

"Gotta go, Margaret. Thank you."

"But…"

Charlene hung up and said, "Pig Game"

"What's that?" Larry asked.

Charlene looked at him, unaware that she has spoken out loud. "The Pig Game"

"You're losing it."

She typed into the google search bar. "The Pig Game is the oldest high school rivalry west of the Mississippi."

The very first link to come up was 'Fresno High School.'

"I think I know where Crawford went to high school."

She clicked on the link and found the high school phone number. She placed the call, made her request, and was transferred to Human Resources.

The man who answered in the main office sounded like one of the high school students. Charlene told him what she was looking for and could hear his fingers rapidly tapping keys.

"Do you have a SSN, Detective?" he asked.

"No."

"It would be quicker and easier if you…"

"I don't have one."

He didn't reply, but she could hear his fingers moving even more quickly over the keyboard, until he finally let out a soft sigh.

"What's wrong?" she asked.

"No one by that name has ever been enrolled in this school. Like I said, if you have a Social Security Number…"

"I don't."

Charlene slammed her open hand down hard on the desk. "Let me speak to your oldest teacher."

"Pardon?"

"The teacher on the top of the seniority list, the one who's been there the longest, let me speak to him or her."

"I'm sorry, but Mrs. Danton is in class."

"Great, here's my number. Have her call me on her break."

Less than thirty minutes later, her desk phone rang.

"Detective Taylor."

"This is Agatha Danton, head of the English department at Fresno High School. I was told to give you a call."

"Yes, Mrs. Danton, thanks for returning my call."

"Certainly."

Although Charlene had never met or seen the English teacher, from her voice, Charlene pictured a tall, thin, wrinkled woman, with her grey hair in a bun and her nose in the air.

"I'd like to ask you about a former student. Sarah Crawford."

Danton was quiet and Charlene could perceive uncertainty. The teacher didn't speak for a long while. Did Danton even remember Crawford? What were the odds that she would remember Crawford from years ago in a school enrollment of twenty-four-hundred students?

"What would you like to know?"

"So you remember Sarah?"

"Yes."

"We're trying to track her down."

"Has she down something wrong?"

"We would just like to ask her some questions."

"Well, she sure wouldn't return to these parts."

The phrase was said with such cold callousness that Charlene felt a chill prickle her skin.

"Why is that?"

"That girl has been through too much, especially losing her family the way she did."

Charlene's eyebrows arched. "Go on."

"Sarah had been very close with her father, and after his death I never thought she'd recover. But shortly after, her mother remarried a very nice local businessman and I thought she'd turn it around. But then, the worst happened. Her mother and stepfather were killed in a fire. Sarah was lucky to get out alive, but she was the only one to survive, so some say she was unlucky."

"What happened to Sarah?"

"I don't know. She just left town after that. Too many bad memories I'm sure."

"I'm sure," Charlene repeated, but wasn't convinced. "What kind of student was Sarah?"

"Quiet, reserved, but brilliant when she needed to be. She could be manipulative to get what she wanted, and she had the looks and brains to pull it off. I always thought there was something off about her, but she achieved above average grades and there were no in-school issues."

Charlene wondered about out-of-school issues. "Would you have any idea where she would have gone?"

"Like I said, Detective, she wouldn't have returned. I have no idea about any other family members or where she would have gone."

"Thank you, Mrs. Danton."

"Certainly."

Charlene hung up and logged onto the Internet. "What's the name of the local newspaper in Fresno?" she asked Larry.

"*The Fresno Bee.*"

Charlene found the main page of the website. She clicked on the 'Archives' icon and scrolled as far back as five years. Then she found it.

The tragic story behind the death of Laura and Luther Vincent, Sarah Crawford's mother and stepfather, had made front page news. The computer screen showed a picture of the Vincent house ablaze, with a young woman standing in front. Sarah's name had been withheld from the papers to protect her, so that's why the story never came up in a google search.

Charlene scrolled down and read out loud.

"Local resident watches her home burn to the ground while countless firefighters attempt to rescue her parents trapped in the burning building."

Charlene punched a button, zooming in and focusing on the woman in the photograph. She wasn't identical to the other. The eyes, hair color and style were different, but those were easy to change. But there was no mistake. The girl in the photograph was definitely Ashley Stanley.

"What do you think?" Larry asked, he had moved behind Charlene and was looking over her shoulder.

"I think it's her."

"Me too."

Charlene read the article in whole. Sarah was the sole survivor, the inferno starting from electrical malfunctions in the basement. The young woman stated she smelled smoke while sleeping and panicked. She yelled for her parents then, assuming they were out of the house, escaped the flames. The girl was in shock when officials found her.

The bodies were pulled from the debris the next morning. Dental records were used to make a positive identification. The fire was determined accidental, faulty wiring in the basement.

The article took up two full pages. Laura Vincent was a nurse's aide and Luther Vincent, a well-known businessman. But because Laura had inherited from her first husband's death, both of them had been worth a lot of money.

Charlene had a gut feeling.

She googled the Fresno Police Department and found the phone number. She called and made her request, leaving her pager number for a return call.

She wasn't sure what they'd dig up. If they reported back with what Charlene suspected, then she would have a solid lead to follow.

"So you think Crawford is in Anderson's book?" Larry asked.

"You read my mind."

They both sprinted across the room and found Darren reading *People* magazine. "I need that black book," Charlene said.

"Sorry, Chip, it's in the car. I'll go get it."

The captain had set up a work table in the Detective Bureau for the team, so they could be readily available when Larry and Charlene needed them, and that's where Darren was set up. It showed how important this case was.

Charlene sat and waited. Papers, files, and folders were piled neatly on his table. Darren's attention to detail and his fine-honed sense of organization was impressive. There were mounds of text books, reference books, and magazines on police procedures and crime scene steps. It looked as if Darren was studying to be a detective.

A copy of *Entertainment Weekly* and a James Patterson paperback novel topped the pile.

"Think he's gay?" Larry asked.

"Larry!" Charlene said, giving him her best scolding look.

"Look at how organized, clean, and thin he is."

"Got it, Chip," Darren said, holding the book in the air while running in.

"Great. Is there a Sarah Crawford in there?"

Charlene waited as Darren looked up the name. "Let's see, Crawford, C... Yep! Got it, Sarah Crawford, right here under 'C'." He looked up at Charlene, regret in his eyes. "Sorry, Chip. That was one I couldn't track down. Damn it!"

"It's okay, Darren." Charlene didn't chastise him. It looked as if he was hard enough on himself. Instead, she grabbed the book. There was nothing written beside the name, no number or address. If Sarah Crawford was indeed Ashley Stanley, then she had been another notch on Anderson's bedpost. In her interview, Stanley had denied knowing Anderson outside of UCLA.

"What's this about?"

"Not sure yet."

She looked at Larry while they returned to their desks. "You were right."

"This guy really got around."

Charlene's pager went off. She glanced at the number and saw a Fresno area code. She picked up her desk phone and dialed.

"Fresno Police Department." She recognized the voice of the man she'd spoken to earlier.

"This is Detective Taylor returning your page."

"Yes, Detective, I found what you requested. If you give me a fax number, I'll send it to you immediately." The man sounded cheery, pleased he could assist. "And if you give me an email address, I can also send you the taped news footage. We have it saved in the archives."

She gave him the fax number and email address, and thanked him. She sat back down at her computer and read from the website, refining her search on Sarah Crawford.

It was almost an hour before Charlene heard the beep of the department fax machine.

"Fax for you, Taylor," someone hollered from across the room.

"I'll grab it," said Larry.

He crossed the room and corralled the pages one by one as they slid out. She watched him as he read the papers on his way back to the desk.

"Anything?" she asked.

"Laura Vincent had pressed sexual assault charges against her second husband three times. Each time the cops arrived, she changed her mind, dropping the charges after she and her husband sobered up."

"The third time the nine-one-one call was made by the daughter. When police arrived, she was in hysterics."

"I'd love to find out if Sarah herself had been abused," said Charlene.

This proved that Sarah Crawford, AKA Ashley Stanley, would have witnessed abuse three times—her own or her mother's, her USC roommate, and her UCLA roommate. Her childhood trauma, and the added insult of her friends having undergone the same treatment, by the same man that she had once dated, or at least slept with, had to add fuel to the growing fire inside her.

Charlene examined the dates of the charges. The third incident occurred only three days before the fire broke out.

When her email in-box beeped, indicating a new message, she scrolled down, finding a subject line, *Fresno Fire*. She clicked on it and opened the message. She opened the attachment, hit the playback button, and waited for the screen to run its course.

A dark haired man, well dressed, with parted hair and too much makeup, stood looking into a camera. A microphone was clipped to the collar of his vest. The caption read, *Tom Steele, Fresno Local News*. Charlene turned up the volume so Larry could hear.

"Late last night, just after midnight, a raging fire started at 264 Sycamore Street, home of Luther and Laura Vincent."

The frame changed, going back one hour earlier, showing the fire. The camera turned to a young woman, standing on the side of the screen, a thin blanket thrown over her shoulders. The anchor man continued.

"This seventeen-year-old, the lone survivor, silently watched as brave firefighters from the Fresno Fire Department attempted to stop the inferno. She stood back and watched as the house she grew up in burned to the ground in a flood of ash.

Forty-four-year-old Laura Vincent and forty-nine-year-old Luther Vincent were trapped inside on the second level, unable to hear their daughter's screams."

The camera zoomed in on Crawford.

"Can you tell us what happened here tonight?"

Sarah Crawford turned to face the camera. She started crying and grew hysterical.

Charlene thought that Crawford turned it on with the nonchalance of an accomplished actress. Of course, it was just Charlene's opinion and there was no way to prove any of it.

Even with the close-up, the screen was still too fuzzy, so making a one hundred percent identification, comparing Sarah Crawford and Ashley Stanley, was impossible. On the screen, Crawford had long dark hair, brown eyes. Stanley has short blonde hair, which could be dyed, and green eyes, which could be contacts. The women were the same age, same height and body type, but so were three-quarters of the women in California.

The coverage changed its focus, and two headshots of the victims came on the screen. The anchorman continued.

"Laura Vincent less than two years ago suffered the death of her first husband. Lawrence Crawford died suspiciously one night outside a local bar. People in Fresno knew him well, the son of millionaire developer Michael Crawford. Laura was remarried less than one year ago to Luther Vincent. Vincent is a well-respected businessman in Fresno and the deaths of these two upstanding citizens will greatly impact the community. This woman," the camera focused on Sarah Crawford, *"is now the last in line to inherit the estate of Michael Crawford."*

The screen blinked back to the original picture of the anchorman standing in front of the remains of the burnt house.

"As you can see behind me, the arson investigator, along with Fresno CSI, continue to sift through ash and debris, but this case has already been deemed unsuspicious. The fire started from faulty wiring in the basement of the house. What lies ahead for this family, only time will tell. This is Tom Steele for Channel Six news."

Charlene closed the icon. Things were starting to heat up. But it still didn't connect the dots for the Anderson murder.

Chapter 24

She had spent all of Wednesday in the office, going through the paperwork that came with an investigation. She didn't want to do that again today.

After a long, sleepless night, Charlene sat down at her desk on Thursday morning and took her first sip of coffee when Larry came rushing over holding a folder.

"A nine-one-one call came in last night we need to hear. The techs are analyzing it now."

They headed to the small, overcrowded audio/visual room hidden in the back corner of the building and entered without knocking.

"Rewind it and play it from the start," Larry ordered.

The techs stopped the tape and did as they were told. Charlene and Larry pulled seats close to the speakers.

"This call came in to nine-one-one last night at 11:38 PM. We traced it to a phone booth on Motor Avenue." The tech pushed play as the room fell silent.

Charlene heard the operator's voice. "Nine-one-one dispatch, what is your emergency?"

Light traffic could be heard in the background and then someone spoke.

"Yeah, I got news about yo' dead white boy."

"Who is this, Sir?"

"Shit…" then it was silent. Loose change fell to the booth floor. "I seen a car."

"You said something about a dead body, Sir?"

"Yeah, shit…I don't know. That teacher. I seen a car near the house. Listen man, I seen it befo'."

"Who is this?"

"Listen, this Nelson Porter. You gotta listen."

From the caller's voice/tone, grammar, vocabulary, and attitude, Charlene pictured an adolescent male, somewhere between the ages of fourteen and eighteen, African American and from the time of the call, the kid was either homeless or a gang member. He sounded scared and gang members don't scare easily.

"Just calm down, Mr. Porter. Where are you now?"

"I don't know, don't you cops got some sorta trace to find me?"

"Just stay where you are, Mr. Porter. I'm sending a black and white immediately."

"I seen dat white bitch. Shit…" Then there was silence, followed by a click of the phone.

The tech walked over and shut off the recording. "That's it. Like I said, we traced the call to a phone booth on Motor Ave. We sent a car but that kid must have taken off. We have an APB out on Porter."

The 'white teacher' had to be Anderson.

Charlene read the report. The police couldn't find Porter, and no one was around to confirm his call. LAPD hadn't had a black and white in the vicinity at the time, and it took officers almost forty minutes to reach the location. When they couldn't find him, the cops looked up Porter and made an appearance at his home on Overland Avenue. Porter wasn't there and his grandmother hadn't seen him all night.

The GRIT—Gang Related Information Tracking—file on Porter was complete. The fifteen year-old African American lived with his grandmother. His mother had died from a drug overdose and his father was serving time at California State Prison for drug trafficking. The oldest of five kids in an extended family, Porter was a trial member with the Bloods, an LA West Side gang. He had spent some time at Central Juvenile Hall, aka Eastlake Juvenile Hall, down on Eastlake Avenue, so there was a picture on file, although it looked a few years old. Charlene knew it was only a matter of time before Porter got into serious trouble or got himself killed.

Charlene had to find that kid.

By 10:45 AM they were on the Santa Monica Freeway. For cops, most call-ins were suspicious and unreliable, but with the Porter house only a couple of blocks from where Anderson was killed, the killer could have parked there and moved on foot.

During the ride, Charlene couldn't get Porter's young, innocent voice out of her head. Whose car did he think he had he seen?

"You heard Porter say something about a white chick, right?" Charlene said.

"Yeah, I heard that part," Larry answered.

Who was the 'white chick'? Had Porter seen Beverly Anderson or Margaret Connors? And there was also Bianchi's unidentified daughter, although at this point, she wasn't a suspect. Charlene had nine suspects for the Anderson murder and five of them were female Caucasian.

They pulled into the short driveway of a shabby, run down bungalow with white siding that had been torn off. The front step was leaning to the left and the paint was peeling. The small front yard was caged in by a poorly painted fence and bicycles, toys, and car parts polluted the lawn. The screen was ripped out of the storm door.

As they approached the front door by a grassy pathway, the detectives heard loud banging inside the house, followed by a woman's yell. Charlene looked at Larry and then knocked on the door.

After a couple of minutes and two more knocks, the storm door was opened by a small black child, wearing nothing but a diaper. The toddler, no more than two years old, stared at Charlene with curious eyes.

"Who dat?" A large, dark skinned woman, with salt and pepper hair rolled into a bun, waddled up behind the infant. She was chain smoking a long, filtered cigarette and eyeballed Charlene. "Can I help you?" she asked in a sarcastic tone.

Charlene flashed her badge. "Detective Taylor, LAPD."

"That suppose to impress me?" the woman asked.

Charlene knew the type, no formal education past fourth grade, but had grown up on the streets and could handle herself.

Grandmother Porter stared at the detectives, hands on hips, waiting for a response. She clearly intimidated any visitor who came to the door. Charlene noticed two children running rampant in the background.

Larry pushed past Charlene. "Detective Baker, can we come in?"

"I s'pose you here for Nelson?"

They followed the woman into what looked like a living room. Toys and dirty diapers cluttered the floor and they were greeted by the stench of urine and cigarette smoke. A long cigarette burned in a Buddha-shaped ashtray on the coffee table.

They didn't sit and weren't offered a seat.

The elderly woman sat down and continued with her hobby of smoking. "Nelson ain't here, ain't seen 'im since yestaday."

The woman fished out a Kleenex from inside her bra and blew her nose loudly.

Charlene looked at Larry, then back at the woman. "Do you know where Nelson is, Mrs. Porter?"

"That's Ms. Porter," she said, giving Larry a subtle wink. She looked back at Charlene. "You deaf, or just don't undastand English? I ain't seen 'im since yestaday." She shook her head. "What dat boy done now?"

"He might have some information for us."

Larry disappeared from the room and moved to the back of the house.

The woman chuckled, it sounded like a hiccup. "He don't know nuthin'."

"Do you have some names of friends he may be with?" Charlene asked.

The woman gazed off into the corner of the room, as if looking for something in midair. Her eyes moistened.

"I do my best to bring 'im up. He a good boy, just mixin' wit bad company, that all, bad company. He come and go as he please. I can't control 'im."

A two-year-old girl with curly brown locks and a dimple-face toddled into the room, and Grandma heaved her up with a single arm, slapping her on her lap. She started bouncing her knee as the child giggled with excitement.

Larry returned from the back and shook his head at Charlene. "Do you have a recent picture of Nelson, Ms. Porter?"

"Child, dat boy neva sit still long enough to get a pickcha." Then she thought about it. "How's bout his school pickcha?"

"That'll do."

The woman gently set the child on the floor and left the room. The child got to her feet, wobbled, and approached Larry, tugging at his pant leg. Larry pulled away. "Beat it, kid."

The woman returned and handed Charlene the photograph. "Here, child, dis from last year."

The detective looked at the picture. "Cute kid."

"Oh, he a handsome devil dat one, but dats just it, he a devil. Look like his papa but act like his mama."

"Can I keep this?"

"Sure, I got anotha."

As they were heading to the car, Larry's cell phone rang.

"Baker," he answered. "Yeah thanks. What's the address?"

He hung up and looked at Charlene. "They found Porter. Palms Junior High School"

"Should we tell the grandmother?"

"No."

Larry got behind the wheel and Charlene plugged the information into the car's mobile computer terminal—MCT—checking the GPS for directions.

"He won't be talking."

Cop cars were parked diagonally outside the football field at Palms Junior High School on Woodbine, cherries flashing, and the first officer at the scene was taping off the area. A cop was stationed at the gate preventing unauthorized vehicles from entering, so Larry showed his ID, signed the log book and followed the trail left by the ambulance and police cars.

They parked and approached the group standing around the body, choosing the most unlikely path the killer would have taken, not wanting to contaminate the crime scene. Charlene saw their contact in black sweats, with an LAPD vest on, kneeling beside Porter. A tech was documenting the scene.

Detective Rodriguez, a thirty-five-year-old Latin detective with short cut, curly dark hair and the beginning of a beard, from the Gang Related Crimes Division of LAPD, saw Charlene and Larry and nodded in their direction. He took off a pair of big sunglasses that were covering squinty eyes. When he stood, he was a full head shorter than Charlene.

"I was told to expect you. Is this your kid?"

Charlene and Larry stepped past Rodriguez.

Charlene nodded. "Yeah, that's Nelson Porter." She looked at Larry. "Someone got to him before us."

"Looks like a gang shooting," Rodriguez said.

The boy was rail thin. He wore a red bandana overtop a shaved head, a short sleeve, black *Rage Against The Machine* T-shirt and ripped jeans. Charlene could see a self-made snake head tattoo, the symbol for the Bloods gang, on his right forearm. The pockets of his jeans were turned out.

"Any thoughts?" Charlene asked.

"We think they came in from behind the bleachers. The fencing has been cut and pulled back, allowing a small hole for trespassers. We'll have to find out from the field crew when that hole was made. No signs of defensive wounds or a struggle. Porter was looking at the shooter, about three feet away. Bang, bang." Rodriguez held out his thumb and index finger, making a gun. "Two shots to the chest. Looks like they robbed him too."

"Murder weapon?"

"Nothing yet."

"Bullet size?" Larry asked.

"Have to wait for Ballistics to confirm, but from the holes in his shirt and chest, we're thinking six mm."

Charlene was circling the body. "You're sure this is gang-related?"

"Looks that way. This is Crypts territory, and they don't take kindly to strangers, especially from a rival gang. But Porter should have known better than to be here, especially alone."

"How do you know he was alone?" Larry asked. "Time of death established?"

"Between one and three this morning. Groundskeeper found him."

"What time was the nine-one-one call?" Larry asked.

"At 11:38 PM," Charlene replied quickly.

Maybe Larry was thinking the same thing. Anderson's killer had time to hear about the nine-one-one call, find Porter, and silence him.

"Who else knew about the nine-one-one?" Charlene asked.

Rodriguez shrugged. "Probably everyone who was at the station last night."

Could be a leak in the department.

She turned to Larry. "What was Porter doing out of his territory, alone? Gangs don't run by themselves, there's always a group of them together. How could a tough fifteen-year-old gangbanger get lured into this field and be such an easy target? He had to have trusted the person."

Larry didn't have an answer.

Rodriguez said, "I'm going to be conducting interviews with some of Porter's gang buddies."

"Keep us informed on that," Larry said.

"Do you want to come along?" Rodriguez asked, but Charlene had already turned and was walking away. Her thoughts were elsewhere.

Larry and Charlene stopped at the edge of the end zone and discussed the case.

"I know we have a lot of suspects in this case, Larry. Carl Minor could have found out about Porter through a leak at the department. He has the money to buy the information. He then could have paid someone to take out the witness. Old, rich men like Minor do not tolerate failure, and Beverly's marriage looked bad for her father."

Larry nodded. "Marcus Lopez has ties with the local gangs, could have received the information from one of his gang buddies and he also has the strength to drag a kid onto a football field and finish the job."

Charlene cut in. "Alberto Bianchi also has many contacts, probably someone on payroll from inside the department. The mob has their own way of finding out things, legal or otherwise, and their own way of solving problems. Putting down a street punk would be like picking apples for them."

Charlene shook her head. "Larry, I know these three guys are suspects, but I don't know."

"What are you thinking?" Larry asked.

"Porter claimed to have seen a woman. Call it feminine intuition or female instinct, but I like a woman for this murder. And not just this one, but Anderson's also. It feels personal, like a crime of passion, two bullets close range. Someone hated Anderson and really wanted him dead. A woman could have lured Porter out here and with Anderson's history with women, his murder just feels like a woman scorned. And we have a long list of those. Anyone can fire a gun."

Larry added, "Whatever Porter saw or knew is now gone forever."

Charlene thought about Larry's statement. A teenage boy with a perpetual boner, hormones kicking in, testosterone pumping, could have easily been lured by the likes of Jessica Philips, Ashley Stanley, Sandra Philips or Margaret Connors, who were all attractive women. Maybe even by an older woman like Beverly Minor, popular these days with young men who saw them as 'cougars.'

Porter, a young street thug, could have been intimidated and followed anybody in a high powered job, such as a cop with a badge. Maybe Carl Minor had someone working for him on the inside.

"Get Brady on our suspects," Larry said.

Charlene opened her cell. "Darren, track down our suspects and find out where they were last night. Check alibis too." She snapped shut the phone.

Charlene and Larry headed back to the precinct where they spent the early part of the afternoon going over interviews, crime scene reports, and possible tips from call-ins. Eyewitness accounts are usually only fifty percent accurate, but this time, they were all dead ends.

They put Barry and Clayton on Marcus Lopez for some counter-surveillance, keeping a loose watch on him. With Porter's death, Charlene and Larry felt that Lopez, an ex-gang member himself, was more dangerous than ever and needed a tail, even though nothing incriminating had been recovered from the search warrants for Lopez's car and home.

With Bianchi being watched by the Feds, and Lopez by the LAPD, those two were in check.

Charlene checked bank statements she had subpoenaed from each suspect. No large sums had been withdrawn or deposited into any of the accounts, meaning no one had hired a professional assassin to take out Anderson or Porter.

Everyone's finances were accounted for except Carl Minor, who could have a number of different accounts in countries that no one knew about. Charlene was sure that he, or his accountant/lawyer, would know all the loopholes in the system.

The ballistics report indicated the bullets pulled from Porter didn't match the bullets from Anderson. Charlene wasn't surprised. The killer wanted these two murders to look unconnected, and that's how LAPD was handling them.

Charlene was at her desk, rereading the case file on the fire in Fresno, when she overheard Berkley and Harris sitting at their desks on the other side of the partition.

"This is victim number five, but it's different. This is by far the most gruesome scene yet, and he seems to be speeding up between murders. Almost as if it was a hate crime, like this was personal."

She stood up and peered over at them. "Who was the victim?"

Both cops looked at her. They knew Charlene had found the locket. "Another B-lister. The woman's name is Tanya Louise Stockton."

T.L.S.

The cop continued. "After we put the woman's picture on the news, her mother called and gave us the address. We showed up at the vic's apartment and found the body."

"When was she killed?" Charlene asked.

"Coroner said three days ago. And she was the worst I've seen yet."

Charlene sat back in her seat. She hadn't been told about this latest victim and she'd never been updated on the FBI's profile of the suspect. Charlene was going to have to go get that information because it certainly wasn't coming to her.

She had to put the Slayer out of her head and focus on her case. The longer it went unsolved, as leads grew cold and hours passed, the chances of finding the killer decreased. Charlene's overtaxed mind was running on fumes at this point.

Her gut told her that Ashley Stanley, AKA Sarah Crawford, was somehow involved. But after reviewing crime scene photos again, trying to place Stanley at the scene, Charlene just couldn't prove it.

Stanley left the ball field early, giving her time to commit the murder. Her alibi was weak, but so were the alibis of every other suspect. Stanley had motive. Anderson was allegedly her former lover and had raped her two best friends, making Stanley relive what Charlene believed was her own abuse. But every suspect had motive.

It took a special kind of person to commit a cold-blooded murder. Because of the fire report, Charlene believed that Stanley had it in her. But believing it and proving it were two different things.

Charlene leaned back in her chair and breathed out discouragingly. She needed a drink.

"What are you thinking?" she asked Larry.

He removed his bifocals and rubbed the bridge of this nose. "Honestly, murderers aren't normally organized, but Anderson's killer is beyond methodical. What about you?"

Charlene didn't say anything, because she couldn't begin to organize the chaos running rampant through her mind.

"Let's discuss the suspects, acting as if the Anderson and Porter murders are connected, which we both think are."

Larry grunted his agreement.

Charlene started. "Jessica Philips, the lover, the 'other' woman, the young, naïve college girl who thought her professor, who she put on a pedestal, would leave his wife. She was looking for a fairytale ending that never worked out. She was at home that night. No one saw her leave. She had means and opportunity and no alibi. Anderson probably told her he'd never leave his wife and then he raped Sandra, just to prove he could."

"Sandra Philips," Larry intervened. "The rape victim. I can't say I know what she's going through, but I know what I would do to the bastard who did that to me. She has skills in handling a weapon, owns a gun and, although she has an alibi for that night, could have left that meeting at any time and then returned."

Charlene's turn. "Beverly Anderson, the jaded wife. Abused both mentally and physically. If not her, she has the money and resources to make it happen. The prideful, scheming wife who had her own lover."

They were in police mode, completing each other's sentences now.

"The lover," Larry continued. "Marcus Lopez. He looks and plays the part of the tough guy. Muscular, tattooed, with a sordid past. He's a former gang member accustomed to violence. He's admitted to a fight with Anderson near the time of the murder and his ties to gangs could get him close to Nelson Porter."

Charlene couldn't resist. "Carl Minor, billionaire, with an ego the size of the Hollywood Hills. He's admitted to not liking his son-in-law and was probably embarrassed by his daughter's marriage. 'No one treats a Minor like that.' Again he has the money to hire a pro and knowing his reputation, he wouldn't think twice about pulling the trigger on that. It would also avoid a large court settlement."

Larry quickly moved on. "Eric Connors' daughter was a rape victim. As a father myself, if something like that happened to my daughter, I wouldn't blame Connors one bit for taking the law into his hands. From what you told me, that incident changed that family's life."

"If we mention Eric Connors, then we have to mention Margaret, who was the rape victim. But I don't like Margaret for this, after seeing how she reacts around other people."

Charlene continued. "Alberto Bianchi, a perpetual criminal, violent, egotistical, with a mean streak longer than the Golden Gate Bridge. He wouldn't think twice about having Anderson or Porter offed."

"That leaves us with Ashley Stanley."

"Yes," Charlene said. "Ashley Stanley or Sarah Crawford. Whoever she might be."

Larry smiled a crooked smile. "What are you thinking, Taylor?"

"I think it's time to turn up the heat and get serious about finding Crawford."

Larry nodded.

"There's no trace of her on the internet, but you can't totally hide from your past. Someone, somewhere, knows her."

Charlene called Fresno High School and was transferred to the school's guidance counselor, who had worked for the school since 1995. When a man's voice mail answered, Charlene identified herself. She wasn't sure what kind of warrant she would need to get high school files.

"This is Detective Charlene Taylor with the LAPD. I'm calling about one of your former students."

The detective left a short message, gave the counselor her cell number then hung up.

The alcohol helped, but it was only a crutch. Case files were scattered on the bed and floor.

She called Andy's number but he didn't pick up.

She sat alone in the dark, lights off, TV on with the volume down. The Dodgers were at home, only two and a half games back, playing the division-leading Giants. The sky looked dark and dreary, but the game played on.

She squeezed her eyes shut, tried to focus on work as she fought back tears as well as unconsciousness.

Why did she always do this? How could she make things right in her life?

Her pathetic self-loathing was interrupted by her iPhone chime. She didn't recognize the number.

"Detective Taylor, this is Ben Cross, Guidance Counselor at Fresno High School. Sorry for calling so late. I played your message over a couple of times, thinking about your request, contemplating my call. That name brought back memories."

"You remember Sarah Crawford?" Charlene had finally gotten to her feet and was searching for a pen.

"Yes. The name has never slipped my mind."

If Charlene had been worried about subpoenaing the counselor, those concerns vanished.

"She was manipulative in every sense of the word—beautiful, mature beyond her years. She used her beauty to control the high school boys who were no match. As far as intelligence, Sarah was a head above her classmates. Could have been valedictorian if she had applied herself, but her grades were never that important to her."

That word manipulative had been used by two different people to describe Sarah Crawford.

"In 2007, she had accused a boy of rape. Of course, we took the incident very seriously. I knew the boy, knew his family personally, and he was not the type. We held an internal investigation, interviewed the parties, and discovered that the story had indeed been fabricated. Sarah admitted it after weeks of inquiry. My opinion, Sarah was pushing our limits, seeing how far she could take it…seeing what she could get away with. It seemed that she took pleasure in other's pain. I had many a conversation with her, and she was sly. She could turn it on when she wanted to.

"I love my job, love my students, but Sarah Crawford was one of a kind. It scared me to think what she was going to turn into. I lost track of her after she left, as I do with most of my students. Life goes on, students move on, and if they don't stay in touch, then I don't see them again."

He wasn't done. "That woman could have done anything she wanted to with her life, but I was worried about the direction she was headed. I have hand-written notes on all of our talks, including my personal and professional opinions."

Charlene asked, "What about her home life? Did she ever mention anything about being abused at home?"

"She hadn't mentioned anything in any of our talks." The counselor sounded genuinely surprised. "She was usually quite open in our conversations, sometimes a little too much, as high school girls tend *not* to be. She was very open with me about things like drugs, alcohol, and sex."

"So she never said anything?"

"It would have been difficult for her. She had lied once about it. She probably thought no one would believe her. Her stepfather was held in high esteem in Fresno. I certainly never noticed any evidence of physical abuse. But I did notice subtle shifts in her behavior. When I questioned her about them, she just waved it off as maturing," he added in a defensive tone.

Charlene asked him to send copies of his notes to the department, thanked him, and said goodbye.

The last thing she remembered as she drifted into unconsciousness was the Dodgers' eighth inning rain delay.

Chapter 25

Her eyes jerked open, a notion buffeting her awake. An idea had been teasing at the back of her mind, and now it had surfaced. She sat up on her futon.

Outside, thunder cracked. She could hear huge raindrops pelting the roof of her building.

Her mouth was dry, spit caked at the corners of her lips. A tiny soldier beat a steady drum in her head. She bit her tongue, trying to reclaim the dream.

It involved baseball, the Dodgers. Dust flying as a player slid for home plate. The umpire with his arms stretched, making the 'safe' signal.

It was dark, even the TV was off. Had she turned it off before falling asleep? Charlene didn't think so, at least didn't remember doing it. She blinked a couple of times, her eyes adjusting to the blackness.

She stumbled out of bed and reached for anything to grasp, anything to steady herself. She couldn't find it and fell hard, cracking her elbow on the hardwood. She cursed under her breath. The room was spinning. What time was it? The digital clock on the wall was blank, the power was out. Charlene searched for her iPhone. She knew it was on the floor somewhere, maybe under the heap of clothes.

She found it, turned it on, and the light helped her find her bearings. 11:11 PM.

She staggered to the sink. Setting the phone on the counter, leaving it on for the light, she ran the water. She splashed some on her face, drinking in the refreshing wetness.

She speed dialed her partner.

"Larry?"

"Jesus Christ, Taylor. Do you know what time it is? Don't you sleep?"

"Larry," she mumbled. "I have it."

"Have what?"

"Meet me at the Anderson crime scene."

"What? Now?"

"Just do it."

She hung up and called her friend Dana Davis with the Forensics Unit, giving her the same instructions.

Charlene fumbled in the dark for some clothes. She dressed quickly, chaotically, locating her car keys after ten minutes. She grabbed a bottle of Tylenol and a bottle of water for the road.

Charlene wasn't sure how long she'd been or if she was late, but Larry and Dana were both waiting when she pulled the Volvo curbside. They were seated in their cars, shielded from the rain, windshield wipers up high.

Charlene's head pounded and her stomach rolled. She felt dizzy and thought momentarily about making herself sick. She got out of her car, pulled her jacket over her head, and sprinted to the front door.

Dana followed, holding a large, metal case with a password protected lock. She was dressed in an LAPD sweat suit and her blonde hair was parted in the middle, the sides hanging down and curling under her jaw line. Her shirt accentuated her large breasts that had acquired Dana the nickname, "Double D." It wasn't just her initials.

Larry looked as if he'd just rolled out of bed, which he had. His hair was messy, his tie crooked, and his suit wrinkled.

"I assume you guys know each other?" Charlene said hoarsely.

Dana smile. "Yep, Larry and I go way back." She playfully punched Larry on the arm, as he tucked his chin into a chest like an embarrassed six-year-old. His face flushed red. Dana had that effect on men.

"You smoke, Davis?" Larry asked.

"Sorry, Larry." She turned to Charlene. "This better be good, Taylor. You got my ass out of bed in this weather for this. I'm graveyard shift this weekend," Dana teased.

"Did you make sure to leave him cash for the cab ride home?" Charlene responded with a smile.

Dana grinned but didn't bite at the jab. "The boss will have a heart attack if he knows I snuck this out," Dana said, referring to the metal case.

As Charlene unlocked the door, she noticed Larry trying not to stare at Dana's breasts, but his attempt was pathetic

"So this is your famous Professor scene. Wish I could've been here from the start," Dana acknowledged, looking around the house.

"Why weren't you on this one with me?"

"No idea, I was working that night, but the boss sent a newbie instead. First time that's ever happened."

The apartment was still blocked off. They dodged the police tape, stepped into the crime scene area and advanced to the taped body outline.

"Don't step on your tongue, Larry," Charlene whispered.

"Fuck you, Taylor."

The power wasn't working, but they each had a standard, LAPD issued flashlight.

Charlene knelt beside the body outline, turning and waving to Dana to join her. Larry stood behind the women. Finally, he gave an annoyed grunt and stooped beside them, his bones cracking as he bent.

"Are you going to tell us why we're out here in this shit-storm, Taylor?" Larry asked impatiently.

Charlene stared at the white chalk dust speckled across the floor, running her fingers gently through it. At first notice, she thought it was just chalk from the chalkboard, but now she had second thoughts.

"Taylor?" Larry asked again.

"Dana," Charlene said, extending her hand. "Give me something to pick this up."

"What the hell is all that stuff?" Larry asked, eyeing the equipment Dana had removed from the metal case and finally taking his eyes off her chest.

"This is an adhesive specimen mount. It lifts powders from surfaces for spectroscopy analysis in lab. And this," Dana added, "is an adhesive lifter. It lifts and preserves trace materials and deposits."

Dana handed Charlene a set of tools, and she used it to pick up the substance and transfer it. Dana ran the material through the process.

"It'll take a few minutes to analyze."

While the analysis was underway, Charlene removed her ball cap and studied the tiny indentations in the floor.

"I need a smoke," Larry complained.

While he shoved his hands in his pockets and started to pace, Charlene had time to stand and circle the body outline, trying to position herself the way she suspected the killer had moved. She followed the marks on the floor, walking towards the body, then back to the door.

Dana observed Charlene. "Uh-oh, Larry, your partner has that lip in her mouth again."

Larry nodded and opened his mouth to say something but a buzzer sounded. They all stared at Dana's machine as she pulled on the read-out, removed the paper and handed it to Charlene.

Charlene looked at it but she wasn't trained in this field. "What does this mean?"

"Well, this machine isn't one hundred percent accurate. It would be more enhanced if we could take the specimen back to the lab. But I know you detectives always want everything done yesterday. So, from the initial reading, that powder," she said, pointing to the floor, "is calcium oxide, containing traces of..." she looked back at the sheet, "magnesium oxide, silicon oxide, aluminum oxide, and iron oxide."

"I get it, lots of oxides. So what does that mean?" Larry was all the way in now.

"So it's not chalk dust?" Charlene asked

"Not the kind you find in school," Dana answered.

"Are you two going to tell me what's going on?" Larry crossed his arms.

"It's lime, Larry," Charlene said. "Baseball lime. You see those dents beside the lime? Like little scratches on the hardwood." Charlene got down on her knees and used the flashlight beam to follow the trail. "I believe those dents were made by metal baseball cleats."

Larry bent to the floor, then snorted and nodded, giving his trademark grunt of approval. He suppressed a smile.

"I went back to our initial interview with Jessica Philips. She said that every Friday the cleaning lady came. If the cleaning lady had done her job, then Ashley Stanley was in the house that night, after her ball game."

Larry smiled. "You know, Stanley has moved out of town, and might be getting ready to run for good."

"Let's go now."

They'd stopped by the department to pick up a car to make it more official.

Larry drove, wipers on full speed, as the drops came down like pellets. Charlene gripped the door handle as Larry steered recklessly through the deluge. He squinted, making Charlene even more nervous. The pellets hammered down, making the road slick.

Charlene was sweating profusely. She wasn't sure if it was the booze oozing from her pores or the intensity of the moment.

The rain had slowed them, but Larry pulled into the motel parking lot in forty-eight minutes and killed the engine. They sat looking out the windshield at the L-shaped motel, barely visible through the rain.

Last confirmed, the girls had moved out of the Hilton and were staying in a motel outside of LA, in Harbor City—the Philips sisters sharing one room and Stanley in another. They'd already called the night manager on the way over.

"You up for this?" he asked.

Charlene looked at her partner. "Yeah. Motel manager said there's only one door, plus a window in the back."

"I don't see Stanley's jeep," said Larry, a look of concern etched on his face.

"Manager confirmed she hasn't left the room."

"I'd like to wait a few days, find more concrete evidence and be able to arrest her. Why do we have to do this now?"

"I'm afraid she'll run. I just want to spook her a bit to see how she'll react."

"Okay," Larry said. "If Stanley is our killer, she might be armed. We don't know if she still has the murder weapon or if she tossed it."

Charlene nodded.

"Take one of these." Larry handed Charlene a pack of breath mints. "You reek of booze. I don't want any red tape bureaucracy bullshit getting in the way of this arrest."

She accepted the package and popped one.

They got out of the car, walking slowly in the rain, the drops hitting them like BBs. Adrenaline spurred Charlene on, her heart frantically beating.

She tried to peer inside the window, but the lights were off and the curtains were drawn.

"The emergency generators are powered so Stanley must have the lights off," Charlene warned.

"She could be asleep. It's past midnight," Larry said.

"Or she could be playing possum."

Charlene flicked her holster button open as a precaution.

She pressed the file under her arm and rapped on the door. She thought she saw the curtain move, but didn't see a face. Charlene put her ear to the door and heard footsteps drawing near.

The door was slowly opened. Stanley was in a housecoat, hair a mess and her eyes barely squinting open. Charlene noticed the suspect had bare legs with running shoes and short white socks.

"Miss Stanley, may we come in?"

"Has there been a break in the case?" Stanley asked hoarsely.

"Actually, yes, there has been."

Stanley let them in. Charlene followed her closely, while Larry stood in front of the door, blocking passage.

"What a miserable night. You both must be freezing. Would you like some coffee? It'll only take a minute."

"No, thank you, Ashley."

"It's no trouble. The machine is in the bathroom."

"No, thank you, Ashley." This time Charlene's voice was sterner.

Charlene noticed three suitcases sitting beside the door. Stanley sat on one of the side-by-side twin beds, not looking at the detective. Charlene sat on the other, across from her. Larry looked like a bouncer standing watch at the bar entrance, arms folded, lips clenched.

"We've come upon some new evidence in the case." Charlene waited for a reaction.

Stanley stared at Charlene, but didn't move or speak.

"We found ball park lime and cleat marks around Ken Anderson's dead body."

Ashley shrugged her shoulders. "I'm in a ball league and I walk around the house in my cleats all the time."

Charlene nodded. "Anderson was killed on a Friday night. Jessica told us that every Friday you have your house cleaned. That means you were in that house sometime that night."

Stanley didn't respond. Charlene looked at Larry, who nodded.

She removed the papers from the folder. "This is a report filed by the Fresno Fire Department two years ago. Two people were killed from a fire caused by faulty wiring. The daughter made it out alive and received a healthy insurance policy and inheritance."

Charlene showed the picture. Still no movement from Stanley. Stanley's calm demeanor put Charlene on edge, second guessing her theory.

"I also found police reports from the Fresno PD filed by your mother, the third one filed by you. Fresno PD has agreed to reopen the investigation into the fire, based on my theory." This was a lie, but Stanley didn't know that.

Stanley looked at the ground.

"I know what you've been through, Sarah." With the mention of her real name, she looked at Charlene for the first time.

She rose from the bed. Larry motioned to move towards her, but Charlene held him back with a finger in the air. Crawford turned her back to the detectives.

"This is all very interesting. Are you sure you won't have that coffee, Detective?"

Crawford made towards the bathroom.

"Stop right there, Sarah. Turn around." Charlene had her hand on the butt of her gun, which was still holstered. She looked at Larry, who already had his drawn.

"Turn around and put your hands where we can see them," Larry said.

There was no reply, no movement.

"Listen to him, Sarah," Charlene added.

Crawford slowly reached inside her robe.

"Hands in the air, Sarah!"

It was too late. Crawford pulled something from her robe and turned.

Before she saw anything else, Charlene was whiplashed by Larry's bulk, as he tackled her to the ground. His full weight landed on Charlene's chest, knocking the wind out of her as two deafening pops went off and bullets lodged into the drywall behind them.

Larry raised his gun over the edge of the bed and fired a blind shot.

It took a few seconds for Charlene to find her breath. "Drop the gun, Sarah. It's over!"

The detective slowly, cautiously, lifted her head and gazed overtop the bed. She heard the bathroom door slam and the lock slide into place.

"Bathroom, Larry," she said. Then they heard glass breaking.

"Window," he confirmed.

As Charlene crept down the hall, gun ready, Larry left through the front door. No sound came from inside the bathroom. She stood beside the doorframe, took a deep breath and kicked in the door, splinting the sides of the frame. She quickly sidestepped out of range. On three, she moved, squaring her shoulders in the doorway, gun pointing in.

The room was empty, the window wide open. Crawford's peach colored robe lay on the floor. Charlene pulled back the shower curtain and searched the room to confirm it. When she looked out the window, she could see the back of Stanley's shadow as the suspect fled towards her jeep parked strategically behind the motel.

"Shit," Charlene muttered.

She grabbed her radio. "Larry, Stanley's jeep is parked in the back, that's why we missed it."

As she was reattaching her radio, two shots echoed outside. They weren't from Larry's Smith & Wesson Model 15 revolver.

"Larry!" She gasped, grabbing the two-way radio again from her belt and sprinting from the bathroom.

When she stepped outside, Charlene tried to shield the rain with her hand. She rounded the corner of the building and saw her partner leaning against a post, holding his right shoulder. She went to him. "Larry, you okay?"

"Just great, Taylor! That bitch shot me!" He winced.

It looked like the bullet had just barely grazed the skin. His sleeve had a speck of a blood stain.

"It's far from the heart."

"Fuck you, Taylor! Go! Get that bitch!" Larry commanded, pushing her away.

Charlene noticed the blood dripping through his shirt now. He would lose use of his arm for a while, but not fatal. For a cop, it was a routine bullet wound.

Charlene scanned the parking lot but couldn't locate Crawford. She was calling in Larry's injury when she heard the squeal of tires, followed by a black jeep speeding by, jumping a concrete block and almost clipping the detectives.

Larry grimaced as he reached into his pocket to retrieve the car keys, throwing them at Charlene. It was an unwritten rule, but understood throughout law enforcement, the police were trained never to leave their partner.

He said something else, motioning with his hand, but Larry's listless voice was lost in the clamor of the rain.

It took Charlene a good ten seconds to get to the Crown Vic., fire up the engine, and wheel out of the parking lot, trying to keep Crawford's vehicle in her sights. She grabbed the car radio.

"Officer down, I repeat, officer down." She gave the address and requested backup, reading off street names as she tried to keep one eye on Crawford.

The rain started to come down harder, making visibility near zero.

Thunder cracked as lightning split the sky.

The rain pounded on the windshield so hard that vision blurred. Charlene was hunched over the steering wheel, peering around droplets of rain.

Traffic was minimal. But with every car that passed, a wall of water washed up past the driver's window. Charlene somehow managed to keep Crawford's taillights in view.

Crawford was handling her vehicle like someone who'd practiced this run before. And that's what worried Charlene. If Crawford had a preconceived plan, then she had the advantage.

Charlene checked her rear view mirror and saw three black and whites following. The black silence of night was lit up by flashing cherries and whining sirens. She looked to the sky, through the deluge, but couldn't see any sign of the aerial surveillance she'd requested. The storm might have kept them indoors.

Crawford seemed to be driving with a plan. She took the first exit onto the Pacific Coast Highway, maneuvering her jeep expertly around the sharp corners.

At the last minute, Crawford swerved the jeep, leaving the highway and merging onto I-110 South. They were only on that stretch for what seemed like minutes, before Crawford merged onto CA-47 North, heading towards the Vincent Thomas Bridge, a suspension bridge that linked San Pedro with Terminal Island. Crawford busted through the toll booth onto the bridge.

Charlene was well aware of the statistics. Because of the low, four foot railing along the VT Bridge, it's the location to almost a thousand suicides, second behind the Golden Gate Bridge. Charlene felt panic turn to dread.

She bit down on her lip and punched the accelerator. As she gained ground, the jeep's brake lights flashed in front.

Charlene picked up the radio. "Suspect slowing down, all units stay back. Suspect is armed."

What was Crawford doing? Once stopped on the bridge, she would be surrounded by water. She was trapping herself.

Suddenly the vehicle stopped, but the motor continued to run. Crawford still had a weapon and would use it, so Charlene brought the car to the side of the road and put it into park. She didn't turn off the ignition.

Charlene picked up the radio and ordered a blockade at the far side of the bridge, but there was no telling how long it would take. LAPD squads should already be on the way.

The night, teaming with the rain, made it increasingly hard to make out the black jeep. Charlene saw the jeep's interior light come on for only seconds, then she thought she saw a shadow moving away from the vehicle.

She had to make a decision.

She grabbed the radio again. "I'm moving in on foot. Stay in your vehicles in case Crawford takes off."

With her gun drawn and aimed at the jeep, Charlene made her way in the blinding rain, shielding her eyes as best she could. She approached the jeep and couldn't see movement. She moved to the driver's side, gun aimed in place, and opened the door. Vacant.

She looked around, but the bridge's solar powered lights did very little against the pounding of the rain. When lightning split the sky again, providing a few seconds of bright light, Charlene spotted Crawford sprinting towards the median, hurdling the barricade.

Charlene took off after her. She radioed her team to follow, motioning in the direction Crawford was headed.

The rain ripped into her eyes. Puddles of water splashed around her as she ran, soaking her shoes and pant-legs up to the knees. Charlene could hear her colleagues barking out instructions and barricading the bridge. She used her hand to shield the rain.

Charlene called out to Crawford, but the thunder and pelting rain drowned out her words.

Crawford leaped the median and crossed the two lanes. One car skidded, swerving to avoid hitting Crawford, only to crash through the short railing, finally stopping with half the vehicle hanging over the side.

Crawford made it safely across and then turned and tauntingly waved Charlene and the others to follow.

The width of the bridge was fifty-two feet. Crawford had no place to go.

Charlene was right on her now. Her regular workouts had prepared her. She was breathing heavily, not from exhaustion, but the intensity of the moment. Out of the corner of her eye, Charlene saw one of the officers throw a flare down on the highway.

She looked for backup, and when she turned back, Crawford was gone. Charlene felt sick. There was no place to go. How could she have vanished? She looked around frantically, turning to the officers who shook their heads and shrugged.

Some officers were down on their knees, checking under vacated cars. Another bolt of lightning briefly illuminated the night, giving off enough light for them to spot Crawford. Officers pointed towards the railing, where Crawford had perched herself. She stood on the railing, looking down into the black water of the Los Angeles Harbor.

Now Charlene understood. She holstered her weapon and took off in a sprint as more flares were ignited.

The LAPD had contingency plans for this kind of situation. Charlene's job was to distract Crawford, while someone could sneak up on her. Usually they would have someone hanging out of a helicopter, with a loud speaker, but the weather had eliminated that plan and everything had happened so suddenly they didn't have time to prepare.

Charlene also knew that the media, who followed on police scanners, could show up at any time, which would really put a kink in the procedure.

Charlene was now close enough to get a good look and communicate with Crawford.

"Don't come any closer, Detective," Crawford said. She motioned to the officers behind Charlene. "Move them back."

"Okay, Sarah, just relax. Don't do anything stupid." Charlene turned to the officers, motioning for them to stay back. Charlene saw the gun still in Crawford's hand.

"Throw down the gun and come down, Sarah."

Crawford looked at the gun in her hand, as if seeing it for the first time.

"I can help you, Sarah." Charlene thought the relentless wind might blow Crawford right off the ledge.

"My parents got what they deserved, Detective. I made sure of that. Ken did too." Crawford showed no emotion.

"Come down, Sarah."

"It's too late, Detective." Crawford turned towards the water.

"Wait!" Charlene yelled. "Talk to me, Sarah." Charlene needed to stall until they could get more men in position, maybe a boat in the water.

Crawford looked around the bridge, as if noticing the chaos for the first time. As if she was in a trance.

She didn't move, but seemed to relax, ever so slightly. She turned only her head to face Charlene, the rest of her body still facing the water below.

"I blamed my mother for my father's death. Maybe not directly, but I could never forgive her after that." She sighed, almost trying to find the nerve to continue. "After Dad's murder, Mom changed. She took the money and used it for drugs. She married one of her dealers six months later."

"Luther Vincent was a drug dealer?" This news surprised Charlene. From the news coverage, Vincent had been a respected businessman. Crawford had no reason to lie now.

Crawford snorted a chuckle. "Had everyone fooled. My mother wouldn't listen. She was only interested in what Luther could provide for her."

Charlene took a step closer while LAPD maintained a perimeter around Crawford. "When did the abuse start, Sarah?"

Sarah shot her head up, a look of surprise registered on her face. Then she smiled.

"After the wedding. My mother sided with Luther. So I took matters into my own hands."

"The fire?" It wasn't a question, rather a conclusion.

Crawford nodded. "That was the easy part. Getting away with it was the challenge. I was surprised at how easy it was to eliminate all traces of Sarah Crawford, as long as you know the right computer guy. School records and internet sites aren't very well protected."

Charlene tried to step closer but Crawford shook her head and waved the gun.

"What about Ken Anderson?" Charlene asked.

"I thought I'd seen the last of him when I left USC. But I was wrong. He brought back a lot of bad memories."

"And then Sandra…" Charlene said, reading it in Crawford's eyes.

"Then Sandra," she said and nodded.

"So you took care of that problem too?" Charlene asked.

Crawford didn't look at Charlene. She had her eyes trained on the cops that had now surrounded her.

Without looking at Charlene, Crawford said, "Ken got what he deserved."

"Look at me, Sarah," Charlene said.

When she did, Charlene saw that Sarah was crying. It wasn't the rain, but genuine tears.

"I'm finished talking, Detective."

Crawford turned, threw the gun on the ground, and without another word, flung her limp body over the side of the bridge.

"No!" Charlene yelled, reaching helplessly over the edge. Sarah's body spiraled down, disappearing into the dark rain, and Charlene could barely hear it splash in the black water.

Charlene leaned over the edge as officers joined her. She waited for minutes, waiting for the body to float back to the surface. But it didn't.

Chapter 26

Charlene sat at her bureau desk six hours after Sarah Crawford's suicide. When she'd returned to the precinct immediately following the event, she had explained it all to her captain—the evidence from the scene, the real Sarah Crawford, the Fresno fire and then her subsequent confession to the killings.

Case closed.

She'd gone home for a shower and four hour nap, before returning to file the paper work. A suspect had died, so Internal Affairs would be brought in to investigate.

Charlene's blood/alcohol level hadn't been tested, but she was confident that she was of sound mind. She was aware, alert, and had made accurate decisions. The alcohol she'd consumed had been hours before the confrontation, before her nap, so the booze had had time to wear off.

She would be questioned, interrogated, but Charlene knew she had done all she could and had handled it the right way.

She tried to relive the moment. She had received the confession for the murder, or had she?

Charlene tried to replay Crawford's words, but with the craziness of it all—the confrontation, the storm, the gun shots, the car chase, and the ultimate suicide—Charlene wasn't sure what exactly she'd heard.

It was still a blur.

Crawford admitted killing her parents. But had she confessed to killing Anderson? She'd said the professor got what he deserved. Did that mean she'd given it to him?

Why confess to one murder and not another, especially if you planned to commit suicide?

"Think," Charlene said, a little too loud.

"What?" an officer passing by asked.

"Nothing."

The captain, basking in the glow of Carl Minor's praise, received his accolades. His team had successfully solved a high profile case.

Charlene had all of the case notes in front of her, trying to put it all together. But something was eating at her.

The image of the motel shootout was still clear in her mind. How had Crawford missed?

She jumped to her feet, took all of the files from the Anderson case, and grabbed the coat from the back of her chair, flinging it on as she ran from the office. She got into her car and headed back to the motel.

She parked in the same spot where they had last night and got out of the car. The scene had already been processed so the room was empty. She dodged the police tape and entered the tiny, single room.

She walked across the shaggy carpet and stood in the exact location where she had been standing when Crawford had turned and fired. Charlene had been less than fifteen feet away from the shooter.

Charlene turned around and looked at the wall behind her. The bullets had already been dislodged and taken back to the department for analysis, but the holes were still there, high and to the right of where Charlene had stood. The bullets nowhere near the intended target.

She pulled out her cell phone and called Larry, who was still in the hospital getting treated for his 'scratch.'

"Larry, it's Charlene, how are you doing?"

"I've been better."

"I'm at the scene. Do you remember when we were inside the motel room and Crawford turned on us?"

"Yeah, what about it?"

"How far would you say Crawford was from us?"

"I don't know, fifteen, twenty feet. Why?"

"I'm looking at the bullet holes in the wall behind us. They weren't even close. What about outside?"

"What about it?"

She walked out to the parking lot and stood beside the car. "Tell me about the shooting."

Larry grunted. "Crawford had somehow snuck up behind me and fired two shots. The first missed, but the second got me, grazed my shoulder. It had almost missed as well."

"How far away was she?"

"Same thing, maybe twenty feet at most."

"And you're a big target," Charlene said.

"Up yours, Taylor. Is there a point to all this?"

"I'm still not sure. Gotta go, Larry. Take care of yourself."

"Yeah, yeah."

Charlene hung up. In both instances, inside the room and out in the parking lot, Crawford had exhibited very poor shooting accuracy.

She opened the Anderson folder, used her coat sleeve to dry an area of the car hood, and laid the file down.

The bullet holes in Anderson, a direct quote from the coroner, "bullet placing was the result of perfect shooting." And Anderson had been moving when he'd been hit. Had it been a lucky shot? Maybe one, but two, highly unlikely.

The gun used last night was Sandra Philips' .32. Charlene would have to ask Sandra how Crawford had gotten it.

Charlene closed the file and got into the car, her bones tired and muscles sore. She thought about how this one case had affected a lot of lives.

Would Jessica Philips ever fall in love and trust another man? She was a murder suspect in the media. Would she ever be able to live that down and lead a normal life in LA?

Sandra Philips would never be the same again. Hopefully someday, someway, the young woman could push past it and live a happy, normal life. It would take a long time and a lot of hard work for the internal scars to heal.

Beverly Minor was now a widow. Out of her husband's shadow, away from the violence and abuse, both mental and physical, the woman could now move on.

Carl Minor had avoided a major financial crisis. He also had lost a son-in-law he never liked. The real-estate tycoon would go on, business as usual.

Marcus Lopez's affair had never gotten out. He had dodged a bullet and hopefully had learned his lesson. He'd admitted his mistake and vowed to change. Charlene hoped, for his family's sake, he would. Lopez had had a tough childhood, had beaten the odds, and had a lot to appreciate in life.

Alberto Bianchi was still under investigation by the FBI, CIA, and IRS. He would always be a major player and always under suspicion. His daughter still hadn't surfaced and might never. Bianchi was smart and would probably never be caught or outwitted by the legal system.

Even though Margaret and Eric Connors might never get over what Anderson had done to their family, and wonder what life would have been like if they'd never met the man, they might be able to sleep better knowing Anderson was gone and feel a sense of retribution and maybe even closure.

Everyone seemed better off with Ken Anderson dead.

Sarah Crawford's life had been altered after her father's death, even before she'd met Anderson. She was a lost soul, who had never found her role in society. Charlene wasn't a religious person, but Crawford had needed help, maybe spiritually.

Larry would survive. The gunshot had sliced the deltoid muscle in his left shoulder. He would be in a sling and require physiotherapy to regain strength. But there were still some things Charlene wondered about Larry and her father.

And Charlene would move on to the next case. This one was deemed a success. She was already being given high praise and commendations for her exceptional work, but she still didn't feel right.

Three people had died. Ken Anderson, a man who lived a reckless lifestyle, tearing down anyone in his path. Maybe he wasn't a good man, but he didn't deserve to die. Sarah Crawford, a woman living through pain and torment, mentally unstable, abused her whole life, had taken her own life. Nelson Porter, a street punk who never had a chance, a witness in the wrong place at the wrong time who'd seen something he wasn't supposed to.

What had he really seen? Charlene hadn't had time to ask Crawford.

Although Crawford's body had yet to be found after the record-breaking rainfall, it was only a matter of time before the Harbor was drained. Maybe a week, maybe a month, but eventually her body would turn up.

Crawford's belongings were searched and no weapons were found. She must have discarded the Anderson murder weapon.

Even though *she* was frustrated, Charlene was proud of her small team. Maybe she could have done some things differently, but she would learn from her mistakes. Reflection was part of the job, as well as getting better with each case. You never stopped learning.

Twists and turns were always part of a roller coaster case. So many suspects, all with motive and opportunity, no alibis, and so little evidence to follow.

She started the car and headed back to the office thinking about the pile of papers on her desk. There was always a pressing case file waiting.

Chapter 27

Charlene was filing away the last of the Professor case on Friday when her name was called from across the lobby. She looked up to find a young, thin, red-headed officer with her head stuck inside the department door.

"Detective Taylor, you have a visitor."

Charlene wasn't expecting anyone. She dropped what was left of the folders and exited the Homicide department, crossing the lobby floor. A woman, in baggy sweatpants and a windbreaker, wearing a cap with a ponytail stuck out the back, stood alone at the front desk.

The woman surprised Charlene when she turned around. "Margaret," Charlene said.

"Hi, Detective Taylor." Margaret's eyes dropped to the floor. "I asked my father to drop me off. Can we talk?"

"Of course."

Charlene led Margaret Connors to her desk in the Homicide division. Charlene knew that Margaret coming to the precinct, alone in public, was a major breakthrough. Maybe Anderson's death had given her a new sense of self-confidence.

Charlene borrowed the chair from Larry's desk and pulled it over. Margaret sat down and Charlene took her own seat, waiting for her visitor to speak.

Margaret looked as if she had something to say, but her attention was focused on the busy office, the cops milling about, papers bustling, and phones ringing.

"Margaret," Charlene had to say her name to get her attention. "Would you like something to drink?"

Margaret shook her head, clasped her hands together, and dropped them into her lap. She began to play with her pinkie ring.

Charlene sat back, relaxing her muscles. After sensing the appropriate time had lapsed, she tried again. "What can I do for you?"

"My dad wanted to come in with me. But it's time I start living my life again." She hesitated and then continued. Her voice was a whisper. "I heard you caught the person who killed Professor Anderson."

"That's right. It was Sarah." Because it had all gone down in the wee hours of the morning, the newspapers had already gone to press and there was nothing mentioned in today's editions, although the TV and radio personalities were all over it.

Charlene continued to tell Margaret about the connection between Sarah and Anderson, the fire killing Sarah's parents and the Sandra Philips' rape.

Margaret listened and when Charlene finished, the rape victim shook her head, her slender neck and scrawny shoulders followed along. "I don't believe it."

"I'm sure it's difficult to digest," Charlene said.

"I just don't buy it. I don't believe that Sarah is capable of that. She..."

"Don't forget about the fire. She admitted it to me," Charlene argued.

"I know, but this is different."

"Why don't you tell me what you know about Sarah?"

"Well, after my...incident...with Professor Anderson, Sarah was supportive, but never to the point of wanting to extract revenge." She used the word 'revenge' while making air quotes. "Sure, she was upset, but we often talked about how to get over this and never once did she mention getting back at him. She didn't hate the guy and thought that if he sought help, he could change. She called it a disease. It was almost like she felt bad for the guy and knew all about it." Charlene wanted to tell Margaret that Sarah had been abused herself, but didn't see how that would help, so she let Margaret vent. She also didn't mention that Sarah herself had slept with Anderson.

"Sarah tried to help me through it, mentally, until I quit school and moved back home. She visited a few times, but eventually she just disappeared. We lost touch after that."

Charlene was taking notes, but none of it made sense. None of what Margaret said matched the information Charlene had received in her investigation. From Detective Jackson's words, Sarah wanted vengeance, wanted Anderson to pay, wanted blood.

Margaret stopped and took a deep breath.

Charlene was thinking of what to say next when Margaret spoke. "Sometimes I wish he would've killed me."

Charlene felt a sickness within her, but didn't say anything.

"I'm serious. Just because he didn't, doesn't mean he didn't end my life."

Charlene believed Margaret.

"Did you ever see a gun in the dorm room?"

Margaret shook her head. "Sarah didn't like guns. Actually after the incident, we took a women's self-defense course. One part of the program was to attend a shooting range." Margaret released a quiet giggle. "Sarah was the worst shot in class. Not even close to the targets."

Charlene believed that, remembering Crawford's sporadic shooting at the motel.

"But I was obviously wrong about her. She seemed to have fooled a lot of people."

Charlene took Margaret's hand. "Sarah's life was one big lie. She was a pro in the art of deception."

Margaret nodded. "I guess. What I really came by for was to see if there would be a service for Sarah."

"Once we find Sarah's body, since she has no remaining family to identify the body, her inheritance will all go to the state to pay for a funeral, if there is one. I can direct you to the proper authorities when the time comes."

"Thanks." Margaret stood up and reached out her hand and Charlene accepted it. Even her handshake felt firmer and more confident. As she was about to leave, the sound of a deep-throated laugh in the back snapped Margaret's head.

Charlene turned to follow Margaret's gaze.

"Is that Officer Jackson?" Margaret asked.

Charlene saw Adrienne Jackson, in street clothes, standing at the end of the hall sipping coffee and talking with another detective.

"I hardly recognize her out of uniform, but it looks like her."

"How do you know Detective Jackson?" Charlene asked.

"She was one of the cops assigned to my case. She came to my dorm room, followed me to classes, and even came to my parents' house when I moved back. She was pretty disturbed when we dropped the charges."

Charlene wondered what Jackson was doing in street clothes, in the Homicide division at that moment.

"Why don't you sit back down, Margaret?"

Margaret Connor's testimony planted a significant seed of doubt.

After seeing Margaret out, Charlene sat at her desk and thought about what she'd heard. She'd faxed Jackson's picture to Dean Brown at USC. The dean had confirmed that Jackson was the female officer who had been investigating the Anderson rape.

Charlene picked up the phone and called the front desk.

"Henry, who is Adrienne Jackson partnered with?"

"That'd be Bobby Johnson."

"Great, get a hold of him for me."

"I'll have to page him."

"Tell him to call me at the office, ASAP." She hung up before receiving acknowledgement.

Charlene jumped from her seat and rushed across the room, hoping that Darren was still in, but didn't expect it on a late Friday afternoon, after they'd successfully solved the Anderson case. She found his seat was empty and she cursed under her breath, checking the entire room. She went through the numerous books and papers on his desk and tried to open the drawers but they were locked.

She called out to no one in particular. "Has anyone seen Darren?"

"Check the bathroom." The words came out of the pack, and Charlene couldn't tell who said them.

She rushed across the lobby and slammed her way into the men's restroom. She found Darren standing at the urinal, pulling up his zipper.

"Jesus, Chip, what the hell are you doing in here?"

"Do you still have that black book?" Charlene hoped he hadn't already filed it downstairs and marked it as evidence to go into the vault. It would take some explaining to get it back out.

"Of course."

"Great, I need to see it."

"You couldn't have waited five minutes? Do I have time to wash my hands?"

Darren unlocked his desk drawer and pulled out the book.

"How far did you get?"

"All the way to 'S'," he stated proudly.

"Did you find Adrienne Jackson in there?"

"You mean Detective Jackson, from Rape?"

"The same."

"Why would she be in there?"

"Did you find her name or not?"

"No. Why?"

"Damn it."

Charlene returned to her desk where her phone was ringing. She picked up after the fourth ring, "Detective Taylor, Homicide."

"This is Detective Johnson. I was told to give you a call."

"Thanks for calling, Detective. Is your partner with you?"

"No, we're off tonight. I'm at home with my family. What's up?"

Why is Jackson at the precinct on her night off?

Time to ask questions without raising suspicions. "Sorry to bother you at home, but this will only take a minute. I was hoping to ask you a few questions about your partner."

"What about her?"

Charlene knew the LAPD partner bond—a trust that couldn't be broken. She had to tiptoe.

"The captain was thinking about promoting Jackson to Homicide and he wants me to get some info on her."

"Oh, sure," the officer said, seeming to loosen up. "What can I tell you?"

"Just tell me about her."

"Okay, well, Adrienne's a damn fine detective. She'd be real good on your staff, real capable and all. She's thorough, assertive, and I trust her with my life more than anyone I know, including my wife." He hesitated, as if checking to see if his wife was around.

The detective had an accent that Charlene couldn't place.

"How would you define Adrienne?"

"That's easy, tough as nails and merciless."

Strange adjective to describe a partner.

"What about her abilities?"

"Top notch! She can shoot better than any cop I seen. Perfect accuracy every time we go to the range, including moving targets. She's relentless, persistent, and overall, I'd say she's the best cop on the force. And you can quote me."

Charlene remembered watching Jackson at the shooting range.

"What about family?"

"Never mentions much about her parents. I know she's divorced. Said she made some bad decisions. Says she's making changes and trying to better her life and the world as a whole. Don't really know what that means."

"What mistakes did she make?"

"Well, Detective, you know how partners are, we confide in each other. She said the divorce was her fault. She'd fallen for another guy, acted on impulse, and because of her stupidity she'd lost a man who truly loved her. At the time, she thought she was in love, but quickly found out the guy wasn't who she thought he was."

"Did she say who this guy was?"

"Nah, just some doctor."

Anderson wasn't a medical doctor, but he did have a PHD.

"What kind of gun does Adrienne use?"

"Berretta 92, LAPD standard issue."

"Any other weapons?"

"Oh yeah, she has a complete arsenal at home, loves guns."

"What about a nine mil?"

"Don't know for sure, never saw the arsenal. Probably though, the nine mil is a pretty common weapon. These are pretty unusual questions."

Charlene had to recover. "That was a personal one. Love weapons myself. Thanks for your time, Detective."

"No problem. And great job on the Anderson case. Adrienne told me you found his killer."

"Thanks."

Charlene hung up and punched Jackson's name into the employee database. She scanned down with a jaundiced eye, looking for anything relevant. Then she found it.

Jackson's father was serving time on a rape conviction at California State Prison in Lancaster. Charlene ran his prison ID number thru NCIC and the State Department of Justice to find out more about the case.

It was Adrienne who'd come forward and testified in court against her own alcoholic father. The man had not only abused his wife, but he'd also taken advantage of his only daughter, Adrienne.

Charlene scanned the rest of the pages, impressed by Jackson's impeccable record as a cop and her remarkable shooting scores. Johnson was right. Jackson *was* one of the best the LAPD had.

As Charlene was searching the file a second time, she caught it. Jackson was her maiden name, gone back to after the divorce. Only a short time ago, she'd been married and taken her husband's name, not legally, but socially. She picked up her phone.

"Darren."

"Chip, I'm just on my way out. Can this wait 'til tomorrow?"

"No, it can't. I need another name checked."

"Fine, who is it?"

"Adrienne Turner."

"Who's that?"

"Is her name there?"

"Hold on."

Charlene could hear Darren flipping through pages while humming the theme to the Flintstones, and then he came back on the line.

"Ten-four, Chip, she's here. I hadn't gotten around to checking the 'T's', figured the case was closed and all, so I don't know much about Turner. Want me to look her up?"

Charlene blew out her breath, not realizing she'd been holding it in. "No, don't worry about it."

"What's this about anyway?"

"Probably nothing, thanks." She hung up before there were more questions.

Chapter 28

Charlene sat at her desk, reviewing the information she had on Jackson.

Jackson had a history of sexual and mental abuse. When her father had abused her mother and possibly Adrienne, it was Adrienne who'd stepped forward. He was now behind bars.

According to her partner, Jackson was divorced because she had cheated on her husband with a doctor, possibly Ken Anderson because her name was in his black book and even though he wasn't a medical doctor, he had a PHD. But there was no date in the book to indicate when Jackson had crossed paths with Anderson. Was it before or after the Connors rape?

Jackson had been at the head of both rape investigations and, from what Charlene knew about Jackson, the woman took things personally. The cop also had a collection of weapons at home, more than likely with a nine millimeter in her arsenal—maybe even the weapon used to kill Nelson Porter.

Charlene also had reports from a number of sources confirming Jackson's insatiable desire to protect rape victims and her avid quest for justice.

Charlene thought about her talk with Jackson, how the detective had so quickly pointed out Ashley Stanley's mental state after the Philips rape—a convenient name-drop.

Finding Jackson's name in Anderson's black book told Charlene that Anderson had probably dated the detective and then dropped her unexpectedly, leaving a bad taste in her mouth, because she'd left her husband, a man who truly loved her. Then the rape happened, with Jackson working the case. The second time, with Sandra Philips, Jackson made sure it never happened again. It was all speculative though.

What else could Charlene do to prove it?

Also, the fact that Nelson Porter, a street-smart gang-banger, was lured late at night to the football field, probably by someone in an authoritative position, with a badge, gave Jackson more opportunity. Porter must have seen the cop's car around the city, recognized Jackson from the streets and knew something was up when he saw her vehicle parked outside his house. Street gangs were always on the lookout for cops.

Being a detective with access to the police scanner and having friends on the force, Jackson would've been following the investigation and found out about Porter's nine-one-one call and intercepted that dispatch.

Charlene knew she had something, but did she have enough to direct her investigation towards one of LAPD's own?

The day-workers' shift had ended, and Charlene knew that Henry would be gone. It helped that a rookie would be manning the night log book.

Charlene approached the front desk, where a prematurely balding twenty-something year-old was texting on an iPhone.

"What's her name?" Charlene interrupted his finger-tapping.

He looked up. "What?"

"The girl you're texting. What's her name?"

The kid's face reddened.

"Don't worry," she said and winked. "Your secret is safe with me."

He smiled at her. She had him.

"I need you to look something up for me." She gave him the dates and asked him to print out the names of everyone on duty from this precinct.

The kid didn't ask questions, just quickly put down the iPhone and performed his duties.

Charlene checked if Jackson had been working the night of Anderson's murder and she hadn't. Then she checked the night that Nelson Porter had been killed, again to find that Jackson was off. This meant that both nights she didn't have a partner looking over her shoulder.

"Thanks."

Charlene headed back to her desk, thinking about what she could do next that wouldn't raise any red flags.

She needed an ally, someone with the balls or authority to influence this hunch. She couldn't go to the captain yet. She didn't have enough to warrant an investigation into an LAPD detective.

She called Larry at home.

"I don't think Sarah Crawford was our shooter."

Larry choked on what he was drinking. "I have a hole in my arm that says different."

"It's a flesh wound, Larry."

"Fuck you, Taylor. This is a legitimate injury. Who knows when I'll return?"

Charlene rolled her eyes. "Anyway, I mean the Anderson shooter. I think I know who it was."

"Whoa, whoa, Taylor," the drama was about to begin and Charlene prepared herself. "First, you get me shot because you're certain Ashley Stanley's the killer. Now you tell me you could be wrong and want my help?" he said with heavy sarcasm.

Charlene sighed audibly, and then told Larry what she had on Jackson.

"Those are some heavy accusations."

"I know. That's why I need you." Charlene might as well grease him up, but it wasn't her style.

Larry's hesitation told Charlene that he was thinking it over.

"Okay, first thing you need to do is find someone new to the department, someone who hasn't been around long enough to know the shit storm this will cause and doesn't have too many friends to backstab. Someone you can trust."

"And who might that be?"

"Brady."

"Darren?"

"He's perfect. He doesn't have any friends anyway and he'd love a chance to sniff your panties a little longer."

"Do you think Darren would help me nail an LAPD detective? The LAPD is his whole world."

"Tell him there's a blow job in it for him."

"Good idea."

"Taylor, I was just kidding…"

Charlene hung up.

LAPD policy required detectives to always work in pairs. Even though this wasn't official business, Charlene realized that having someone with her would help answer questions when they came up later…and they would.

Darren wasn't at his desk when Charlene went to get him. She knew he still lived with his parents and looked up the number and address in the database. She called from the car.

Darren was waiting on the front step when Charlene pulled into the driveway of a rundown brick bungalow. With a toothy grin and in plain clothes, the young cop leapt into the passenger's seat.

"Where we off to?" he asked.

"Surveillance."

"Finally, some real action."

Charlene had already looked up Jackson's address. After the divorce, Jackson had moved into an apartment near the end of East Third Street, past Indian Street, a major east-west thoroughfare.

Charlene parallel parked at the curb on the opposite side of the street, a hundred yards down from Jackson's residence, near the intersection of South Lorena Street.

There were a couple of kids on the sidewalk, performing tricks on homemade skateboard-ramps. The teenagers never gave the cops a second glance, but Charlene realized they could create a problem.

Jackson's car was parked across the street from the building.

After ten minutes, Darren said, "You gonna tell me what's going on? Who are we watching?"

"A possible suspect."

"What case?"

"Anderson."

Darren's eyebrows arched. "I thought that was closed?"

"I've reopened it."

Darren smiled. "Does the boss know?"

Charlene let out her breath. Time for some trust, which wasn't easy for her. She told him what she suspected and what she could confirm. Darren listened without interrupting.

When she was finished, he said, "Cool, dirty cop. Just like the movies."

Charlene rolled her eyes and prayed Darren didn't blow this.

"So what do you want to listen to?" Darren asked, fiddling with the stereo knob.

"I don't care," Charlene replied, not looking away from Jackson's apartment building.

Charlene couldn't see herself sitting in the car for long with Darren. She'd go stir crazy and want to choke him.

"We need to get Jackson out of the apartment."

Darren shrugged and sat back. "Why don't you call something in?"

"What do you mean?"

"We both know the type of person she is. Jackson is controlling. She needs to be involved."

"Good thinking."

Charlene spotted a payphone, which are rare, and placed a fake call reporting a possible rape. She felt bad doing it, but knew that Jackson would be hell-bent to respond.

She gave an address close enough to Jackson's apartment to entice the detective and make Charlene's phone booth location seem more reliable, but far enough away that Jackson would be gone long enough for Charlene to search the apartment.

Charlene got back into the car and waited.

"Think she bought it?" Darren asked.

Before Charlene had time to answer, Jackson sprinted from the building, slinging her jacket over her shoulder. The detective jumped into her car and sped off, fishtailing and almost colliding with an oncoming vehicle.

Charlene grabbed the car door handle. "Let's go. We might not have long."

She crossed the street with Darren close behind. She caught a break when a man was coming out of the building when they got there. She sidestepped to avoid him and then gently wedged her foot between the door and frame, keeping it from locking.

They stepped inside. There were no other people around. She approached a line of mailboxes and buzzers, reading the names on the mail slots. Jackson's hadn't been updated but Charlene already had the number.

"Okay, Darren, I'm going up to the apartment. Here is my phone with Jackson's number already punched in. You wait outside. If she comes back, hit send and let it ring twice, then hang up. Got it?"

"Got it. Call, ring twice, hang up. I'm not an idiot."

"The jury is still deliberating."

"What if Jackson has caller ID and sees your number?"

"Shit, good point. I never thought of that."

"I have them once in a while."

She thought about it. "Do you have your phone?"

He nodded.

"Here's my number and don't get any ideas. Call it if you see her. I'll keep it on vibrate not to raise alarms to her neighbors."

She headed for the staircase.

A warrantless search was illegal, but Charlene knew that not a judge in California would grant her one on what she had.

She took the stairs to the third floor, avoiding elevators and cameras.

Charlene rapped lightly twice on the door to make sure no one was there. She wasn't sure if Jackson had a roommate or a lover. When no one answered, she snapped on a pair of gloves and ran her hand around the door frame and lifted up the camouflage door mat looking for a hidden key. It was common knowledge that most cops were less cautious than the average public. No key.

She pulled out a tiny, steel device and worked the lock on Jackson's door. It took less than a minute to gain access to the apartment. Like most cops, Jackson didn't have much of a security system, a standard lock with no alarm.

Charlene let herself in and closed the door gently. She stood and listened, making sure again that Jackson didn't have someone inside. She followed the front hall, checking the perimeter and taking an extra minute to scan the one bedroom apartment. Everything was in perfect order—unbelievably clean and well managed, almost unused. Even the bed sheets were drawn tight with military corners.

Charlene was heading back to the bedroom when a sound from the kitchen almost emptied her bladder. She followed the noise and found a police scanner plugged in on the counter. So that's how Jackson was always one step ahead.

She started in the bedroom and hit pay dirt.

When the detective opened the bi-fold closet doors, she found a stash of weapons hanging neatly, individually placed and fastened to the wall. No shelves or drawers with clothes and shoes, only guns.

She quickly took inventory, moving from weapon to weapon, but didn't see a nine mil. If Jackson had used it on Anderson, then it was conceivable that she'd discarded the evidence. But Charlene knew Jackson. The weapon was part of her arsenal and Jackson was just arrogant enough to think she'd never be caught or even suspected.

With the closet a dead end, Charlene searched rapidly but methodically, inspecting the rest of the bedroom. She turned the bed, checked the laundry hamper and went through drawers, careful to replace everything as she'd found it.

She checked behind the toilet and under the sink, moved to the tiny kitchen, checking the fridge and freezer and then into the den. She found an old wooden chest with rusted hinges at the end of the sofa. It had been covered by a ratty blanket. Charlene removed the blanket and opened it.

The chest contained stacks of photo albums but no gun.

With the rest of the apartment already checked and no sign of the murder weapon, Charlene lifted out the photo albums and gently set them on the coffee table. There wasn't a speck of dust on any of them.

She was about to open them when the phone rang. She froze, staring at the portable on the coffee table, perspiration specking her forehead and upper lip. Had Darren forgotten? The phone reached three rings and when the answering machine picked up Charlene heard Adrienne's partner, Bobby Johnson's voice.

"Hey, Ade, just checking if you've heard from Homicide. Let me know."

Charlene quickly leafed through the books. She found old black and white photographs of who must have been Jackson's grandparents and mother when they were children. No pictures of her father or his family.

She saw a young Adrienne Jackson participating in events, playing with other kids and as Charlene thumbed through the first album, she watched Jackson grow from a small, innocent pigtailed girl, to a pimple faced teenager and then to the adult she was now.

Charlene's attention was interrupted by footsteps in the hallway. She left the album open on the table and gingerly moved towards the front hall. She saw the shadows of two feet, through the crack under the door, stop just outside Jackson's apartment.

Had Darren forgotten to call? There was always a chance that Jackson had someone else living there, who Darren didn't know, and they were now returning.

An anxious moment passed. Charlene tried to stay as quiet as possible. The feet hesitated in front of the door and then continued down the hall. Charlene shook her head and returned to the chest.

She anxiously flipped through the second album. Charlene scrolled through newspaper clippings from Jackson's father's entire trial, from arrest, to first testimony, to final sentencing. There was a picture of a younger Jackson on the stand.

As Charlene read on, she found other clippings from rape trials, infamous names that Charlene recognized, men who had become celebrities because of *Court TV*, whose trials were covered by the national media.

Charlene studied the clippings, wondering if Jackson sat up at night, alone, reliving these nightmarish stories through the clipped articles. Did she live with her inner demons, and was it these articles that motivated her, kept her striving until every monster on the streets was erased?

Was Anderson her first or were there others?

She found Anderson's murder file and articles in another book, on the first page. Unless there was another book not there, this was her first victim and Jackson had bought a separate book, planning to fill the pages.

Charlene felt sick to her stomach. Jackson was a deeply disturbed individual who needed help. Charlene was outraged that a fellow officer, an unscrupulous LAPD detective, would try to take the law into her own hands.

But wait. *I'm doing the same thing with my dad's case.* That was different, she told herself.

Charlene replaced the albums in the same order. She made sure that everything was in place and left the apartment, locking the door on the way out. She took the elevator down to the main floor and found Darren on the sidewalk, showing the teenagers a couple of tricks on the skateboard. They were high-fiving each other when Charlene exited the building. So much for staying inconspicuous and out of sight.

"Let's go," she said.

Chapter 29

Back at the department, they sat at Charlene's desk.

"You mean that's it?" Darren asked.

Charlene put up her finger. "Let me think."

There was one other possibility, but it was a long shot. If the gun wasn't there, then she'd have to tail Jackson and hope the detective led her to it. But that was like a Hail Mary.

The precinct was quiet. Except for a few stragglers writing out daily reports and conducting interviews, the building was empty.

Charlene jumped to her feet with Darren right behind. She approached the front desk where the same freckle-faced officer was still on his iPhone.

"I've forgotten the combination to my gym lock. What should I do?"

The young officer looked annoyed. "You'll have to wait and get it tomorrow when HR opens up."

"But I need in there now."

"Then you'll have to call someone to come in and open it."

Charlene sighed. "You don't have an electronic swipe key?"

The officer nodded, looking back down at his iPhone and laughing at a text he'd just received.

"I do, but I don't have authority to let you in."

"Listen, Officer Austin." Charlene read the pin on his shirt. "Do we really want to call one of your superiors at six o'clock on a Friday night to come in, because you're too busy texting to let me in?"

He looked back at her and slipped the phone into his pocket. "I guess not."

"All I need is my combination. That's it."

Now it was the officer's turn to sigh. "Fine."

He led them to Human Resources, and using his swipe key, let them in.

"Thanks," Charlene said as she shut the door and left the two men outside.

She hustled across the lobby to the filing cabinet. She knew that security cameras videoed every part of the office, but she had the excuse of needing her lock combination, which happened to be in the same cabinet as Jackson's.

She found the code easily, as well as Jackson's locker number, and let herself out. Darren was by himself when she exited.

"Get what you need?" he asked.

Charlene nodded.

They took the stairs up to the Rape Special Section department. Charlene had Darren wait outside the woman's change room, to knock for a warning. There weren't many women on the force, and Charlene hadn't seen anyone in the lobby.

She entered the locker room, checked the aisles, but saw no one. She didn't hear running water, the showers were all off, and after checking the stalls, determined she was alone.

A breach of department security.

Charlene entered the three numbered code and the lock unfastened. She opened the squeaky, steel locker and found the inside unusually neat, almost military style. Jackson's uniform, freshly dry cleaned, hung neatly on the hangers, her shower kit and other bathroom facilities were lined perfectly, side by side, on the top shelf, and workout clothes were folded and placed neatly on the locker floor. Freshly shined shoes rested on top of the folded clothes.

Charlene delicately removed the contents. At the bottom of the locker, hidden underneath the piled workout gear, was a Smith & Wesson, nine millimeter semi-automatic. The smell of fresh oil told Charlene that the weapon had been recently cleaned.

She gently picked up the gun by the barrel and set it on the bench. Then she replaced the other items and shut the locker, replacing the lock. When she walked out, Darren was standing at the door, talking with another officer. He saw the gun and smiled, saying nothing. The colleague nodded, smiled and walked away.

"What was that about?" she asked.

"Nothing. Is that it?"

Charlene shrugged. "Let's find out."

Charlene felt her pulse and breathing slow to a normal pace when she'd left the building, the gun bagged and tucked safely away.

She called Dana and told her she was on the way over.

Once they had parked, Charlene practically jogged across the lot and into the Hertzberg-Davis Forensic Science Center. Inside the building, they speed-walked past the Criminal Justice main office and took the elevator to the fifth floor.

They found Dana, in her white lab coat, hairnet, safety goggles, gloves, and surgical mask, in the Trace Evidence Section of the lab examining a swab through a microscope. Charlene waited for the technician to make eye contact.

Dana looked up, turned off the scope light, and removed her rubber gloves. Then she removed the rest of her gear and walked over.

"What's up, Char?"

"Do you have any pull with Forensics?" Charlene asked.

"A little," Dana replied with a wink.

Charlene was the only one who knew that Dana was seeing a guy from the Forensics Unit. The LAPD frowned upon inter-departmental relationships. Darren stood back and said nothing, but Charlene noticed him examining Dana's breasts.

"Do you want the microscope, Darren?" Charlene asked.

Darren looked up quickly, his face reddening.

"What do ya need?" Dana asked.

"I need this tested with the bullets pulled from Anderson." Charlene handed the bagged weapon to Dana.

"Is that the murder weapon?"

"Not sure."

"When do you need it by?"

"Yesterday."

Dana grimaced. "Oh boy."

"What's wrong?"

"Derek will lecture me about how other cases take precedence. He has already been complaining about the ever-growing back log. Detective Mitchell has been breathing down his neck about the Adams case." Dana smiled. "I guess I'll just have to offer him something in return that he can't refuse."

"That's my girl. I'll be at my desk. And Dana, don't log the test."

Dana didn't question Charlene.

As Charlene and Darren turned to leave, Charlene felt a sharp elbow jab her side. She turned back towards Dana who mouthed the words, "He's cute."

Dana winked. Charlene rolled her eyes and walked away.

Back at her desk, time passed and silence engulfed them. She was a bundle of nervous energy. She understood that these things took time, but Charlene couldn't stand the waiting. She could have used a drink.

She did anything she could to pass the time—read the sports section, did a Sudoku, doodled on a pad, and watched Darren.

He pulled a tiny mirror from his pocket and checked his hair. Maybe it was Dana's comment, but, for the first time, Charlene noticed he wasn't a bad looking guy.

Darren read from an Archie comic, looked at reports, and quietly wrote notes down in his pocket notebook. His handwriting was impressively neat for a man.

She could hear his phone vibrate constantly, and when he checked his alerts, found that he was on a Hollywood entertainment site.

When there was a noise at the door, they both turned anxiously. Dana strode in, carrying the gun.

Charlene got up and met her half way. "What did you find"?

"It's a match. We tested the bullets pulled from Anderson, and after conducting several tests, we found, without a doubt, the bullets were fired from this gun. Forensic evidence doesn't lie." Dana handed the bag to Charlene. "I'll let you label it."

Charlene felt a surge of blood to her temples. "Thanks, Dana. I owe you one."

"Actually, that's two now."

Dana handed Charlene the report.

"Hey, Dana, if anyone asks, this didn't happen."

Dana smiled. "I figured as much."

When Dana disappeared, Darren asked, "What now?" His voice was animated.

"We put the weapon back."

"What? We can't do that. It's evidence."

"Yes, Darren, illegally obtained evidence. It'll never hold up in court."

Darren seemed to sag. "So what do we do?"

"I'm not sure. I have to put this back. Then I'll think of something."

After replacing the gun, Charlene sat at her desk, unsure of her next move. She had everything she needed on Jackson, but how could she make it legal. She still didn't have enough legally obtained information to obtain a search warrant. Or did she? Everything was circumstantial.

Darren couldn't sit still, which annoyed Charlene and disrupted her concentration. He constantly checked his appearance in a mirror.

She called Larry. "I'm stuck."

"You think you have problems. Mary-Anne is drivin' me nuts. She won't leave my side and she thinks I smell like smoke. And I haven't had one since I got shot. I'm under constant, twenty-four-hour surveillance and I can't sneak away."

Charlene told Larry everything she'd found since she'd last spoken with him.

Larry grunted. "And now you don't know what to do with it."

"Exactly."

"Let me make a couple of calls. Sit tight."

Charlene sat at her desk, rereading Jackson's profile.

Jackson had been involved from the start. If Margaret Connors' rape had been filed and Jackson had signed off on the case, Charlene would have discovered her involvement from the beginning. But as circumstance happens, Jackson was a silent player.

Anderson's rape of Margaret Connors set off a chain of events that had spiraled out of control.

When her phone rang, Charlene picked up after half a ring. "Hello?"

It was Larry. "You got your search warrant, Kid."

"How'd you do it?"

"Never mind, it's done. Should be getting to you any second now. Signed, sealed, and delivered." She could sense Larry's smugness through the phone.

As if on cue, the department fax machine chimed and spit out a piece of paper. Charlene set the receiver down and retrieved the fax, reading it over on the way back to her desk.

"Thanks, Larry."

"Keep me posted. I'd like to be there when you nail Jackson, but that won't happen."

Charlene let a few silent seconds go by before catching her breath. "Hey, Larry?"

"Yeah, Kid?"

"About last night."

"No need, Kid. That's what partners do."

She smiled and her eyes started to tear. She swiped at them and looked around the office to make sure no one was watching.

"I need to say it."

But Larry was adamant not to let Charlene put herself in a situation of desperation. "I know, Kid. You want to thank me, but there is no need. You would have done the same thing for me."

"No, it's not that." She paused before continuing. "I was just going to say that…you move pretty fast for a fat ass." Charlene smirked.

"Fuck you, Taylor. Now go nail that bitch!"

Charlene hung up, still smiling, and immediately dialed the captain's cell number.

She told him everything from her initial suspicions to obtaining the search warrant, excluding her illegal searches.

Silence ensued as the captain took in everything he'd just heard. He sighed audibly.

"Make it happen. I'm on my way in."

Chapter 30

Extensive prep was needed, but by eight o'clock, they were ready to take down Jackson.

With the captain's blowback warnings ringing in her ears and because the department's dirty laundry would be a city-wide affair, there had been a number of calls to make—superiors, colleagues, CSI, the DA, and anyone else who needed to be around for the arrest, investigation, and interrogation.

With the captain looking over her shoulder, Charlene ordered an eight-man unit at the scene. She had a CSI member use the warrant to clean out Jackson's department locker and another one to join her at Jackson's apartment. She gave strict instructions that no one use their unit radio and no police reports on scanners.

The car was parked down the street among a row of cars so as not to stand out. Charlene didn't like the way they were scrunched in.

She sat in the passenger seat. Darren, who had helped in finding the evidence against Jackson, was in the driver's seat and the CSI tech sat in the back.

Charlene had two undercovers posted outside the front of the apartment building, two covering the back exits, and another two men planted inside, one in the lobby and one on Jackson's floor.

There had been no reports or sightings of Jackson and there was no telling how long this stakeout might last. Darren looked as if he might burst at the seams from sitting that long.

Darren must have seen Charlene fidgeting and biting her lip for the last hour.

"What's wrong," he asked.

"I don't know. It doesn't feel right."

"What do you mean?"

"Darren, we're about to bust another cop for murder. How do you think this will go down? We won't be looked at the same again in the department."

He put his hand on top of Charlene's to stop it from shaking. "You're doing the right thing."

"I hope you're right."

Thirty minutes passed with no sign of Jackson.

"What if she doesn't come home tonight?" Darren asked.

"Then we wait all night," Charlene replied.

Darren exhaled forcefully, and the techie in the back moaned under his breath.

"There she is." Charlene nodded towards a dark-colored, 2004 Ford Taurus slowly moving towards them. The same make and model Jackson had on record.

All three of them ducked down slightly when Jackson passed.

Because they were now ducked down, Charlene had to adjust the rearview mirror to see behind her. "There's no underground parking so Jackson must be looking for a place to put the car for the night."

Jackson pulled past the building about a hundred yards before finally finding a spot. They watched her parallel park, get out of her car, and use the remote to lock it.

Charlene spoke into her radio. "We'll wait for Jackson to get into her apartment before taking her. Stand down."

There was also the chance, since Jackson was familiar with the precinct, that the detective might recognize a face or vehicle.

Charlene had had a brief discussion with her captain on the best way to handle it. Because of Jackson's reputation and stellar record with the department, as a professional and personal courtesy, the captain told Charlene to do it with as little noise and exposure as possible. But to Charlene, the captain's decision had more to do with the media this would attract.

They watched Jackson walking towards the building then she stopped in midstride.

"What's she doing?" Darren asked.

Charlene didn't answer, but continued to watch using both the side and rear view mirrors.

Jackson pulled a phone from a clip on her belt and brought it to her ear.

"Suspect got a phone call," one of the undercover cops outside the building reported to Charlene.

With the phone still tucked to her ear, Jackson started to gaze around the area. Charlene could see the detective's lips moving, but had no way of knowing what was being said.

Just then, Charlene could have sworn that Jackson looked right at the parked car, hidden amongst a group, almost making eye contact with Charlene through the mirror, before the Rape detective pocketed the phone, turned and took off in a sprint.

"We're so busted," said Darren.

"Shit!" Charlene already had her hand on the door handle. "We have a runner."

She knew that by the time Darren pulled the car from the curb and turned it around Jackson could be gone. So Charlene's only instinct was to run.

"Try to cut her off, Darren."

It took Charlene only seconds to exit the car and hit top speed, her legs pumping hard like a trained sprinter. She didn't need to radio her team because they were already moving like a pack of wolves.

Although Charlene was in good shape from her years of hardcore running, she knew that Jackson worked just as hard in the gym, and with the lead Jackson had, there was no way Charlene would catch her outright. She had to strategize and try to anticipate Jackson's route.

At the next corner, while her colleagues continued straight through the stop light, Charlene weaved to the right, and flowing against traffic on Lorena Street, tried her best not to bump into the crowd on the sidewalk.

She had her badge out as she ran, hoping that it would cause pedestrians to open up a free lane for her. She had hit a nice pace, her arms and legs moving in unison, sweat beads pelting her face. She could feel her shirt dampen, and even though her legs began to tingle, her pace never slowed.

As she hit the next corner, she could hear a rush of excitement from a crowd of people, screams and bellows. Charlene dropped her head and raced towards the cries.

At the next corner, she heard honking horns and sirens. Bursts of static hung on her radio as her team revealed Jackson's location, trying to stay one step ahead of the suspect.

Then, over the heads of the upcoming crowd, Charlene spotted Jackson, who was sprinting full tilt towards the same corner. It was as if they were on a collision course. Charlene gritted her teeth and took a deep breath.

Timing it just right, they hit the corner at the same time. Charlene threw herself headfirst into Jackson, her shoulder crunching Jackson's side, just above the hip bone. The force of the jar sent both women reeling, hitting the ground upon impact.

Adrienne was barely able to pull herself up, and Charlene got to her feet as well.

"It's over, Detective," Charlene said.

Jackson smiled. Her teeth and lips bloodied from Charlene's shoulder check.

Before Charlene could say anything else, Jackson pounced on her like a panther, clawing and ripping at Charlene's skin. Charlene brought up her arms to shield her face, but Jackson was out of control, like a shark smelling blood.

The pedestrians on the sidewalk had all stopped and were watching the two women trying to tear each other apart.

Jackson went for Charlene's eyes, trying to dig her fingernails into Charlene's sockets, but Charlene was able to block the attempt and flip Jackson over her, both women landing hard on the concrete ground.

Jackson jumped back to her feet, spurred on by what seemed like a rage erupting from deep within. Charlene, sore and aching, still sitting on the ground, was able to reach her ankle holster and pull her secondary weapon.

But before she could aim the small caliber weapon, Jackson had already turned to run. As she bounded into the oncoming traffic, the Rape Detective was cut down at the waist by a speeding motorist.

Jackson flew into the windshield of the Jetta, before flipping up onto the roof and then rolling off the back. The accident caused another as vehicles screeched to a halt, the smell of burnt rubber permeating the LA air. The white Volkswagen now had a red strip down the middle, smeared in Jackson's blood.

Charlene ran to Jackson, who was curled up, lifeless on the road. Charlene carefully rolled Jackson onto her back, using her jacket to prop up her head.

Jackson opened her mouth and then closed it. Blood from internal bleeding curled out between her lips.

"Don't move, Adrienne," Charlene said.

"You're making a mistake, Detective," Jackson mumbled between tight lips. "Who else will stop these scumbags?"

Charlene didn't respond. She looked down at Jackson, knowing that the pity and pain showed in her face. Jackson managed to smile again.

"Men like Anderson need to be stopped. The victims deserve justice," Jackson coughed out. "Who is going to do that, the legal system? Prison doesn't change these guys, they can't be rehabilitated. It only makes them hungrier."

"What about Sarah Crawford and Nelson Porter?" Charlene asked.

Jackson looked genuinely concerned. "Crawford was a killer." Jackson grimaced as she spoke. She coughed out a speck of blood. "Porter was collateral damage," she said. "He got in the way."

Charlene felt sick to her stomach. She didn't want to talk anymore.

Jackson closed her eyes and never moved again.

Charlene waited until an ambulance arrived, although by that time there was nothing they could do. Before they wheeled Jackson into the vehicle, Charlene unclipped Jackson's cell phone. She scrolled through the incoming calls and dialed the number from the last incoming call.

It was answered immediately.

"Did you make it?"

Charlene recognized the voice. "Detective Johnson?" she said, but the call was immediately disconnected.

So it had been Jackson's partner, Robert Johnson III, who had called to tip off the detective. She considered writing that into her report, but doubted she could prove it, as the phone conversation was never recorded and it was his word against hers.

Charlene slumped her shoulders and put Jackson's phone in her jacket pocket.

By the time she got back to Jackson's apartment building, three patrol cars were blocking the entrance and six uniforms were standing around, smoking and talking.

She approached the group as they turned. Some nodded, others never made eye contact. She had just played a major role in the death of another cop, and there was no telling what the reaction would be.

The adrenaline that had once coursed through her was gone. She was tired. "Make a call and have Detective Jackson's car towed to the lab," she said to the group.

She took the elevator upstairs and entered Jackson's apartment. The area was full, everyone doing their job.

As she floated in a dream-like state through the apartment, she saw that Jackson's old wooden chest was open and the albums were spread out on the table. It was as if Jackson had been waiting for them, or maybe reliving her nightmare.

Charlene sat alone at the end of the bar, sipping at her third Jack and Coke, this one a double. She ached in muscles she didn't even know she had.

Darren had offered to join her, almost begging to have a drink together, but Charlene, although tempted and told Darren that, had declined.

She remembered the hurt in his eyes, knew it took all the gall he had to ask her out. She had tried to let him down easy, told him she didn't get involved with cops, but she knew that she had still wounded him.

She took another healthy drink from her glass and tried to wash away Darren's pitied eyes.

Normally a drink soothed the pain, but tonight's round hurt.

After all was said and done recovering the evidence against Jackson, legally, enough to obtain what the DA thought would have been a guilty verdict, then the CSI team combing Jackson's apartment, car, and locker, finding not only Anderson's murder weapon, but also the weapon that was used to kill Nelson Porter, Charlene had left the office.

While she was on her death bed, Jackson had never tried to deny the accusations. She was a stone. Her words wouldn't leave Charlene's thoughts.

Jackson saw herself as an avenging angel.

As the lead investigator with the Rape Special Sections, CAW—Crimes against Women—with the LAPD, Jackson had opportunity and access to all of the information on both victim and suspect. She'd already compiled a list of DSOs—Dangerous Sexual Offenders—a "hit list" of her own.

Charlene thought about how Jackson had manipulated the Anderson case from the start, guided Charlene and Larry in the direction she needed. Dropping hints along the way, like Stanley's name, in just an unsuspecting way, had been brilliant. And Charlene had bit on it.

She drained what was left of her drink and ordered another.

When all the evidence came into play—the female hair fibers found on Anderson matched a sample from Jackson, the scrap books, Jackson's past, her involvement throughout and finally the murder weapons—not a jury in the world would have acquitted her.

But how would they have reacted to a cop? Would they have been lenient to someone who had been loyally protecting this city? Would they have taken pity on a woman who had been abused herself and was trying to exact revenge for women across the city? Or would they see a cop, someone who was in an authoritative position, abusing her power?

LAPD techies had gone through Jackson's computer files and had found a short list of suspected rapists who had eluded justice. Jackson had a hidden agenda and a plan.

Maybe Jackson thought that what she was doing was the right thing by bringing down evil. Charlene felt a pang of guilt, because Jackson, in her own, albeit illegal, way, was trying to help the women who had been affected by these individuals.

But Jackson was dangerous. She had the trained skills, the means and the opportunity. She had everything to be the perfect weapon. A cop with ulterior motives—a personal vendetta.

She looked around the sparsely occupied barroom. From the row of bikes parked in front, she thought she recognized her stalker's motorcycle, but she didn't see his face amongst the crowd.

Charlene was beginning to feel the buzz she'd longed for when she saw Andy walk through the front entrance. He looked at her but didn't smile, making his way over.

She watched him cross the room and he was about halfway when Charlene's iPhone rang. She saw an LA area code number displayed that she couldn't place. She answered the call, still looking at Andy.

"Good job, Charlie," the voice said. "Detective Jackson had to be stopped."

Charlene gulped, bile rising in her throat. "What do you want?" Andy was now standing beside her.

"I thought he was out of the picture?" The Celebrity Slayer paused and then added, "We're not done yet."

She felt her blood rise. Charlene left the barstool, staggering before gaining her balance by grasping the rail. She walked by Andy who gave her a stunned look.

"Where are you?" Charlene asked into the phone. She covered her bare ear with her hand, desperately attempting to discern the background noises on the phone.

"Never very far," answered the Slayer.

Charlene was looking around the bar, trying to notice if anyone else was speaking into a phone. But, of course, there were numerous people—a well-dressed woman in her mid-forties by the pool table, a man by the bar who looked barely legal enough to drink, and a waitress on her break.

Anyone on a phone in the bar could potentially be the Celebrity Slayer, but none of them fit the profile.

Then an idea popped into her mind. Because this was the first time a number had appeared on her phone from one of the Slayer's calls, she hung up. She knew that would irritate him.

She immediately redialed the last incoming call and looked around the room for someone's phone to ring. When she didn't notice anyone reaching for a cellular device and no one answer on the other end of her call, Charlene hung up.

The phone rang again suddenly, but instead of answering, she flipped off the ring tone and slipped it into her pocket, feeling the vibration through the thin denim. She was through playing his games. She was going to play her own.

Book IV

The Lone Ranger

Chapter 31

The department was buzzing when Charlene got to work later than usual the next morning. Her phone vibrated and, for the first time, she noticed she had eleven missed calls.

She didn't dare remove her sunglasses that were now saving her pupils from the bright light of day. She and Andy had stayed up late to talk things out.

She almost got knocked over on her way to her desk by a speed-walking Fed, as there were half a dozen FBI agents milling about the room and all of her superiors were huddled inside the captain's office. Something was up.

Larry was still off from the gunshot wound, so she flagged down Darren to find out what the ruckus was about.

When Darren got to her desk, she asked, "Is this about the Jackson case?" She finally removed her glasses and squinted from the fluorescent lights. Her headache thundered.

"You look like hell," Darren said.

"Darren!" Charlene let out her breath and motioned to all of the extra law enforcement scattered throughout the precinct.

"The Celebrity Slayer struck again last night. I think they have something."

His last sentence almost floored Charlene. She jumped from her seat and hustled over to the conference room where the special-agent-in-charge was preparing for a conference call.

"Detective Taylor," the AIC said. "We've been calling your cell phone all morning. You probably want to get in on this." He handed Charlene a thick, stapled package of papers.

Charlene accepted the photocopies and stepped into the 'incident' room, smelling fresh coffee, bagels and muffins. She poured herself a cup and grabbed the first available chair.

Once everyone was seated and fed, the meeting got underway. There were no introductions.

"Late last night we received a nine-one-one call from a concerned neighbor on Maple Avenue."

Charlene sipped gingerly at her coffee, her head spinning like a top. Her eyelids were half closed but when she'd heard the address, her eyes bulged. That was just around the corner from the bar she'd been at.

The AIC continued. "The woman was outside with her dog and was sure she'd heard screams from one of the large estates on her street. A black and white was sent to check it out but there was no response after multiple attempts at contact." He looked down at a report before continuing. "Officers Decker and Piper used the computer terminal in the car to look up the home owner and noticed it was a former B movie star, fitting the Celebrity Slayer's murder victim profile. That was enough for them to enter the home without a warrant."

"Invitation or probable cause?" Charlene asked.

The AIC looked at her captain, as if seeking verification. The captain nodded.

"Officers Decker and Piper noticed a drip of blood on the door knob," the AIC confirmed.

Charlene highly doubted that. In her mind, there was no way that the Slayer would make such a careless mistake, after so many perfect murders.

The AIC went on. "Our team set out like they've done for every scene, but this time we caught a break."

The AIC turned on a projector that was attached to a laptop, enlarging one of the images that were in Charlene's handout.

When Charlene saw the latest Celebrity Slayer victim, probably the most gruesome one yet, she felt last night's binge drinking come up. She caught it at the top of her throat and swallowed it back down.

"We found a partial fingerprint on the victim's left breast."

Charlene covered her mouth, as if that would stop the spewing. She quickly looked away, dropped her head beneath the tabletop, and inhaled three quick breaths.

"Are you okay, Detective Taylor?" the AIC asked without inflection. "Maybe you would like to step outside for some fresh air?"

Charlene looked back up, all eyes on her, especially her captain, who was now burning a hole through her.

Charlene cleared her throat loudly. "I'm fine."

"The print was quickly removed and brought back to the department for a run and retrieval through the AFIS database. And we hit pay dirt."

"Hold on," Charlene interrupted. "So you're telling me that this guy has been killing for months, hasn't left a hair follicle, scale of skin, fingernail, or even a thread of fabric and now he leaves a fingerprint?"

"That's what we're saying, Detective. Is there a problem?"

"I just find it hard to believe."

"Maybe you should see where this is leading before jumping to your own conclusions." He turned back to the group. "Let's move on."

Every member in the situation room collectively turned the page in their booklet, so Charlene did as well.

"The print belongs to Sean Cooney."

Charlene's head shot up. Sean Cooney? She'd heard that name before.

"I know that name," Charlene said. But before waiting for an answer, she buried her head in Cooney's bio, while the AIC highlighted the details out loud.

"Cooney is former LAPD and had been fingerprinted, that's why he already had a ten-print card in the system. He served twelve years—six as a patrol officer, four in Vice working undercover, and two in Robbery/Homicide. In fact, Detective Taylor, I believe your father and Cooney were partners for a while."

Charlene's stomach rolled and her chest tightened. She didn't look up from the paper but knew that all eyes were focused in her direction.

But no one seemed to expect a response from Charlene.

"During his twelve years," the AIC said, "he had multiple encounters with Internal Affairs. IA investigated him on counts of suspect beatings, illegal evidence removal, questionable interactions with criminals, and monetary income discrepancies. After so many accounts, the LAPD slowly pushed him out, starting with suspension for CUBO, until Cooney eventually transferred his pension and moved on. For the last twenty years, using the skills he learned on the force, Cooney has been head of security at the Armand Hammer Museum of Art and Culture Center at UCLA. When Cooney was still LAPD, rumor around the precinct had it that he was secretly dating a B-list movie star. It was never confirmed, and we don't know who she was, but she apparently broke his heart. This is his stressor and direct link to the Celebrity Slayer victims."

Charlene was thumbing through Cooney's LAPD stats and noticed that he had been her father's partner for eight months in 1998. Charlene couldn't ever remember her father talking about Cooney, so then how did she know the name?

"We know that ten years ago Cooney sold his home in Burbank and bought a hunt camp just outside the Santa Monica Mountains, known for its variety of wildlife. We don't have a current photo, just the one from his LAPD days."

Charlene looked at Cooney's head shot, in his LAPD blues. He had angular features, cords of muscle in his neck, and he'd been bald since the age of thirty.

The AIC went on to detail Cooney's last twelve hours, but Charlene was too focused on the material in her hand.

This just didn't feel like the guy, to Charlene. It was true, he fit the profile. And it was true her father had thought that a cop was involved in these murders. But the information she read wasn't what she was expecting. But what was she expecting?

"The tactical team has worked through the night to put a plan together for a crash raid on Cooney. We will move in when it's all set up."

Charlene had so many questions that she couldn't sort through them all in time to fire them at the group.

Was anyone else surprised that after all of these murders, the Slayer finally left a print? There was nothing else on this guy. What is his motive? Did he have opportunity?

It was as if this case was so huge, had a life of its own, that all of the standard questions that came up in a case were disregarded because the cops, media, and whole city had a hard-on to catch this guy. They finally had a lead.

Just then the AIC and captain's phones rang simultaneously. They both answered.

The AIC listened for less than a minute, hung up, and addressed the audience around the conference table.

"We're ready."

Darren was sitting on the edge of her desk when Charlene left the conference.

"What happened?" he asked.

"It's about to go down."

"I want to come," Darren insisted.

She knew she owed Darren from his work on the Jackson case and she was still too sore from her brawl with Jackson to drive. She threw him the keys.

"You drive."

Chapter 32

The Santa Monica Mountains, one of a group of mountain ranges in Southern California, was located along the coast of the Pacific Ocean and was just under an hour's drive from the LAPD Headquarters, which meant that Charlene would have enough time to bounce ideas off Darren.

"I just don't buy it," Charlene started. It was only she and Darren in the car and they were following a row of law enforcement officials trying to remain inconspicuous in regular morning traffic. "How could he mess up like this? He hasn't left a shred of evidence, and now he leaves a partial print? That's sloppy. Not his style."

Darren smirked. "You sound like a fan."

"I'm serious, Darren."

"You know as well as I do that even the greatest criminals mess up eventually. You've been to enough crime scenes to know that eventually luck runs out. Mistakes happen and it's our job to find them when they do."

Charlene shook her head, still not buying it. "Does this guy seem right to you?"

Darren shrugged. "He's a former cop, trained to kill. From his record, he has obvious anger issues, been known to become abusive. Never married, no kids. His former lovers have come forward and said that at times he could turn violent. He hates the LAPD. He has a high-status position of authority at work. Lives in a remote location, secluded from neighbors. Sounds like a hand-picked, Taylor-made candidate for the FBI profile. They must be gloating their asses off."

"I know, you're right. But I spoke to this guy on the phone. I have a feel for him."

"Geez, Charlene, it sounds like you have a thing for this guy. Like you almost hope he's not the guy."

Charlene grimaced. "It's not that. I don't know. I'm just tired."

"Late night?"

"More like early morning."

"Ouch. There's Advil in the glove box."

Charlene opened it and pulled out the bottle, noticing an older, slightly crumpled picture at the bottom of the compartment. Charlene, knowing Darren still lived at home, didn't want to embarrass him so she didn't mention it.

She opened the bottle and shook a couple into her mouth, dry swallowing the capsules.

"Maybe once you see this guy, his place, your mind will change."

"Maybe."

She still had the printout package on Cooney and filtered through it. "I had the sense from this case that the killer had been abused by a female power figure in this life. But there is no mention of any females in Cooney's life. Mother died of natural causes many years ago, he was never married and no mention of a current girlfriend or life partner. Sure he's had previous relationships, but nothing long-term."

"I think you've been watching too many *Criminal Minds* episodes. Not every killer is an archetype. But the FBI did mention that Cooney used to date a movie star."

"So they say." She pulled a paper from her jacket pocket and unfolded it. "That's where I've seen Cooney's name before."

"Where?" Darren asked.

"My father's notes. He had made a list of cops he thought could be possible suspects as the Celebrity Slayer. Cooney's name is on it."

"Can I see that?" Darren asked.

She handed him the paper and he placed it on the wheel, trying to read it as he steered. "Dr. Gardner is on here."

"I know"

He gave it back. "Now do you believe it's Cooney?"

"Maybe," she repeated resolutely, but she was far from sure.

Charlene turned away from Darren, looking out the window and admiring the beautiful California scenery. She could see why Cooney had left the city for the countryside.

As they left the smog-infested city, bypassing West Hollywood, passing Runyon Canyon Park and Universal City and hitting the 101, they passed the small Californian countryside Charlene never got to see.

It was very much Andy Griffith-Mayberry style, roadside farmland of everything she loved to eat from avocados to strawberries to garlic. When they veered off the main highway at Agoura Hills and left civilian life, that's when the beauty of the scenery really emerged.

They had established a meet site about a mile and a half from Cooney's mountain retreat. Darren pulled into the parking area behind the other vehicles, and Charlene exited the car before it had even come to a complete stop.

She wasn't allowed near the huddled members, but she could at least get as close as possible to hear and see the plan.

She stood behind an opened car door, holding the neck of her jacket tight. She hadn't been prepared for the bracingly cold wind that came off the ocean coastline as they moved closer to the mountains. The temperature had plummeted ten degrees since she'd left the office.

Through binoculars, Charlene inspected the cedar-shingled cabin. She didn't have a feeling either way this time.

Was that the killer's home? She wasn't sure.

They had moved in closer, now about five hundred yards from the unmarked dirt road to the small, well-built cabin.

The Feds and Tactical team leaders stood together, sipping coffee from a thermos. This was a one shot deal, maybe their only shot. LAPD SWAT had joined forces with the FBI Tactical Unit.

She could hear two of the SWAT members approaching the car. They stood shoulder-to-shoulder. One was holding heat sensor binoculars and the other had a FLIR—Forward Looking Infrared Radar—attached to a tripod.

"We don't see any signs of movement in the house."

A chain link fence surrounded Cooney's property, and SWAT had cut through it at multiple locations. They had a double perimeter set up around Cooney's camp, and inner and outer circles in case he made a run for it. The only vehicle Cooney had registered was a 1999 navy blue Ford f150 with twin exhaust pipes, and it was parked in front of the cabin.

"Do you think he's been tipped off?" the SWAT leader asked the Fed in charge.

"Never know. He still has some loyalty on the force. A lot of guys are still pissed off at how it all ended with him."

The SWAT leader put his hand to his mouth. "Take your positions. Cooney has three guns registered. A Blaser R93 German Hunting Rifle, a pump-action Remington 870, and a 9X19 mm Walther P99 Handgun. But he's a former cop, so he could be more heavily armed."

Charlene watched SWAT fan out to form an arc, moving into position. If she hadn't been looking for them, she would never have seen them camouflaged against the forest of trees and long grass. The Evasion and Search—E&S—tactics unit was ready to seize the cabin and take it over.

Charlene swept the binoculars over the house, a tingling sense of anticipation flooding her body. No movement. The wooden blinds on the first and second level were all closed.

She didn't notice herself holding her breath when the order was given.

"Move in."

Charlene scanned the remote area, watching the team moving in unison. She looked for any danger signs, anything out of place that could be considered a hazard. She kept her eyes trained on the cabin.

The unit, in combat crouches, crept towards the cabin. The division moved simultaneously, covering each other. The no-knock forced entry was all about timing and synchronization.

Half the team took the back of the building. They had the cabin surrounded. There was still no movement inside. The team was close now.

Then it was time.

Charlene gritted her teeth as they stormed the cabin. The front lock was quickly picked. The door was eased open, and still no sound from inside. She could feel her own adrenaline rush as members, one by one, slipped inside the cabin. Some of the unit went through the doors, others climbed through windows. There was SWAT on the ground, the roof, and inside the cabin. But still no shots were fired.

Charlene could hear the controlled chaos on the leader's transmitter. Rooms were cleared, voices shrilled, but still no gun shots. An inordinate amount of time had passed, and Charlene considered the limitless possibilities.

Radio bursts punctuated the air as each room was cleared, and the final radio cackled with a voice saying, "Cabin's clear. We've found a woman in the basement cellar."

It was over in less than a minute.

"Should we call in the EMTs?" the AIC asked into his mic.

"Don't bother. It's too late for that."

"Any ID?"

"Negative."

"Cooney?"

"Negative."

Everyone who had been waiting on the perimeter began to work their way towards the cabin. Charlene followed, anxious to see inside the lair of the Celebrity Slayer.

As she neared the hunt camp, Charlene's attention was drawn to the surrounding woods. There was something on one of the trees.

She called out to a uniformed officer who was heading to the cabin from the outer circle, "I'm going to check out that tree."

The officer turned and looked, and then turned back and shrugged. "Go for it."

She stared at the tree as she walked towards it, a shiver creeping up her spine. Clearly carved on the side of the tree were the letters SC. Cooney had whittled his initials into the bark. The sharp, jagged shaped lettering chilled Charlene to the bone.

She was turning back towards the cabin when out of the corner of her eye she spotted another tree, with more carvings.

She moved further away from the group and headed into the thicker brush, where someone had spent a lot of time brushing trail and wearing it down. There were footprints, which could have come from anytime, and evidence of an all-terrain vehicle.

This tree had the initials CH. Who was CH? A friend, a lover, a victim? Charlene ran her fingers over the letters, feeling the scratchy, rough wood surface.

Further down the path there was another tree, with even more initials. This time it read DB. Charlene wondered how many trees had been stamped. She went to the third tree and stared at the letters. It would be almost impossible to know who DB was. She would have to cross-reference the celebrity slayer victims with the carvings.

Charlene searched the surroundings and didn't notice any other carvings in the vicinity. She wasn't sure just how far from the scene she was. She couldn't see or hear any of the team.

It was eerily quiet. No animal noises, the sirens had faded, and there were no radio bursts. All she could hear was the rapid beat of her own pulse. The fine hairs on the back of her neck prickled.

"You're losing it, Char," she whispered.

As she turned to head back, Charlene felt a cool breeze blow down the back of her shirt, heard a soft thud behind her, and the ground around her feet vibrate.

She turned to find Cooney, hitting a three-point landing. He must have been in the tree. He was gripping a knife with a serrated blade. He sneered, homicidal rage on his face.

He was an imposing figure and looked nothing like the head shot she'd seen only hours earlier. He was broad-chested, his jaw covered by a thick red beard, and he was wild-eyed. A sheen of sweat peppered his face, and his tight T-shirt was pasted to his body.

As she was reaching for her gun, his strong bicep wrapped around her throat, blocking her air passage and lifting her off her feet.

She clawed and grasped at the camouflage-sleeve, scratching at his thick, hairy knuckles, drawing blood. She flailed her feet back and forth, kicking wildly, hoping to connect with a shin. Wrestling with all of her strength, she could feel her attacker's grip loosen just before a sharp rap on her skull drained her fight.

"Nice to see you, Charlene," his voice dripped contempt. It was the last thing she heard before the blackness surrounded her.

When she regained consciousness, she could feel herself moving, but knew she didn't have the strength to move her limbs. Struggling to open her eyelids, Charlene barely made out the brushy trail as she was being fireman-carried, hands tied behind her back, through the forest. She fought to stay conscious, trying to count seconds in her head, replaying images in her mind of the recent events. The pressure mounted on her skull and the pain numbed her senses.

The sun had gone down, cooling her warm cheeks. She wasn't sure how long she'd been out, or how far away from the camp she had gotten. It was a blur, a dream-like trance. The one thing she did know was that she wasn't going down without a fight. It was now all about self-preservation.

She didn't dare move suddenly or quickly change positions. She had to make her abductor believe she was still unconscious and not a threat.

Charlene tried to bend her body indiscernibly in a way that her hand could reach her ankle holster. It was getting there ever so slowly, and she thought that her movement hadn't been noticed. She was just inches away now, the end of her fingertips slowly pulling up the bottom of her pant leg. She was there and grabbed for the weapon, but it was gone. Cooney must have already snared it.

She remembered her phone in her pocket, but reaching in that direction would surely be noticed.

Charlene shrank back into her original position, her heart and hope dropping in the process.

She felt her carrier's pace slow and she sensed he was getting ready to stop. Before she had another thought, her body was flung violently onto the ground and then hauled up aggressively by the shoulders of her blazer.

Then she was pinned to a tree, feeling the sharp, rough bark against her back. She kept her eyes closed. She couldn't see, but could feel the killer's warm breath on her skin, his cigarette odor blowing in her nostrils.

The man spit, a snarl in his voice. "You can stop pretending, Detective. I know you're awake, your breathing has changed."

He grabbed her by the throat and squeezed, manipulating his thumb on her thyroid cartilage. When her eyes opened, she came face to face with a trained killer. Even behind the green and black camouflage face paint, there was no mistaking the eyes of Sean Cooney, the same man who had stared back at her from his picture in this morning's meeting.

When Cooney looked into her eyes, seeing the fear that lay there, he smiled and brought the large hunting knife to her throat. The knife was already stained with blood.

She noticed his nostrils flare as he smelled the air.

"I love the smell of fear on a woman."

His forehead was dotted with perspiration beads, and he licked his lips. He smelled like sweat, cigarettes, and cheap cologne.

"I wanted to kill you long ago but now I'm glad I didn't. I'm going to have a little fun first. I've done a lot of hunting in these parts, bobcats, gray foxes, coyotes, and even mountain lions. But hell, Charlene Taylor, you'll be my prize pig." He ran his free hand up her side, squeezing her breast and massaging it roughly.

She closed her eyes, grimaced, and turned away. Then she felt his mouth on her neck, his tongue making a trail up her cheek. He pulled her hair hard, trying to turn her head to face him, but she fought it, the muscles and veins in her neck bulging. He was too strong to fend off for long minutes.

He twisted her head painfully, holding her jaw in one hand, squeezing her cheeks to pucker her lips. With her eyes still closed, she could feel his lips touch hers and hold them there, his tongue darting in and out.

So Charlene did the only thing she could think of. She felt around for his bottom lip and when she found it, she bit down as hard as she could. Clenching her teeth viciously, she shook her head back and forth like a wild animal until she could taste blood. Cooney let out a yelp and pulled away, leaving part of his bottom lip lodged between Charlene's red-stained teeth. She opened her eyes to find a stream of blood leaking from Cooney's gaping mouth.

"You bitch!" he stuttered, bloody spit flying from the open wound. "You're going to pay for that."

He stepped forward quickly and threw a sharp right fist that she didn't have time to dodge. His callused knuckles struck her nose, and Charlene could hear cartilage crunch under the weight of the blow. Her eyes instinctively watered, blinding her.

"There," he said and chuckled. "Now that face has some *personality*."

He sheathed his knife and with strong hands, grabbed her by the shoulders, spinning her around and pressing her head into the bark-covered tree. He smashed her face into the rough wood. She could feel her skin scratch, the bark tearing into flesh and blood dripping a line down her neck. She could feel the broken bone in her nose move even further out of place as he applied more pressure.

She felt like screaming, but didn't want to give him the satisfaction of hearing her pain. She knew guys like Cooney got off on that. So she swallowed her panic.

When he finally let go, she turned her head away, taking three quick, staggered breaths to reduce the pain, keep from vomiting, and avoid more involuntary tears. The fight was almost completely out of her now, her adrenaline gone, the exhaustion settling into her weary bones.

But the break from her nightmare was short lived when a thin, leather strap was wrapped around the back of her neck, pulling her tightly against the tree as Cooney fastened it at the back. He removed one handcuff, then pulling her angrily against the tree, refastened it, her arms now hugging the tree. Then a second cord was thrown around her waist and fastened as well.

He moved back around her. She could no longer see him, but could hear his footsteps snapping branches. She took some pleasure in hearing him breathing hard, the wind whistling through the hole in his bottom lip, knowing that she had put up a valiant fight and had at least made him work for this kill.

"Let's have some fun," he whispered into her ear. He pulled the iPhone out of her back pocket and rammed it three times against the tree, shattering it to pieces. "We'll be here for a while."

Charlene tried to yell, wanted a scream to burst from her throat, but the strap was so tight around her that it almost cut off her air passage. She could feel her heart pounding against her rib cage.

Using the knife, he cut the back of her shirt down the middle and tore it from her upper body. Then he cut open her bra and snapped it off. The bark of the tree scratched at her breasts and torso. He unhooked her belt and pulled it out through the loops, then undid her pants and pulled them down to her ankles, her panties coming along with them. She was now fully naked, tied face-first to the tree.

He whistled. "Nice ass and tramp stamp. You're the kind of girl I've been waiting for." He spread her legs. "I'm going to have some fun with that. It's just you and me now, Charlene. No more interference. Besides, I heard that you like it rough."

Charlene swallowed hard, dread almost stealing her breath. She could feel beads of nervous sweat slip down the middle of her back. "Why me?" she asked in a voice that sounded like a child's.

"You were handpicked."

Charlene closed her eyes, the paralyzing pain heightening her senses. She heard his belt buckle dangle and metal zipper. When she felt his big hands grab her firmly by the hips, she bit her lip and said a silent prayer.

Her ears perked up, picking up something in the background and then she heard a pop.

Cooney released his grip.

"What…why?" She heard his voice, like a little boy, then a gurgling sound, as if someone was talking under water.

Another quick pop followed, echoing around her, and she heard a crumpled sound from behind. She couldn't turn her head, but could no longer hear the whistling of Cooney's breathing. Charlene's chest heaved.

Footsteps behind startled her and she felt a soft cloth draped over her naked shoulders.

With her face turned and still strapped to the tree, Charlene peered down and saw a short, thin shadow of a man on the ground. The man walked behind the tree and finally appeared in Charlene's line of site.

"You okay, Chip?"

Charlene was never so happy to see Darren. Then the lights went out again.

It was well after dark when she came to. Generators had been brought in and portable lights set up to better see the scene.

After he had freed Charlene and covered her, Darren had used his radio to call for help. The densely wooded area was now populated by half of the LA and Federal law enforcement units.

A sheet was draped over Cooney's body, and Darren was being put through the ringer by the investigative officers on the scene.

Charlene watched from a nearby stump where she sat while being examined by a young African-American EMT. She pulled her knees tight to her chest under her chin, shivering from the cold of the moment.

"We'll need to get you back to the hospital. That nose looks pretty bad. It's so far out of place that we might have to re-break it to set it. The bump on the top of your head and dilated pupils tells us that you could have a concussion. Expect some short-term memory loss from that."

"I want to see inside the cabin first," Charlene answered.

"Look, I think that your best bet is to go to the ER for—"

"The cabin first," Charlene stared at the EMT, who just shrugged.

"Whatever." The EMT left to pack up his things.

When she noticed Darren finally alone, he looked at her and she motioned him over.

"I guess you deserve a thank you," she said, although it didn't come easy for her.

Darren smiled and blushed. "You're welcome."

"How did you find me?" Charlene asked.

Darren shrugged his shoulders. "I was heading in behind you when the cabin had been cleared. I saw you detour and head towards the woods. I remember your instinct from the Jackson case, so I followed you."

Images of the scene came and went, but were relived in foggy detail. Seeing Cooney's initials, following the path, something coming down hard on the back of her head, being dragged through the forest, the confrontation, strapped to the tree. It all seemed so surreal now.

She checked her watch. She couldn't be certain because everything was a blur, but she could have sworn at least three hours had passed since her ordeal.

Darren must have seen Charlene check her watch. "I couldn't get to you any quicker. I had lost you at one point and then when I found you again, I had to wait for the perfect opportunity to strike, to get Cooney in a vulnerable position, the safest way for you too. I had to make sure you were out of harm's way before I countered."

Charlene nodded, although she was groggy and none of it made perfect sense to her at this point.

"I want to see Cooney's body," she said.

"Sure."

"You okay, Detective?"

Charlene looked up to find her captain standing behind her. She nodded. "I'll survive."

"Good. Get to the hospital and get checked out. We'll handle things on this end. Good work, Kid." He started to walk away and thought of something. "I called Detective Baker and told him what happened. He wants you to call him when you can."

"Sure, thank you, Sir."

Charlene checked her pockets and then remembered that Cooney had smashed her phone.

"Can I use your phone?" She extended her hand towards Darren and the officer handed it over.

"Can I get some privacy?" Charlene asked.

Darren nodded and backed away, turning to join a group that was hovering over Cooney's body.

She dialed Larry's number and he answered on the first ring.

"Hello?"

"Larry, it's Charlene."

"I tried to call your phone but you wouldn't pick up." Upon hearing her partner's grumpy voice, Charlene felt a warmth and coziness sweep over her. "You avoiding my calls?"

"I've been kind of busy."

Then his tone softened. "The captain called and filled me in. You okay?"

"I'll get by."

"Do you need anything from me?"

"No, Larry, I think I'll manage, until you can get back on your feet." But it felt good to hear him ask.

"Well, don't let this go to your head. Just because you stopped one of the most wanted serial killers in the history of the LAPD, don't let it inflate your ego."

She laughed, which hurt her whole body. "I'll try not to."

"Good, I'll be back soon. Remember, you're still number two. Great work, Kid."

"Thanks, Larry."

She hung up feeling better. She slipped the phone into her pocket and attempted to get up, which was a feeble effort.

Darren returned, holding two steaming cups of coffee. Charlene waved it off. "I want to see Cooney."

She placed a hand on Darren's shoulder for support and got to her feet. She felt like she was standing on rubber legs.

He took Charlene softly by the arm and helped her limp across the grounds. Every part of her ached as she slowly made her way to a blanket-covered Cooney, sprawled out on the cold forest floor.

Darren borrowed a flashlight from an on-scene officer. He knelt down and lifted off the blanket. Charlene remained standing and looked down.

"What happened to his lip?" Darren asked from his knees.

"Sharp incisors," Charlene said, with no hint of a smile in her eyes. She inspected Cooney.

Rigor mortis had set in. The bullet had pierced Cooney's throat. His blood-stained hands were still on his neck, and coagulated blood had gathered at the openings. Cooney had tried to stanch the bleeding by pressing his palms against the wound. That's why he'd only been able to sputter a few words before he started choking on his own blood. That was the gurgling sound she'd heard.

"Through the throat." Charlene noticed the bullet hole in the side of Cooney's neck. "Nice shot."

"Thanks. Lucky one. I had to go for the kill shot. Couldn't risk wounding him and having him pull a gun on you."

A second hole was between Cooney's eyes.

Charlene looked down on Cooney and didn't see a weapon or holster. She thought of the game of cat and mouse they'd been playing, and this was the conclusion. It was still hard to believe.

Standing over his dead body, she felt a cold resolve. Seeing Cooney now brought back a flood of memories from only moments ago and how close she'd come to death. Feeling lightheaded, she steadied herself against a tree.

"I want to see the camp," Charlene said.

"Look, Chip, the EMT said you need to get to a hospital."

"Darren, I don't think a broken nose, a bump on the head, and some scratches will put me in the ICU tonight. Do you?"

Darren didn't respond. They found an ATV and after receiving permission, headed back down the path towards the cabin.

The cabin had a funny dream-like quality when she entered. As she walked through the Celebrity Slayer's lair, she just couldn't pick up the sense of the Slayer's presence. It didn't feel like his style.

Maybe it was the fact that the cabin was overcrowded with professionals attempting to conduct searches and investigations. FBI, LAPD, CSI, SWAT, and anyone else they could find bunched into each room, taking inventory, dusting, collecting evidence, and doing whatever else they could to chip in. This was a big one.

There was barely enough room to move, and any form of contact sent a shock bolt of lightning pain through her whole system.

"Are you sure you're okay, Chip?" Darren asked for the fourth time. "You don't look good."

Charlene nodded as she entered another room. "I know the guy I talked to. Our conversations were personal, almost intense to the point of erotic. This furniture," she pointed around the inside of the camp, "it's so impersonal and plain."

"The FBI is calling Cooney a psychopath, so there probably is no rhyme to his reason."

The stripped wooden floors were badly scratched and the rustic cupboards were lined with old findings like kerosene lamps, tin pots, and hunting survival supplies. Dirty dishes were scattered across the counter and on an old white, two-burner stove.

They left the main floor and took a set of stairs down to the dank cellar. Charlene spoke as they moved. "And the way Cooney spoke to me out there, showed nothing of the person I spoke with on the phone. The guy I conversed with had a passion to him, a sensual fire in him like he knew how to talk and treat a woman. Cooney was like an angry, wild animal."

"He knew he was going to be caught, and you did rip off his bottom lip. Maybe he felt at that point he had nothing to lose," Darren said.

"Maybe," Charlene answered, but she wasn't buying it.

They walked through the basement and found a team of technicians examining the woman's mangled body, or the pieces that Cooney had left behind to be attended to.

The victim had been hogtied to a chair in front of a stone fireplace. She had been so close to the fire that the hairs on her arms had been singed off. The room still smelled of her sizzled flesh.

"Any idea who she is?" Charlene asked.

Darren shook his head. "Not yet. Might never know. We have very little to work with. But they'll do what they can with what is available and run a cross reference check with missing persons. Hopefully they will find out, and someone somewhere will get some closure."

Charlene knew that the victim had been a heavy meth or heroin addict from the multiple track marks on her arms. Her eyes were deep set and almost black. She had multiple piercings—snake bites under her bottom lip, a curved barbell in her left eyebrow, and several ear rings, big and small, in both ears.

"TOD determined?"

Darren shook his head. "ME will have to check on time of death when we get her back. Looks pretty fresh though."

Charlene nodded. She had seen enough, plus she physically ached.

"Let's go."

Chapter 33

After surgery to repair a broken nose, a zipper of stitches on the top of her head, tender ribs bandaged, scratches, cuts, and burns creamed and wrapped, and a prescription for enough drugs to tranquilize a small horse, Charlene was released from the hospital the following evening with only a minor concussion diagnosed. They'd kept her in for twelve hours as a precautionary measure.

It took some persuasive talking for her mother to let Charlene stay at her own place without a chaperone. She was given time off from work, but something was eating at her.

After stopping at the pharmacy to fill her prescription, she arrived home and immediately ignored the *do not take with alcohol* label on the pill bottles. She opened a bottle of beer and used it to chase a few of the anti-inflammatories, muscle relaxers, and painkillers.

She dropped on the futon and rested her head, visions of Cooney dancing in her brain. She squirmed under a blanket and pulled it up to her chin, gripping it tight while shivering.

He isn't right.

How could Sean Cooney, the disgusting, low-life, sleaze-ball who tried to rape her in the woods, be the same guy who she spoke to so frequently on the phone? Did she have no sense of the Celebrity Slayer at all? Could she not characterize a suspect, picture and profile the kind of man she thought he had been? Had she just fantasized about him, wanted him to be a certain way to appease her own way of thinking?

She let out a breath and took another drink, allowing time for the booze and pills to kick in. She closed her eyes and saw Cooney's face, a mask of terror, a beast who thought of women as garbage, only meant to be on this earth to satisfy his insatiable desires.

"Maybe I'm wrong," she said to herself.

Everyone seemed to think Cooney was the perfect suspect, as Darren had said, Taylor-made to fit the profile.

Darren.

Charlene smiled when she thought about him now. Had she been underestimating him this whole time? He seemed to have something about him now.

Was she really starting to have feelings for Darren after his relentless pursuit? Or was she just in a vulnerable state, and this was some sort of gratitude to Darren for saving her life? Was she hero struck? Charlene fidgeted on her seat cushion, a strange desire rising from within her.

She erased Darren from her thought process and moved back to Cooney.

She called Larry's cell. "It's me."

"I heard you did good, Kid."

"Thanks, but I'm not feeling it."

"What do you mean?"

Charlene told Larry about her doubts, about her frequent conversations that didn't add up, and her gut feeling that it wasn't Cooney.

Larry sighed. "You know what your father used to tell me, Kid? You find the truth by following your emotions."

She found herself back at Cooney's hunt camp. She hadn't remembered much about the drive, the pills and booze kicking into overdrive and slowly turning her into a walking zombie. But this wasn't the first time she'd had to manage on a buzz.

Her body screamed in defiance as she slowly, unsteadily pulled herself from the car. The cabin had yet to be cleared, there was still work to be done, but at least now Charlene could walk through it alone. She scoped the whole place again, without touching anything—seeing it clearly for the first time as it had been left by Cooney.

As she moved around, she felt the phone on her hip vibrate. She checked caller ID and saw her mother's cell number.

She answered. "Hi, Mom."

"Honey, how are you feeling?" Her mother's voice sounded sad.

"I'm fine. Just relaxing." Charlene continued to walk the cabin.

"Let me guess…on the futon, legs up, watching the Dodgers game."

"How did you guess?" Charlene asked.

"That's funny," her mother said, "Because I'm standing in your apartment right now."

Charlene squeezed her eyes shut. "Sorry, Mom, I just had to step out."

"Please call me when you get home, honey."

"I will, Mom, I promise."

Charlene hung up and looked at her new phone. Although her other one had been smashed to pieces by Cooney, a communications technician in the department had been able to save all of her data and contacts and transfer it to a new one while she was in the hospital.

She trudged through slowly, jumping at the smallest noise or shadow. Her nerves were frayed.

She didn't notice anything on her first swipe, so she snapped on a pair of disposable gloves, delving a little deeper.

She checked each room methodically, flipping each bedroom, cleaning out closets, running along crevasses, and searching waste baskets. She was looking for any kind of connection between Sean Cooney and the Celebrity Slayer, to either dispel or prove her theory that Cooney wasn't the Slayer.

She was going through the bookshelf when she stopped, terror seizing her. On the third row, fourth book from the left, was a hard cover copy of the entire volume of *Brownstone's Police Manuals*. It wasn't the fact that Cooney had these books in his library—most of the cops on the force owned a set. So it was no wonder they were over-looked by the crime scene team as potentially significant.

It was the fact that the spine on all four of these paperback had been stained. The same coffee stain Charlene had mistakenly deposited on her father's set of manuals twenty-years ago as he was studying to become a detective.

Were these her father's books?

Charlene removed the first manual and flipped it open to the introduction page and written in perfect penmanship at the top of the page was an inscription.

To Marty,
Good luck, make us proud.
Love Brenda, Jane, and Charlene

There was no mistaking her mother's penmanship. These were her father's books, but how did Cooney come to have them? Had he borrowed them to study for the detective exam? Did he steal them from her dad's desk at the precinct? Did he take them after he'd killed her father? There was no way for Charlene to ever find out.

Charlene was thumbing through the manual when something slipped from between the pages and fell to the ground. She bent over and picked up a black and white, four-by-six photo that looked to be at least thirty years old.

It was a picture of a stunning, breathtakingly beautiful woman. She was well made up, with an old-fashioned, V-neck cut gown and a pearl necklace with matching earrings. Her hair was in a tight bun, accentuating her long, smooth, graceful neck, high cheekbones and clear, milky skin. She had over-plucked eyebrows and was posing like a model or actress, without actually looking at the camera.

The writing on the back of the photo told Charlene that the woman's name was Deloris. But that was all it said.

Charlene turned the picture back over and stared at the woman. There was something eerily familiar about her. Charlene had seen her somewhere before.

What was her connection to Cooney? Was she a wife, mother, lover, sister, aunt, daughter? In the files, Cooney was said to be unmarried with no children. The AIC mentioned that he allegedly had a girlfriend a long time ago.

She tucked the photo into her coat pocket and placed the books at the entrance, to return to their rightful owner…her mother.

After thoroughly searching the rest of the cabin, Charlene gave up, frustrated and sore. The pills were starting to wear off and she needed to get off her feet with a drink and a fresh dose of meds.

Charlene lay on her futon watching the Dodger's game. Her legs were outstretched, and she had a cold drink in her hand. She had eaten a big supper, taken her regular dosage of pills, and was finally physically relaxed for the first time in weeks.

But mentally, she just couldn't get there. She thought more about Sean Cooney and the Celebrity Slayer, and the more she thought of it, even though she had no proof, the surer she was that Cooney wasn't the Celebrity Slayer.

He just hadn't done enough in those woods to show Charlene he was the same man she had spoken to. His personality didn't fit. He wasn't smooth or patient. He was the total opposite of what Charlene was expecting.

And what about when he called her by her name? On the phone, he had called her Charlie. He knew that was what her father had called her and knew it upset her. In the woods, Cooney had called her Charlene.

And what about the tattoo on her back? The Slayer had mentioned it, but Cooney had acted as if it was the first time he had seen it.

Then Charlene remembered the phone call at the bar the night before the whole Cooney incident went down. The call had come from an LA area code, the first time a phone number had ever appeared from the Celebrity Slayer's calls. Was that a sign he was slipping up? Did he want to be caught? Why now?

She retrieved her phone from the kitchen island and clicked through the call log until finding the number. She wrote it down and called the phone company. After identifying herself and making a request, the operator went to search.

"Yes, I'll hold," Charlene said, her body vibrating with anticipation.

Five minutes turned to ten before the customer service rep. came back on the line.

"Detective Taylor?" she said.

"Yes?" Charlene bit down on her lip.

"The phone belongs to a Martin Taylor. It was registered and opened two days ago." The operator read off Charlene's parents' address and details.

Charlene felt numb, her mouth too dry to speak.

"Detective Taylor?"

Charlene hung up, her nerves tingling, her body quivering. She felt suddenly cold and alone. Was this some sort of sick joke? Was that why he had used a phone number this time, rather than hiding it with a private caller message? Had he wanted Charlene to find that out, taunting her?

Charlene felt a sudden nausea and felt like vomiting. She rushed to the bathroom and brought up everything that she could.

She wiped the corners of her mouth, rinsed it out with tap water, and returned to the living room, thinking. He probably hadn't planned on using the phone long, since bills would have started arriving at her parents' house.

There had been no cell phone recovered on Cooney or from his cabin. And there were no other phones, except his landline, registered under his name. Was this Cooney's sick joke or someone else's? If it was someone else, did they still have the phone on?

There was only one way to find out.

She hit redial on her phone and watched the numbers pop up one by one, searching and dialing. As she pressed the phone to her ear, listening to the ringtone, she thought she could hear a ringing from somewhere in her apartment. She froze.

That was impossible. She hung up and the ringing stopped. She hit redial again and again the same ringing came from another room in the apartment. Her heart almost leapt out of her chest. Was he in her apartment?

She pulled her gun from the holster and kept the phone pressed tightly to her ear. She clicked off the safety and tried to follow the sound. She could hear it growing louder as she stepped out of the living room and into the short hallway. She headed towards the bathroom and could hear the ringing through the door.

She shut off the phone and clipped it to her belt. The ringing in the bathroom stopped. She held her weapon with both hands and gently pushed open the door. The bathroom was empty. She checked behind the shower curtain, nothing.

How could that be?

She removed her phone again and hit redial. This time the ringing was loud and she looked down at her feet to where her jacket was crumpled on the floor. She picked it up and chaotically went through the pockets, finding the phone. She pulled it out and felt it vibrating in her hand with each ring.

How had he slipped it in her pocket?

Then Charlene shivered and saw her reflection in the mirror, paling with each new understanding. She remembered who had put it in her coat.

She had.

Charlene moved to the bedroom and sat on the futon, staring at the phone in her hand. Her mind was swirling. She shook her head, trying to focus.

What was happening? How was this connecting? This was the phone she had borrowed from Darren.

Was Darren somehow involved? It didn't make sense. Why had that call been connected to Darren's phone?

She tried to recall everything she knew about him.

He'd transferred from the Hollywood division, where the Celebrity Slayer had started his rampage. He moved to the West LA branch, perhaps knowing that Martin Taylor was working the Slayer case. Charlene remembered how Darren had admired and looked up to her father.

Darren had spent many hours with her father, questioning him endlessly. Charlene just thought it was Darren's way of becoming a better cop, preparing him to be a detective someday, and maybe, in the back of her mind, she thought it might also be Darren's small way of getting closer to Charlene.

Darren had also been partnered with Charlene's street partner when she'd been off for her father's death. Is that how he, the Celebrity Slayer, knew so much about her personal life?

Had Darren killed Charlene's father?

Was that how someone, Darren—a friend, a colleague—had gotten so close to her father in the alley without Martin Taylor's cop instincts going off and survival mode clicking in?

Did this make sense at all? Or was the combination of booze and drugs playing with her mind?

She could picture Darren's desk at the precinct—clean, in perfect order, and lined with textbooks on procedures and techniques. Charlene's short time profiling suspects told her that murderers often read up on police procedures and crime scenes.

She'd known all along that Darren had a thing for her. Had that overlapped with her phone calls with the Slayer, who had an obvious attraction and desire for her?

Was that why Darren so readily and willingly asked to be a part of Charlene's team on the Anderson case and then, later on, on the Jackson case? It wasn't for personal reasons, to be close to Charlene, but to find out what she knew about the Celebrity Slayer case. Had Charlene mentioned to Darren that she was secretly working the Slayer case? She didn't think so, but she couldn't be certain. She had showed him her father's list.

Charlene all of a sudden felt sad and alone.

Was she disheartened at the thought of Darren not actually being attracted to her physically? Surely she didn't really need someone that badly, wasn't so emotionally vulnerable that she had actually longed to be wanted by Darren. Maybe she *did* enjoy the attention that Darren was constantly giving her, watching her and wishing to be with her. She could always feel Darren's wandering eyes on her in the precinct. Maybe she missed that.

What was wrong with her? She couldn't be that fragile and filled with self-loathing.

Charlene opened another beer, disgusted with herself. But she had to forget about that and stay focused on this case. It wasn't about her.

She recalled a conversation she'd had with Larry about how perfect the Slayer killings had been, which was very unusual for an amateur. The fact the killer had left behind nothing for the cops to work with was uncanny, especially for a newbie which the Slayer presumably was. A cop would know exactly what the crime scene teams would be looking for and how to avoid leaving any trace evidence.

The weapon that had killed her father had a silencer. Not many people owned silencers, but cops would have no problem accessing such items.

Martin Taylor thought it was a cop.

Cooney leaving a print was just too easy. Had Darren set Cooney up? How had Darren known Cooney was the perfect fall guy, unless he'd been following him? Perhaps they were working as partners?

Darren was also known to be good with computers. He could have easily hacked into her account at work, of that she had no doubt.

Charlene tried to bring up their phone conversations in her memory. Had the Slayer said something, maybe imperceptibly to indicate he was a cop or at least knew the law?

He always knew exactly what happened to her at work and knew it quickly. Like when she beat up the child abuser, made detective, saw the shrink and got cleared for duty. Darren would have the means to access that information.

Darren knew what bar she was going to the other night. He had wanted to come along but she'd turned him down. So he killed his next victim close by.

What did she really know about Darren?

He was methodical, hard-working, and over-prepared. When Charlene had asked him for a brief description on the Philips' rape, he'd handed in a twelve-page document.

Larry had described him as a young go getter who was crazy to have transferred from Hollywood. Everyone knew that the Hollywood detectives had it easy compared to a West LA cop. Why would someone move into the center of the crime universe?

He was shy, quiet, didn't have many friends on the force, and still lived at home with his parents.

Charlene got up and went to the closet, retrieving the final document from her father's notes. A man's size eight shoeprint. Charlene didn't know Darren's shoe size, but she knew he was short and thin, and probably close to that size.

Darren was very self-conscious about the way he looked, carried a mirror, and his uniform was always freshly pressed. Mommy must be taking good care of him.

It was starting to make sense, the dots starting to connect. But why did Darren hate celebrities?

Chapter 34

Three hours of troubled sleep, her dreams haunted, interrupted by the nameless woman from the picture in Cooney's cabin. Where had Charlene seen her before?

She had been given time off, but Charlene needed to go in to use the department computer terminal. There was too much to do. Too much at stake.

She wasn't sure how she would react to seeing Darren.

Whom could she trust? She couldn't take her ideas to the captain, especially only days after having accused, and ultimately, killing a fellow cop. Some of the guys on staff still weren't over it, even if Jackson had been guilty. She couldn't go after another cop already on hearsay and circumstantial evidence. On a Taylor gut feeling.

Before leaving the apartment, Charlene put together a folder of the key findings from her father's files. She threw everything in a duffel bag and locked the door on her way out.

The precinct was unusually quiet, and few officers acknowledged her presence. The captain would be the only one to know that she had been given time off, but she doubted, with the captain knowing about her work ethic and insatiable desire to succeed amongst her male counterparts, that he would question her coming in on the day after she'd been released from the hospital.

She moved slowly to her desk, still stiff and tender from Cooney's ambush. She threw her coat on the back of the chair and headed to the coffee room. She was thankful that she didn't see her captain, and she was even more thankful that she hadn't yet run into Darren. She still wasn't sure what she would do.

The coffee room was empty, and she took a few moments to enjoy the silence before mixing herself a coffee and heading back to her desk. She sat down at her computer and booted it up.

Charlene wondered what detectives and crime scene teams were working the Cooney murder, and who would be in control of those files. Since she had been a major part of it, getting her hands on those notes wouldn't be a problem.

She picked up the phone and dialed the medical examiner's office. She knew that Lloyd Webster had been called in to work the scene, because she had remembered seeing him on site. She was quickly transferred to his office where she was told he was just getting ready to leave.

"Hi, Lloyd. It's Charlene Taylor from RH."

"Hi, Charlene, how are you feeling?"

Webster was in his sixties and loved his work so much that he would probably die before he'd retire. His wife had passed away ten years ago, he had no children, and the job was all he had.

"I've been better, but on the mend."

"Good to hear." Charlene could picture Webster smiling at the other end. "What can I do for you?"

"I was hoping to find out about the woman found in Sean Cooney's basement two days ago."

"I sent in my report last night," he said, sounding surprised.

"I know, but I haven't had a chance to read it yet. I took a chance that you might be in and I'd get the information directly from the master." Charlene grinned.

"Oh, you young ladies really know how to sweet talk us old guys. What specifically would you like to know?"

"What can you tell me?"

"Typical Slayer victim. Many cuts, deep and long strokes. We matched the wounds from her torso, back, and chest—because of depth, length, width, and serration—to the knife Cooney was about to use on you. You're a very lucky girl, Charlene, lucky to be alive today. You're lucky that Officer Brady found you when he did. Who knows what would have happened in another minute."

She had spent so much time thanking Darren and owing her life to him, that she had not thought about how Darren had stumbled upon her. It was very convenient. He said he had followed her into the woods.

She thought about the bullet hole in Cooney, one to the throat and one between the eyes. Both kill shots, or at least deadly enough to immobilize Cooney and leave no doubt about the prospect of ever having Cooney talk to the cops.

Had Darren followed her into the woods because he knew Cooney would be there? Was Darren's plan to save Charlene's life in hopes she would be so grateful that she would fall in love with him?

"Detective, are you still there?"

Charlene was snapped to attention and realized she was still on the phone.

"Did you find anything different?" she asked. "Anything not corresponding with the other victims."

"We did find evidence of sexual assault prior to death."

Charlene was stunned. "Sexual assault, but there was no sign of forced penetration in any other victims, was there?"

"Not that I'm aware of."

Either this girl was special to Cooney, or this piece of evidence bolstered Charlene's theory that Cooney either wasn't the Celebrity Slayer or was working with a partner.

The Celebrity Slayer was a known exhibitionist. He wanted his victims found. Cooney had brought this girl back to his camp with the idea of never having her found. She was like his prize. Charlene had to find out who this girl was and if she meant something more to Cooney.

"Thanks, Lloyd." Charlene hung up and went to search for the case file.

She knew that a copy of the file would already be stored since the case was now considered closed even though loose ends would still have to be tied up. It was all a formality, and with Cooney dead, a case number would be given but it would be worked on at a leisurely pace.

She grabbed the thick stack of papers and took it to her desk to study.

The victim's name was Courtney Benedict, thirty-four years old from Anaheim. She had started out as a "fluffer" in the porn industry in the late eighties before turning mainstream in the early nineties, appearing in minor roles for six low-budget films. She then vanished from the big screen.

There hadn't been a thorough background check on her yet because there hadn't been time, and Charlene wasn't sure if there ever would be. Charlene was almost hoping that Benedict would have had no connection to celebrity status, strengthening her claim that Cooney was a separate case.

The victim and weapon matched, but the only anomaly was the sexual assault.

Cooney might be involved, but Charlene was sure that he wasn't the voice on the other end of the line of their phone conversations. In most cases like this, detectives would look up a serial killer's parents or children. Often these urges are DNA linked, and when children see a role model commit certain actions, they tend to follow. But Cooney's parents were deceased, and he had no children.

There had been no weapons, other than the knife, found on Cooney. Darren had told Charlene that he had to wait for a perfect moment to take out Cooney before he pulled a gun on Charlene.

She paced across the room and ducked her head in her captain's office. "Are the Feds still around?"

He looked up from an *LA Times* crossword. "They flew out this morning. What's up?"

"Just some final touches on the Slayer case."

"It's closed and it's not your case. Anything you need, get from Berkley and Harris."

"Right."

Charlene went back to her desk and sat down. She looked around the room and saw no one paying attention. She then tilted her computer screen down and to the side, where no one would have a clear view of what she was working on.

She punched Darren Brady's name into the computer.

Darren's head shot, in police blues and his uniform hat, came onto the screen, as well as a short bio about when he'd joined the force, his transfer, and his credentials. Charlene scanned the short write up and scrolled down.

Then she saw it.

Darren's mother was a former child movie star, B list. This was Darren's connection to the victims.

Charlene did a search on Wikipedia and found a page dedicated to Darren's mother. It was a very short page with very little information. Charlene wondered who had set it up.

Candace Hayes was born as Deloris Marie Wyatt on June 21, 1955 in St. Louis, Missouri.

There was very little on Hayes' early life. A single child to immigrant parents, Hayes grew up in a poverty-stricken life before being discovered by a talent agent at a county talent show. She moved to LA at the age of seventeen to pursue a career as an actress/model.

The 'Personal Life' section told Charlene that Hayes was married in 1990, had a baby boy that same year—Darren—and divorced in 1994. Darren's father died of natural causes three years later.

"Longer than most celebrity marriages," Charlene muttered.

There was nothing in the 'Current Projects' section. Candace Hayes seemed to have vanished from the spotlight and made a quiet, secluded life for herself. She sounded like the perfect candidate for a Celebrity Slayer victim.

Charlene scanned the filmography but didn't recognize any of the over twenty movies Hayes had played in. Her last movie was in 2003. She hadn't been in anything in over ten years.

When Charlene scrolled down to find a picture of Candace Hayes, her breath caught in her throat and she started to hyperventilate.

It was her.

The woman from the photograph.

That's where Charlene had first seen the woman's face. It had been in the glove compartment of Darren's car when they had been driving to Cooney's camp.

Charlene pulled out the picture she'd found at Cooney's and compared it to the woman on the screen. Although the picture on screen was taken in 1990, there was no mistaking the beauty of Deloris Wyatt.

Charlene opened a new tab and googled images of Candace Hayes and the pictures were identical. Now the question was why did Cooney have a picture of Darren's mother?

This was another piece involving Darren, but what did she really have?

She had Darren's phone, which she knew was in her father's name. She had Darren's mother's photograph which she'd found at the crime scene. She had Darren's history with the B-film industry.

She needed more and had come prepared.

She pulled out a piece of notepad paper where she'd jotted down a summary of details on each of the Celebrity Slayer's murders, including dates and particulars. She searched the LAPD precinct database for the shift schedule and cross referenced the murder dates with Darren's past schedule. She created a timeline of whether Darren was working, on call or off. The dates matched up pretty well. All of the victims had either disappeared or been killed on a night that Darren was off.

Then Charlene looked at the dates again and thought of her own interaction with Darren. She noticed there had been a lag in the murders, long spaces between a few, and Charlene realized this was when she and Darren had been working together and getting along well. The most gruesome had happened when she'd refused to take his calls and the last one, the probable setup of Cooney had come the same night Charlene had turned Darren down on his after work drink offer.

His invitation, combined with her refusal, had probably pushed him over the edge.

Did it make sense or was she grasping at straws?

She knew she was right, but didn't have enough to prove it or to convince anyone else. She knew the Slayer, knew his inner, dark secrets. He wanted to be heard. He wanted his story told. She needed to confront Darren, or at least try to persuade him into talking. Charlene was sure that he would talk to her. She had felt a special connection with him on the phone that she was sure she hadn't dreamed up. Charlene sensed that Darren felt it too.

That was her in.

Chapter 35

Two hours later, Charlene found herself at Darren's doorstep, rapping on the front door of the low, prewar bungalow.

What are you doing here, Charlene thought to herself.

She looked around the neighborhood but saw no one. She rapped again.

Charlene had spent the last couple of hours going over her plan. She wasn't sure how confident she was, but she was out of resources, and this was her last resort.

The first step was getting in the door.

She was about to knock a third time when the door opened and Darren stood in the doorway, his hair messed and his eyes squinting.

"Chip," he said. "What are you doing here?"

Charlene pulled the cell phone out of her pocket. "I forgot to give this back to you." She handed the phone over to Darren.

"That's where it is. I thought I had lost it. Thanks." He took the phone and slipped it into his jeans pocket.

Charlene stood on her tiptoes trying to look around Darren and into the house. "Were you sleeping?" she asked.

Darren grinned. "Taking a nap. I didn't realize how exhausted I was after that whole Cooney thing. But I guess I don't have to tell you that." Darren smiled at her so she returned it.

Charlene wasn't sure how to react. Here she was, eye to eye with possibly the most famous serial killer in the history of the city, and she didn't feel one bit threatened. She could actually feel herself drawn to Darren.

Is this insane?

"Yeah," she said. "Even standing for long periods of time is hard."

Darren took the bait.

"Chip, I'm sorry. Would you like to come in and sit down?"

"Well, maybe for just a few minutes." Charlene limped past Darren and into the front foyer, where the floor was covered in a vintage shaggy carpet.

"Here, let me take your coat." Darren slipped Charlene's coat off her shoulders gently while Charlene wiggled out of her boots. "Please, have a seat and make yourself comfortable." He motioned towards the living room.

Charlene stepped inside and felt as if she'd entered a time machine. The inside of the house was outdated and in need of a makeover.

She examined an old-style upholstered sofa and found part of a cushion that wasn't too littered with cat hair and sat down.

"Sorry about the mess," Darren said when he joined her in the living room. "My mom went out for the afternoon and cleaning isn't exactly her thing."

Charlene licked her lips. "All of these pills the doctors have me on really dry out my mouth."

Darren jumped to his feet. "Would you like a drink? I just bought beer."

Charlene smiled. "That sounds nice, Darren. Thanks."

He turned to leave but stopped. "Wait…can you drink alcohol while on those pills?"

Charlene winked. "It will be our little secret."

Darren smiled. "Okay."

When Darren left the room and entered the kitchen that was connected by a swinging door, Charlene got up and began searching the room for anything.

She checked the book shelves, drawers, end tables, piano bench seat and anywhere else that had a hidden storage compartment. The retro living room was littered with pictures of Candace Hayes in costume, on stage, behind the set, and some modeling poses.

"Man, this woman loves herself," Charlene mumbled.

She could hear Darren fidgeting in the fridge, pulling out two bottles that clanked together. She heard them land on the counter and then the fizzled sound of the cap being twisted off.

Charlene looked around the dim-lighted room and felt that the only thing missing was a disco ball hanging in the center. She rushed back to her seat, but had a few extra seconds before Darren entered the living room carrying two sweating brown bottles. He handed her one and then took a seat opposite her.

Charlene took a long drink and let the cold, smooth liquid swish in her mouth and slipped down her throat. Then she chased it with another.

"So how long have you and your mother lived here?" she asked.

Darren looked around the room. "As long as I can remember. It's not much, but it's home." He took a drink and so did Charlene.

"When was that picture taken?" Charlene motioned to a black and white photograph of Darren's mother on a book shelf above the television.

Darren looked at the picture. "Oh, probably about twenty years ago. She hasn't taken many recently, although I think she has aged very well compared to most women her age."

Charlene nodded, looking around the room for any sign. A few minutes passed without a word exchanged. Charlene took another drink.

"So when are you coming back to work?" Darren asked, almost as if uncomfortable with the silence.

"As soon as I'm healed up."

He smiled. "You love your job, don't you?"

Charlene nodded. "I do. What about you?"

"I couldn't see myself doing anything else." He raised his glass in the air. "To the job!"

Charlene raised her glass and repeated, "To the job."

They both drank.

"I never really got to thank you, Darren, for saving my life."

Darren blushed, his cheeks reddening and a self-effacing smile curling on his thin lips.

"No need, Chip."

"No, really. How you were able to find me and take down Cooney? That was real brave police work." She took a drink.

He raised his glass. "You would have done the same thing. You've had a tough time. First your dad, then the Anderson case, your run in with detective Jackson and now Cooney. I bet it hasn't been easy following in your father's footsteps. I'm sure everyone has been comparing the two Taylor detectives."

Charlene brought her hand to her eyes, rubbed them, and shook her head. That sounded familiar. Had the Celebrity Slayer said that on the phone?

"Oops," Darren said. "Did I say that out loud? You must be confused, Charlie."

Charlene looked at the bottle in her hands, was having trouble focusing on the label, her vision going in and out, the letters on the bottle a blur of fuzz.

She squeezed her eyes shut, closing and opening them rapidly, but the visual disturbances continued to grow. She bent down to peer inside the bottle neck but the liquid looked normal. Confusion set in. Was she getting drunk on one beer?

She felt light-headed and a bit woozy. Her muscles began to relax involuntarily. She tried to grip the bottle, but it slipped from her hand and fell to the carpet. She could hear the liquid pouring out, but the muscles in her neck wouldn't allow her head to bend and look down. She attempted to pick the bottle up before it made too big of a mess, but when her brain demanded her muscles to move, they ignored her and remained motionless.

"Are you alright?" Darren asked. "Let me get that bottle."

"I'm sorry," she said. "The bottle…" but her voice trailed off. She didn't recognize it. In her mind her speech sounded slurred and slow.

She watched him get up, walk over, bend down and pick up the bottle, setting it on the coffee table that had two ashtrays with burning cigarettes.

Charlene felt lazy, relaxed and totally at ease. Almost sleepy. That's when she realized it…Darren had drugged her.

He walked around behind her, and Charlene could feel him drop his hands on her shoulders. He leaned down and she could smell his breath and feel it on her neck.

She tried to go for her gun but her reaction time was slow, as if moving on a film reel at a slowed-down pace. Darren already had her weapon. When had he taken it?

"You should have left it alone, Charlie," he whispered in her ear. "Cooney could have been your man. The case would have been closed. We could have been together. But you're too much like your dad."

He walked back around and knelt in front of her. This time, when Darren looked into Charlene's eyes, she saw something she had never seen before…pure evil.

She was paralyzed. She tried to scream but her vocal chords were useless.

He retook his seat across from her and sat back, steepling his fingers and bringing them to his face, perfectly relaxed. He smiled, pulling a tiny vial from his pocket and holding it up for her to see.

"How do you feel?"

She didn't respond.

"It's a chemical restraint concocted by a Colombian cocaine drug lord. The cartel gives it to people who steal from them, so the thieves can watch themselves being dismembered, limb by limb, by power tools. Colorless, odorless, tasteless and the best part, it escapes the body in twelve hours leaving no trace."

So that's why victims weren't found until a day or two after they'd been killed, to give the drug time to wear off. There was never any sign of drugs in their urine or bloodstream.

Darren smiled. "A poison that will render the victim totally paralyzed, while still keeping them alive and aware, was never thought possible, biologically speaking. Muscles require nerve impulses, and we would suffocate if, say, the diaphragm was paralyzed.

"They call it El Insensible. The English translation is The Unfeeling. I know, not very creative, but blame the Colombians."

With his left hand, he grabbed Charlene by the right wrist and pulled her towards him. He bent his knees and back and flung her over his shoulder, slid his right hand between her legs and straightened his knees in a squatting exercise to lift her off the ground—as if he'd done it many times before.

"Dead weight," he grunted.

Charlene could do nothing but stare at the shaggy carpet. She tried again to cry out, to swing and flail her arms and legs, but her body was out of her control and was not cooperating with her brain signals.

She watched carpet change to linoleum tile as they moved through the swinging door and crossed the kitchen to the back of the house. She heard a door swing open and saw the tile being replaced by wooden steps as they descended into darkness.

As they reached the bottom, the dank, dark dampness and cold air hit her.

Darren flicked a light switch at the bottom of the staircase, and Charlene was gently laid onto the top of a steel, bloodstained table. She could smell stale urine and feces. Her limp body trembled.

"I had big plans for us, but when you looked me up this morning, I knew it wouldn't work between us. I was very disappointed that it had to end like this."

He must have seen surprise in her eyes. He pulled a small device from his pocket and held it up to her. It looked like a USB flash drive.

"You know, China has some of the most sophisticated hackers in the world. It's amazing what you can acquire on the internet. The week you were promoted, I set up this redirecting hardware on your computer. I just accessed your account by decoding your password, 'DADDYS GIRL'." He smiled. "Then I installed this onto your computer, hoping you wouldn't notice it and you didn't.

"All of the activity from your computer was sent to my laptop here at home so I could track anything you searched. When I saw my name pop up during your internet trail, I figured you'd made the connection."

He shook his head and wagged his finger. "You shouldn't have looked up my mother. Now look what you've made me do."

He rounded the table and moved behind her. She was unable to turn or move her head to follow, but she heard what sounded like steel utensils being dropped on a metal tray. She could feel goose bumps jump on her bare arms.

Charlene felt like a newborn baby—helpless, out of control, unable to communicate or express herself. But, unlike a baby, she couldn't move, not even squirm. Terror seized her chest and tore at her insides. She could hear her own heartbeat hammering her chest bone. Tears and perspiration ran down her cheek, splashing onto the stainless steel.

"How rude of me," Darren said, taking her head in his hands and rotating her neck so she could now see on the other side of the table.

"Don't cry," he said, swiping away a tear on her cheek with his thumb. He had turned her head to the side so she could see him walk over to a tool bench that was strapped to a wall. He opened three drawers. "I just wonder how much you put together." He looked back and smiled, removing some tools.

He held up a knife, a menacing looking jagged-edged blade that was at least ten inches in length. It was still stained. "I used this one on Sophia Harding." He smiled proudly. "She was my first and a real screamer. I was sloppy, as most newbies are. But man, I was *hooked*."

He dropped the weapon on the metal table and picked up another. This one was a smooth-edged blade, shorter and thinner, looked more like a knife used to skin wild game. He sighed. "Elizabeth Jenkins. A pretty little young thing. Bright eyed and bushy tailed, ready to take on the world. It's a shame she picked a profession that tore apart families."

He set that weapon down and stared at the array of cutlery, shining in a row, placed neatly on the table. "You know, I could go on and on about each weapon, but that would bore you. I know what you really want to hear."

He returned to the table and pulled a chair up to the edge, but didn't sit down. He began to smooth out her matted hair, running his fingers gently through the strands and planting his face in her hair. He breathed in softly. With one hand, he massaged her scalp gently, twirling her hair, and he used the other to trace his fingertip over her face, gently running up and down and around, in a tickling fashion. He gently kissed the side of her neck, sucking and nibbling softly.

"I'm going to kiss every square inch of your body," he whispered. "I'm going to treat you like a princess, the way you should be treated."

As valiantly as she tried, Charlene still couldn't move. She tried to wiggle, tried to struggle, to scream, to claw, to bite, to scratch, but her body parts were immovable.

"But before I do that, I want you to know everything."

He sat down, crossed his legs and clasped his hands together, resting them in his lap. "I guess I will begin with my mother.

"She was a beautiful woman, built to be a star. What she was never meant to be was a wife or mother. I believe she'd always been goal-oriented, and having children was probably seen as something that would only interfere with achieving success in film."

He got up and went to the wall, pulling a dust-covered wine bottle from a rack-full that was attached to the wall. He blew on the cap, twisted off the outer tin layer, and using a cork screw, removed the cork. He poured himself a healthy portion and returned to his seat, sipping gently.

"Delores met my father in the summer of '87. He was in LA on leave from his military duties. One unexpected pregnancy later, a shotgun wedding, and an unwelcomed bright-eyed baby boy joined the scene. But my birth never slowed down my mother."

He took a sip and continued. "She continued to live the fast life, shooting movies all over California, drinking excessively, doing drugs, and being the life of parties. My father quit the army and became a stay-at-home dad. I remember as I got older, three and then four, hearing the shouting matches, living in a house full of hate and contempt. Delores would stay away for months at a time, only to return when it suited her, trying to be the wife and mother that she couldn't be. My dad was soft, weak, and always took her back."

Darren drained the remainder of the glass in one big slug and refilled.

"My father hung on for years, but it finally reached the boiling point in '94. After years of unfaithfulness, Delores fell in love with one of her flings. My dad had had enough and kicked her out for good. But the deceit didn't just break up our family, it broke my old man's heart. He tried to carry on, start over, but less than a year later he died of a cardiac arrest. But the stupid, lonely old man either forgot to change the will, or had never gotten over my mother, because he left everything to her. She moved back in, this time bringing home her lover in the process, Mr. Sean Cooney."

Charlene understood that his father's death had probably accelerated Darren's maturity, and changed his way of thinking.

"We all knew that it was only a matter of time until Delores got tired of Cooney and moved on, either dumping him or cheating on him. Cooney was like a father to me. We attended sporting events together, he taught me how to hunt and fish. That's why I wanted to be a cop, to follow in Sean's footsteps. But eventually, as it always does, a good thing came to an abrupt end.

"In 1999, Delores fell for a guy from the set of one of her movies. It crushed Sean. But it hurt me even more. First my father then Cooney. I had just turned fifteen, curious and quiet, and unsure of my place of belonging in the world. I wanted to explore."

Darren didn't smile or laugh. Charlene thought that he must have lost it some time ago and had only been clinging on by a thread. How he had managed to make it this far, Charlene had no idea. Self-delusion maybe?

He turned and refilled his glass. Charlene again tried to wiggle her wrist and thought she felt her fingers move, maybe telling her that she was getting some feeling back in her muscles.

"When I hit high school, I noticed the changes. School bored me. I began to set traps in the back yard, catching squirrels, cats, chipmunks, anything that came around. I loved to watch the pain I could inflict without actually killing them. I'd push the limit a little further each time. My mother either never saw the changes or chose not to. She was too wrapped up in herself to notice anyone around her. But Sean noticed."

"He worked with me, taught me skills, self-control and other things that could help me. I moved from small animals to bigger ones, wild game, Sean and I hunted out by his camp. He used to rent it back then. I felt alive when I killed. I enjoyed seeing the animals suffer. I remember returning from the hunt and masturbating three or four times a night. I was obsessed with it. I didn't need women, had no use for them. I had the thrill of a lifetime.

"But it all changed for me when my mother left Sean. He changed too. That's when we decided to up the stakes." Darren smiled. "I had to kill her."

"We took to the streets, starting with lowlifes, those who wouldn't be missed. But I soon wanted more. The torturing of my victims escalated with each new kill. I longed for the thrill of the hunt."

To Charlene, there was no sign of remorse in Darren's voice or facial features. It was as if it all brought him peace of mind. He was emotionless.

"We evolved, learned from our mistakes, and increased the danger, steadily moving up until we reached our ultimate destination."

He hesitated and took a drink, draining half the glass in one swallow.

"I hated what the lifestyle had done to my mother and my family. Celebrities are pure evil, the lowest form of disloyalty, greed, and corruption. It's not their fault—it's the lifestyle. There are too many temptations, too many easy-way-outs. So Sean and I took matters into our own hands. We made a difference. As Gandhi said, we were the change we wished to see in the world."

Darren picked up a flashlight and shone it towards a board that Charlene had missed in the corner of the room. It was plastered with newspaper articles and pictures.

"We didn't select major celebrities. That's just too risky. We settled for the bottom feeders. I kept track of the media, followed television reports, subscribed to magazines, and collected all of the newspaper clippings."

For the first time, Darren's face showed regret. His rueful smile didn't look faked. "I didn't mean to kill your father. That wasn't part of the plan. I always liked him. He took me in, showed me the ropes. Hell, I moved from Hollywood to learn under him. But, he got too close. After I killed him, Cooney wanted to kill you but I wouldn't let him. I convinced him to keep you alive."

Darren seemed to hesitate, as if giving Charlene's dad a moment of respectful silence.

Charlene took it all in. Darren was the alpha-dog. He had killed her father, he was the mastermind calling the shots, and Cooney had been his loyal servant.

"Excuse me," he said.

Charlene's eyes shot open, only to find that she was still on the steel table. How long had she been out?

Her memory was blurred. She was no longer shivering. Her body had acclimatized to the cold and her nose must have grown accustomed to the stench because she no longer noticed it.

She remembered Darren suddenly leaving, as if he heard something or had an idea, bolting from the room, up the stairs and through the door. Now, Charlene could hear his footsteps on the floor boards above her. What was he doing?

Tension mounted with each creak she heard from Darren above her. She tried to breathe deeply, tried to calm down, focus, concentrate and think of a way out. But it seemed hopeless.

The door at the top of the stairs opened. Charlene could see the beam of light from the kitchen. When she heard footsteps descending the stairs, she hoped it was anyone other than Darren.

"Oh good, you're awake. You must forgive me, Charlie. It was very rude to just leave you like that. It won't happen again."

He sat back down beside her and resumed the talk as if there had been no interruption.

"Sean had wanted to kill you right from the start. He knew that he could never have you, and that's what tortured him. I remember him telling me stories about when he was partnered with your father, you would always be around and he had wanted you. He would get hard just talking about you, rather immature and disgusting. But I was the reason you were spared. I saw something in you that I had to have for myself."

Charlene wondered if Darren was looking for a *thank you.*

"I really felt we made a connection during the Jackson case. I thought that there was potential there and a spark that you felt too."

Charlene tried to move her lips, attempted to answer but could not. Her mouth was dry.

"That's when the plan to set up Sean came into focus. I knew that as the Celebrity Slayer, I could never get close to you. But with that case out of the way, we could pursue a relationship and be together forever. But I was wrong. I followed you into those woods and when you saw my initials carved into the tree, I thought I'd been exposed right there. I guess DB never registered." He chuckled. "I was just lucky I could get to Cooney before he talked to the cops. When I discovered you were investigating me, I knew that it had to end.

"I knew that Charlene Taylor, the Lone Ranger, the determined, bull-headed female investigator who didn't trust men would come knocking on my door. It has always been Charlene Taylor against the world."

Charlene fought to struggle and felt more movement, albeit small. She was regaining the feeling in her muscles and the control to act on her own. But her strength was still limited.

Darren must have noticed it because he looked down at Charlene's wrist.

"Looks like we're almost out of time," he said. "It's time for us to become one with each other. I know you like to be on top, always in control of everyone and everything. But I'm going to do this nice and slow, make sure we both get what we need."

Rather than using the knife to cut through her clothes, with gentle fingers he slowly unbuttoned and opened her shirt, revealing her black lace bra. The bra snapped at the front, so he easily unhooked it and let the elastic pull away and drop to the side.

Darren gently rubbed her nipples between his thumb and forefinger, licking the tips and moistening her nipples until they grew stiff. Charlene fought it as much as she could.

"That's my girl," he said, smiling as Charlene's nipples grew hard and pointy.

He began fondling her breasts, gently kneading them in a circular motion. He bent over and kissed her nipples, taking them in his mouth and sucking them lightly.

Then he climbed up on the table over her, moving up towards her neck, kissing and sucking playfully. He gently swept aside her hair and nibbled at the crook of her neck. Charlene could feel his warm breath and the skin on her throat goose-bumped. His breathing quickened and she could feel the swell of his hardness through the thin pant fabric against her thigh.

She knew the end was near.

He looked into her eyes. "I've been waiting a very long time for this, and I know you have too. It just feels right."

A tingling sensation returned to Charlene's tongue and she knew that she was regaining some feeling. She coughed, trying to mouth words, but all that came out was a choking sound.

"Just relax," Darren said, placing his hands around her throat and massaging her Adam's apple.

Again she coughed and then slurred words spewed from her lips.

"Shhh. Let it happen."

"K..k..k..itchen….b..b..b..asement," Charlene blurted out.

Darren chuckled. "Kitchen, basement? Man, that drug has really gotten to you."

He got back off the table and to his feet. He traced his fingertips down the middle of her sternum, between her breasts and around her belly button. His hand roamed inside her belt, feeling underneath her pant fabric, lingering under her panty waistband and running smoothly over the stubble of pubic hair.

He walked down to the front end of the table. He removed her shoes and then her socks, placing them neatly on the floor at the end of the table. He returned to her view and unfastened her belt buckle, pulling the belt completely through the loops. He snapped the leather strap with a loud *crack*.

Charlene felt warm, flushed, dizzy, nauseated. She wanted to vomit. Her head spun, as it all felt like a dream.

"This is what I've been waiting for. The moment is killing me." He gently stroked her cheek and whispered intimately into her ear. "We need each other, Charlie. We're a team."

He unhooked her pants and unzipped her metal fly. Charlene raised her hips ever so slightly off the table to allow Darren easy access to pull down her pants to her ankles. He pulled them completely off, folding them neatly and setting them on the chair.

She could see Darren look into her eyes as his hand roamed on her inner legs, slowly moving upwards, finding her inner thigh.

"Help me," Charlene whispered quietly. She felt like a helpless child.

Darren looked into her eyes. "I am, my love."

"I'm not talking to you."

She held her breath, waiting for it, and then she saw it in his eyes—that moment of recognition, of total vulnerability and betrayal. As if he knew he'd been beaten.

Darren's eyes widened, bulging almost out of their socket. Anger erupted in his eyes.

"What the fuck is this!" he spat, his face now pale with rage.

He violently tore the black thong from her waist, ripping it from around her leg. That's when Charlene heard the *clunk* on the metal table between her thighs. Darren reached down and then brought his hand over her face so she could see it clearly.

He held a mechanical device—a short wire connecting a tiny microphone and square transmitter. A piece of black tape dangled uselessly from it.

"You bitch!" He stared with open fury in his eyes.

He turned and grabbed the closest knife from the table behind him. He turned back and held it with two hands over Charlene's chest, looking into her eyes, ready to thrust down and end her life.

Just then Charlene heard a noise in the background, behind Darren. Darren turned his head to look towards the door, and as his mouth opened, a loud shot snapped Darren back.

When he looked back down at Charlene, a look of disbelief registering on his face, she saw blood trickle from Darren's mouth. Another shot blew Darren completely off his feet, back against the wall.

Charlene waited, listening to footsteps on the concrete floor, first tramping around the room then coming towards her. A blanket was flung over her naked body before she saw her partner, Larry Baker, looking down at her. She was never so happy to see his ugly mug.

Larry's smile was strained. A single earpiece dangled from his lobe and a wire snaked down into his jacket pocket. "We got him, Kid."

Then she passed out.

Epilogue

Moving On?

Within hours the Brady house was swarming with officials.

Charlene was seated on a gurney, strapped to an IV, being carefully looked over by a team of medics as Larry watched over them. Her partner had a serious look of concern on his face.

"I'm glad you know the drug that was used, because we've never seen it before. Rohypnol, which is a major component of this drug, can last up to eight hours depending on how much was administered, but we believe it is starting to wear off. The IV should speed up the process," the EMT said.

They had been talking to her for the last fifteen minutes but very little was registering. Charlene felt confused and a little dizzy, almost like being hung over.

She tried to jump off the gurney but her legs gave out. The EMTs stabilized her with strong arms. "You need to stay on the gurney." He re-administered the IV and Charlene watched the liquid commence dripping.

She felt woozy, uncoordinated and a little sluggish, but she brushed away his arms and sat up.

She heard her captain's voice. "Is she able to speak?"

Charlene looked at Larry. "I don't remember much."

A medic immediately jumped in. "That's one of the side effects as the drug wears off, victims are unable to remember what happened while under its influence. We call it retrograde amnesia."

"It's okay," Larry said, holding up the portable taping device. "It's all recorded here."

He handed the wire to the captain.

"I think I'm going to be sick," Charlene said, pushing the EMTs away and stumbling behind the parked ambulance. She proceeded to dry-heave hard.

"Take care of her, Baker," the captain said. Then he turned and joined a crowd of reporters who had been gathered behind the police tape.

Larry stood behind Charlene, holding back her hair as spit hung from the corners of her mouth. She wiped it away with her sleeve and straightened her body, standing upright for the first time in hours.

"I feel like I got hit by a bus," she told Larry. "My limbs feel like they're being controlled by someone else."

Larry only nodded. "Sorry it took me so long to get in there. I couldn't find you and I didn't want to alert him. When he came upstairs, I thought I was a sitting duck. I had to hide and lay low until he disappeared again. Thank God you gave me that signal, the basement through the kitchen."

"Yeah, Darren thought I was just talking gibberish."

"What *do* you remember?"

Charlene shook her head and rubbed her eyes with the palms of her hands. "I'm not sure. It comes back in snapshot images. My mind is playing tricks, flashbacks coming and going.

"It was like I was under his spell, trying to fight him with the strength of an adolescent girl. Like he was a puppeteer, making me do whatever he wanted and I was obliging him. I was scared out of my mind."

Then Larry did something that even Charlene, as a gifted detective, never saw coming. He wrapped his big, strong bear-like arms around her and squeezed. Charlene found herself doing something she would have never bet she'd do, she leaned into his hug. They stayed there for long minutes, taking in the moment, leaning on him both physically and emotionally. She felt her eyes water and in that instant, Charlene thought of her father.

"Are you sure he's dead?" she asked, referring to Darren Brady. Her face was still buried in Larry's chest and her voice caught in her throat.

"It's over," he answered. "Your father would be so proud of you."

"You really think so?"

"I know so."

"So it's really over?"

"You tell me, Kid."

Charlene pulled away and looked into Larry's face, wondering what he meant.

Then he said, "Can you finally move on?"

She asked herself that very same question.

~ * ~

If you enjoyed this book, please consider writing a short review and posting it on your favorite review site. Reviews are very helpful to other readers and are greatly appreciated by authors, especially me. When you post a review, drop me an email and let me know and I may feature part of it on my blog/site. Thank you.

Luke

luke@authorlukemurphy.com

Message from the Author

Dear Reader,

Thank you for picking up a copy of *Kiss & Tell*. I hope you enjoyed reading this novel as much as I did writing it. My goal was to please anyone who loves thrillers, strong female protagonists and a fast-paced crime investigation. I hope I succeeded.

This is my "baby". Although *Kiss & Tell* is my second published work, it was actually the very first story I ever wrote, back in the winter of 2000. It took about four months to write, but it was nowhere near ready to be published. I tucked it away for the next twelve years and just opened it back up after I'd published *Dead Man's Hand*.

This is a work of fiction. I did not base the characters or plot on any real people or events. Any familiarities are strictly coincidence.

The idea for K&T came after helping my girlfriend write a short story for one of her college courses. I took one of the characters we had created and I ran with it.

I never had a chance to visit LA, but I used many sources, from the internet to speaking directly with locals. *Kiss & Tell* became real from taking advantage of experts in their field and adding my wild imagination.

For more information about my books, please visit my website at www.authorlukemurphy.com.

You can also "like" my Facebook page and follow me on Twitter.

I'm always happy to hear from readers. Please be assured that I read each email personally, and will respond to them in good time. You can direct your questions or comments to the contact form on my website. I look forward to hearing from you.

Regards,

Luke

Novels by Luke Murphy

Dead Man's Hand

Kiss & Tell

About the Author

Luke Murphy is the International bestselling author of *Dead Man's Hand* (Imajin Books, 2012).

Murphy played six years of professional hockey before retiring in 2006. His sports column, "Overtime" (Pontiac Equity), was nominated for the 2007 Best Sports Page in Quebec, and won the award in 2009. He has also worked as a radio journalist (CHIPFM 101.7).

Murphy lives in Shawville, QC with his wife, three daughters and pug. He is a teacher who holds a Bachelor of Science degree in Marketing, and a Bachelor of Education (Magna Cum Laude).

Kiss & Tell is Murphy's second novel. He is represented by The Jennifer Lyons Literary Agency.

For more information on Luke and his books, visit:
www.authorlukemurphy.com

'like' his Facebook page at:
http://www.facebook.com/pages/AuthorLukeMurphy

Follow him on Twitter at: www.twitter.com/#!/AuthorLMurphy

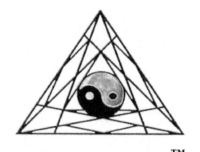

IMAJIN BOOKS^{TM}

Quality fiction beyond your wildest dreams

For your next eBook or paperback purchase, please visit:

www.imajinbooks.com

www.imajinbooks.blogspot.com

www.twitter.com/imajinbooks

www.facebook.com/imajinbooks

IMAJIN QWICKIES^{TM}
www.ImajinQwickies.com

CPSIA information can be obtained
at www.ICGtesting.com
Printed in the USA
LVOW04s0923150516

488339LV00015B/637/P